Fana

Standing Strong

Salome Kassa

Cover Art by Kristi L Johnston

www.KristiJohnstonArtworks.com

Table of Contents

Dedication

I thank God for his blessings. This book is dedicated to my indomitable grandmother and to women like her who face adversity on a daily basis, but no matter what, they keep going.

My parents – I still try to emulate their ethics and goodness.

To my children and grandchildren who brought me parental joy and challenges.

To my former husband.

To my cherished siblings, aunts, uncles, cousins, brothers-in- law, sisters-in-law and nieces and nephews.

My great gratitude goes to my wonderful friends who have remained my cheerleaders and confidants. Some of you read *Fanaye: Standing Strong* and gave your valuable criticism. Thank you so much!

Last but not least, I want to thank my wonderful mentor and friend Jennifer, a generous soul, who brought out the writer in me.

Acknowledgments

To my wonderful editor Barbara Field, thank you for your keen editing.

To the union writers' group, I value the camaraderie and advice.

To Yalin, my immeasurable gratitude for your tremendous help with my novel and your friendship. You believed in my ability as a storyteller when I didn't. You made my life much more pleasant. To the Public Library, which has been my home from the time I came to America until now including spending hours there while writing my novel.

To all the people I have encountered in my normal life that made my life comfortable, I thank you.

About the Author

Salome Kassa, who is just as strong a woman as her grandmother has discovered a passionate writer within herself. Her first book, *Fanaye: Standing Strong* is an example of her wit and grit. She is grateful for *A History of Ethiopia* by Harold G. Marcus, Berkeley University of California Press, 2002. He had written the story as a true historian. It refreshed Salome's history and allowed her to produce a story of her own. Nega Mezlekia notes from the Hyena's Belly, New York: Picador USA, 2001, were of great help to her as well. It gave her a clear understanding of how her people in Ethiopia went through hell during the communist regime of Mengistu.

Fanaye: Standing Strong is the story of a daring woman who survived and prospered in the tough, totally male-dominated world of Ethiopia in the first half of the 20th century. Her story inspires and instructs women today who face the many forms of sexual oppression. It will also resonate with male readers as they will feel deep empathy for this courageous protagonist.

Chapter 1: Fanaye

It was a cool September evening, with the wind whistling among the trees and hyenas roaming in search of prey or cadavers. That night, the village of Dow-Dow in the province of Wollo was chilly, dead quiet, and pitch dark, as though life outside of the hut no longer existed. Fanaye, a lean and strong thirteen-year-old girl, lay on her thin cot listening intently to the eerie sounds of the night that filtered in through the thatched roof of her hut, barely audible against the vibrant snoring of her father sleeping nearby. It's a good thing Mother and Aylahu do not snore, she thought as she rolled over and covered her cold body with her cotton blanket. Her thoughts drifted into the coming morning. She only wished that her mother, Hewait, would allow her to go to the neighboring village by herself to visit her favorite cousin, Yenanish. The two girls were inseparable friends, and they often wondered why their families didn't live in the same village in the first place.

As soon as Fanaye woke up in the morning, she felt anxious, knowing it would take a great deal of effort to convince her mother that she was old enough to make the trip on her own. Still, she sprang out of bed and dashed outside to look for Hewait but was intercepted by Ato Toshoma, her great-grandfather, who was sitting on a stool in front of the hut and sharpening his spears in anticipation

1

of his imagined enemy encounters from the past. The spears were at least as old as he was. Since the war of Adwa in 1896, he always seemed to be expecting the enemy to show up unexpectedly at his door at any time and was eager to tell a story or two about his early youth and struggles with the Italians who had invaded Ethiopia. Fanaye was normally his most avid audience, but today, she had no time for his stories.

Ato Toshoma beckoned with his hand and called out, "Fanaye, Fanaye! Come! Come here and sit beside me." As usual, sharpening his spears had put him in one of his deeply patriotic moods.

Fanaye cringed. "Oh no!" she mumbled to herself, impatient to get on to more important things. "Not now." Still, she was reluctant to disobey him. She always had a great deal of respect for elders, especially for Ato Toshoma.

"Yes, Telku Abaye, father of my father," she said, although she remained motionless.

Her great-grandfather gestured again with his free hand. "Come here and sit down," he said.

Finally, she sat obediently beside him. Pointing to the tip of his spear, Ato Toshoma said, "Fanaye, do you see this edge? It's still sharp, even though it is as old as I am." He laughed, as he always did, appreciating his own humor. Fanaye had heard this countless times. She smiled politely, accepted the spear from his old trembling hands, and began to examine its point, pretending to be looking at it for the first time.

"Yes, thank you, Abaye. I remember. You showed me before how to sharpen the spear."

"You remember? You remember? But how can you remember? You were born yesterday! I remember! When the Italians came... young people don't know—they've never seen war before."

Fanaye started to protest, to prove to him that she had listened and understood every word he'd said when he surprised her by suddenly grabbing the spear from her hands and waving it high above their heads. "This spear drove our enemies out of Ethiopia," he shouted. "We defeated them at Adwa, and we can defeat them again. But we always have to be ready. That is what I've learned. They may come again!" He thrust his spear upwards. Fanaye noticed that her great grandfather's normally bent back had straightened, and his dim eyes were lit up.

"I know, Telku Abaye. We must never trust the Italians, I know."

"You, Fanaye, you must always be ready. Do you understand?" He held Fanaye's chin, staring deeply into her eyes.

"I agree. I'll always be ready," Fanaye said while pondering a way to escape. She was touched by his display of emotion, but as hard as she tried, she couldn't bring herself to care much about what had occurred so long ago.

Suddenly, Fanaye thought, "You taught me so much about those enemies, Telku Abaye, but I'm afraid my brother doesn't seem to get it. He really needs to learn this lesson." She leaped up and called out loudly, "Aylahu... Aylahu!"

Clueless, her younger brother came running and asked what she wanted.

"Telku Abaye wants to talk to you," Fanaye said with a mischievous smile. And then she dashed off to look for her mother.

Fanaye found her mother, Hewait, squatting by their small garden and tending to the vegetables. She threw her arms around her and kissed her over and over. Her mother said with a knowing smile, "Okay, okay! What is it you want?"

Fanaye was always amazed at how nothing passed unnoticed by her mother. She scratched her head and jumped straight to the point. "Emaye, can I go visit Yenanish, please?"

Her mother dismissively said, "Since when do you go alone?"

"I'm old enough now to go there by myself, and I really want to see Yenanish. I won't stay long, I promise. I'll be back before sunset."

4

Hewait remained firm. "You can wait till Sunday, so we can all go together."

But Fanaye kept at it, begging while also looking as pathetic as possible. Hewait hated to disappoint her children and found herself yielding at the end. "I just don't see any urgency in your seeing her today," She raised her mud-covered hands up in the air, but just this time, I'll let you go," she said. "But don't you ever ask me again!"

To show appreciation, Fanaye offered to bring her the firewood first. With that, she ran inside their hut and grabbed her sturdy shama, a large cotton shawl women wear. "I'll be back with lots of wood," she called out, running out the door.

Her mother raised her head. "Be sure not to go anywhere near that crazy monkey."

Fanaye paused. "What crazy monkey?"

"They say there's a sick monkey running around, in and out of the village. They're trying to catch it and do away with it. Those monkeys can be really dangerous. Promise me you won't go near it!"

Fanaye promised and then was gone in a dash. Not too far from her home, she entered the familiar woods near the outskirts of the village. She gathered up large pieces of firewood to save time. But halfway through her task, she heard loud noises coming from the village. At first, she ignored them, but when the roaring grew louder, she decided to investigate. She spotted a thick bush and hid her bundle of firewood under it.

Fanaye moved rapidly but stealthily through the trees and bushes, back to the village where the sounds were emanated. At the center of the marketplace, she saw a crowd of men gathered in a circle, shouting, pointing, waving their arms, and throwing stones. Many local farmers had come from the surrounding areas to barter their goods. Vegetables were traded for fruit and millet, barley and teff for fish or eggs, even several chickens for a young goat.

She quickly found the cause of the uproar. Surrounded by the menacing crowd, a tiny grey monkey squealed, snarled, and scrambled around frantically in circles. The poor creature looked demented, with foam dripping from its mouth as it bared its teeth and lurched with anger at the crowd. This had to be the crazy monkey her mother had warned her about.

Fanaye didn't understand how a crowd of grown men couldn't quickly grab that small monkey and put him out of his misery. Why were they torturing the pitiful creature instead? With disgust, she watched their unsuccessful attempts to kill the little creature with stones. The monkey howled in distress, and the men shouted in frustration: "There! There! Catch him!"

The monkey leaped onto a tree and, nearing the top, jumped up and down.

On a sudden impulse, Fanaye decided to take the matter into her own hands to end the monkey's agony. She calmly pulled out her slingshot from inside her belt, slipped a hefty piece of rock into it, took careful aim, and released the stone with deadly accuracy. The stone hit the monkey on the head with an audible thud, killing it instantly. The crowd gasped when the frantic monkey went limp, fell all the way to the ground, and there remained silent and motionless.

At first, no one wanted to get too close to the monkey in case it was only stunned. One step at a time, the men closed in on the poor creature with their sticks and rocks. After looking at it for a moment and ascertaining that it was dead, the men raised their fists in the air and shouted in triumph, "Yaznaw! Yaznaw!"

Fanaye shook her head, put her slingshot back into the folds of her belt, and headed back to the woods, hearing, just before she left, the men arguing with each other as to whose rock had felled the crazy monkey. With a smile on her face, she slipped out of the marketplace. So much more to tell my cousin later, she thought.

To make up for her lost time, Fanaye rushed to where she'd hidden her bundle of wood. To her relief, the wood was still there. She swung the bundle over her shoulder and hurried home, where she stacked the wood against their hut as quickly as she could and then went inside, shouting, "Emaye, I brought the wood!"

"Thank God you're safe; I knew you wouldn't go anywhere near the mad monkey. Did you hear anything?"

Fanaye pretended she was clueless. "No, I heard nothing." Then she asked, "Can I leave now?"

Hewait nodded somewhat reluctantly. Fanaye hurried to the wicker basket, where she kept her clothes. She picked out a white, short-sleeved, ankle-length cotton dress with strikingly bright embroidery that ran all the way down the front to the hem. Dressing up was unusual for Fanaye, who preferred to walk around in plain clothes, but today she wanted to put on her Sunday best, mostly to please her mother, who always complained about Fanaye's tomboyish appearance and negligent way of dressing. If her mother approved of the way Fanaye looked, she was less likely to rescind her agreement to let Fanaye travel alone.

While Fanaye was getting dressed behind the bamboo partition at the back of the room, her uncle, Ato Tesfaye, an elderly man in his seventies, barged into the hut. As her mother listened to his exciting story of where and how the monkey's killing had taken place, Fanaye sneaked past them, trying to look as casual and inconspicuous as possible, and stepped outside, not even saying goodbye as she left. She was just glad that she didn't have to hear the rest of her uncle's elaborate recitation of how the dangerous monkey had died.

Chapter 2: In The Woods

On her way to her cousin's house, Fanaye walked through the familiar village in which she knew everyone. Huts were scattered on each side of a narrow footpath. Some of the huts were pointed at the top, while others were flat. Some were big, and others were small. For some reason, she had never noticed these details before. On one dusty patch of land, four boys were playing Gena, a native game similar to hockey. One of the boys, Tesfaye, froze when he saw Fanaye and stared at her with his mouth agape. When the others turned to see what was distracting him, they too saw Fanaye all dressed up as if she were going to a wedding or some other festive event. A second boy called out, "Hey, Fanaye, look what you did to Tesfaye. He lost his mind. He can't move!" They all laughed. Fanaye ignored them.

Farther down the path, Fanaye's girlfriend, Amsalu, appeared at the doorway of her hut and called out, "Fanaye, come and let me show you the new doll I'm making!"

But Fanaye was not to be distracted. "I will, but on my way back." She smiled and continued with her purpose.

The rest of her trip was uneventful as she cut through familiar territory, half walking and half running, going up and down rolling hills, through woods and meadows, and eventually arriving at her cousin's village in the afternoon. As she approached her cousin's hut, Fanaye's aunt,

Turunish, came out of the door carrying a bucket of barley. She was surprised to see Fanaye and looked around to see if Hewait had come with her. She hugged Fanaye and kissed her on both cheeks. Then she drew back, looked at her from head to toe, and exclaimed, "Oh, my dear, look at you. How well dressed you are! But what's the occasion? And where are your parents?"

"I just felt like coming over to visit you."

"And Hewait let you come all by yourself?"

"Well, I'm old enough now, you know."

At that moment, Yenanish appeared in the doorway and cried out in surprise and delight when she saw Fanaye. She hugged her cousin and then turned to her mother. "You see, Aksta, Hewait allowed Fanaye to go by herself. Won't you let me do the same?"

"We're not going to talk about that now," Turunish responded. "Go and give Fanaye some whey. She must be very thirsty from walking in the sun."

The two girls wrapped their arms around each other's shoulders and giggled as they walked into the hut.

"Tell me how it's possible that Aunt Hewait allowed you to come by yourself?" Yenanish whispered. "How did you convince her?"

"Well, it wasn't easy, I can tell you that." Suddenly Fanaye's mood shifted. "But first, I have to get something off my chest. Something terrible happened on my way here."

"What? What happened?"

In a hushed tone, Fanaye said, "You may not want to hear this, and it's not what I wanted to happen... but I killed a crazy monkey."

"What?! Why did you kill him... did the monkey threaten you?"

"No, no, no. He had gone crazy, so everyone was out to kill the poor thing, but they were too clumsy to do it. They were just torturing him! I hated to see that, so I wanted to end his misery by killing him."

Yenanish had no doubt about Fanaye's capabilities but was surprised to hear she'd killed a monkey. "How did you do it? How did people react?"

"I used my sling to kill him. They didn't even know I did it. Every man there was busy claiming he'd been the one to throw the fatal rock."

"I wish I'd been there," Yenanish said. "Why do I miss all the exciting things?"

The two cousins lost no time catching up on whatever juicy gossip they'd heard that was worth a laugh. But soon, Yenanish stopped laughing, and a serious expression came over her face. Fanaye wasn't accustomed to seeing her cousin look so glum. "What's the matter? What's going on?"

"I'm very upset," Yenanish admitted. "I'm not sure yet, but I think my father has agreed to marry me off to that wacky and ugly Bekale."

"But did your Ababa Gebra say so?"

"Not yet."

"Well, let's hope not. I don't think your father would give you away to him."

When Yenanish did not seem convinced, Fanaye added, "No way! You're not going to marry that crazy boy. If your father insists, I'll kick Bekale so hard he'll fly off to some unknown land, never to be seen again. See, the problem is solved."

Yenanish laughed, her good humor restored. "You're right!" She said and grabbed Fanaye in an embrace. Then she took Fanaye's hand. "Let's go and see Thitina."

They walked to a neighbor's hut. Thitina, a somewhat reserved and chubby little girl, was a friend of both Yenanish and Fanaye. When Thitina saw how dressed up Fanaye was, she wanted to change into her own fancy dress. The three friends fussed over their clothes, braiding each other's hair, and played Gebeta, a board game. After they had been at Thitina's house for some time, Turunish retrieved her daughter and niece.

It was then that Fanaye realized it was getting late, and she needed to return home immediately. When she told Turunish and Yenanish, they exchanged puzzled glances since they were under the impression that Fanaye planned to spend the night. Then Turunish shook her head adamantly. "No, you are staying here tonight."

"I can't! I promised Emaye I'd be back before dark. I really have to go now."

"But it will be getting dark soon," Turunish pointed out. "I don't want to send you back by yourself so late in the day. I'm already surprised that my sister let you come here alone in the first place. No more talking about it. I'm the adult here. You can go back in the morning."

Out of respect for her aunt, Fanaye consented and ended up staying overnight.

The next morning, after eating the delicious breakfast her auntie had prepared for her, Fanaye got an early start heading back home, not wanting to upset her mother any more than she probably had.

At first, her journey passed uneventfully. When she arrived at a crossroads outside of Yenanish's village, she wavered a moment before deciding to take a shortcut through the thick woods. This was much more of a forest than an outcropping of woods. The total absence of people began to strike her as unnerving. She moved as swiftly as possible, often jumping over fallen tree trunks or pushing aside branches with her bare hands. More than once, her beautiful dress got caught and tangled in thorny bushes. What I wouldn't give to be in my usual everyday dress right now, she thought. The air was filled with the constant chirping of birds, and the occasional screaming of monkeys seemed to mock Fanaye's uneasy progress through the foliage.

The forest seemed without end, and she regretted her decision to take the unknown path. But despite her uneasiness, she continued to move forward. At one point, the sounds of the birds diminished, and the forest became thicker. An instinctive fear filled her with inexplicable nausea, and she suddenly felt the urge to run. At that same moment, she thought she heard a faint whisper behind her. She wheeled around. To her horror, she came face to face with a menacing-looking stranger with long, matted hair who leered at her with hungry eyes. A blade glimmered in his hand. Fanaye drew a sharp breath, tense and vigilant at the stranger's every move, sensing a pervasive undercurrent of violence.

The man watched her, smirking in amusement at her growing terror. Fanaye moved back a few steps and heard more voices coming from deeper in the woods. Shiftas! She remembered the stories about bands of bandits who lurked on the roads between towns, robbing merchants and unlucky travelers. She removed her silver cross from her neck. "Here, take this and let me go," she pleaded.

The stranger's tangled hair partially concealed his face. "Keep your cross," he said. "If you're good, I may let you go."

Laughter rippled through the woods. The man stepped closer to Fanaye, and she had nowhere to go. He cocked his head towards the woods. "Your choice: me or them."

"Please just take this and let me go," Fanaye pleaded again.

"Are you crazy? They are dogs. I'll at least let you live. Get down now!" He looked around, pushing her down with his open hands. Fanaye's mind raced. She obeyed and got down on the ground, but before she could lie back, he'd already mounted her. Fanaye didn't resist since his knife was at her throat.

She played along and waited to make her move. She lay on the ground meekly while the man fumbled to open his pants. Then Fanaye kicked him in the groin. He howled and dropped his knife in the dirt. They both scrambled for the blade, Fanaye desperately stretching her arm towards it, clawing the ground and gasping as her attacker dragged her backward. The man lost his balance and faltered. Sensing her advantage, Fanaye managed to get up and grabbed the long cane hanging from the man's side. She then swung the stick at the man's head, giving him a thorough beating. He tried in vain to defend himself and to grab the cane back, but she continued to deliver several well-placed blows.

Laughter exploded around them. Frightened, Fanaye swung around and saw three other men, all of them even more menacing-looking than the first stranger, who was still moaning on the ground. Unlike the neighborhood boys who bullied and teased her, these men were not to be easily gotten rid of or easily negotiated with. Quickly her fear turned to anger. Right then and there, she vowed that she'd rather die than let these terrible men have their way with her.

Pointing to Fanaye, the ringleader said to the man on the ground, "Ah, so here you are, with your little secret. How long were you planning to keep her from us?"

The other two men laughed.

"You couldn't even manage her, so let me show you how to do it," the ringleader boasted.

He moved forward and wrestled Fanaye down to the ground as she struggled and spat at his face. He then attempted to mount her while pinning her arms onto the ground. Fanaye bit her lip and, with all of her strength, brought her right knee up, slamming it into his crotch. He howled with pain and loosened his grip. Still straddling Fanaye, he slowly released his hold on her. Taking advantage

17

of this, Fanaye suddenly reached over and picked up the cane. The ringleader turned back to Fanaye just in time to see the blow coming. She swung the cane, whacking him repeatedly. Badly hurt and stunned, the ringleader did not have a chance to brace himself against this second onslaught. The remainder of the men laughed and took in the scene with amazement and disbelief.

Finally, a tall man who had not yet approached her spoke. "Hey! Are we going to stand around and watch our leader get beaten to death?" With that, he grabbed Fanaye from behind and knocked her once again to the ground. He kicked her hard and then punched her viciously. Fanaye tried to knee him in the groin, which only fueled his anger. He attacked her as if she were a man. Fanaye fought until she could no longer muster enough strength. Then everything went black.

It was at this moment that they all heard the sound of what they thought to be horses trotting through the wood's silence. "Let's get out of here. I hear people coming," ordered the shiftas' leader. The men scrambled and dispersed into the woods.

Chapter 3: The Crumpled Body

Major Kebada Adafraw drew in a deep breath. He loved the cool freshness of the morning. He and his men had awakened at dawn to get an early start on surveying the area and making their report about the possible expansion of the Italian military into Ethiopia. Now, on their return trip, Kebada had given each man permission to visit his family. He'd chosen these men because they were from this area and because of their familiarity with the region.

Absentmindedly, Kebada patted his horse's neck. It had been a long journey. They'd traveled all the way from Addis Ababa, and now they were to return to the capital. Military life was never easy, and now things were strained with Eritrea. Rumors continued to spread that the Italians were crossing their agreed-upon borders in Eritrea and were trying to steal into Ethiopia, infiltrating into as far as the northern regions. The ungodly Italians were becoming increasingly greedy.

Kebada cursed under his breath because, in the past, their great King Menelik had been deceived by the thieving Italian hyenas. Menelik had foolishly traded part of the motherland to them—and for what? For weapons that soon rusted and rotted. Now, thirty years later, Italians were sniffing around for more. Well, by God, he wouldn't stand by while his people were betrayed once again!

Kebada's horse perked up his ears. He knew his mount well enough to trust its instincts; he reached for his pistol and scanned the trees. The horse cocked his head to one side, so Kebada also focused in that direction. A faint moaning was coming from a grove of trees off the path. Kebada dismounted, tense and on his guard. A trace of smoke lingered in the air. As he stepped into the clearing, he made sense of the scene in seconds: a smoldering campfire, signs of a struggle, and the crumpled body of a young girl propped against a tree, groaning. Shiftas did this, he thought. From the number of footprints he saw, Kebada figured there had been at least three men. The fire had not been out for long, either. Maybe they intended to come back.

He covered the girl with her shama, trying to decide what to do first. She moaned again and rolled over, wincing as though each limb had its own separate agony. Her lips were covered with blood, and her cheek was bruised. He realized one eye was swollen shut while the other was open. She cringed and clutched her torn dress.

"Shhh," Kebada said. "Don't be afraid. I won't hurt you. Here." He tried to help her sit up and brought his canteen to her lips to moisten them. She lay unmoving and unspeaking, her expression vacant. "Please try to get up and come with me," Kebada whispered, gesturing to the woods encircling them. "They may still come back. I have to get you out of here."

Fanaye's body convulsed with a surge of fear as she struggled to her feet. The effort was too great, and her knees gave way. Kebada stretched out his arms to prevent her from falling. "Can you walk at all?" He asked, afraid she might mistake his intentions if he tried to pick her up. He realized she was still in shock. He passed his hand in front of her face. Nothing. No response. Kebada had no choice but to carry her. He bent down and looked into her empty, staring eyes. Then he scooped her up with his left arm, keeping her wrapped in her shama as if she were a child. He balanced her against his chest with one arm, and with his right hand, held his pistol at the ready. His eyes searched the shadows among the trees as he struggled to make his way towards where he had left his horse.

When Kebada emerged from the grove with his odd-shaped bundle, the horse whinnied. "Shhh," Kebada said, hoping his calm voice would keep his horse quiet. He wasn't sure about the best way to get the girl mounted. She was badly hurt, and with her arms dangling at her sides, he doubted she'd be able to straddle the horse on her own. So, he hoisted her over one shoulder like a sack of teff, long enough for him to jump up into the saddle. Then he settled her in front of him, cradling her against his chest.

The horse moved forward. As they rode along, the sun flashed in and out between the shadowy branches, like a child playing peek-a-boo. In about a half-hour or so, Kebada saw a village ahead. He directed his horse to the nearest hut, where he heard a shriek and saw a tiny, stooped woman rushing toward him, beating her chest.

"Mariam, Jesus, enata menow? Menow?" The woman clawed at her faded yellow dress, ready to tear it apart. "What happened?"

"No, no, no, she's not dead," Kebada assured her, holding his hand up.

The woman was stunned and confused. When her fist loosened on her garment, it slid down her chest and now hung limply at her side. "She, she..."

"Yes, she's alive!" Kebada exclaimed.

"Mariam, Mother of Jesus!" The woman collapsed to the ground in hysterical tears.

A farmer stomped into the frontyard and found himself in the midst of an unexpected tableau: an imposing figure on horseback loomed over his wife while she knelt in the dirt and wailed uncontrollably. The man had heard rumors that certain city officials could ride up and demand whatever they wanted from you—livestock, grain, even the land itself. His wife must have refused him, and so they would pay the consequences. The farmer slowed his pace, knowing instinctively that one wrong move could be deadly. He dared not challenge the stranger.

"Sir, please, forgive my wife," the farmer said. "We have very little, but whatever we have is yours. Long live the King!"

"You don't understand. I found your daughter!" Kebada pointed at his bundle. The man was bewildered, for he had no daughter, but he felt it was unwise to contradict Kebada. So he took Fanaye from Kebada's arms and carried the limp girl into his hut. Kebada dismounted, helped the distraught woman to her feet, and walked her to the rotted door.

While his wife was busy tending to the girl, the farmer cleared up the misunderstanding. "You see, sir, we never had any daughter," he explained. "We have two sons. We've never laid eyes on this girl before."

"Probably she's from another nearby village then," Kebada said. "Her family will soon come looking for her, without a doubt. Until then, this is for your trouble."

He held out a handful of genzeb to the farmer, who knew he must pretend to refuse such a generous gift at first, or he would appear heartless and greedy. "No, no, I cannot take your money," the farmer said, pushing Kebada's hand away but hoping he wouldn't change his mind. "This is God's work."

"Please, you must," Kebada insisted.

"No, sir, I cannot accept."

"For your family then?"

The woman came outside and emptied her basin of water into the yard, and wrung out a rag.

"How badly is she hurt?" Kebada asked.

"She's not hurt so bad that she won't heal. The worst is she doesn't speak. Her eyes are open, but she doesn't see." Then the small woman returned inside to tend to Fanaye.

"We want to help the girl," the farmer told Kebada. His voice softened. "But, sir, if this girl cannot speak, how will she tell what happened? Her family will look for her, and when they find her here in a household with two young men, they will think one of my boys did this to her. They may even accuse us of hiding her here because of it! If she can't identify her attackers, even my neighbors will become suspicious of me, and my family name won't mean anything anymore!"

"She's young and will recover," Kebada responded. "Don't assume the negative. They will be grateful you have cared for her and will be glad to see her alive."

"Maybe she'll speak against my sons if her memory is damaged. Then my being helpful will cause bloodshed between our two villages. Sir, we are not cruel people. We want to help, but only if you stay here to tell our side and protect us from malicious rumors."

Kebada explained this was impossible. He had to report to Addis Ababa and was already delayed. "I can stay one more night only to see if her condition improves."

The following day, color had returned to Fanaye's face. "How are you feeling today, young lady?" Kebada asked.

She remained oblivious to Kebada standing before her.

This confirmed all of the farmer's worst fears that she might never recover and that her condition could bring trouble onto his sons and leave them all destitute. "Even if she recovers, her own family may wish her dead," the farmer told Kebada. "This poor girl will never marry. There's no future for her here. Take her to the city when you go. No one knows her there. She could work, maybe even get married. Have a new life!"

"Your mind moves too fast, my friend. Give her time. She may recover yet."

But the farmer insisted that he'd seen similar situations. At one time, a mother had lost her daughter and was never able to speak or care for herself again. She became a burden to her remaining children, and her husband left her, as she was no longer any use to him.

Kebada considered his options and realized he didn't have any, except to do his duty. He needed to move on, but the farmer had been so convincing that Kebada was now conflicted. He didn't want to see the girl he'd rescued abandoned or unable to lead a normal life. In the end, he begrudgingly decided to take Fanaye along to Addis Ababa. He hoped that the maternal instincts of his servant, Tsega, would prove invaluable during this young woman's recovery. Perhaps, at some point, the girl would speak again and then could return to her own village.

Chapter 4: Where Is Fanaye?

Hewait began to worry about Fanaye when it was growing dark, and her daughter still had not returned home. She reminded herself that it wasn't a good idea for Fanaye to come back by herself so late in the evening, and this rationalization made her feel better. Turunish must have kept her overnight, Hewait thought. A wise decision.

When Thanaw, a tall, slender man, Fanaye's father, and Aylahu came home and didn't see Fanaye at the dinner table, Thanaw asked where Fanaye was. Hewait explained that she had gone to Turunish's house to see Yenanish. Her husband raised an eyebrow and said, "Oh, how come? Did your sister come and take her along?"

"No, she went by herself."

"Since when do we allow her to go by herself?" Thanaw asked, his voice turning harsh.

Hewait had already regretted letting Fanaye go off on her own, but she tried to sound casual about it. "She did all her chores and some extra too, and I wanted to make her happy," she said. "Just this one time, I wanted her to feel like she is now almost the woman that she is."

Thanaw shook his head. "I just don't understand you," he said. "I know you let her get away with her wishes easily, but this was a big mistake, sending a young girl off like that."

Aylahu didn't understand either that his mother had let Fanaye go off alone, but he said nothing since he didn't want to upset Hewait anymore than she already was. If anything, Aylahu wanted to defend his mother against his father's accusations; if he'd dared, he would have told his father not to speak to his mother in that tone of voice. As it was, the matter was dropped for the night.

The next morning, Fanaye still did not come home. Hewait spent most of the day anticipating her daughter's return, but the whole day passed, and Fanaye was nowhere in sight. The sun had already sunk behind the horizon, and the moon was creeping up, just a sliver of a crescent, casting a meager light that was hardly enough to placate an anxious Hewait. Fanaye not showing up the day before was understandable; it might have gotten late, and Turunish had kept her from leaving. But, what about today? Why wasn't Fanaye home? It's almost nighttime, and she still isn't back, Hewait thought, her mind racing. What should I make of this?

She went in and out of her hut repeatedly, trying to see if Fanaye was coming in the distance. At one point, she noticed someone approaching, and her heart leapt, thinking it was Fanaye. But when the figure came closer, she realized it wasn't even a woman but a male neighbor, the elderly Ato

Wendema. "Oh, excuse me," Hewait stammered. "I was expecting my daughter, but..."

Ato Wendema smiled a mostly toothless grin, trying to make her feel at ease. "Oh, believe me, I understand," he said. "These days, children are very defiant. They test our authority, don't they?" He then bowed and continued on his way. This must be the case, and Hewait became upset that Fanaye had so blatantly disobeyed her.

Soon it was completely dark, and there was no sense in entering and exiting their home anymore, but Hewait still stood outside for some time. Slowly, her anger at Fanaye dissipated and was replaced again by fear and deep anxiety. "Tethelfas behone!" she moaned aloud. "What if she's been kidnapped?" She smacked herself hard in the mouth to knock out the dreadful thoughts and to punish herself for not trusting God. She knelt down on the ground and prayed. "Please, Heavenly Father, the Holy Ghost, please, I beg You, don't let anything happen to my Fanaye! Please, God, forgive me for doubting You."

She felt better momentarily, but as time passed with still no sign of Fanaye, fears and panic returned. Her heart felt as though it would explode out of her chest. To distract herself, she started compulsively cleaning the house, scrubbing the pots and pans, sweeping the floor, and dashing outside to look again for Fanaye. Under ordinary circumstances,

Hewait would never sweep the floor in the evening; this was believed to bring bad luck.

Aylahu was oblivious to his mother's ordeal. He was relaxing nearby in the living room area and stroking the strings of his kirar. When he no longer felt like playing, he lay down the instrument and noticed no aroma of his mother's cooking. There was also no wood-fire in the stove, as there normally would be at this time of day. He called out, "Emaye! Emaye! Where are you?"

A jittery Hewait came back inside and threw herself against her slender boy's shoulders, squeezing him so hard that Aylahu was startled. "What's the matter, Emaye?"

"Nothing," she answered, not wanting to upset him. She also had the superstitious fear that if she expressed her fears aloud, they would come true.

Aylahu sensed Hewait's anxiety. He straightened himself up, stuck out his chest, and with as much authority as he could muster, said, "Look, I'm not a kid anymore. I'm grown up now, almost a man. Tell me what's bothering you."

Hewait managed a smile. "You're my big boy," she said, hugging him again. She couldn't help thinking it seemed like only yesterday when Aylahu was peeing all over her, and now he sounded like a grown man at the age of ten. Hewait glanced upwards and prayed quietly, "Please, dear God, let

Fanaye's head be resting peacefully on a pillow at my sister's."

"Remember, I'm the second man in the family, after Ababa," Aylahu reminded her. "I'm ready to protect you." On a sudden impulse, he asked, "How come Fanaye isn't home yet?"

She dismissed him absentmindedly with a wave of her hand. "You must be hungry," she said. "I'll make dinner."

Hewait placed several pieces of wood on the stove to start the fire. Her hands trembled, trying to kindle the wood, and she was only able to produce embers. "Aylahu, please help me get a fire going so I can warm up dinner," she called out, exasperated.

Aylahu took over, and in no time, the fire was blazing. "There, Emaye, fire!" he said proudly. But when he looked at his mother, he saw her forehead was perspiring, and her face was distressed. "What's wrong?" he asked her again. "Is Grandmother sick?"

"Well, your grandmother is feeling her age," Hewait muttered. "She has been sick a great deal these days."

The whites of Aylahu's eyes shone in the dim light. "She's always sick," he said. "Tell me the truth. Is she dying?"

"Oh, God, no!" Hewait said, flinching, and made the sign of the cross with her right hand.

Yet Aylahu sensed something was still wrong. "Has something happened to Ababa?"

Hewait shook her head. "Your Ababa is fine," she said. "Probably he's with his friends right now drinking tej."

Because she was so worried, Hewait forgot to warm the leftovers, despite the fire Aylahu had built for that purpose. She served him a cold dinner, which he ate anyway, not being the type to complain. Mother's too distracted, he thought, perplexed. Halfway through his dinner, he noticed she hadn't eaten anything. "Emaye, please sit by me and eat your dinner," he pleaded.

Hewait felt a fervent need to hold him close, but she held herself back, fearing that her raw emotions would scare him. She sat down next to him and attempted to eat but struggled with every bite. Aylahu sent covert, sideward glances at her, trying to read her mind as she fidgeted and nudged the food around on her plate. Finally, he pushed his own plate away and said, "I have no more appetite."

"What's the matter, son?"

"I wish Fanaye were here to cheer you up," he said. "I'm not good at this."

A lump swelled up in Hewait's throat. "I wish I knew where she was," she whispered and broke down crying.

Aylahu was bewildered. "But didn't you say she's at Auntie's house?"

"Yes, but she should've come home by now," Hewait said between gasps and whimpers.

Just then, she heard Thanaw's heavy footsteps outside the door, sounding like someone dragging a heavy load. He walked in, his face more tired and red than usual. "Greetings, dear ones!" he said.

Hewait relaxed when she saw her husband so happy. She removed his shama from his shoulders. "Aba-yea!" Aylahu called out.

Thanaw beckoned the boy with his hand, so Aylahu dashed to his father's side. Thanaw embraced him and kissed him on the forehead.

"Leja, my son, wash your father's feet," Hewait said.

Though he was growing sleepy himself, Aylahu took the bucket of water from his mother's hand, untied and removed his father's sandals, and washed his father's tired feet. When Aylahu finished, Thanaw said, "Yebarkeh, bless you, my son."

Soon, the three retired to bed. In no time, the two men started snoring, their rhythmic breathing rising and falling in tandem, like a competition to see who could make the loudest and strangest noises. Hewait, on the other hand, couldn't sleep and kept on praying throughout the night for her daughter's safe return.

At dawn, as chickens squawked and roosters flapped their wings and crowed, welcoming the morning sun, Hewait dragged herself from her mat and stretched her weary body. The sun's rays filled the cramped hut with filtered light. At least the day is bright, she thought. She went outside and washed her face, then scattered a basketful of seeds for the chickens. She watched the mother hens vigilantly strutting around their chicks, pecking away at the aggressive ones. Whether human or animal, a mother was always a mother, and nothing in the world could take the place of her children. This thought briefly comforted Hewait.

Her husband and son left the house to perform their chores—Thanaw tended to the corn crop, while Aylahu took the herd to graze. Hewait ignored her daily chores. She just sat outside, waiting for Fanaye to come home.

Zenait, her neighbor and friend, came by carrying an empty jug on her back. She asked Hewait why she was sitting around and not ready to go fetch water. When Hewait didn't answer, Zenait asked, "What's the matter, my friend?"

Hewait shook her head and told Zenait she wasn't going out to fetch water today.

"But what's the matter? You look worried."

Hewait explained how Fanaye should have returned home yesterday before nightfall. She didn't know if Fanaye had been cajoled into staying longer at her aunt's place. "I don't know what to think."

Zenait smiled. "Your worrying is probably premature. If that's your reason for not going, come on, let's go get the water. When we return, I bet you'll see Fanaye."

Hewait hesitated, but to please her friend, she went inside and carried out her jug. Even as she walked, Hewait couldn't shake off her worries. They'd only walked a little way before Hewait stopped and said, "I can't explain it. I have a terrible feeling something's wrong."

"Ah, my friend, you worry too much!" Zenait said. "As I said, she was probably enjoying herself and decided to stay longer. You know how children are." But Zenait understood she could not persuade Hewait to continue on with her to fetch water, so the two women embraced.

As Hewait started back toward her hut, she continued to fear the worst until she was half walking and half sprinting, desperately picturing Fanaye waiting for her when she arrived.

"Fanaye, leja, Fanaye!" she called out when she arrived back at the doorstep. There was no response. She thrust the door open with her shoulder, shouting, "Fanaye, dear, where are you?" But Fanaye was not there.

She accidentally dropped the empty brownish clay jug from her back. It shattered into tiny fragments that scattered across the mud floor, but she was too distracted to worry about picking up the broken pieces.

She rushed out of the house and started toward her sister's village, a two-hour trip by foot. She ran most of the way like a mad dog, her netala flying in the air, mumbling to herself, "Leja, my daughter Fanaye, come home safely." She tried to console herself by thinking she was being foolish. Of course, she's at my sister's house, playing with her cousin, she thought. That's what girls do.

After walking and running for what seemed an eternity, Hewait arrived, covered with sweat and filled with ominous premonitions, at her sister's hut.

The dogs greeted Hewait with enthusiastic barking. "Lucky dogs!" she quipped. "You don't know how good you have it. Not a worry in your bones."

Yenanish run out to greet her, shouting, "Auntie, Auntie!" But then she noticed her aunt's downcast, sullen expression. "Are you okay?" she asked. "You're out of breath. Did you run all the way here?"

Hewait ignored all of Yenanish's questions. "Where's Fanaye?" she asked, her heart pounding.

Yenanish looked confused. "What do you mean, where's Fanaye? She left yesterday morning."

"Are you telling me Fanaye's not here?" Hewait grabbed hold of Yenanish's hand.

"You mean she never came home?"

Hearing the commotion, Turunish hurried outside. The moment she saw her sister so distraught and out of breath, she immediately assumed the worst. "What's wrong?" she asked with fear in her voice. "Who died?"

Hewait began to wail. "Fanaye never came home!" she cried.

Turunish shook her head in disbelief. "Could it be that she decided to visit one of her other cousins or go to Mother's?"

Hewait knew that Fanaye would never do such a thing, and she said so. Turunish took Hewait by the arm and gently tried to lead her inside, but Hewait pulled her arm free. "Do you really expect me to sit while my daughter might be in danger?" she shouted. "I need to find her!"

They decided to go check at their mother's house first. The walk felt endless to Hewait. She kept praying, then blaming herself, then hoping they would find Fanaye unharmed. When they finally arrived, they saw that their mother had company, an elderly woman who appeared more youthful than she was. Their mother was lying on a cot. "Did Fanaye come here?" Hewait called out.

"Not yet," their mother said.

Hewait started wailing again. "Please, calm down," her sister pleaded. "Fanaye is where she should be, at her house. You'll see. Let's go."

The walk back to Hewait's hut was long and arduous. The heat baked the ground; the women could feel the heat through their sandals. Overhead, the sun-scorched with a blinding light that made it uncomfortable for them to keep their eyes open, especially for Hewait, whose vision was already blurred from continuous weeping. They covered their heads with their netalas.

Turunish tried to make small talk, hoping to distract her sister, but to no avail. Hewait was cursing herself for letting Fanaye go off. Her daughter's tomboyish nature hadn't been a problem when she was younger. It had become a problem only when she reached puberty when Hewait's relatives began to tell her that if Fanaye continued acting like a boy— running around and chasing a ball, tackling kids and climbing trees—men wouldn't be attracted to her, and she wouldn't be able to find a husband.

"But she was a special child, wasn't she?" Hewait said aloud, as though Turunish could have read her thoughts. Then again, she let loose a loud howl, unable to control her body's shaking; her legs felt as if they might buckle from under her. Turunish held Hewait closely while she convulsed and cried. When her sobbing subsided, they continued walking. Soon Hewait became nearly catatonic. Each step was a struggle. After a few minutes, she could no longer continue and collapsed on the forest floor.

Worried, Turunish knelt to comfort her, but Hewait remained unresponsive. As luck would have it, a group of men in the distance, probably walking home after a day's work, had heard her cries. When Turunish caught sight of the men, she pleaded, "Please help! My sister has fainted. I need to get her home."

The men rushed over and looked at Hewait lying prone on the ground. One man, fearing the worst, gently felt her pulse. He shook his head, worried. "Tell me!" Turunish cried. "What's wrong with her? Why has she fainted?"

"Have you been walking for long?" the man asked in a cautious tone. When Turunish said they'd been walking for an hour, he said, "So she's clearly exhausted. She needs to rest. How far do you live from here?"

When Turunish said they lived another hour's walk away, the men said they could help get her home. The youngest and strongest of them lifted Hewait and threw her over his shoulder, her body limp and her legs dangling as they made their way to Hewait's hut.

When they arrived, they found Aylahu sitting by the door with his neighbor, Mengustu. "Aylahu, Aylahu, please open the door quickly," Turunish called.

"What's wrong with Emaye?" Aylahu exclaimed with fear in his eyes.

The man carrying Hewait set her down, where she lay like a wet rag. Aylahu bent down and shook her, unable to accept seeing his mother completely bereft of energy. He longed to see her behave as she usually did: laughing and talking incessantly and even screaming in anger. Aylahu remembered seeing dead people being readied for burial, crumpled up and squeezed into wooden boxes. Petrified that his mother would die, he began pounding his chest, hardly aware of his actions.

"This can't be happening!" He lowered his head and whispered into her ear, "Emaye, please wake up. Don't die. I promise to be good and to take care of you." When she didn't respond, Aylahu pinched her cheek and pulled up one of her eyelids. He saw the white of her eye.

Finally, Hewait stirred and moaned faintly. "Fanaye, come home," she mumbled.

"Aylahu, dear, she is alright," Turunish assured him. "Go fetch your father and tell him to come home immediately."

The boy resisted. Why should he leave his mother's side if Fanaye was fine? "But you heard her speak," he protested.

Turunish held his hand and gazed into his eyes. "Of course, she's fine. Just go and fetch your father."

"Ababa won't like being called from work early."

40

"He'll like it less if he's not told Fanaye is missing," Turunish said. "You're old enough to know, too. Hurry now!"

Aylahu appeared stunned. "Is Fanaye really missing? How can that be?"

"That's why we need your father right away, so he can organize a search."

In a daze, Aylahu sprinted down the dirt road. The midday sun blazed relentlessly, its white-hot light forcing Aylahu to shield his eyes with his hand. He tried to comprehend all that was happening—first, his sister had gone missing, and now his mother was in a frightening condition, too weak to walk or talk.

He saw his father working in the cornfield, waving at him and smiling from a distance, which momentarily comforted Aylahu. "You came to help your Ababa?" his father fondly said when Aylahu reached him.

"No, Ababa, I came to get you," he said. "Aksta Turunish needs you home right away."

Thanaw's back stiffened, and his face tightened. "Has something happened to your mother?"

Aylahu shook his head and explained that Fanaye was missing. As Thanaw listened, the veins in his neck began to stand out like thick olive branches. "No one knows where

41

she is since she left Aksta Turunish's house," Aylahu said, looking straight into his father's eyes.

Thanaw looped the rope and tied the mule to a sturdy pole. "Son, don't worry," he said, managing a thin smile. "Everything will be okay. Fanaye will turn up someplace we haven't expected. We'll find her."

Aylahu nodded. He wanted so much to believe that Fanaye was safe. "She's not lost, right, Ababa?"

Thanaw patted Aylahu's arm in response.

When they arrived home, they found their small hut filled with neighbors, friends, and relatives, all witness to Hewait's wailing, her breasts slightly bare and bruised from beating herself with her fists. No one could comfort her. Many of their family members and friends had gone out in search of Fanaye and had promised to bring her back. "My daughter!" Hewait kept crying with a weakened voice. "Precious jewel, where are you? Find my girl!" Still unable to stand, she swayed back and forth in anguish.

Turunish, profoundly upset by her sister's grief, sat on one side of her. How could she free Hewait from the tentacles of the dark place that was claiming her, even though? It would not be a happy ending. Turunish patted her sister's hand and adjusted the cold cloth on her forehead. Thanaw sat down next to Hewait on her other side. "Hewait, please stop lamenting as though our daughter were dead," he pleaded. "I swear to Almighty God I'll find her, but I need your support. I don't want you sick and useless. You need to take care of yourself and our son. I will go from house to house and town to town until I find her. Have faith!"

Fanaye's father stood, thanked his guests for coming, and apologized for having to leave. His two brothers, Yohanes and Delka, stood up simultaneously and said they would go, too.

Several more men also volunteered to help search for Fanaye. The women remained behind to console Hewait, fussing over her and holding her hands. Others left to gather roasted chickpeas, barley, dabo kolo, and dry meat for the men to take on their journey.

Chapter 5: The Journey

Throughout their journey to Addis Ababa, Fanaye kept screaming and punching Kebada's back. He became so fed up with her raving and ranting that he cursed the shiftas for driving her crazy. If only she could remember where her village was, or if he could find someone willing to take her in until she fully recovered. Finally, after more screaming and shouting, her voice turned coarse, and her throat began to ache. Full of rage, she pushed against Kebada's back and jumped off the horse, falling to the ground and bruising one of her knees. She lay on the ground for a moment, her head down, feeling helpless.

Because it was late afternoon and Kebada was exhausted, he decided to set up camp right there and rest until dawn. "Young lady," he said, "why don't you rest in the shade under this tree and take a nap. I'll do the same." He curled up under the tree and soon drifted off into a deep sleep. Fanaye waited until she was sure he was sleeping, then she tiptoed into the forest. She didn't know where she was headed at all. She just knew she had to escape this evil man.

When she tried to run, her legs felt weak and rubbery, so she limped as briskly as possible through the trees. For a while, the forest seemed pleasant and benign, with nothing but small arboreal creatures and birds making a racket in the treetops. But then the forest grew thicker and more ominous looking, with sunlight no longer penetrating through the thick canopy of trees. All of a sudden, the chatter of small creatures ceased, creating an eerie silence. She stopped and frantically tried to gather her wits as she struggled to overcome the panic building up inside of her. When she heard a familiar sound like coughing nearby, she knew it could mean only one thing: a leopard was lurking somewhere in the vicinity. Terrified, she turned around and limped as fast as she could, her instincts telling her to go towards where the forest seemed less dense—back to where Kebada was. She lurched forward fast as she could, casting nervous glances over her shoulder from time to time.

The sound of footsteps and snapping twigs woke Kebada. He saw Fanaye hurrying toward him and said sleepily, "I hope you got some rest, too." Fanaye, breathing hard from all the running, said nothing in response. She merely gave him a scornful look, then haughtily turned her head away.

They rode through the quiet forest. Occasionally, the trees grew so thick that they had to duck to avoid the branches. After twenty minutes, they reached a large meadow. To the right, they saw a number of scattered huts and to the left, a green pasture that stretched further than their eyes could see. Luckily, with only a little effort, Kebada found the home where he'd stayed more than a year ago. It had been recommended by one of his fellow officers because it was fairly large, and the owner was a patriotic man. Kebada steered the horse toward the second hut on their right.

As they approached, Kebada saw his host-to-be, a very tall and skinny man who looked like a walking skeleton, standing near the entrance. The skinny man recognized Kebada immediately and greeted him. He bowed and said, "Welcome to our humble village. Please come into my place and get some rest."

Kebada thanked him. "Would we be welcome to stay overnight?" he asked.

Remembering the reward he'd received last year for putting Kebada and his companion up, the man was quick to respond. "Of course, sir. My wife and I would be delighted to have you as our guests. Our place is humble, but it's yours." He smiled, remembering all the heroic stories Kebada had told everyone last year, which filled the man with a sense of pride. But he didn't know what to make of Fanaye. Was she a relative or a maid?

Fanaye found herself in a large hut that looked similar to her parents', except her parents were not there. Her mind was too foggy to determine where she was and what was going on. Then, in desperation, her mind cleared. She was not in her own home and was still with a very dangerous man.

Once they were seated, the man's wife appeared with a small basin and water jug so that Kebada could wash his hands. Next, she reappeared with a masob, the traditional straw tray with raised edges, in which was a millet dish—injera—with some wate, a sauce. After she served the men, the wife brought a smaller masob to where Fanaye was sitting and joined her to eat. In between bites, the woman attempted to make small talk, but Fanaye was not at all in the mood. "Do you know that I've been kidnapped?"

The woman was at a loss. "By whom?" she inquired.

"By that man over there." Fanaye pointed at Kebada. "Please take me to my home!" she whispered.

The woman, not knowing what to make of this confused and weak-looking girl, simply shook her head, incredulous that someone as respectable and reliable as Kebada would do such a thing. But she needed to find out the truth. When she had the chance, the woman approached Kebada and whispered, "Sir, is something the matter with the girl?"

Kebada explained what had happened to Fanaye in the forest and how she'd apparently lost much of her memory. He asked if they'd be willing to keep Fanaye and take care of her until she fully regained her memory and remembered where she lived.

His hosts listened to Kebada's story and were sympathetic, but they said they couldn't take her into their

47

home indefinitely. "Sometimes, doing good can cause more harm," the skinny man pointed out and then suggested that perhaps it was best if Kebada took Fanaye along with him. "Maybe it's the girl's fate to end up in the big city!" the woman brightened.

Kebada wasn't sure about his hosts' reasoning, but he couldn't force his request upon them, so he let go of the idea of leaving Fanaye with them and hoped that during their long journey, he'd run across someone who'd be willing to help the poor girl.

Early the next morning, the wife prepared a simple kita, a flat barley bread usually eaten for breakfast. During the long goodbyes outside, the woman handed Fanaye small dried injera she'd packed for their journey. Kebada mounted his horse, pulled Fanaye up behind him and, waving their final goodbyes, rode off into the forested hills surrounding the house.

By the afternoon, the weather had turned so sunny and dry that Kebada decided they needed rest. Just as they dismounted the horse and settled down, he heard a strange strangled sound, like an animal in distress. He picked up his rifle and neared the patch of weeds where the sound emanated. There, a very badly wounded pregnant deer lay on the ground, her body heaving with each breath. Kebada stared at the deer for a moment, then aimed his rifle and shot her.

The animal shuddered and then stopped moving. Fanaye looked at Kebada in horror. "You cruel monster!" she shouted. "You just shot a poor animal for no reason."

"No, I put her out of her misery. She was going to die anyway, but she might have suffered for hours that way."

Fanaye eyed Kebada suspiciously. "I don't believe you," she said. "I think you killed her because you're a mean person."

"I assure you, shooting her was the best thing to do." He looked gently into Fanaye's eyes. "Why don't you take a rest while I prepare our meal?" he suggested.

Fanaye was willful. Kebada worried that she'd wander too far and get lost. "Listen," he said, "I hope you're not planning to do anything foolish."

Fanaye ignored his comment. She walked by the horse, stroking it as she passed, and looked for a suitable place to lie down. Meanwhile, Kebada knelt beside the deer and skinned it with a sharp knife. When he finished cutting up the meat, he started a fire to barbecue it. Fanaye noticed none of this because she had fallen into a deep sleep. A few hours later, she was awakened by Kebada holding a chunk of meat in front of her face and saying, "Get up and eat! This is going to be the best meal you'll have till we get to Addis Ababa."

Fanaye shivered with revulsion. She glared at Kebada and thought, he has to be one of the evilest men in the world.

"If I were you, I'd eat," he repeated, but she steadfastly refused.

For days they traveled over rolling hills and meadows, through forests and thick bushes, and stretching plains. On the ninth day, Kebada spotted a lake in the distance. They could use some rest and cooling off since the day had been exceptionally hot. After tying the horse to a tree, he walked to the edge of the lake. Out of respect for Fanaye, he only took off his shoes, rolled up his pants, sat on a jutting rock, and dipped his legs into the cool water. He scooped up some water and splashed it across his face and over his head. "Feels good," he said to Fanaye and then left to give her privacy.

But Fanaye had her own plans. When she was sure he was out of sight, she jumped into the lake and swam out at a rapid pace.

Kebada returned to where he'd left her, but she was nowhere to be seen. He looked around, growing increasingly uneasy. Where had she gone? Then he spotted a small still figure floating in the water a good distance away. He couldn't even tell for sure if it was her, but he had to find out. So he quickly took off his shoes, pulled off his clothes, and jumped into the lake.

He swam as fast as his body allowed. If the floating figure was Fanaye, was she dead or alive?

By the time he reached her, he was out of breath. When Fanaye was within his reach, she glanced back, saw Kebada closing in on her, and swam further away, leaving Kebada wondering where she found the strength to keep swimming like that. Just a week ago, she'd been almost dead; who would believe that near-catatonic girl was the same one who was now swimming like a dolphin? He imagined that she was fueled by fear and desperation to escape the predator— namely him! He hoped her memory would return soon so she'd realize he wasn't the villain. But right now, he had to catch up with her and restrain her so he could get her out of the lake.

It took a great deal of effort for Kebada to catch up to Fanaye. When he came within grabbing distance of her, he acted with caution. He waited for an opportune moment, then suddenly grabbed her by the wrist. Once he had gotten hold of her, he held her at arm's length and slowly towed her, against her will, all the way to the shore. At first, Fanaye struggled and tried to break free, but Kebada had such an iron grip on her arm that she eventually resigned herself to her fate and submitted to getting pulled to shore.

Once they reached the shore, both Kebada and Fanaye collapsed on the ground from sheer exhaustion. Soon they

51

both fell into a deep slumber, which lasted undisturbed throughout the night.

The following morning, Kebada calmly told Fanaye, "I'm trying to help you whether you believe me or not. And also know this: I want you to return to your family just as much as you do. I didn't want to take on this responsibility, but for the time being, you're under my care, and all because of a decision I made that I now regret."

His somber talk only confused Fanaye, but she didn't fight him as they mounted the horse. In silence, they rode along for several more hours.

A few days later, Kebada noticed signs that they were approaching the outskirts of Addis Ababa. It didn't cross his mind how odd they might look traveling together, with her face still bruised and hair matted. They traveled for several hours before Kebada stopped at a place to get food and beverages. Kebada found people staring at them with puzzlement and suspicion.

They sat in a dimly lit dining area, which suited Kebada just fine. As soon as they sat down, a young man of about twenty came to their table, bowed, and said, "Good day, sir." He avoided looking at Fanaye altogether, acting as if Kebada were dining alone. Kebada couldn't help but wonder if he had made a big mistake by traveling so far with this young girl. Perhaps he should have tried harder to find her parents.

But he remembered that the farmers had convinced him of what was best for the girl, so with the assurance of this recollection, he vowed not to question his decision anymore. When dinner was served, the girl would not eat despite Kebada's insistence. For the most part, she just sat beside him like a rag doll, leaving Kebada to his thoughts.

As they approached the city, Kebada chose to go through the back streets and winding alleys to be less conspicuous. He didn't want to draw the same kind of attention they'd had to endure while dining. Fanaye had also seen the way people had stared at them in the inn. She'd waited for someone to step forward and come to her aid, which no one had. Her spirit was too trampled to fight this man. But when they finally arrived at a fenced-in house guarded by soldiers, Fanaye assumed there were many people in the house who would help her. She would tell them the story of what this man had done to her.

In the early evening, Tsega, Kebada's housekeeper, heard a commotion outside the door. Kebada had returned unexpectedly after one of his long absences... but he was not alone. He was with a very young girl who cowered behind him, looking frazzled.

Perhaps a new servant, Tsega thought, although she couldn't figure out why that would be the case. She was curious, but she didn't have the privilege to ask such questions of her master. She figured that later she'd learn everything that she needed to know.

"Welcome home, sir," she said and politely stepped aside to let them in.

Kebada casually told Tsega that the young girl would be staying with them for a while and that she should take care of her. "Yes, sir," Tsega replied, bowing and heading towards the back of the house. She passed the tiny pantry area and came out the back door to the servants' quarters, which were humble but sturdy, consisting of several small rooms under a flat roof, including a storage area and an outdoor fire-pit used for cooking. She grabbed a small gourd of water and a small basket of kollo—roasted barley—and dashed back to the main house. "Sorry, sir, I had no idea you'd be back this evening," she told Kebada, "so I didn't prepare a meal."

"No need to apologize," he said. "This will do for now."

Kebada sat in his favorite chair while Fanaye curled up on the floor in a corner, her head resting on her bent knees, her feet flat against the wood floor. While Tsega washed Kebada's feet, she glanced at the girl, noticing her coarse clothing and braided hair. This girl was certainly not from Addis Ababa, and she didn't look well either. Tsega understood feeling confused and lost, coming to a big city from a small village. She remembered how difficult it had been for her back when she had first arrived with her mother, fresh from the village. The city people had called her a getharay girl, a villager.

As she dried Kebada's feet, she assured herself again that he was not in need of any more servants. After all, hadn't she managed quite well on her own for years? Although she was aware of becoming a bit older, she doubted he'd just dismiss her after all her years of faithful service. No, certainly he must have brought this girl to ease her load, to assist her!

Fanaye didn't even look up when Tsega brought the food to the table. "Come and sit down here," Kebada said, pointing to a nearby stool. Tsega's eyes widened in surprise. Definitely not a new servant if he's inviting her to eat with him at the table, she wondered. Maybe a distant relative? Perhaps a niece?

When Fanaye refused to look up or budge, Kebada gave up and asked Tsega to show the girl to a spare room. "She's very tired," he said. "So, why don't you help her get washed up before she goes to bed? And I hope you don't mind staying overnight for a while to assist the girl."

Although it was inconvenient to stay at the house, Tsega knew she had to accept his request. She'd never contradict him, for he was a good man and, as her employer, gave her the freedom she needed. Besides, she much preferred to work for a master than for a mistress since she generally found men less fussy and demanding than women. With a slight bow of her head, she said, "Of course not, sir."

Tsega took Fanaye by the hand and gently led her to the spare room, but Fanaye was too startled and distracted to respond, noticing that the rooms were way too bright. They shone like the day, but the light was different from that of the sun, as though lightning had flashed. And all that light, she saw, came from a small, round object that dangled from the end of a twisted string attached to the middle of the ceiling. This frightened her, making her wonder what kind of witchcraft was it and what it would do to her.

"This is your room now," Tsega said cheerfully. "We'll look after you. Don't worry." Her assurance helped Fanaye feel somewhat comforted. Tsega went off to get Fanaye something to eat, but when she returned, Fanaye had fallen asleep with her clothes still on. Tsega covered the girl with a wool blanket and then watched her sleep. What was going on in this girl's mind? She was frightened and unsure, to the point of being in a state of shock. Perhaps I can help her, Tsega thought as she quietly closed the door behind her.

Fanaye slept all night and through most of the following day. When she finally woke up, she was still confused and frightened, not understanding where she was or how she had gotten there. Her head pounded, and her mouth was dry. Everything was unfamiliar and strange. Just then, the door

56

opened, and Tsega walked in with a smile. "Good morning, you must have been very tired. It's good you rested well. Now let me take you to the shintbet, and I'll bring you some water to wash yourself."

Fanaye couldn't remember the woman clearly from the night before, but Tsega's warmth made her feel safe, so she meekly followed the woman. On the way, "Where am I?" she questioned.

"You are in Addis Ababa, in Basha Kebada's house. Don't you remember that Basha Kebada brought you here?"

Fanaye said nothing. The two women were exact opposites. Fanaye was tall and robust, while Tsega was thin and fragile-looking. The girl had honey-colored skin, while the woman was as dark as roasted coffee beans. "Let's talk over breakfast," Tsega suggested. "You didn't eat a thing yesterday. You need to eat."

"I don't want to eat anything in this house," she said. "I've been kidnapped."

Tsega looked confused. "You were not kidnapped. Basha Kebada would never do that."

"But he did! Believe me, he did. I want to go home. Please get me back home."

"Maybe your family has given you to him."

"No, he just took me."

"Yenilaje, dear child, that can't be. You need to eat and get some more rest." Tsega took Fanaye by the hand, sure that a little food and sleep would restore her memory of what had actually happened.

Fanaye would not leave her room as long as Kebada was nearby. She feared him, unable in the aftermath of her trauma to distinguish who had harmed her. For some reason, she remembered only Kebada's face from the incident in the forest, and so she believed he'd been one of her attackers, not realizing he had actually been her rescuer. Day after day, Tsega explained in vain to her that Kebada had found her after the attack and brought her to Addis Ababa to help her recover, but Fanaye remained unconvinced. She believed that Kebada had simply tricked his housekeeper.

A few days passed with little change in Fanaye's behavior. She stayed in her room if she heard Kebada's voice. She hardly ate and didn't talk. Either she sat on the bed and sulked all day, or else she raved and ranted, furiously pacing the room and banging on the walls with her fists, crying, "I want to go home; take me home!"

On these occasions, Fanaye's hair would fly in all directions; her eyes would be as red and swollen as her knuckles, which hurt from banging on the walls, and her voice cracked from shouting and screaming. After these outbursts, her beautiful face resembled that of a sick person.

58

Tsega, listening to her charge's crying and wailing, thought that the girl was losing her mind.

One morning as Tsega was serving Kebada his breakfast, she begged him, "Sir, please, do something before something terrible happens to her."

"Do you think I want to keep her here against her will? I told you I don't know where her village is. Until she remembers the name of her village, I can't do anything."

The subject was not mentioned again for several days. Then one morning, as Tsega swept the floors, Tamru, Kebada's assistant, knocked on the door. When Tsega answered, Tamru went straight over to Kebada, saluted sharply, and handed him an envelope that gave Kebada his latest orders. He needed to travel and would return in several weeks. Tsega quickly packed for the journey.

"Tsega," Kebada said by the door, "please find a way to help the girl." And as an afterthought, he added, "Have the tailor come and make her new clothes, also."

Tsega wasn't sure how she could best help Fanaye. She'd conjured so many stories in her head about Fanaye and what had happened to her, but the mystery remained of who the girl was and how she'd come to be there. But one thing was certain: the girl insisted she'd been kidnapped. Later that day, she asked Fanaye one more time if she remembered when she'd last left her parents' house.

The girl's face darkened with a deeply troubled look. "I couldn't tell you just like that," she said, "but I'll bet if we just got going, I could find my village. You and I could find it together."

"Every village has a name, Fanaye. What's the name of yours?"

"I can't remember, but I can show you; I'll know it when I see it."

By now, Tsega was convinced that something was clearly amiss. I should have known better, she thought. Basha Kebada is not a kidnapper. Why would I doubt him for even a second? She reminded herself that if he wanted a woman, he could have his choice of mistresses from among the sophisticated city crowd.

Tsega's days became filled with new routines with her new charge, some of them challenging. Fanaye remained adamant that she'd been kidnapped and refused to socialize with anyone. When she spoke at all, she bitterly condemned Kebada and sometimes, by implication, Tsega as well. "Why is he keeping me here?" she asked pointedly. "Can't you both see I'm dying to get back to my family?"

When Fanaye protested like this, Tsega would cringe and grimace with empathy but would also repeat what she'd already told the girl many times before: that Basha Kebada wasn't a bad man; that what he was doing was for her own good; that he would send her back when the right time came.

Hoping to prod Fanaye's memory of the past, Tsega offered a memory of her own. "You know, Fanaye," she began, "when I was a young girl about your age, I loved my mother's dabo. She knew exactly how to make it, just what to add to it and what not to, so it was always delicious. And she'd never share her cooking secrets." Tsega cocked her head to one side and asked, "How about you? What did you like most from your mother's cooking?"

Fanaye's expression was tight and impassive. "Everything," she said.

Although Fanaye was still angry at Kebada, Tsega continued to believe that, in time, the girl would come to terms with her situation. Even if Fanaye had been kidnapped, this was not at all an uncommon practice, and many kidnapped young girls went on to have perfectly normal and even happy marriages. Still, Tsega couldn't help but wonder, at the back of her mind, if Basha Kebada had taken Fanaye to be his mistress.

Chapter 6: Softening

When Kebada returned from his trip several weeks later, he was startled and drew his horse to a halt. A beautiful and well-dressed young woman gathered wildflowers in his yard. It took him a moment to realize this young woman was Fanaye. She wore an elegant, ankle-length cotton garment color-shot with citron and magenta, with threaded Coptic cross embroidery. The design fell straight down the center to the hem. The fabric wrapped around her like a shawl from the nape of her neck to her ankles. It fell softly across the curves of her body, accentuating her sensuality as she moved. With her hair freshly braided and reaching her shoulders, Kebada couldn't help but marvel at the transformation of the wounded creature he had first brought home with him.

He dismounted his horse and walked cautiously toward her. "How are you, Fanaye?" he asked, "you're looking well." He reached out to touch her shoulder. He hadn't meant to do so.

Fanaye shivered at his touch. When she looked at him, Kebada couldn't help but notice the improved color in her cheeks. "I'm a little better, sir," she said. "I'm strong enough to return to my village. Will you take me back?"

"Which village would I be taking you to?"

Fanaye shook her head sadly. "I'm sure I'd know the way, if…"

"When you're fully recovered and remember the name, we'll take you back."

"My mother's name is Hewait, my father is Thanaw, and my brother's name is Aylahu."

"It's good that you remember their names." Kebada hesitated. "Do you remember the day we met?"

"No."

"Well, it's been six months."

The conversation was too much for Fanaye. She turned away from him and ran into the house. He could hear her yelling at Tsega in the kitchen or perhaps to no one at all, "I will never see my parents again! I hate this man! He took me from them!"

Kebada stood there helplessly, hoping Fanaye's memory would return quickly and wondering how he could make sure it did.

As the New Year approached, Kebada came up with a gift idea of buying Fanaye jewelry, hoping that it would cheer her up. One quiet weekday afternoon, he stole away to a well-known jeweler.

As soon as Kebada entered the store, the owner, Guma, greeted him as one would greet a dignitary. He was a short and stocky man who stooped, which made him appear even shorter. "Sir, I'm at your service. What would you like me to show you?"

Kebada desired to look at some fine jewelry. He deliberately lowered his voice because he didn't want to call attention to himself, even though no one else was around. "No rings or bracelets," he said. "Just necklaces."

Guma pursed his lips and, with a deferential bow, slipped into an adjacent room. Soon he returned carrying a white cotton bag, which he set down on a smooth round table. He slid his hand into the bag and took out a handful of sparkly necklaces. With his white but crooked teeth flashing, he said, "Sir, I believe you can find what you want from these selections, since I carry only the very best."

Indeed, Kebada had never seen such a rich selection of beautiful jewelry. Still, he felt more comfortable leaving the choice to an expert, so he asked Guma to pick for him.

Guma knew his merchandise well. He made room to lay out a select few of the necklaces for Kebada to consider. "These are the most exquisite necklaces, made by the best craftsman," he said. "He takes his time in making them, but once he's done, there's nothing else that is comparable to them." After a brief pause, he subtly expanded on his sales pitch. "Sir, I just know your wife will be more than happy having any one of these, since she will never see any other women wearing the likes of it."

Kebada nodded his head, and, after staring at the necklaces for some time, made his choice. Like a good salesman, Guma tried to persuade Kebada to consider some matching bracelets and rings, but Kebada repeated, "Just the necklace." He then asked, in his direct manner, how much the necklace cost.

Guma claimed to offer him a steeply discounted price for which his profit would be marginal. Without a word, Kebada took out the money from the front pocket of his coat, counted out the exact amount, and handed it to Guma. He then thanked him and walked out.

Afterward, feeling the necklace's subtle weight in his pocket, Kebada hoped the gift would show Fanaye his sincerity and lessen her anger toward him. She was just a young woman, after all, who, like others, would be happy with such a thoughtful present. But he knew she wasn't the type who was easily impressed. In fact, she might consider his generous gift a bribe. But he quickly brushed that thought aside. He hoped he was wrong.

As more time passed, Fanaye remembered that people from her village would travel to big cities, even to Addis Ababa, and return with items they couldn't get in the village. An idea formed in Fanaye's mind that she believed was clever, an idea that would help her escape from Kebada's captivity. Although she was growing fond of Tsega and would rather not misguide the older woman, Fanaye knew that she had to look out for herself. Tsega's loyalty would always be to Kebada, and part of Fanaye's clever idea was to act cheerful and agreeable to Tsega, even pretending to enjoy her ridiculous city cooking, as a way to convince Tsega to take her to the main marketplace.

Fanaye's fourteen-year-old mind never considered that, in a big city like Addis Ababa, there could be several open market areas. In a marketplace, she might run into one or two people from her village. She would immediately tell them what terrible things had befallen her. After hearing her story, these people would surely help her return to her village and reunite with her family. She still didn't remember her village's name or even its whereabouts but, in her child's mind, surely someone would recognize her face and know the village she came from.

Fanaye plotted a strategy to get to the marketplace, knowing that she had to be extremely careful. It wasn't easy to just run away. Even if she managed to sneak out of the house without Tsega noticing, she couldn't slip past the two guards who were always on duty at the gate. On one occasion, Fanaye had tried testing them by dressing as Tsega to see if they might mistake her for the housekeeper. But the difference in their heights betrayed Fanaye.

Harsh reality set in when Fanaye considered—then rejected—the high-risk move of climbing over the high fence that surrounded the property. Frustrated, maybe the only way to leave this place was with Tsega's help. But as kind as Tsega was, getting her cooperation was out of the question. Helping Fanaye escape would cost Tsega her job, and her family depended on her meager income. Besides, Kebada had been good to Tsega, and she had expressed her gratitude to him often.

Fanaye had only herself to depend on. But there must be a way out and, to seize the opportunity when it presented itself, she had to be constantly vigilant. Thus, her mind was constantly in turmoil. Frustrated about how to escape, her helplessness first turned to anger, which eventually gave way to a deep sadness.

As Kebada became more preoccupied with how to help Fanaye, he decided that sharing a familiar activity such as gardening might trigger her memory, or at least make her more comfortable in his home. With this in mind, he planted a small garden on one side of the house large enough to grow a variety of vegetables and flowers. "Are any of you knowledgable in vegetable gardening?" he asked his guards.

One young man who came from the country and had worked on his father's farm immediately lit up. "Yes, sir!" he said.

Kebada sized him up and was impressed with his well-built, strong body and his large, calloused farmer's hands. "What's your name, young man?"

"Alula, sir," said the young soldier as he snapped to attention.

A faint smile hovered over Kebada's face at the young man's display of enthusiasm and self-confidence. "Where do you come from?"

"From Gonder, sir, and I've been here for just a little over a year." Then, as if he anticipated Kebada's next question, he added, "Before I joined the army, I was a farmer, sir."

Kebada was satisfied. This young man would be perfect for the job. "Come then," he said. "Let me show you where I want you to cultivate a garden."

Chapter 7: Alula

Fanaye acquired a daily routine. At sunup, she and Tsega headed behind the outhouse and, sheltered from view, washed their privates. Before bed, they'd clean themselves again. In the morning, they'd sip their coffee and, when the cups rattled and were empty, Tsega would enthusiastically tell Fanaye's fortune from the coffee dregs at the bottom of her cup, turning the cup over to divine the future for her. Fanaye didn't really believe Tsega's interpretations, but welcomed them as something to pass the time. Tsega would begin the ritual by reciting something like, "You'll have two children and a handsome, powerful man for a husband. The boy will look like his father, and the girl will resemble you. You'll be happy with your family."

But talk of family only made Fanaye nostalgic. Strangely, she still couldn't remember the name of her village, but she could visualize the faces of her family and remember their names. Fanaye pictured her mother surrounded by neighbors, either at her or someone else's home, drinking coffee, chatting, and laughing about some harmless incident or joke, most often after listening to her friend Martha's dramatic stories. Then she imagined her mother attending weddings or celebrating the birth of a child. Did these celebrations remind her mother of the loss of her daughter? And what about Yenanish? Did Yenanish miss

69

her? Fanaye wondered if her cousin had gotten married yet. She couldn't picture Yenanish as a married woman, even though she would be considered eligible for marriage. As for her father, Fanaye imagined him sitting quietly and listening to her mother as she told him about church gatherings, weddings, celebrations, visits to sick people, and funerals. He would have nodded his head up and down in consent and from side to side in disapproval. And her little brother... she smiled at the thought of him. She missed his mischievous laughter and good nature, even the teasing and the tricks they used to play on each other.

Fanaye still believed that Kebada had kidnapped her since she still had no recollection of how they'd met. The incident was locked away in some hidden memory. Yet Kebada behaved so kindly that, along with Tsega's conviction of his innocence, Fanaye sometimes wondered if she was wrong about him.

One morning, after one of their coffee rituals, Tsega suggested they cook lamb stew "the city way." She cut the meat from the bone in perfect pieces. "You will grow to like the life here," she told Fanaye. "Let me teach you how to cook."

"I don't want to get accustomed to it here. I'll never like it!"

Tsega placed two onions in Fanaye's hands. "Chop these, please. No arguments. Let's just cook. Making food is good."

Fanaye quartered the onions rapidly and washed her hands, thinking she was finished.

"Where are you going? Finish chopping the onions so I can sauté them," Tsega said.

"Don't you see I am finished? That's the way my mother does it."

Tsega laughed and showed Fanaye how to chop the onion into small fine pieces, her hands moving swiftly. Where she stood, Fanaye's eyes began to tear from the onion. "Please finish it," Tsega said patiently and handed the knife back to Fanaye. And then, changing the subject, she said, "The gardener is coming again today."

"Finally, the land will be useful," Fanaye said, careful not to show her enthusiasm. "I'd like to help in the garden, too. Then you'll see how wonderful the vegetables will taste."

The gardener, Alula, labored the entire morning working on irrigation ditches, yanking out rocks and weeds, while sweating furiously in the hot sun. Fanaye stared through the window as Tsega brought him water to drink. Alula smiled, showing his bright white teeth, and said, "Thank you."

Seeing his big smile made Fanaye smile, too. She wished she handed him the water. Before he left, he washed his face and tucked his shirt in so he looked respectful. Then she looked over the garden. Seeing it slowly taking shape lifted her spirits.

The following morning, Fanaye awoke to one of those gorgeous balmy days in the dry season: the sun shone in a perfectly cloudless sky, the leaves were still on the sun-dappled trees. It was neither too hot nor too cool. Birds chirped in the nearby trees. Fanaye stretched lazily and climbed out of bed. Kebada had already left before sunrise. After spending a few hours tidying up her room, eating a bit of dabo for breakfast and helping Tsega with household chores, Fanaye drifted into the living room. Through a window that opened onto the side of the house, her eyes again fell upon the handsome young man now patting down dirt under his big hands. He'd removed his shirt, his bronzed torso gleaming with sweat and his strong muscles rippling as he dug the ground with his hoe. Fanaye was captivated by the well-defined sculpting of his body. Her excellent eyesight caught every detail of his physique and movements. She missed nothing.

One time, when Alula paused, stood upright to catch his breath, and wiped the sweat off of his face, Fanaye hurried to the kitchen, telling Tsega, "I'll take some water to the gardener today. He is working so hard, and you are busy, too"

Tsega didn't have time to question the young girl's motives... so Fanaye quickly filled a glass and went outside.

"Here is some water." She handed the glass to Alula. After they stood in silence for a moment, with him gulping down the water and her blinking under the blazing sun, she asked, "What kinds of vegetables are we going to grow here?"

"Cabbage, kale, tomatoes, and carrots. Maybe some peppers and pumpkins."

"I'm from a village, too, and I can help in the garden."

"You can't work here. This isn't work for a lady like you."

"Are you from my village?" she asked.

"I could be. There are many villages. I'm from Gonder."

"How far is that?"

"A five-day trip by mule." Out of politeness, he didn't ask where her village was, although he was curious.

Alula had been working in the garden for three weeks, and it showed great promise. Each morning while they had coffee and breakfast, Tsega and Fanaye watched him from the window. "My goodness, that young man is so strong!" Tsega said, seeing the way Fanaye looked at Alula.

"Yes," the girl said in a deliberately subdued tone. "How wonderful that we'll be eating fresh vegetables right from the backyard. He must be very hot though. He keeps wiping his face. Do you think he'd like some water?"

"Who wouldn't be thirsty on a day like this? Let me go give him water," Tsega said, knowing that Fanaye wanted to serve him and curious to see how she'd react.

"Don't bother yourself," Fanaye said softly. "I'd like to see the garden's progress. I'll go."

The next day, anticipating Alula's arrival, Fanaye kept checking her hair in the small wooden mirror hanging in the hallway. She brushed her teeth an extra time. Right before going outside, she grabbed the gold cross that Kebada had given her, but which she'd never worn. She stared at her reflection, admiring the necklace, pleased by how the cross complemented her complexion. Then she watched discreetly from the window as Alula spoke to one of the guards. Even when he squinted in the sun, his eyes remained sparkling and intense. As usual, seeing Alula's dazzling smile made her smile. She hoped the guard would leave soon so she could go join him.

After a few more minutes of chatting and pointing to the garden, the guard left. Fanaye waited a minute longer before bolting so that Alula wouldn't think she'd been watching. She stared at him as he bent to pick up dead leaves and move some tools, his movements so graceful that they looked choreographed. Fanaye's face glowed with pleasure as she watched him. Being so absorbed and distracted, she didn't hear that Kebada had come home unusually early.

The house was in such complete silence that, at first, Kebada didn't think anyone was home. He headed for his bedroom, but as he passed by the main room, he caught sight of Fanaye frozen by the living room window. Careful not to startle her, he slowly approached her, curious to see what she was watching with such fascination. He coughed audibly, yet Fanaye still remained oblivious to him. Kebada followed Fanaye's gaze to Alula toiling outside and was seized by a sudden and uncontrollable fit of jealousy and rage. "So you're wearing the cross I gave you for the eyes of my coolie out there!" he exploded with a twitch in his eye. "Not in my house!"

He stormed outside and stomped towards the clueless Alula, who was digging up some weeds. When he saw his boss, the young man hastily straightened up and stood at attention. "Your job here is finished," Kebada said curtly. "You'll be transferred to another post. Check in with my assistant for your orders tomorrow morning."

Alula froze, confused. "Sir, were you not happy with my work?" he asked.

"Just be sure to show up at the base for your next order," Kebada said and gruffly walked away.

Tsega found Fanaye in a miserable and mournful state, her eyes red and swollen from tears. At first, she was baffled by what could have put the girl into such a gloomy state when Fanaye had seemingly been making progress, but it didn't take her long to figure out that Fanaye's mood had something to do with the sudden disappearance of Alula.

To Fanaye's chagrin, he vanished on that day. But the brief romantic longing haunted Fanaye for years. That nothing ever happened between them made the fantasy even stronger.

Chapter 8: Lesson

Fanaye stared up into the evening sky, lost to her memories. The sun had disappeared to its unknown resting place and magically, the sky had turned pitch-black. A few white stars delighted her, as if she were seeing old friends. Heavenly bodies—particularly Venus—had always fascinated her from the time she was a little girl. "Do the stars grow and become big like the moon?" she had once asked her mother. "Are the sun and the moon the parents of the stars? And who is the mother and who is the father?"

Overwhelmed with the questions, her mother had shaken her head and frowned. "Fanaye, my love, you ask questions only the wise men can answer." Fanaye hadn't been satisfied with that response, so after dinner, she'd sat by her father and asked, "Ababa, can you tell me about the stars? Are the sun and the moon their parents?"

Unlike his wife, Fanaye's father was impressed with her fanciful curiosity and was very eager to teach his daughter about the stars. "Let's go outside and talk about them!" he had said, taking her by the hand as they left the hut. Outside, he'd questioned her, "Fanaye, why do you think the sun gives more light than the moon?"

Fanaye had just shrugged.

"Think," he'd said as they sat side by side on the stone stools.

"I know! The sun is the ababa, right?"

"In a way, yes, the sun is the master of the moon and the stars and everything else that we see in the sky."

"Like you are for our family?"

"Yes, like I am," he had said with a smile, amused by the comparison.

Fanaye remembered Mescal, one of the biggest holidays. It's Epiphany Day, a celebration of the baptism of Jesus Christ. Most families—including Fanaye's—would stay overnight, where the priests and altar boys would pray, sing praises and dance. The priests and altar boys would wear their best colorful garments of silk and fine cotton, and dance joyfully, moving this way and that, holding colorful open umbrellas. The ceremony would go on throughout the night. In the early morning, the miniature Ark of the Covenant, known as Tabot, would be carried out, led by the priests to a river. After the sermon, the priests would dip their crosses in the river and sprinkle water on the crowd. Some would go in the river and bathe to renew their baptism. After the ceremony, there would be a big feast with family and friends where lamb or chicken—drenched heavily with ghee and spiced with herbs—would be cooked, plus all kinds of vegetable stew. A big round of dabo (wheat bread), and lots of small dabos were handed out to visiting children. Of course, tela or mead would be served. Whatever food was left, it would be donated to the poor at the church.

Fanaye had never appreciated the holiday that much, but now she would do anything to be near, even stay up all night at the church celebrating.

Tsega gently touched Fanaye's shoulder, interrupting her dreamy reverie. "I think Kebada is coming."

Shortly thereafter, they heard his unmistakable, deep voice. "Good boys, good boys," he was saying to the barking dogs; they always seemed to bring out his soft side.

Fanaye's stomach knotted at the sound of Kebada's voice. She closed the door to her room, flung herself across her bed, and sobbed quietly. After a while, Tsega knocked at the door and announced that she had something to tell her.

"I swear on my ababa's name, it had better be something good that you are going to tell me, otherwise don't bother," Fanaye warned her defiantly. Tsega opened the door and came in anyway, as if she had not heard the warning. She then gently wrapped her netala around both their shoulders. Fanaye turned to her with a serious look and said, "You know, Tsega, I am truly thankful for your kindness. So, tell me anything you want, but don't let it be anything about Kebada."

"Thank you, but I want you to know that people often think about their pasts in much better ways than they actually were in reality. They glorify it, as though everything was as perfect as angel's wings."

"So, you're saying I'm glorifying my past?"

"No. That's not what I meant. I just want you to look more towards your future."

Fanaye insisted, "But what do I have to look forward to? My future seems as bleak to me as the dark clouds in the sky."

"I'm old enough to be your grandmother, so I'm going to speak as if you were my very own daughter. Have I told you I have three sisters? My youngest sister Aster has a very pretty daughter Aberach, as pretty as you are. Unfortunately, my sister lost her husband to illness—"

"There's no use trying to distract me," Fanaye interrupted, losing patience. "What's so important that you want to tell me?"

Regardless, Tsega told Fanaye the full story of her sister Aster after her husband died and left her with four children. Because Aster was struggling financially, she wanted Aberach, who was thirteen, betrothed to a good provider. A longtime family friend named Terefa was acquainted with a man who was a widower and looking for a new wife. He was a man so well off that he probably could have supported ten families. He thought Aberach might make the perfect choice for this man.

When Terefa mentioned the widower to Aster, she grew so excited that it didn't occur to her to ask about the man's age. A few weeks later, the prospective groom arrived at her house along with him. When she first saw the man in his sixties, Aster assumed he was the groom-to-be's father. This can't be, she told herself when she realized the old man was the prospective groom himself.

After much agonizing and vacillating back and forth, Aster reluctantly agreed to the marriage. When Aberach learned of the arrangement, she became terrified and cried inconsolably for days. Aster was very remorseful about what she was doing to her daughter, but she couldn't see any way out of it. She resented Terefa placing her in this situation, tempting her in a time of dire need with the promise of a good life for her daughter.

"As it turned out, my niece's husband was not only very old, but also a cruel and physically abusive man," Tsega concluded. "He also denied Aberach any share in his wealth. They have been married for over ten years. You see, Fanaye, some people are having an even more difficult time in their life than you."

"But why are you telling this story to me? What's this story got to do with me?"

"Ah," said Tsega wisely, "I told you this story to show you how different your case is from this poor girl's. Whereas her husband was old, ugly, cruel, and miserly, Kebada is just the opposite. You should thank your God that he has sent you a wonderful man, a man who is handsome, respected, generous, and loving. Not many men are like him. You may be too young to appreciate all this, but I wish you'd trust me and believe me on this."

Fanaye was quick to respond. "So, I knew it was going to be about him!" But she didn't press the issue any further and was, in contrast, quiet and pensive for the rest of their time together.

Chapter 9: Marriage

At the age of fourteen, Kebada was dumbfounded to discover that his father had arranged a marriage for him without his knowledge, to a girl named Negat with whom he had no desire to spend the rest of his life. Although he'd told his father outright and refused to accept Negat as his wife, his father, resolute as an engraving on a stone slab, wouldn't change his mind. Long ago, he'd promised Negat's father that when their children reached the appropriate age, they would get married, and breaking that promise now would sully his reputation.

Kebada realized that the only way out was to openly defy his father, which would discredit and belittle his father in the eyes of Negat's father and all his peers, and deal his pride and dignity a death blow. So Kebada reluctantly agreed to go through with the marriage, hoping that in some way, things would work out between him and his wife. The wedding took place on a depressingly overcast day, which perfectly reflected Kebada's mood.

Their relationship began as a platonic one. On their wedding night, the couple finally parted from the family and guests and retreated to their bedroom. Negat became acutely aware of Kebada's emotional withdrawal and obvious lack of desire. She was utterly hurt and rejected. "You can have the bed," she said in a melancholy voice. But Kebada refused and let her take the bed while he slept on the floor in the farthest corner of the room.

The next morning, Negat woke looking disheveled and very much like a drunk. Her eyes were red with dark circles under them, and her beautiful and elaborately designed wedding dress was wrinkled and damp with perspiration from having slept in it all night. When Kebada looked at his new wife, he couldn't help but pity her and wondered what would become of them as a couple. Would he eventually learn to love and desire her, at least enough to fulfill his husbandly duties?

Over the next few weeks, Negat finally swallowed her pride and faced the problem that clearly lay between them. She decided to speak up, no longer able to endure the silence that separated them like an invisible wall. She dragged herself up from bed one day, draped in a sheet to hide her nakedness, and approached him beseechingly.

"What is it?" Kebada asked guiltily.

"Please... don't tell anyone!" she pleaded.

"Tell what?" he asked with a frown.

She lowered her head, staring at the Coptic cross that was woven into the carpet under her feet. Then, with nervous hands moving up and down in sharp, choppy movements, she said, "That you reject me as your wife."

84

Kebada hadn't expected her to be so direct. "I didn't reject you!" he said. "I've just been rejecting marriage! Marriage is not for me."

Negat's expression brightened slightly. "You mean you don't hate me?" she asked. "This is how you would feel no matter who the bride happened to be?"

Kebada nodded and repeated that his problem had nothing to do with her.

Negat had grown up witnessing her own parents' loveless marriage. Her mother had skillfully managed to hide her own marital disappointment for so many years, accepting her life as a dream she couldn't control, in which her role was simply one of compliance and subservience. She was the epitome of the good wife as a second-class citizen, like countless generations of Ethiopian women before her.

Following her mother's example, Negat gathered the pieces of her broken heart and went on to become the perfect wife in every other respect, doing her best to perform her domestic duties during those rare occasions when Kebada was home for a few days at a time. All of these adjustments seemed to pay off; a form of understanding and friendship began to grow between Kebada and Negat. Kebada acted on his guilt and dedicated himself to giving Negat the satisfaction of motherhood. Despite her loveless union with

Kebada, Negat bore him three healthy children. These children became the entire focus of Negat's life. When Kebada announced one day that he'd been assigned to Addis Ababa, the capital city, and that he would have to live there most of the time, returning only occasionally to visit her and the children, Negat agreed without complaint.

They had been married for twelve years, and all went relatively well between them, until one day a nosy neighbor came to Negat with disturbing news. "I saw a pretty, young girl at your husband's home. Who could that be?" Negat's heart raced, but she managed to respond, "Oh, the girl... she's his new housemaid. A distant relative."

It wasn't uncommon for some married men to have mistresses, but that wasn't the case for Kebada at all. It was unknown whether he had had any mistresses earlier, but with Fanaye, it was completely different. Being the perfect gentleman, Kebada wouldn't dream of taking advantage of a helpless young girl in his custody, whose very presence in his house was due to a tragic twist of fate.

Negat was not foolish enough to believe that Fanaye was just a servant in his house. The possibility of Kebada taking a mistress had loomed large in her mind since their first night of feigned conjugal bliss. Now, faced with this reality, Negat dealt with the situation in a way she'd learned from her father. He had been a master mind reader with intuitive knowledge that often gave him an advantage in interpersonal situations.

She had learned from her father how to act dumb when that played to her advantage. When she found out about Fanaye, she pretended to everyone that she didn't suspect the girl was Kebada's mistress. She referred to Fanaye in public as Kebada's new housemaid. This made sense since Kebada's faithful servant Tsega was getting rather feeble with old age and had arthritis, and she could indeed use a young and vigorous helper.

Negat knew that confronting Kebada directly on any issue wouldn't be wise. She assumed he was unlikely to send Fanaye away, and might even send Negat packing instead. As Negat quietly resigned herself to her fate, she nevertheless persisted in believing that one day Kebada might learn to love her for her loyalty and enduring care.

While she was determined to show to her friends that her husband's taking in a pretty young girl to his household did not bother her, when she was alone in bed at night, she burned with jealousy, afraid that someone might accidentally discover the truth about his "live-in maid." She imagined the shame and humiliation she'd feel. The women who envied her privileged life would gloat and have a wonderful time celebrating her misfortune.

One night, as she lay on her bed in solitude, with a hint of moonlight filtering through the windows' louvered shutters, she felt more depressed than usual. She kept comparing herself to Fanaye, thinking of what irresistible physical attributes the girl might have that would make her vastly more appealing to Kebada. Quietly, Negat prayed to God to be her judge and resolve this matter for her.

Chapter 10: Confused Feelings

Kebada had just returned from another one of his trips, soaking wet from the heavy rain and glad to be home. But as soon as he stepped into the house, he was greeted with a mournful cry coming from Fanaye. "What's wrong with the girl?" he asked Tsega, startled.

Tsega removed Kebada's wet coat, frowned and shook her head. "She's in a lot of pain," she said. "This has happened before. I'm hoping the medicine woman will come soon."

"Is she sick?"

"It's a woman's issue."

"How long have you been waiting for the medicine woman?"

"Makonen already went to get her. She'll be here soon."

Kebada stood by Fanaye's door. "I'm sorry you're not feeling well," he said. "Be patient. The medicine woman is on her way."

The room was quiet. "The hot-water bottle is easing her pain," Tsega said.

Tsega let in Weizero Sunqua, a tall, dark woman who was the local herbalist. The medicine woman followed Tsega to Fanaye's room. "How are you feeling?" she asked as she reached down and gently poked Fanaye's belly.

Fanaye pushed the woman's hand away, but Sunqua continued making her examination. "Oh, it hurts so much," Fanaye moaned.

When Weizero Sunqua finished her examination, she explained why she caused Fanaye pain. "I was releasing the stagnant blood," she said. "I have herbs to help you." Then she turned to Tsega and said, "Let's go to the kitchen to prepare the medicinal herbs. She'll be just fine."

Tsega boiled water while Sunqua mixed herbs and requested a few clean cloths. When the herbal tea was ready, the two women drained its liquid and used the boiled twigs and leaves to make a poultice to use as a compress.

They returned to Fanaye and Sunqua handed her the large cup of hot herbal mix. "Drink all of it," she instructed, and sure enough, soon after the first treatment, Fanaye's pain eased, and she started to feel a little better.

Sunqua turned to Tsega and said, "Make sure to reheat the poultice as needed, and press it down. Give her a cup of the tea every three hours and let her rest."

Meanwhile, Kebada had been sitting in his chair in the main room. He opened his eyes as the medicine woman exited Fanaye's room and bowed to him. He stood up and said, "Thank you for helping her."

Sunqua asked, "Do you want me to come back to see how she's doing?"

"If you think it's necessary," he answered.

"The woman has all the instructions. I left enough medicine for her. The young lady will be fine. It's just the women's curse."

Toward midnight, Fanaye's symptoms returned with a vengeance. Her moans awoke Kebada from a deep sleep, and her loud cries finally drew him out of his bed. Quickly, he put on his robe and went to the kitchen to call Tsega, but on the way to the kitchen, he remembered that earlier in the evening he'd given her permission to leave so she could take care of her sick mother.

He went to the kitchen, rekindled the charcoal, warmed up the medicinal tea, and poured it into the large cup. He had never done that before. He knew that Fanaye wouldn't scream unless she was in great pain.

He knocked on her door, but no response. "Fanaye, it's me! I brought you the tea the medicine woman had prepared for you." Still no response from Fanaye. "Are you decent?" he called. "May I enter?"

"No, I don't want you to come in." Fanaye shouted.

"I am trying to help you. You sound like you're in great pain."

"I am not, and don't come."

"Okay, I'll just leave the tea by your door."

Finally, after a while, when she could no longer bear the

pain, Fanaye slowly opened the door. By then, the tea was already cold.

Toward morning, Fanaye's scream woke Kebada. Once again, Kebada knocked on her bedroom door. "Is there anything you need?"

"No, thank you." But she sounded as if her voice, too, was in pain. Regardless, he decided to offer her tea again, so he went to the kitchen and returned shortly with the warm poultice and tea in his hand. This time she shyly accepted it and thanked him. Kebada could see that she was too preoccupied with her misery to feel self-conscious in his presence. As soon as she placed the poultice on her stomach, the warmth brought her a measure of relief.

Seeing Fanaye in pain, Kebada felt helpless, not quite knowing what to do. Her feet were sticking out from under the blanket, and when he moved to cover them, his hand brushed against one foot. It was icy cold. Impulsively, he massaged her toes, trying to warm them. He felt his body heat rising. As if Fanaye sensed this, she jerked her foot away, making Kebada realize that his good intentions could be interpreted as taking advantage.

Actually, Fanaye was feeling new sensations throughout her body. The warmth from Kebada's hands on her toes had been sending tingles all the way up her spine and spreading to her abdomen. In only a moment, she had turned from cold to hot, and a pleasant sensation had replaced the pain that she'd never felt before.

The only man who had ever excited her before was Alula. For a moment, Fanaye forgot whom she was with. Kebada's touch had made her feel entirely different than the touch of the medicine woman. Maybe she was an unusually sexual person? To hide her pleasure, Fanaye turned her face toward the wall. Only an hour before, she would never have imagined letting Kebada lay a hand on her. She was certain she would never care for, much less desire, this selfish man who had separated her from her family and caused her so much suffering.

She felt a pang of guilt since she'd been brought up as a virtuous girl who was not supposed to enjoy a man's touch. She wanted to be like the women who screamed and wailed as if they were in labor when their virginity was taken from them on their wedding nights.

Traditionally, the bridegroom's best man would be obligated to stand outside the bedroom door, waiting to hear the bride's screams. Then he would enter the room holding a white cotton cloth, which the bridegroom would use to wipe some blood from the deflowered bride as proof of her chastity. Then the best man would run off with the cloth, proudly waving it around for all to see, shouting, "The bride is a virgin! The bride is a virgin!" Upon hearing the good news, the family and friends would celebrate, singing and dancing while the bride and the bridegroom remained in their conjugal bedroom. In fact, the bride and the groom would remain in the room for three days and nights, with only the closest family members allowed to enter for short periods of time to chat or serve food.

If a girl lost her virginity to another man prior to her wedding night, she was beaten by her husband, kicked out of the house, and sent back to her parents, where an equal punishment by her father would be waiting for her. Her treatment would be as bad as that of any common criminal. Also, her entire family would be disgraced.

A premaritally deflowered girl would have very few options. Most girls in that situation would have to run away to big cities to build a new life, outcasts from their families and villages. Unfortunately, most of these young girls would end up working in bars as prostitutes, or as house servants in strange towns where no one knew them. Fanaye knew that if she were to yield to her feelings of desire, her own future would be no exception. But now, she was profoundly confused and conflicted by her feelings towards Kebada, as well as by the contradiction between her pristine upbringing and the strength of these new emotions. Try as she might, she couldn't explain them away as anything but unanticipated—and overwhelming.

Chapter 11: The Incident

In a typical Addis Ababa rainy season, it rained hard all night without a minute's break. The deluge continued throughout the early morning, making it difficult to say exactly when the sun had risen through the dense clouds and stubborn rain. The ground became soggy and turned to mud.

Fanaye drifted in and out of sleep, calmed by the rhythm of the rain as it beat down on the roof, just as she had done when she was a child in her village. She felt as if she was inside a dream.

Kebada had been up for hours, oblivious to the pouring rain, going in and out of the house, checking on the horses, and giving various instructions to the guards.

Finally, he sat down and ate a little bit of kitfo and washed it down with a strong cup of coffee, but didn't touch the eggs Tsega had scrambled. She knew he never liked to eat anything heavy in the morning, but that never stopped her from trying to tempt him. She picked up the untouched eggs and handed the plate to Tamru, Kebada's assistant. When Kebada finished his breakfast, he called out, "Tamru, let's go!"

He and Tamru headed to Wal Wal in Ogeden to investigate rumors that foreigners were building a fort. Reports had increased that the Italians were gradually

95

encroaching into Ethiopian territory. The Emperor had given orders to determine whether the rumors were true or not.

It was still raining by the time Kebada and Tamru arrived at Wal Wal. Kebada had previously assigned two young soldiers to check out the situation there, but the information they'd provided had turned out to be incomplete and dubious. So, in spite of his high rank and the risk to himself, Kebada decided to go there personally to collect the needed information.

While surveying the scene, Kebada and Tamru were accosted by Italian militia. "What are you doing here?" a guard demanded.

"I'm standing on my country's land, watching foreign troops illegally build a military fort," Kebada responded defiantly.

Italian soldiers surrounded Kebada and Tamru.

"You must leave this site immediately," the guard said. "You don't have permission to be here."

"I don't need your permission," Kebada snapped. "You're invading our land." Then he turned to the nearest Italian soldier and asked curtly, "By the way, by what right are you building these fortifications?"

The Italian soldier instantly became angry. "We're just following our superiors' orders," he said. "Who the hell do you think you are to ask these questions?"

The other soldiers tightened the circle around Kebada and Tamru. Sensing the imminent danger to their lives and having accomplished their original mission, Kebada turned to Tamru and, with an air of superior authority, said, "Let's go and not waste our time anymore. These people disgust me."

They walked towards the small grove of trees where they'd tied their horses. Kebada was relieved to notice that the Italians had remained where they were and were not following them, since he had no intention of engaging in combat with them. The two men mounted their horses and galloped away when a gun fired. A bullet whizzed past Tamru's head, which caused him to lose his balance and fall off his horse. Laughter rang out behind them, followed by another shot. Tamru remounted and spurred his horse to catch up with Kebada whose horse was now darting through the copse of trees, as another shot was heard.

Once out of the range of the Italians' gunfire, they rode in silence for an hour. Then Tamru noticed something odd: Kebada's head was swaying back and forth in an unusual way. Tamru shook his reins and rode up alongside him. Slowly Kebada raised his head, his eyelids drooping, rain pouring down his face and neck. As he turned his head, Tamru saw the blood on his sleeve. "You've been hit!" Tamru said.

"Nothing to worry about. It's a mosquito bite."

But after a while, Tamru watched in horror as Kebada became semiconscious and collapsed forward onto his horse's mane. After making sure that Kebada wasn't going to fall off his horse, Tamru quickly leaned over and took the reins from Kebada's limp hand. They then journeyed back home, riding as carefully as possible.

Chapter 12: Feeling

Fanaye watched as Tsega settled herself on her stool. Dinner was over, the table was cleared, and the day's work was done. Their evenings together had almost become a ritual. Fanaye knew what would happen next: Tsega would methodically draw her thumb and forefinger together on her lower lip, not pinching but pulling, as if this would help her find the right topic for the night's conversation—the latest from Addis? A story about her family? Maybe the traditional Tarik and Mesalee folk tales?

Whatever topic she chose, Fanaye knew that Tsega's story would eventually revolve around marriage and children. Tsega would pretend to have chosen each particular story at random, and Fanaye would act as if the moral of the tale had nothing to do with her life in Kebada's house.

Tonight, with good humor, Fanaye ended Tsega's story by saying, "… and so they got married with a great celebration, and everyone danced and sang joyously, wondering why they had ever waited so long to join in holy matrimony."

"Ah, Fanaye, what will your wedding be like?" Tsega went on. "Don't you dream of it? Of your children and grandchildren, too?"

"Yes, Tsega. I do. I think of marriage sometimes."

Tsega clapped her hands together and smiled.

"My mother and father will host a great celebration for my wedding," Fanaye continued. "Very likely they have chosen a husband for me already. It's only a matter of time before I return to my village and all my dreams will come true."

Tsega's smile faded slightly, but then she tilted her head and nodded knowingly. "Yes, going home is a beautiful dream. But, child, what better husband could your mother and father choose for you than this man who has already lavished the wealth of his whole house upon you? You have everything!"

To that, Fanaye was quick to respond. "Everything but freedom! Tsega... I just want to go home! Why won't he take me home?"

"Nevertheless, you're in good hands here. Not everyone is a gentleman like Kebada. I notice how the other men look at you, eyeing you up and down, like a ripe melon."

"A gentleman?" Fanaye huffed and, as she rose from her stool, tried to block from her mind the memories of his gentle hands massaging her aching feet, and how her body had thrilled to his touch.

"Yes," Tsega said. "See how he cares for you? He's a man of honor."

Fanaye began to pace back and forth. "What honor? He kidnapped me!"

"Evil men kidnap for lust," Tsega challenged her. "Did Basha Kebada? No! He saved you from rapists in the woods!"

For the first time, Fanaye considered that Tsega could be right about that, but her pride wouldn't let her admit it. Instead, she loudly uttered the worst thing she could think of: "Who will save me from him? I wish he were dead!"

Tsega spat and crossed herself. "Lord, have mercy!" she cried.

At that moment, the dogs started barking ferociously, startling both women and drawing Tsega to her feet. Fanaye rushed to the window. She could make out the gate and two lanterns but not much else. "I wonder who is coming at this hour," she said.

The sleeping guards, awakened by the loud noise, knew that frantic banging on the gate was not a good sign. They rushed to the gate and peeked through the slats. "Open up!" a voice shouted.

They recognized Tamru's voice as they struggled with the rain-soaked plank that barred the gate. "Hurry!" Tamru hollered. Finally, the guards managed to free the swollen board and fling the gate wide open.

"Get the medicine woman!" Tamru shouted to the guards. He quickly dismounted his horse and held Kebada's horse by its bridle. The guards were stunned to see Kebada, weak and powerless, slumped against the horse. With the aid of one of the guards, Tamru carefully helped Kebada dismount from his horse, picked him up into his arms, and headed towards the house, while the guard, Wondosen, took the reins of Kebada's horse and began heading to the stable.

Tamru shouted again. "Go get the medicine woman, now!"

Tsega, trembling, unbolted the door. Fanaye stood immobile behind her. At the sight of Kebada's limp body, both women cried out. Tamru shouted, "Don't just stand there, staring! Get moving! Boil water, rags!"

Tamru carried Kebada into his bedroom. Tsega rushed to the linen basket and took out some clean white cotton fabric and tore it into strips, all the while praying, "Jesus Christ, Mary Mother of Jesus. Have mercy."

Fanaye covered her mouth and sobbed as she dropped to her knees. "Good God!" she whispered. "Forgive my evil words! I take them back. I don't want Basha Kebada dead. I will do anything, God! Please."

Tsega returned and Fanaye, not wanting to be caught on her knees in prayer, grabbed some wood for the fire.

The guard Abtu made his horse gallop with the speed of a cheetah, but his overworked horse could not sustain the pace after having ridden so long from Wal Wal earlier in the day. The ground was unstable, covered with mud and pebbles. The rain clouds had passed, and now the charcoal-colored sky was sprinkled with a few nameless small stars, just enough to help Abtu see where he was going. A few scattered houses were visible in the distance. At last, he saw Weizero Sunqua's house, with its familiar kerosene light burning in the window.

She was busy mixing herbs to take to a sick, pregnant woman in the morning when she heard the approaching galloping horse. She cocked her head just as she heard a desperate call, "Weizero Sunqua, quick! Basha Kebada has been shot! You must come right away!"

The medicine woman grabbed the lantern. One entire wall of her hut was filled with containers: red and black clay jars of different shapes and sizes, and stuffed sacks, some no bigger than handkerchiefs while others were large as shamas. She had no need for labels on the jars. Sunqua swayed from side to side, mumbling and sniffing, searching for the right ingredients. Like a dog hunting, she leaned forward, her neck stretched out and her nostrils flared.

At last, she reached for some bitter green herbs. "Yes, you're my reliable one," she cheerfully shouted. "You will help Basha Kebada."

After Sunqua had gathered her supplies, she put on her netala, which covered her from head to knees. "I think I have everything now," she said as she stepped outside.

"Good God, let's go!" Abtu said.

He helped Sunqua mount the horse first, and then jumped on himself. It helped that she weighed so little. They took the same path lit by those same small Ethiopian stars that guided them through the darkness. For some time they rode in silence. Abtu was too focused on finding his way to make conversation. Besides, he felt awkward being so close to this strange woman—he feared her mysterious powers.

"You ride like a woman!" Sunqua told him. "Hurry up!"

"The horse is going as fast as he can."

"It's not the horse, it's you!" She kicked the horse's belly sharply with both heels, causing the startled animal to leap into a full gallop.

The gate to Kebada's house swung open quickly as they approached. "They're waiting!" Wondosen said, putting his arm out to help the medicine woman dismount.

"I can manage, thank you." She got down and hurried toward the house.

Tsega met her at the door, crying out for Sunqua to save Kebada. The women stepped into Kebada's bedroom, where Fanaye was sitting on a stool in the corner, while Tamru paced around the room. Fanaye stood up when Sunqua entered, and all eyes turned expectantly towards the medicine woman.

Before the medicine woman could say anything, Kebada spoke, his voice soft and strangely tender: "Emama, you are back. I thought you were dead, but not anymore?"

Sunqua frowned. She bent down and unwrapped the crude field dressing so she could examine his injury. The bullet had gone straight through his upper left arm. There were two small holes, one where it had entered and the other where it had exited. But he had lost much blood. She looked intently into his eyes, and her intuition, inherited through generations of healers and further developed from years of experience, told her that Kebada would survive. She tossed off her shama and announced that she needed more hot water, some clean pieces of cloth, and a small bowl.

Tsega and Fanaye quickly left the room, and in no time they returned with the items. Sunqua happily informed them, "Look, he is sweating and shivering at the same time. The sweating is good. It will pull out the poison. Now let's see if we can bring down the fever. It's making him delirious." Sunqua knew that a clean shot like this one would hurt, but after the bleeding stopped, the wound would probably heal. But infection could set in later and, if so, the wound would fester. She reached into her pack and drew out a thin piece of bone. Dipping it into the herbal salve she'd made, she motioned Tamru to the bed. "Hold him tightly," she said.

Tamru held Kebada down firmly, while Sunqua pushed the bone into the bullet hole all the way through Kebada's arm, and then quickly pulled it out again. Kebada groaned. Sunqua wiped the area, covered the wound with an herbal compress, and wrapped it securely with cotton fabric. After she finished tending to Kebada's arm, she leaned closer and observed him for a while. Then she reached into her pack for little pouches filled with crushed herbs, and handed them to Tsega. "Make tea for him, with these," she said.

Tsega nodded, took the medicine, and thanked her before leaving the room.

Sunqua whispered to Fanaye, "What Basha Kebada needs now is your medicine. Be near him tonight. You are full of life. With you beside him through the night, you will keep death far away. Don't worry, my dear. I must go back home now. Make sure to change the poultice whenever it gets soaked. I'll return in the morning with fresh salve and powders."

"I'll do anything you say," Fanaye responded.

"Dehna daaru," Sunqua said. "Good night. Remember: tea every hour, change the poultice every three hours, and keep him warm. I'll see you in the morning."

After Sunqua left, Fanaye hesitated and lifted the covers, slipping into bed next to Kebada. She wiped his brow. Tsega, feeling that her prayers had been answered, thanked Sunqua for making this happen.

Fanaye had never seen Basha Kebada so helpless or heard his voice so weak. She handed the teacup to Tsega and gently repeated, over and over, "Eshee, eshee. It's okay, it's okay," until Tsega managed to bring the cup of tea to his lips.

Despite Fanaye's and Tsega's diligent and constant care, with every passing hour Kebada grew weaker and more delirious. "Emama!" he kept whispering.

Fanaye kept wiping his brow, trying to soothe him. "Eshee, eshee, don't worry."

The women kept vigil throughout the night. Tsega went back and forth to the kitchen to keep the water boiling for herbal tea, although it was difficult to get Kebada to drink the full cup every hour. Fanaye continued to wipe his brow and tried to keep the covers over them both, but he kept pulling and pushing them away. Tsega tried to lift his head while Fanaye brought the teacup to his mouth, but Kebada was restless and kept turning away and muttering, "I... need to get up... but the way is not clear..." Whenever Tsega and

Fanaye changed the poultice, he would fade in and out, sometimes cursing the Italians, other times fighting off the imaginary attackers pushing at his blankets.

"Don't you touch her... bastards... I'll kill you... Fanaye? Are you alright?"

"I'm alright. I'm here, Basha Kebada! I'm here. Eshee, eshee, eshee." Fanaye wiped his forehead. Then he fell into a deep slumber.

A sudden image came to Fanaye then as the memory she'd been repressing returned with sharp clarity. In the forest dense with trees, she remembered Kebada whispering, "Shhh, they may be close by. Be quiet." She recalled the ugly bandits, the shifta who certainly would have raped her if Basha Kebada hadn't come to her rescue. Tsega had been right all along—he would never force himself upon her. He had saved her!

When Tsega served the last of the tea, she saw Fanaye nestling Kebada in her arms, the girl's tears falling onto his face, mingling with his own beads of sweat. She looked first at Fanaye and then at Kebada. "Basha Kebada, please drink," she said and held the cup to his lips, but he refused it.

Then, Tsega's caressed Kebada's head, then Fanaye's as she helped the girl settle back in under the covers. Tsega tucked both of them in and, then sitting on the stool next to the bed, leaned her head against the wall for a few moments' rest before sunrise.

Hours later, when Sunqua returned, she went straight to Kebada's side and unwrapped the gauze from his arm. The sound filtered through Fanaye's exhaustion and confused her. She was vaguely aware that she wasn't alone in bed. Still groggy, she felt a hand resting on her shoulder. A face moved above her and spoke in a whisper, "You have done well. At least he's sleeping now."

Now fully awake, Fanaye sat up. Tsega held the basin while Sunqua dipped a small cloth into the hot infusion and dabbed the wound gingerly. "Why is it still so red?" Tsega asked, frowning.

"We have to keep fighting the poison. This will help." Sunqua soaked the cloth in the murky mixture of herbs and steaming water and wiped the wound again.

The fever hadn't broken. Kebada shivered and muttered—first about the war, then Fanaye, then about his mother—as sweat drenched his body.

"Sweating will purge the poisons from his body," Sunqua said. "Keep a small basin of warm water and herbal infusions to wipe him down." Then she left. For the rest of the day, Tsega and Fanaye had little rest as they changed Kebada's poultice, prepared the medicinal tea, soaked up the sweat and applied the cleansing infusion to his wound. Whenever

109

Tsega or Fanaye touched him, whether to wipe his brow or to lift the healing tea to his lips, he muttered his resistance to unseen foes. Though his words were fierce, his voice was often barely audible. Fanaye sang to him, caressing his hand and patting it absently, as if soothing a child.

For several days, the medicine woman came before dawn and brought all sorts of medicinal herbs and ground bones. Tsega boiled and steeped the herbs, while Fanaye changed the gauze, applied the poultice and kept Kebada warm. Despite their efforts, Sunqua wasn't satisfied. She saw little improvement. It was true Kebada had stopped being restless, but that was probably because now the medicinal tea had sedated him.

The following day, Sunqua unwrapped the wound to see that the stubborn redness was still there. This made her angry; it seemed there was something troublesome beneath this stubborn infection. She threw her shama off and slapped her palms together, rubbing vigorously and glaring at the offending flesh. "Quickly! Bring me hot water in a basin and a kabatto," she ordered.

Tsega went off to gather the items, while Tamru lifted Kebada up to a sitting position. When Tsega returned, Sunqua grabbed the cotton kabatto and wrapped it around Kebada's upper arm, tightening it forcefully. Kebada groaned as Sunqua squeezed the wound, trying to force out

110

the pus. Nothing. Frustrated, she unwrapped the tourniquet and asked Fanaye, "Is there any arakai in the house?"

Fanaye looked at Tsega, who nodded and slipped out of the room. Sunqua fished around in her pouch and pulled out a long, thin bone with a sharp tip. "I must lance the wound to release the poison," she said. Each moment she delayed, she told them the poison would spread in Kebada's body. The infection would claim his arm, but it wouldn't be satisfied with such a small territory either. Sunqua knew she must become like a general and oppose this advancing enemy with every weapon, every strategy, every skill she possessed. "I will not allow it," she said firmly. "Basha should not die like an old woman, weak and sickly in bed."

Fanaye shivered involuntarily when she heard the word lance. The word sounded dangerous. Tsega returned with the arakai and handed it to Sunqua, who smiled reassuringly at Fanaye. "Be brave," she said. "This must be done."

Sunqua held Kebada's head in one of her arms, putting the bottle to his lips with the other while chanting some unintelligible words. She let the arakai run slowly into his mouth to numb him, then dipped the lance into the liquid as well. "Tamru, please hold Basha Kebada firmly. I don't want him to move."

Tamru wedged himself behind the bed and wrapped his arms around Kebada's chest, immobilizing Kebada's arms.

111

At the same time, Fanaye held Kebada's free hand. Tsega was on her knees, praying.

Sunqua grasped the lance, holding it high in the air. "God guide this hand," she said, and without hesitation, pierced the center of the wound, her enemy. Kebada moaned and tried to squirm, but couldn't move because of Tamru's tight grip. With a fierce squint, Sunqua twisted the lance. Kebada's entire body convulsed.

"Yes, I feel it!" Sunqua cried and pulled the bone out triumphantly. "It's done! Bring a cloth and change this water."

The foul smell of the escaping pus filled the air. Fanaye cringed, trying not to retch.

"Open the windows," Sunqua ordered. "We need fresh air."

Fanaye released Kebada's hand long enough to jump up, hug Tsega, and unlatch the shutters to let in the morning light and a soft breeze. Then she took Kebada's hand again, kissed it and pressed it to her heart impulsively for a moment, relieved now that the worst was over. Then she stood up and went off to fetch more water while Tsega gathered fresh pieces of cloth.

The next morning, Sunqua and her nose were very pleased. The redness of Kebada's wound and the strange smell emitting from it were almost gone. She instructed

112

Tsega and Fanaye to give Kebada the salve and powders on changing his bandages, and offering him a small cup of shorba in the morning to see if his appetite returned. "He must rest," Sunqua said. "Sleep is the way he will regain his strength. Keep him warm when the evening chill falls."

Over the next few days, Fanaye and Tsega followed every instruction while Kebada slept peacefully. The ladies slept when they could. Tsega returned to her room each night after she and Fanaye had cleaned Kebada's wound and had changed the gauze together. Fanaye remained sleeping at Kebada's side, continuing to provide the warmth as she'd been instructed to do. In time, she grew accustomed to his warmth as well.

Chapter 13: Dawn

One morning just after dawn, a dull ache tugged Kebada awake. He felt the throbbing of his shoulder meet the beating of his heart. Yet something drew his attention away from the pain—a gentle warmth right below his heart, resting upon his chest. This presence calmed him as he breathed, feeling waves of heat and strength in his soul.

When he opened his eyes, he saw Fanaye nestled at his side. Was this real or a fragile dream? Fanaye, still asleep, snuggled closer to him. Kebada blinked and looked around the room.

He was at home. A few memories washed over him: the bullet entering his arm and the dark confusion of the trees swirling as he had fallen unconscious, lanterns lighting the night, faces swimming before him—Sunqua, Tsega, his mother, and Fanaye. Fanaye, here in the darkness. Fanaye, here in the morning light. Fanaye.

The door creaked open, and Tsega backed into the room with her arms full, holding a tray with tea, a basin of hot water, salve, powders, and fresh gauze. Fanaye stirred from sleep at the familiar footfalls but noticed instantly that something was different. She opened her eyes and saw Tsega staring down with her mouth agape. Fanaye gasped and didn't dare look up at Kebada, fearing the worst had happened in the night. Hadn't she done her best to keep him

114

warm to save his life? She buried her head deeper into his chest, tears flowing freely. A hand rested gently on her hair. "Don't cry, Fanaye," a deep voice said.

She lifted her eyes, startled by the sound of her name. His hand slid down from her hair, across her cheek, and under her chin. Embarrassed by her outburst, she shied from his touch, her face flushing.

She jumped up and ran past Tsega and out the door.

"Thank God! God is good! Basha Kebada, I am so happy to see you're feeling better," Tsega said and set down her tray, adjusted his pillows, and helped him sit up against the headboard. She served him hot tea with a knowing gleam in her eye. "You were very close to death, but Fanaye cared for you night and day."

His heartbeat was stronger. "So... I had to be shot in order to win her heart? Why didn't I think of this months ago?" He laughed and then winced, feeling his shoulder throbbing.

"Here, Basha, have some more tea. Sunqua will be here soon."

Kebada now saw Fanaye in a new light—caring for him. Caring for him at all! And how many days and nights? The morning sun was already at work outside, spreading its heat and pushing the grey fog away. Fanaye sat on a solid stone, warmed by the sun, enjoying the breeze that played around

115

her. A new dream arose, clearing away the dark thoughts that once separated her from Kebada. Fanaye's embarrassment at Tsega seeing her lying in his arms was nothing compared to the rush of desire and heat she had felt from the touch of his hand on her cheek. A strange new fear gripped her. What if Kebada was so grateful for her care that, when he found out her memory had returned, he took her back to her village?

Suddenly, the home was no longer there but here.

Fanaye remained seated outside for some time, savoring the memory of those early morning moments in bed with Kebada. Her cheek tingled as if he were touching her again. She rested her chin on her own hand, dreamily returning his passionate gaze.

"How's Basha Kebada this morning?" a voice asked, interrupting her thoughts.

Fanaye looked at Sunqua, who had entered through the gate. "He's... better," Fanaye said.

Sunqua eyed Fanaye for a moment. "Looking at you, I'd say he's much better," she said and motioned for Fanaye to come inside with her.

But Fanaye's eyes widened at Sunqua's words. How did she know? Would everyone else see her feelings, too? Too embarrassed to go back to Kebada's room after the affectionate exchanges between them, her mind raced for some excuse or delay. "I must boil some water first," she sputtered and then slipped away into the kitchen before Sunqua could reply.

"Bring the basin!" Sunqua called out to her. "Fresh gauze, too." She then pushed open the bedroom door and saw Kebada sitting up in bed, his eyes wide open and alert. What a glow, she thought to herself, surprised. She didn't need her nose to tell her how much he'd improved. He seemed oddly majestic and well-composed, enthroned on pillows and blankets, sipping tea. Sunqua proudly straightened her shoulders, sure that his recovery was due to her salves, tea and powders. When she unwound the gauze from his wounded arm, she saw that the redness, the odor, and the inflammation were gone. Now he would need only time and rest for a full recovery. And, miraculously, he would keep his arm.

When Kebada looked down at his shoulder, he wondered how many days had gone by with him laid up in bed. Then he thought, "Enough, time to return to my post." But when he attempted to lift his back and climb out of bed, the muscles in his arms trembled, and he fell back against the mound of pillows. He was used to pain, but weakness? No. This was unacceptable.

Ignoring Sunqua's protests, he took in a deep breath and tried again but collapsed back onto the pillows for a second time. He cursed under his breath just as Fanaye entered the

117

room with her head down, delivering the steaming basin and gauze that Sunqua had asked for. Sunqua cleaned his wound and bandaged it with fresh gauze. "Basha Kebada, you are getting better, but you are not ready to get up yet," Sunqua chided him. "You've had nothing but tea for days."

Kebada was surprised when she told him he'd been laid up in bed for nearly a week. "That long?" he muttered. "I don't remember—"

Sunqua told him he'd had a high fever for days, and Fanaye and Tsega had nursed him constantly. "Everyone had feared for your life, but God has brought you back to us," she said, securing the gauze tightly around his arm. "Now eat light broth every few hours to bring your appetite back, and your whole body needs massage at least twice a day to get rid of the stiffness."

Sunqua moved things around in her basket and removed a small gourd containing a fragrant ointment. She lifted the covers and showed Fanaye how to massage Kebada, starting with his right foot. Sunqua took Fanaye's hands in hers, and they massaged together for a while. Once she was satisfied with Fanaye's technique, she stepped back to watch Fanaye massage him on her own. "Yes," she said, "very good. Not too much pressure."

After Sunqua and Tsega had left the room, Kebada smiled at Fanaye as she obediently worked on his calf

118

muscles. Although he enjoyed the massage, he felt it was an imposition on Fanaye, who was still shy about such closeness with him. "You don't have to do this," he said. "I'll be fine."

"But Weizero Sunqua said you need the massage," Fanaye's voice shook when she heard Tsega's cough in the hallway, obviously meant to alert them to her presence. Fanaye withdrew her hands behind her back.

Tsega poked her head into the room. "Sorry to interrupt, Basha Kebada, but now that you are feeling better, I must ask your permission to go home," she said. "I must see my mother—as you know, she is a sick woman, and I have been away for many days."

"Of course you must go. Say no more."

"I will prepare everything in the kitchen before I go. I'll be back early, the day after tomorrow, when Weizero Sunqua comes to see you. God cares for you." Tsega bowed and then nodded to Fanaye. "If you need me, send Tamru."

Kebada leaned back against the pillows and pretended to close his eyes, although he could see clearly through the fringe of his lashes. He'd waited patiently for Fanaye for a long time. If she didn't surrender herself to him now, she never would. Two days could mean everything or nothing. We will see, he told himself.

After Tsega closed the door behind her, Fanaye still couldn't look Kebada squarely in the eye. Her hands had stopped massaging, so she willed her fingers back to action, fighting an urge to run after Tsega and beg her to stay. But in time, she felt more comfortable. She touched Kebada's forehead to feel for fever. He smiled, took her hand, and held it lovingly. "Thank you for helping me. By the way, your hands are beautiful, so long and slender."

Fanaye blushed and shyly averted her eyes.

He kissed her fingertips. Then his lips moved, as of their own accord, to the center of her palm where his kiss lingered. "I love this hand."

The tingling sensation spread to the center of her palm, and she felt a rush of burning energy. How strange that she was alone with this man! What's wrong with me? Fanaye asked herself. Am I different than the other women in my village? All my life, I've been warned about the agony that awaits me, the pain that all women endure on their wedding night. She'd been told that on that night, a woman could only expect blood and suffering but was supposed to do her duty no matter how painful. Yet Fanaye couldn't imagine that pain would result from this occasion. Although she was frightened of her feelings for Kebada, she also felt happy.

Early one morning, even before he was fully recovered, a messenger came to the house with orders from Kebada's superiors requiring him to join his unit immediately. A large contingent of Italian forces had been spotted within a day's reach of the city. He was expected to go on a reconnaissance mission to ascertain the enemy's strength, location, armaments, and other details and report his findings to the headquarters. Kebada, still wearing bandages, hastily got up and began to make preparations, packing his gear, issuing orders, thinking, planning.

When Fanaye became aware of what was going on, she thought, "This is my only chance." She had never forgotten what her grandfather often used to say to her. "The enemy may come again at any time, so, Fanaye, you should always be prepared and ready for them." And she had promised him that she would always be ready. When she recalled her grandfather's warning on that particular morning, how right he was, she thought. The more she thought about his warnings, the more resolved she had become to do something to defend her country and her family. On an impulse, she quickly got up and cut her long hair almost down to her scalp. She then fetched one pair of Kebada's old pants and a coat. First, she wrapped her breasts tightly with a cotton shawl to hide her womanhood. When she put on Kebada's clothes and was satisfied that she was close enough to look like a man, she then rushed off to see Kebada.

121

Kebada was almost ready to leave. When she appeared in front of him, he couldn't believe it. "What on earth have you done to yourself? What did you do to your hair? And why are you dressed like that?"

"I am going to fight too!"

"No! You cannot go anywhere. I have enough people to help out with the war effort. You don't need to bother. Just stay home."

Fanaye stomped her foot and shouted, "I am going! I've made up my mind!"

Kebada got impatient. He raised his voice sharply. "Look, don't waste my time, I told you you could not go, and that means you are not going!"

Fanaye was quick to retort, "If you don't want me to go with you, fine. Then I am going by myself. You can be sure of that."

Kebada did not respond. He ignored Fanaye and went on with his last-minute business.

For a moment, Fanaye just stood there but said nothing. You will see, she thought.

No sooner than Kebada and his small entourage departed, Fanaye quickly left the house and sneakily began to trail them. There, she was happy to notice that a group of women also joined the troops. They were wives, sisters, and volunteers who would provide support to the soldiers, such as cooking, carrying ammunition and goods, and tending to the wounded. Fanaye was able to blend in with the women, though she kept a low profile and stayed with the group.

Fanaye's adjustment to the hardships of life in the field was smooth and effortless. While she worked with the women, she felt no need to conceal her gender. Her efforts to look like a man turned out to be quite unnecessary.

Aside from providing all the other services expected of the volunteer women, Fanaye was also making another extremely valuable contribution. Growing up watching her mother gathering edible mushrooms and plants, she quickly recognized which mushrooms and plants were poisonous and which ones were not. So, she was very useful at their encampment, showing the women how to identify the edible ones.

Meanwhile, it wasn't escaping Kebada's attention that Fanaye had adjusted so perfectly to the hardships of her new environment and was working diligently. This filled him with pride and admiration for her. However, Fanaye was getting increasingly dissatisfied with the merely supportive role she was playing for the fighting men. She was dying to actually fight with the enemy. That was what she had intended from the beginning anyway. So she began to look for ways to realize her wish without Kebada's knowledge. But first, she had to learn how to shoot.

123

One day, a wounded soldier was brought in and placed under the women's care. He had a deep wound on his left arm, which could easily get infected. Fanaye carefully cleaned and bandaged his wound and then put his arm in a sling. After a few days, the young soldier was doing much better. He thanked Fanaye elaborately for taking such good care of him and then said he'd love to do something for her if she ever needed anything. This instantly gave Fanaye an idea. She said, "I can already think of something you can do for me. Can you teach me how to use a gun?"

At first, the soldier was somewhat taken aback by this unusual request from a woman, but when he saw the absolutely serious and determined look on her face, he thought, Why not! We can use as many fighters as we can get, man or woman. So somewhat reluctantly, he agreed.

The very next day, the young soldier took Fanaye to a large clearing in the forest, which was far enough from the enemy's location for gunshots to be heard, and there her shooting lessons began. He first showed her how to hold the gun, how to load it, bring it to her shoulder to aim, both in standing and lying down positions. He taught her how to take the gun apart, clean it, and then put it back together. However, when the time came for actual shooting practice before she was allowed to fire, he asked her, "Please take great care and take careful aim before firing since bullets are

124

extremely scarce, so should not be wasted." To his surprise, he saw that Fanaye was almost always hitting the bulls-eye on her targets after a few initial trials. He gleefully announced that her training was over, that she could now consider herself a capable shooter.

Thinking that she had sufficiently learned how to handle rifles, Fanaye approached Kebada one day and directly got to the point. "I am not happy with just playing a support role along with the other women. I want you to let me take part in actually fighting with the enemy."

Kebada was both amused and proud of her gallantry. "That's fine, but how are you going to fight them?" he inquired. "You need to know how to use firearms."

Fanaye was quick to respond. "I wouldn't ask you if I didn't know how to shoot."

Kebada was quite skeptical. "Is that so?" he said somewhat sarcastically. "Now, how did you learn that?"

Fanaye was growing impatient. "Just give me a rifle, and I'll show you what I can do," she retorted.

Kebada thought about it for an instant. Then he left and came back with a rifle and a few bullets on a sudden impulse. He extended the rifle to her and said, "Okay, show me how you load this rifle."

Fanaye took the rifle from his hands and deftly loaded it with the bullets he provided. While Kebada looked at her in

125

disbelief, she quickly unloaded it, loaded it again, and looked at Kebada victoriously. Kebada was truly surprised. "How on earth did you learn that? Who taught you, and when?"

"Never mind," she said. "The fact is, you've seen that I know how to use it."

Right at that moment, while Kebada just stood there not knowing what to make of all this, Fanaye heard a faint rustling of leaves from a tree in the woods about fifty yards away. When she focused on that tree with her sharp eyes, she instantly saw the partly concealed and camouflaged figure of a sniper seemingly taking aim at Kebada. She responded without thinking. She instantly raised the rifle to her shoulder, quickly took aim, and fired. The dead body of the sniper fell through the branches and the leaves and hit the ground with a dull thud.

After a moment of silence, while men rushed in from everywhere to see what had happened, Kebada was deeply moved by what had happened. He hugged Fanaye, then held her at arm's length and said, "You just saved my life! You are my hero!"

Fanaye softly said, "Well, at least now you know that I know how to shoot."

"Had you been a man and an enlisted soldier, you would surely have gotten a medal for what you just did," Kebada concluded.

Figuring out what happened, the soldiers broke into cheers and applause. Fanaye had become their hero as well.

Within the following days, the reconnaissance mission ended. They had gotten all the information they needed about the enemy's strength and position. What remained now was returning to their main units to report their findings as swiftly as possible. So, before sunrise one morning, they packed everything and headed back as stealthily as they had come.

Chapter 14: A Baby On The Way

One morning, Fanaye woke up craving green peppers and onions. When Tsega served barley porridge for breakfast, she told Tsega, "I feel like eating green pepper salad instead." Tsega froze with her mouth wide open, staring at Fanaye. "What's wrong?" Fanaye asked.

"You always refused to eat that before."

"But now I really, really want some. What's the matter, Tsega? You're scaring me."

"No, it's nothing. I may be jumping to conclusions, but..." Tsega shook her head and turned away. "Why don't I go and fix what you want to eat."

When Fanaye's pregnancy became definite, she was at first delighted, but soon her mood turned melancholic. The idea of giving birth without her mother's presence rekindled in her a deep nostalgia for her family and her village. She had never thought she would be giving birth this way. As much as she loved Tsega, she badly wanted her mother at her side and wished she'd tried harder to go back to her village.

It had been over two years since Fanaye left Dow-Dow, and now at age fifteen and pregnant, another fearful thought came to her mind. What if she died during childbirth and left her newborn child behind? Many moms died during labor. Who would raise her baby? Would Kebada give the baby to his wife? If so, would she raise her child as she would her own? Had Kebada been there at that moment, she would've told him that she preferred that Tsega raise her baby. So, one morning she asked Tsega, "If I die, would you take care of my baby?"

Tsega frowned and spat on the ground. "What kind of talk is that?" she cried. "You're healthy and strong and in no danger at all." But Fanaye reminded her that some women died during childbirth. It was an unavoidable fact of life.

"Of course, I'd take care of your child!" Tsega reassured her. "But right now, don't even think about things like that."

Tsega's promise relaxed Fanaye somewhat. She joined Tsega to work in the garden, despite Tsega's protests that she should stay inside and out of the heat. Under the bright sun, Fanaye's good mood returned. Seeing that the tomatoes were still green, Tsega teased. "Not quite ripe yet. Just like you." She extended her hand, and Fanaye placed it on her swollen belly, and they laughed together.

As her pregnancy progressed, Fanaye daydreamed more and more about her mother. Tsega sensed her longing for her family and distracted her. She called to Fanaye, "Come, let me braid your hair." Then, just as Fanaye's mother used to do, Tsega tenderly massaged fresh butter into her hair as she braided it. She also created a variety of dishes out of two tomatoes.

One late afternoon, Fanaye felt her baby kick a couple of times, so she went to bed to lie down. Tsega brought a tray and placed it near Fanaye's bed. "Have some fenugreek tea," she said. "It's time for an afternoon snack. Here is some barley bread. Did you enjoy your nap?"

Fanaye sat up and yawned. "Every time I fell asleep, the baby would kick and say, 'Wake up!' I wonder if I kicked my mom like this."

Tsega placed her hand on Fanaye's big belly. "Oh, the baby is talking to me now, greeting his grandma. Bless you, my Leja. Be patient now. This is what babies do. Your little one will be here before long."

Days passed in the slow routine of spring. The two women hoped Kebada would be back in time for the birth of his child. Fanaye was always counting the days. Eighty-five days now, she thought.

One morning, she was out as usual after breakfast, pulling weeds. Tsega pushed her off with a warning, "You shouldn't be bending so much and squatting. It's not good for the baby or you."

Fanaye continued working. "Don't worry. I don't need much rest. I'm my mother's daughter." She kept working until the day my brother arrived. Other women, like my aunts, did all their chores, too. They didn't spend their time lying around in bed."

130

"That's because they had no choice. You are lucky. We have people to do gardening here."

"The baby and I are just fine," Fanaye said, feeling a little touchy.

"Fanaye, I think the sun is making you short-tempered. Come in and you will feel much better if you lie down in bed for a while. I promise."

Fanaye went inside and lay down on Kebada's bed as Tsega suggested. She sensed that her time was getting close since she felt the baby's weight further down her belly. Tsega fetched some cool whey to soothe and strengthen her. Fanaye closed her eyes.

Kebada had been away now for three months and, while she used to welcome his absences before, she now yearned to see him again. Sunqua had praised her own medicines as the key to Kebada's swift recovery, but deep in her heart, Fanaye knew she'd kept him alive with her warmth and her budding love.

She was uncomfortable, so she rose from the bed. "I have to pee again," she announced.

Tsega had the pot ready for her. "I've made you some barley gunfo," she said as Fanaye squatted over the pot.

A great rush of water left Fanaye, and the pot overflowed. "I'm so sorry," she told Tsega, embarrassed. "I didn't know there was so much water in me."

131

Tsega noted the thick liquid on the floor. "I think you're about to have the baby," she said. "Lie down and let me have a look."

Fanaye lay down on her back with her loose cotton dress pulled up. Tsega peered between her legs. "I think I see a full head of hair already!" she said. "The baby is coming."

Sunqua was supposed to come earlier to check up on Fanaye. Tsega wondered where she was. Sunqua also served as a midwife. Although Tsega was experienced in matters of childbirth, she was uncomfortable with the prospect of delivering Fanaye's first child all by herself. What if something went wrong?

She sat by Fanaye's bedside, rubbing her belly, wiping her forehead, and giving encouraging comments. "Fanaye dear, you're doing just fine; please relax, and soon you'll be joyful to have your own miracle."

When Sunqua arrived, she looked as if she'd already delivered five babies. Her hair was tangled, and her face was shiny with sweat. Tsega ushered her inside and asked if she'd like a glass of water first, but Sunqua shook her head and went straight to Fanaye. "How are you feeling?" she asked, standing over her bed.

"I feel pressure," Fanaye said. "Nothing hurts that much. Will I have more pain later?"

"Some women do feel more pain, but if you don't, it's a good sign the baby will be an easy delivery," Sunqua assured her.

The rest went smoothly. Fanaye's heightened labor and eventual delivery took little time. Once the baby girl arrived, Fanaye was filled with joy that no words could describe.

"The angel cries!" Tsega called out when the baby started to cry. Then she looked heavenward and sang throatily, "Ellil, ellil, ellil," Fanaye couldn't wait to hold the child. Tsega and Sunqua seemed happy about the crying. "Good, she has strong lungs," one of them said.

"I want to see my baby." Fanaye hardly comprehended that the child in Tsega's arms was real.

Sunqua snipped the umbilical cord, then handed the girl over to Fanaye. Together, Fanaye and Tsega spent hours huddled over the child, watching breathlessly as the baby fussed and slept and breathed.

One late afternoon, Tsega heard the trotting of horses. She flung open the door, calling out behind her, "Basha Kebada is here. He's here. Basha Kebada's home!"

Kebada handed the horses off to his assistant and walked in the doorway with a sense of purpose. As soon as he came in, Tsega cheerfully told him, "Sir, you have a healthy girl child!"

She saw how his shoulders and face relaxed at the news. "Very good," he smiled. "And how's the mother doing?"

As Kebada opened the door to the bedroom, he saw Fanaye, her hair cascading over the plumped-up pillows, and the baby lying in the crook of her arm. He pulled up a chair at Fanaye's bedside and sat beside them. For a moment, Kebada and Fanaye said nothing, just looked together at their baby. "I want to call the baby Hewait after my mother," Fanaye told him.

Kebada was reluctant, afraid the name might awaken unresolved emotions in Fanaye. "If you don't mind, why don't we find another name, like Sosina, if you'd like."

"I really want to name her Hewait."

"Why don't we discuss it later?"

"The baby's hungry all the time and wants to be fed now."

"She's beautiful like her mother and smart. She already knows what's good for her. I hope she'll be as strong as you are."

They both laughed.

Tsega entered the room and said, "I brought gunfo for Fanaye and you. For the mother and you too, sir."

Kebada turned to Tsega with gratitude. "What do you think of naming the baby Sosina?"

"I like it!" Tsega said. "It fits the baby just fine."

Fanaye nicknamed her Senafickish, meaning I missed you so. Ethiopians give names to their children in several ways. Some name them after their own mothers or fathers or relatives. Others use biblical names. There are also those who give their children names carrying sentimental meanings, such as Senafickish or Yenanish, you belong to me.

Even as an infant, Sosina clearly resembled her grandmother, Hewait. She even had her grandmother's dimples, which both delighted and saddened Fanaye. At times, Fanaye felt both she and her daughter were cheated by not having Fanaye's parents in their lives since she was accustomed to growing up surrounded by parents, grandparents, and an extended family. Fanaye had been showered with love as a child, and now she wanted the same for her own child. She would have to try and convince Kebada to provide her with a military escort to take her and the baby back to her village since it would be dangerous for her to travel on her own. Even in Addis Ababa, people were getting killed by the Italians. Yet Fanaye was willing to take the chance, despite the war. She hoped Kebada would understand her wish and trust her enough to return to him.

Meanwhile, Fanaye was delighted by every minute she spent with Sosina. She'd carry the baby on her back and go outside; she would point out the vegetables that she liked most in the garden.

Tsega would also come out and enjoy Fanaye's happiness with the baby. "You know, Fanaye, the poor child does not know what you are talking about," Tsega said one day and laughed.

"Who says a baby can't understand?" Fanaye answered her back.

"Save your answers for later. As soon as Sosina starts talking, she will be asking you questions all day long."

During one of Kebada's rare visits back home, Fanaye mentioned returning to her village.

"I understand, I really do," Kebada said, but he shook his head firmly. "Now is the worst time to trek through the country to go anywhere, especially with a child. Our resistance movement has been so successful in killing so many of their soldiers that Mussolini is now furious," Kebada explained. "He's sent thousands of more troops to attack our men everywhere." Now that the Italian army was familiar with the Ethiopian geography and landscape, they knew almost every inroad and pathway. Because of that, Kebada said Fanaye wouldn't be any safer traveling with a squadron of men than she would be traveling with only a couple of escorts, which he couldn't spare in the first place because there was such a shortage of fighting men.

"Fanaye," he said, taking her hand in his, "please be patient and wait until it's safer to travel. Then, I swear to God, I will personally take you and Sosina to your village."

Although Fanaye didn't forget her ache to return to her village, she accepted Kebada's reasoning. Still, she did what she could on her own to find a way to contact her family. Tsega was dismayed that Fanaye continued going to the marketplace as often as she could in the hope of running into someone from her village who could tell her parents that she was alive and well. To Fanaye's bitter disappointment, she never did run into anyone familiar. One day, when she mentioned the name of her village to an elderly farmer, he said, "Oh yeah! There's a shepherd selling sheep who is from there." Then he looked around and said, "But he's not here today. He comes only once in a while. You have to catch him when he shows up."

Fanaye tried many times to find this shepherd but had no luck. Then one day, when at last she found him, her heart raced out of her chest when she spoke to him. But the old shepherd had never even heard of Dow-Dow.

A few years later, Fanaye was now in charge of organizing the kitchen and setting up a budget for each week. When she discovered she was pregnant again, she was overjoyed. Having a second child for Sosina to play with would be a blessing, not to mention that she and Kebada

137

were creating another addition to their own family. Of course, when Tsega heard the news, she was sure it was all part of God's almighty plan.

Tsega entered with a glass of hot oat drink with butter and honey. She carried warm wet rags over her arm and under the tray.

"Thank you, Tsega, but I'm getting up now anyway."

"Well, drink it up before it gets cold, at least."

Fanaye accepted the glass and drank it. "I know I have to drink it. It's good for the baby."

Tsega quipped, "Sosina can't wait! I'm so glad the children will only be a few years apart. They'll be good friends. And Fanaye, please try to stay off your feet more."

"Stop worrying," Fanaye laughed. "Didn't I move around a lot last time when I was with Sosina? And it didn't do anything bad to me. In fact, I think all that movement made the baby's birth easier."

As Fanaye predicted, like the last one, this birth turned out to be as easy as a calf's birth. This time, Fanaye gave the privilege of naming the baby girl to Tsega. The woman was touched by this honorable gesture. All along, she had secretly wished to name the baby Zenite, and so it was.

Chapter 15: Get Them! Get Them!

The struggle with invading Italians had escalated to the point where full-scale armed conflict existed in Ethiopia. War had begun. Fighting now took place on many fronts. Eventually, Italians were also in Addis Ababa. They had begun going from door to door, recruiting able-bodied men to their side. Those who resisted were taken to jail or killed on the spot. All this meant Kebada had to keep an even lower profile, which included sending away the guards at the entrance of his home. He was also away from his home for longer periods of time, making fewer and fewer returns, often in the middle of the night.

Fanaye and her children now lived in the middle of a war. Still, she never lost hope she and her family would one day reunite. Once the war ends, when the children get older and stronger, she'd make the journey to Dow-Dow, even though their trip by mule would be an arduous one, requiring days of riding over mountainous terrain, even during peacetime.

She shared with Kebada her pleasure and happiness with her newfound life. He smiled. "You have no idea how much it pleases me to hear you say that." But after a brief pause, he added, "Although we must also welcome sudden and unexpected changes in life, too."

Although Kebada occasionally visited his legitimate wife Negat and their children, in his heart, he felt he only

139

had one woman—Fanaye. Yet, he remained loving and loyal to his children and provided well for them and their mother. He wished he could spend more time with his children, especially with his son, and bring him back into the fold to be raised by Fanaye, but he knew Negat would never allow it. The only request she'd made of him was that he not make any claims on their son. It hadn't been difficult for him to agree since he was spending more and more time away from home, heading military functions. Meanwhile, the news that Mussolini had allied himself with Hitler was a devastating development, which would only keep Kebada away from home even more.

Every day, the Italian fascist government continued to send more combat troops and equipment into Ethiopia. It wasn't the first time the fascists refused to learn hard lessons about Ethiopians' proud identity. They were surprised they had lost the war in 1887 as a result of Ethiopia's victory at Adwa. The entire modern world was shocked to see a defenseless nation defeat a prominent European power. But sadly, although the war had been won, a great many people had perished then, as many of them were perishing now.

Kebada's energy was depleted, and his sleep was often broken by anxiety over the encroaching enemy. Many nights he would wake up shouting, "Yazew! Yazew! Get them! Get every one of them!" His face would tighten, and intense

140

headaches would follow. Even though he understood the inevitable and irrevocable horrors of war, it was incomprehensible to him how a so-called civilized people could viciously attack another independent nation to claim it as their own.

Fanaye saw the effect the war was having on Kebada, and her worry for him grew stronger. Her most pressing responsibility now was to try to make his home life comfortable and alive with warmth and care.

As the Italian invasion of Ethiopia progressed and newer regions fell under Italian occupation, Basha Kebada was away more and more frequently, sometimes for months at a time. Meanwhile, Fanaye settled into a routine of motherhood, eagerly awaiting those times when Kebada would unexpectedly come home.

One day, when he was at home, Kebada approached Fanaye with a grim face and announced that he needed to talk to her. After Fanaye sat down, Kebada updated her on the war—about the invasion of the Italians, how they were far superior in armaments and manpower. "But they're in a land not their own, whereas we're fighting for life or death in our own country, for our own freedom," he explained. "Many of our fighters have nothing but spears and bows and arrows against their machine guns and cannons. But you will see, again, we will be victorious and win the war in the end."

141

Kebada pointed out that he'd been able to operate out of Addis Ababa so far without arousing the enemy's suspicion, which was why he could return home from time to time, though he was gone for long periods. Due to the great secrecy he maintained around his clandestine operations and comings and goings, they had not been accosted at their residence yet. "But, my dear, unfortunately, that's no longer possible." He explained further that Italians had begun to tighten their control over Addis Ababa and its people, especially over the military and civilian leadership. The regular army units were being dismantled, and large-scale arrests and detention of important military and civilian personnel had become commonplace. They'd even started taking officers into custody without warning. "They just come and rip people away," Kebada said. "At this point, we're forced into guerrilla warfare. Our armed forces will operate pretty much as an underground resistance from now on."

He paused, struggling for the right words. "This means I can no longer operate out of Addis Ababa," he said. "I've already received my orders to leave and report to my secret post at an undisclosed location. No one will know where I am." He looked Fanaye squarely in the eyes. "No one," he repeated.

Fanaye's eyes widened in dismay when she realized what he was saying. "Believe me, this is for the good of our whole family," he added. "Every minute I spend in this house puts all of us at risk."

Fanaye, choked with emotion, said nothing. She secretly harbored daydreams of killing the enemy with her bare hands. Why couldn't women fight too? When she was able to speak, "How often are we going to see you?" she asked. "And what if there's an urgent situation here at home and we need to let you know? What then?"

Kebada reassured her that he'd already made arrangements for someone to stop by the house as often as possible, a different person each time so as not to arouse suspicion, and check with her. If Fanaye had a message for him, she could give it to the visitor, and he'd be sure the message reached Kebada. "You'll know the messenger because when he comes to the door, he'll say, 'God looks out for us.'"

Fanaye nodded. "When are you leaving?"

Kebada sighed and held Fanaye's hand. "Tonight."

A new phase in the lives of Fanaye, Tsega, and the children began after that night. Tsega grew worried and suspicious of everything and everybody. Fanaye, being the strong-willed and self-reliant woman that she was, took everything in stride, managing the house effectively while also taking care of her children. As Kebada had warned, living conditions became much worse for everybody under the increased violence and repression by the invaders. Some people disappeared overnight, never to be seen or heard from again. Frequently, Italian soldiers shot citizens in the streets.

One evening, a week after Kebada left, Fanaye and Tsega heard a loud, persistent knocking on the door. Fanaye bravely answered. Half-a-dozen menacing-looking Italian soldiers pushed open the door and stormed past Fanaye into the living room. They ransacked things, knocking tables over; dishes and lamps fell as they stomped around while the children cried and Tsega prayed. They couldn't find what they were looking for.

The leader of the soldiers shouted something in Italian. The man turned to Fanaye and translated in a curt voice, "Where is he? Where is Major Kebada?"

Fanaye took a deep breath, raised her chin, and, looking at the Italian soldier's face, said in a strong and unintimidated voice, "I don't know where he is. I haven't seen or heard from him... for a long time."

After the petty officer heard the translation of what she'd said, he flew into a rage and babbled some harsh-sounding words to the translator. The other soldiers took out their bayonets and mounted them on their rifles.

"Look here, young woman!" the translator said. "He says if you don't tell us where your husband is, they'll slaughter every living soul in this house! As you can see for yourself, they really mean it, so don't be stupid. Tell them where he is."

This threat, which would have cast terror into any normal person's heart, barely fazed Fanaye. She thought for a moment, then again looked into the soldier's small brown eyes. "Look, tell him to use his head," she said. "Any mother would give away her husband's whereabouts to save her children's lives if she knows where he is. If she's not telling, she doesn't know where he is. I'd do anything to save my children. I'm not giving you information because I really don't know."

It took several minutes for the translator to get this across to the petty officer. At first, the soldier looked a bit confused, but then a subtle smile of admiration crossed his lips. For a moment, he looked down at his feet as if he was thinking hard. Then he shouted orders, and the soldiers noisily filed out of the room. Fanaye slammed the door shut behind them.

Chapter 16: Freedom For Ethiopia

This wasn't Italy's first attempt to colonize Ethiopia. Half a century earlier, in 1885, the Italians had attempted to subjugate them, but the proud Ethiopian people had fought bravely. Italy's modern army had become the laughingstock of Europe after being soundly defeated by 'mere savages' armed with only spears, bows and arrows. And now, the great Mussolini was determined to seek revenge to restore Italy's name as a dominant power. Once again, the Ethiopians fought to the death to defeat the invaders. That much was certain. All Ethiopians were united to oppose the fascists' onslaught.

Upon reaching the training camp, Kebada briefed his lieutenants and sent the new recruits into formation for the long march to the front. The latest intelligence indicated that the Italians were gathering outside Entoto, trying to cut off supply lines.

The recruits were from everywhere. After years of supplying their families with wild game, the farmers brought their own bows and arrows and were proficient in using them. The same could not be said for the city dwellers. Kebada spent entire days training new groups of recruits, mostly novice draftees who were still in their teens and had never held a gun before. He and his drill sergeant taught them basic combat skills.

He knew that the fascists had more guns, more bullets, and more training than his band of recruits, but they also carried with them something even heavier than their metal tanks: arrogance. Kebada relied on this. The enemy always underestimated Ethiopians, whereas he knew that even a seasoned farmer could become the fiercest warrior.

In the afternoon, a courier came galloping through the woods with an urgent message for Kebada from the province of Mekalay. The note read: Report here with your troops. Need reinforcements. Fighting has begun.

After informing his lieutenants of the news, Kebada ordered the troops to follow him to Mekalay. "Tamru, we ride at once," he said. "Men, brothers, we are marching on to Mekalay where we will crush those faithless fascists again! Bring on the rain! We will rip them apart and let God wash their filth away from our land. Freedom for Ethiopia!"

The men cheered and shook their bows in the air as Kebada's horse stomped, reared, and galloped toward Mekalay, with Tamru galloping hard behind.

When they reached Mekalay, many of the soldiers were as enthusiastic as Kebada, who fought bravely for most of the day.

As the day wore on, the men became sluggish and cold under the constant and powerful rain. Some huddled together to stay warm. The same must have been true for the Italians, for battle seemed to subside for a while.

To Kebada's dismay, even some of his lieutenants looked haggard. He urged them on to boost their morale. On an impulse, he raised his gun and shot into the air. "Brothers and sons, we are invincible!" he cried out. "No bullets can stop us from protecting our mother, Ethiopia. She will help us with the rain, stopping their tanks in the mud. This unrelenting rain is our gift from God. He washes them away, as He shields us from their bullets!"

As the men waited for the battle to begin again, Kebada recited the famous speech by King Menelek: "*All have to die sometime. I will not be afflicted if I die fighting our enemies who have come here to ruin our country and change our religion. They have passed beyond the sea, which God gave us as our frontier ... these enemies have advanced, burrowing into the country like moles, but with God's help I will get rid of them.*"

When fighting resumed, tired men surged up in a wave of passion, following Kebada's lead as he charged the front line. Precise and powerful, he wasted no bullets. Each flew straight to its target, hitting heads, chests, and vital organs. The fight went on for hours, and as Kebada had predicted, the enemy fell back. This would have been a perfect opportunity to follow through and chase the enemy as they retreated until every one of them was wiped out. Unfortunately, during the long and bloody ordeal, the Ethiopian forces had also lost many men, and the surviving ones were so exhausted that Kebada decided to call it a day.

As Kebada and his men plodded on toward the encampment, the excitement of winning the battle at Mekalay gradually wore off as the relentless heavy rain and wind did not let up. Tamru was filled with admiration for Kebada. I'm weak and limp like my wet shama, he thought. But he—he is a gift from God. No wonder they call him the Great Basha Kebada!

The following day was clear and bright as if to make up for the harsh weather of the past few days. Kebada and his men went into battle again, but the day's losses soon mounted far above those from the day before. The sun was still glimmering through the eucalyptus grove just past the gates of the compound. Soon it would slip entirely out of view. Another day gone. This last battle was particularly brutal. Kebada had lost almost half of his soldiers, and many of the survivors were injured. He hated retreating, but it was the only thing he could do. They would rally more reinforcements and try once again to recapture the ground the fascists had taken.

The next day, Kebada and his troops restlessly waited to attack and capture the column of Italian invaders that had infiltrated the area. Kebada hid his troops among the thicket of oak and eucalyptus trees. After hours of reconnaissance, seeing his troops weak from hunger and wilting in the scorching heat, he let them return to their encampment to rest and recuperate.

By late evening, someone informed of an imminent enemy attack at Naziret. He hastily brought in new recruits, and with two-hundred-fifty enlisted men, Kebada dashed off to Naziret. Although it turned out to be a false alarm and their trip was for nothing, they remained in Naziret the following day to ensure that the town remained safe. The town chief saw to it that Kebada and his troops were fed.

Halfway through their journey back to Addis Ababa, the night grew dark and cold. Some of the men were more experienced and better equipped than others at making their way through unknown terrain in the dark. A group of about fifteen men fell behind and became separated from the rest. Disoriented and confused, and unsure about how to navigate, they barely moved. The next day, a lieutenant discovered that these men were unaccounted for and reported this to Kebada. Immediately, Kebada ordered a group of soldiers to go out and look for them. Unfortunately, after hours of searching, the soldiers returned empty-handed. The lieutenant of the search party reported, "Since we didn't find any bodies, more than likely they just ran away."

Since there would be no more fighting that day, Kebada assigned one of his lieutenants to command and ordered the troops to return back to their base camp so that he could take off and go home to his family.

When Kebada arrived home, he heard faint giggles and squeals from the garden. At the garden's edge, he hesitated, reluctant to disturb the children's play. Instead, he watched his two little girls as they skipped and chased each other, oblivious to everything but their own delight. Kebada smiled, longing to scoop them up in his arms, aware that there were no guarantees tomorrow would bring such joy. He'd seen entire villages blown to bits by enemy artillery. How could he or anyone defend his precious children from such horrors? His teeth clenched in rage. He would die to protect them!

As he watched the children, Kebada became aware of the strange contrast at the border of his little garden—the fragile sweetness of his children versus the stench of war upon himself. He couldn't defile their innocent sanctuary by setting one foot inside, so he simply remained standing where he was, reverently adoring them from a distance.

But as soon as they saw Kebada standing at the entrance of the garden, his two little girls screamed with glee and raced into his open arms, crying, "Ababa, Ababa!" He kissed them and held them tightly until they squirmed out of his arms and pulled him into the garden.

That night, after he'd finished eating dinner with Fanaye and the children, Kebada went straight to bed. Exhausted from months of fighting the war, he had a recurring dream in which Mussolini approached him wearing a military uniform. Mussolini was alone, marching as if he were in a parade. As he moved closer to Kebada, Mussolini's face changed to the countenance of a grinning hyena. Startled, Kebada gasped and turned away, but the hyena paced in front of him. "I am going to make a feast of you!" He then gave Kebada his notorious salute and disappeared.

Kebada awoke with a start, drenched in sweat. He was relieved when he realized it was only a nightmare, but had a hard time falling back asleep. When he finally did, more frightening dreams came. This time a group of fascists in black shirts called him by name and clapped their hands cheerfully, as though they were glad to see him. Kebada chased them away, but they kept dodging him, still applauding with the same enthusiasm. Kebada then drew his gun and fired at them, but instead of backing off, the men dashed toward him at a faster and faster pace, dodging most of his bullets. Even those few who were hit continued their bloodthirsty cheering as they moved closer to him. With blood dripping from their arms and legs, they chanted, "Long live Mussolini! Long live Il Duce!"

Kebada awoke at the crack of dawn with a splitting headache. Disoriented from the nightmares and almost overwhelmed with fatigue, he nonetheless put on his uniform and checked his list of things he needed to attend to. Fanaye was already awake and busy preparing food for his journey, which wouldn't spoil: Dabo kolo, dried lamb, roasted barley, and sunflower seeds.

He lingered just long enough to gulp down his coffee. He didn't tell Fanaye about his nightmares because he knew they'd distress her. Instead, he offered advice: "Take care of the children and yourself. If anything happens, go to the military office and tell them who you are. They will take care of you." He then clutched Fanaye's hand on a sudden impulse.

Fanaye couldn't understand why Kebada was so personally affected by the enemy's actions; every defeat or setback was causing him great agony, as if he alone had let down his country. Fanaye wished Kebada wouldn't discuss what to do if he didn't return. Such thoughts frightened her, like a prediction of terrible events. "Why don't you stay home today? Can't the men manage without you?"

Kebada took her face in his hands. "Don't be sad," he said softly. "I'm being cautious."

153

"I'm only asking you to do it this one time." Fanaye pleaded.

"I have to go. Not going would be like a bear sending her cubs to hunt for food by themselves in the wilderness."

Their conversation was disturbed by a commotion outside. "Please, Basha Kebada, I don't know what's wrong with Wudu!" Tamru shouted.

Kebada darted out, knowing Tamru wouldn't bother him unless it was important. Kebada saw Wudu, his horse, wildly jerking his head up and down, neighing and digging the ground with his hooves while Tamru tried to control him. When Kebada moved close to his beloved horse, Wudu locked eyes with him and neighed loudly.

"Sir, I don't know what's wrong with him," Tamru said. "He even refused to graze. He tried to kick me when I tried to brush him. You know, ordinarily, he loves that. If I didn't know better, I'd say he was untamed."

Kebada stroked Wudu's neck and calmed him down. "What is it you are trying to tell me, Gwadanya?" he asked as he offered the horse some grass. Wudu ate it obediently.

Tamru shook his head. "He was impossible with me," he insisted. "I tried everything."

"Son, make sure you eat well and don't worry about Wudu," Kebada reassured him. "He's just cranky." Then he went back inside for another cup of coffee.

Wudu again became restless and uncooperative. He neighed so loudly that it woke the children, who ran outside to see what all the commotion was about. Kebada set down his cup of coffee and followed them. He grabbed the reins from Tamru and eventually succeeded in stopping Wudu's wild kicking. Again he whispered into the horse's ears and quieted him enough to mount him.

Sosina and Zenite had watched their father struggle with Wudu. Sosina rushed to her father and stretched out her hand to grab his. Kebada's throat constricted when he looked into her innocent, dark eyes, but he managed a smile. "Ababa, when you are not here, what do you eat?"

"So you want to know what your ababa eats?" he replied. "Let's see. For breakfast, I eat a tiger or two, and for supper, a big lion." He then pushed out his belly like a balloon and patted it with his hand.

Sosina's laugh sounded like bells. "No. You don't eat lions and tigers!"

"And why not?"

"Because they will eat you first."

"You are too smart." Kebada picked her up, gave her a kiss, and then set her back down.

Zenite tugged at her father's tunic. "There you are, my big girl!" He smiled as he lifted her up and kissed her too.

Fanaye came out of the house to say goodbye. Kebada had already mounted his horse, so Fanaye held his canteen up to him, holding back her tears. He bent down and kissed her on both cheeks and whispered, "Everything will be alright. Better days are ahead for all of us. Take good care of yourself." With that, he spurred Wudu gently and galloped away.

A rumor spread that it was a matter of days before the Italian army would completely occupy and take over Addis Ababa. People grew anxious. Everyone, young and old, stood ready to fight for their country. Kebada had already been informed that the Italian commander, Badoglio, and his troops were anticipating a triumphant march into the capital. Badoglio was confident that nothing would stand in his way and didn't anticipate any major challenge to his success. He felt so confident that he kept speaking about having a grand parade march through the city, showing the natives who their future masters were.

Meanwhile, Haile Selassie, the Emperor of Ethiopia, hid at the Lalibela Church in another province far from the capital, his power lost to the enemy. He remained there for three days, fasting and praying in seclusion. Like other earlier monarchs of Ethiopia, he relied on his faith in God for protection and strength. But most Ethiopians were ready to fight, to give their bodies and souls for their beloved country. So, at night, about three thousand men marched to the outskirts of town, planning where they'd hide in order to see the enemy when it approached Addis Ababa. Unfortunately, the enemy had plans of their own: they had already arrived and waited in the proximity of the city to wipe out the Ethiopians like flies.

Once the Ethiopians were in sight, the enemy began firing at them furiously. Ethiopians expected their enemy to have superior weapons and equipment, yet they were willing and able to fight them with their simple weapons and die for their country. They had not counted on the Italians' unprecedented treachery and cruelty, which manifested itself by releasing mustard gas, even though international law had strictly outlawed this practice. The effect of poisonous gas on masses of Ethiopian soldiers was catastrophic. In panic and agony, the blinded men tried frantically to escape the gas, but to no avail. They pushed one another and screamed in pain. Some went into convulsions, rolling on the ground. Others stood apparently in a state of shock, desperately rubbing their burning eyes, while others doubled over with severe abdominal pain. The more they tried to alleviate the effects of the poison gas, the worse it got for them.

Kebada, as well as other commanders, found themselves in a predicament beyond their control. They had anticipated fighting the Italians with all their might and were aware that they'd lose many soldiers, and an even greater number would suffer injuries. But none of them expected the Italians to stoop so low as to resort to outlawed chemical warfare. Even for Mussolini, the attack was brutal and inhumane, indicating a new stage in warfare. It seemed like the Italians were determined to wipe out the Ethiopians at any cost, like exterminating pests to reap a healthy harvest.

Chapter 17: The Turn Of Fate

From her usual seat facing the frontyard, Fanaye saw Tamru and several other men approach the house, carrying something wrapped in a heavy black blanket. For several seconds she watched with a feeling of mounting unreality. Surely they were carrying piles of blankets to keep the family warm if the enemy were to come and turn them out? As the men drew nearer, she couldn't deny that they were carrying a body. Instinct told her the man was Kebada. He must have been badly hurt since he would never allow anyone to carry him if he were able to walk. Fanaye's stomach tightened, and she was glad the children were playing at the neighbor's house and didn't see their father in this state.

Unable to control herself, she dashed out into the yard. "What's going on?" she cried. "Is he badly hurt?" Her pleading eyes shifted from one soldier to another. "Please tell me!"

As they carried the body through the doorway, Tamru took Fanaye's hand. He paused, fumbling for the right words. "I'm so sorry," he finally said, his voice cracking. "We lost him, our greatest hero. He was a true warrior." Then he pointed the soldiers in the direction of the bedroom.

Fanaye sobbed uncontrollably. "I asked him not to go this one time, but he wouldn't listen." She followed the soldiers to the bedroom in a daze and watched as they laid Kebada's inert body down on the bed. Numbly, her fingers touched him, searching for the wound. Then she flung herself across his body and cried out, "God, why did they take him from us? Tsega! Tsega!"

The old woman came running in at the sound of the commotion. She froze for a moment, staring at the body, and dropped to her knees with her hands to her face, howling with pain and misery.

The men stood silently with their heads bowed. After a while, Fanaye managed to rise to her feet. With her hands clenched into fists, she faced the soldiers, her face burning like a flame and veins protruding from her neck. "So, they finally got him," she said, her eyes narrowed into slits. "They don't know what they've done. We will wipe those fascist bastards off the face of the earth!"

Tamru did his best to console her. "Our great leader has left this ugly world behind to join our Heavenly Father, but his spirit will always be with us."

"We will make the necessary arrangements," one of the soldiers said somberly. Then, turning to Tsega, who now stood beside the bed weeping, he whispered, "Maybe you should take her to another room."

The grief-stricken Tsega gently guided Fanaye out of the room. Mesfin, one of Kebada's soldiers, went to the kitchen door to ask for water. He called out for the women, but he retrieved the water himself when he received no answer. He stepped into the kitchen, and there he saw Fanaye and Tsega sitting on the floor in a corner, hugging each other as they rocked back and forth. Stunned, he stood very still, not knowing what to do. Should he comfort them or allow them a moment of solitude in their sorrow? His heart went out to Fanaye, perhaps because she was closer to his age. For a moment, he forgot why he had come into the kitchen as he slowly approached them.

Once she saw Mesfin, Fanaye quickly straightened up. Mesfin bowed as he would have to Kebada and whispered, "I'm so sorry for your loss. This is hard for all of us."

"Tell me how it happened," Fanaye asked. "Tell me he didn't suffer before he died!"

Mesfin described how the fascists had brutally attacked, taking aim at Kebada all at once. "They really wanted to get him, and there was no way we could have saved him," he said. "Some soldiers who tried to shield him from the fire died, too." Suddenly, Mesfin turned toward the wall and punched it hard with his fist. "I should have been there with him!" he said. "I would have gladly given up my life for him!"

Fanaye's anger matched Mesfin's. She punched her fist against her palm, wishing she could get her hands on one of the beasts who had killed Kebada. At that moment, she vowed to make the enemy's lives a living hell.

Despite her own sorrow, Fanaye asked the men if they should transport Kebada's body to Negat, his wife. "Oh no! Definitely not!" Tsega shouted.

Fanaye wasn't so sure. Wasn't Negat entitled?

"But you were the true wife!" Tsega insisted. "Basha Kebada would have agreed with me."

When they asked Tamru for his opinion, he agreed with Tsega, explaining there was no time to spare anyway. According to Coptic religion, a dead person had to be buried as soon as possible, which made sense since bodies would decompose very quickly in the hot climate. So, they decided to bury him in Addis Ababa, at the cemetery of Saint Michael's Church. After the funeral, someone would be sent to inform Negat about Kebada's death.

Because most military men were still away fighting, only those who were in the vicinity of Addis Ababa were able to pay their respects to Basha Kebada. The soldiers and neighbors quietly journeyed to the burial ground before dawn, carrying Kebada's coffin on their shoulders, fearful that Italian troops might be lurking nearby. Luckily they were able to bury him promptly and return to his house to continue the mourning rituals. Following the Orthodox Coptic tradition, they wanted to mourn by staying in the deceased person's house for about a week, but since most of the mourners were soldiers and it was a time of war, the usual tradition wasn't followed. Fanaye didn't have the consolation of having family around to share her grief, with the exception of Tsega and a couple of women.

As was also the custom, Tsega insisted on shaving Fanaye's head. Fanaye refused to do this. "I see no value in it," she said. "I would do so, only if it would bring Kebada back."

The rest of the time, she sat silently. She didn't beat her chest or scream uncontrollably, as was expected of her. Later, some people misinterpreted this as a sign of indifference, and they began to whisper, "Doesn't she care that Kebada is dead?"

"It's amazing that she doesn't even bother to pretend she's mourning," one woman muttered to her companion. "God knows, I've met many women who didn't care a bit about their husbands when they were alive, but when they died—oh! What a show they put on as if their whole world had come to an end!"

A man said to his wife, "She acts like she's not really convinced her husband is dead." To which his wife sarcastically replied, "You're right, dear; he wasn't her husband."

After a few days, a messenger arrived at the house of

Negat's brother, so they could deliver the bad news to Negat. At first, shocked by the news, Negat screamed and wailed as any good wife would. Upon hearing the commotion, the neighbors dropped what they were doing and rushed over to her house. There, they joined her in wailing and lamenting. When they'd released some of their grief, they turned their attention to Negat and tried to keep her from beating her chest, pulling her hair, and damaging herself.

"My hero, my children's father!" Negat cried over and over.

Unlike Fanaye, Negat followed custom and shaved her hair. She wore black from head to toe. However, after only two weeks of mourning, her mood rapidly changed. She planned a trip to Addis Ababa to claim what was rightfully hers before Kebada's mistress got to it. The more Negat thought about her marriage with Kebada and how much he'd been away from their children, the more she was determined to vindicate herself by getting everything he had.

Fanaye had his love, but now I'll have his money, she thought. Fair is fair.

And so she traveled to Addis Ababa, bringing along their son Dawit as proof of her marital status if any was needed. She claimed her widow's pension and had no problem. She was aided by having the necessary paperwork, and in no time, the transaction was done.

The day after the funeral, the sun rose brightly, in sharp contrast to Fanaye's dark mood. Restless, she dressed quickly and, clutching her long gabi, went out into the garden. Her long-suppressed yearning for her family, combined with the sadness she felt over the loss of Kebada, overwhelmed her. Memories flashed by, but the now eighteen-year-old Fanaye turned away from these painful thoughts. She had no time for all that. Still, in spite of her self-confidence, worries kept creeping back into her mind. Eventually, her head cleared when she remembered Kebada's sage advice, "Don't let fear win. Push fear away with a flick of your wrist."

There's no time for melancholy, she told herself, snapping out of her reverie. She needed to take care of important matters, like going to the military office to find out about survivor benefits.

She stood in a long line in front of the military office. When her turn came, she told the young clerk that she was the common-law wife of Basha Kebada and had two children by him.

The man stood up, placed his hand over his heart, and said respectfully, "I am so sorry for your loss. He was our lion."

Fanaye was touched and thanked the man. "Basha Kebada told me to come for benefits if anything ever

165

happened to him."

"Of course, there should be benefits for the family of a hero," he said. "Give me a moment, please, to see what I can find out for you. This shouldn't take too long."

But he took so long that Fanaye began to wonder if he had forgotten. When he finally returned, his face was downcast. "Weizero, I'm so sorry," he informed her. "Unfortunately, only his legal wife is entitled to benefits."

"But what about our children?" Fanaye asked desperately. "I may not have been his legal wife, but they are his children."

The clerk was sympathetic but said there was nothing he could do. "If you petition the court, you might get a positive response," he said. "As you say, they are his children after all, and they should be entitled at least to some benefits." He handed her the appropriate form if she decided to petition.

"I don't know how to read and write," she responded, extending the paper back to him. "So I don't know what to do with this!"

"You must know someone who can help you. Some relative, maybe?"

"I have no one to help me." Then she waved the paper in front of his face angrily. "Take me to the person in charge!" she demanded.

"The Dejazmuch, who is in charge of these matters, isn't

here today. I'm sorry."

Fanaye had no choice but to leave with the matter unresolved. On her way home, she considered what recourse she had if she didn't succeed in getting benefits. The only thing that came to mind was that she could gather wood to make a living. Ironically, gathering wood was the first chore that she was asked to do as a child. Yes, she reassured herself. I can gather wood and carry a heavy load.

But what if she were caught by the enemy? Weren't they known for raping any woman they saw in the woods? In her imagination, she saw herself fending off another physical attack by men. The wretched fantasy made her head feel heavy and sent the blood coursing rapidly through her veins.

Tsega's arthritis acted up. Usually, soaking her feet in hot water with a pinch of cayenne pepper and salt would bring her great relief, but on this particular day, her symptoms were getting worse instead of better. Tsega knew that she needed a stronger remedy. She'd soaked her feet for so long that they had begun to look like wrinkled prunes. Finally, ignoring the pain, she got up, wiped her feet dry, and prepared to leave the house. "I'm going to Fanaye's," she told her mother, who sat in a chair across the room.

Aselafach frowned and shook her head. "I just don't know where the money is going to come from," she grumbled. "Apparently, you choose to work for free."

Tsega knew her mother found it ridiculous that she continued to work for someone who could no longer afford to pay her wages. Still, she had grown tired of explaining that Fanaye was like her own child, that it was her joy to help Fanaye in any way she could during these distressful times. So, without responding to her mother, she gathered the last of her things and walked toward the door. But as usual, Aselafach had the last word. "If you keep listening to your dreaming heart, we'll soon be out on the street, begging," she said. "I hope God will have mercy on me and take my life before things come to that."

When Tsega arrived at Fanaye's place, the two women embraced. Fanaye's face was flushed with gratitude. "Tsega, how good to see you," she said. "Look at me, penniless, and you still want to help me."

"I'm not going to abandon you! You're like my daughter.

"How lucky my children and I are to have you."

"It's not me," Tsega said. "I believe God never takes something away without replacing it with something equally good."

Fanaye nodded and told her that sometimes when she looked at her children, she saw God's miracle and was thankful for His gifts.

"Fanaye, you're so young, but you have so much wisdom."

"Thank you, but now let me put my wisdom into practice."

Fanaye then explained to Tsega how she was going to find work. "I used to gather wood for my mother and was always praised for being quick and for carrying more than others. I can still do that and earn a living," she said, smiling in anticipation.

Tsega's reaction was not what she'd hoped. "You can't be serious," Tsega said, frowning. "A lady like you does not do that kind of work. Please, don't even think about it."

"A lady like me?" Fanaye laughed and then shrugged. "Have you forgotten I'm a farmer's daughter? Where I come from, people do everything for themselves, including gathering wood."

"Let's not forget about a husband!" Tsega reminded her. "You see how Basha Kebada's friends have been eyeing you. Don't tell me you haven't noticed them."

Fanaye wasn't impressed. "They can stare all they want, but that's as far as it goes."

Nothing more to say on the matter. Fanaye headed out to the garden to pick vegetables for the children's lunch. Tsega continued worrying; the thought of Fanaye going off into the woods alone to gather wood troubled her. Just a few days ago, in broad daylight, Italians had raped a young girl who had gone into the woods to do her chores. She was found bleeding and nearly incoherent from the attack.

Chapter 18: Agota Negash

After several attempts at calling from outside the gate and getting no response, a man picked up a stone the size of a grown person's fist and banged at the gate.

Startled, Fanaye grabbed a heavy cane from the house and walked nervously toward the gate, where a strange man was standing. "Who are you, and what do you want?" she shouted, trying not to show her fear.

The man apologized for alarming her and introduced himself as Negash, a friend of Kebada's. "I've come to offer my condolences."

"I'm sorry," she said. "Please, do come in."

Once inside the house, she gestured for Negash to have a seat. Unfortunately, he sat in Basha Kebada's chair, which she still regarded as Kebada's. Negash had removed his coat. He was sitting with his legs crossed as if readying himself for a casual conversation.

"It must be very difficult for a beautiful young lady to be alone with young children and no man to comfort her," he said.

Fanaye ignored his apparent lack of manners. She remembered what Kebada had once said about him, that he was an opportunist who would sell his own mother to get what he wanted. In all the years Fanaye had lived with

Kebada, he'd never invited Negash to the house, making it clear to Fanaye that Negash was no friend of Kebada's. She sensed why he'd come to visit and doubted the wisdom of inviting him inside.

Despite Fanaye's reservations about Negash, she was still a gracious hostess, sitting down with him and asking how he'd come to know Basha Kebada. Negash barely heard her question since he was carefully taking note of all the furnishings in the room. None of it impressed him. This wasn't surprising since Kebada had taken little interest in accumulating material wealth.

When he heard the soft whisper of voices, Negash turned and saw Sosina and Zenite standing in the doorway. He smiled, waved his hand, and beckoned them over. "Children, come in," he said. "Don't just stand there. Come and say hello to your agota, uncle."

But the children remained by the door. Negash got up and walked towards them. "You don't need to be shy around me," he said. With his hands on their shoulders, he steered them into the room, where they sat meekly. He then slipped his hand into his trouser pocket and pulled out a small pouch, which he held in the air by its string. "I have something for you!" he said.

Sosina and Zenite were curious at the prospect of receiving a gift. "But you have to come and get it," he continued, lowering his voice to create more mystery and excitement while dangling the pouch in the air. Tsega set down a tray with a pot of coffee and discreetly left.

The children barely restrained themselves from rushing up to this stranger and grabbing the pouch out of his hand. They looked at their mother for permission to accept his gift. Fanaye was uncomfortable; she didn't know how to refuse the man without offending him.

"Children, I want you to know I was like a brother to your father," Negash said, trying to convince Fanaye to let the children accept his gift. "I think he would want you to call me Agota Negash."

Little Zenite was quite impatient by then. "What do you have for us?" she demanded.

"Ha!" He smiled and gently shook the pouch. "You'll just have to find out for yourself. Come and get it!"

Zenite sheepishly looked at her mother. Fanaye smiled, lifting her chin up. "Go ahead, children, but thank Ato Negash for bringing you a present."

"It's Agota Negash and never Ato Negash," Negash protested. "You're like my own family, and you don't call your family Ato." He pulled out two small silver crosses from the pouch and handed them to each child. Zenite grabbed hers and ran to her mother. Negash couldn't help but notice Fanaye's surprised expression when she saw the silver

173

crosses.

"I think you forgot to thank Ato Negash," Fanaye scolded her. "Go thank him."

Later, after the children left the room, Negash resumed attempts to sweet-talk his lovely young hostess. First, he stared at her face, then dropped his gaze down to her long graceful neck, which he saw was unadorned. "Such an exquisite neck as yours should be complimented by an equally beautiful necklace," he said. "What a pity! We'll just have to do something about that."

Fanaye gave him a half-smile but said nothing. He continued to stare at her, allowing his eyes to move from her throat to her breasts, then to her slender waist and hips. "You know, you and your children need to be looked after, and I will make sure that happens," he said a little aggressively. "Life is tough these days, especially for a beautiful young woman like you. The fascists are causing a great deal of agony for everyone. Our people are being forced out of their own homes."

Fanaye remained polite and reserved as she listened but didn't say anything. Negash sighed, leaned back in his chair, and continued: "The Italians are saying they're determined that Ethiopians have modern homes as if they're really concerned about us. They may not be sincere, but I can see their point. They're saying that they want to bring us out of the darkness of the past into the light of the twentieth century. It's so true. We are a very backward country."

Fanaye almost lost her self-control when she heard this. Still, she knew the futility of arguing with Negash about this hypocritical and deluded point of view. For years, Tsega had tried to tone down Fanaye's blunt and outspoken manner, and Fanaye reigned herself in whenever she felt a strong urge to speak her mind. Nothing could be gained from letting Negash know how she felt about the Italians. Besides, she was fairly certain that he was one of the officials who would decide if she'd receive any compensation. Negash was in the position of authority.

Fanaye was very different from most of the women he'd known. She stood strong and upright, looking directly into his eyes with great self-assurance. Her strength and bearing had gained his respect so much that he decided, right then and there, to pursue her. Yet, there was tension in the room between them. Fanaye wished the children would barge in and break the mood, but they were happily playing outside with their new gifts.

Negash broke the silence. "You look so thin," he said. "Are things difficult for you?"

Fanaye didn't know what to say, so she gave him a blank stare. Negash was put off by Fanaye's silence, but then he wondered if she was too proud and reticent to reveal her difficult situation to a stranger. He reached out and gently took her hand. "I will make sure you never have to worry again. I am going to take care of you and the children. A beautiful lady like you surely needs someone to look after her."

Then, unable to control himself any longer, he lifted Fanaye's hand to his mouth and wetly kissed her fingers. Fanaye stiffened and pulled away. Negash thought she was hard to get. He took her hand again and, smiling, caressed his rough cheek with it.

Fanaye, unable to endure his clumsy attempts at seduction any longer, yanked her hand away from his. "What do you think you're doing?" she asked.

"Oh, dear, dear!" Negash muttered, still smiling. "You're playing hard to get, and I'm going to forgive you, for I'm smitten by your charm."

Fanaye looked unflinchingly into his eyes. "Please, you've come to the wrong house," she said in a strong, steady voice.

Negash recoiled, sensing her repulsion for the first time. "So, you're a daring woman!" he said, at once indignant and imperious. "Don't you know who I am?"

"No, and I don't care!"

"My lady, you are not only daring, you're also foolish!"

"Think what you wish. Just leave."

Negash laughed. "So, you think this house belongs to you and not to the government?" he asked. "You, my dear, have no home. Perhaps it was my mistake. I'm too nice. But don't upset me from now on. I'm going to forgive you today, but next time I'll expect you to be nicer to me so that I can be nice to you in return. Don't forget this man who is going to be your future caretaker."

"And who says I need to be taken care of?" Fanaye shouted as Negash made ready to leave. He ignored her spirited outburst, although he seemed to be taken aback as he left.

That night, Fanaye lay tense between Sosina and Zenite in her cramped wooden bed, thinking hard about their future. She was no longer able to conjure up thoughts of better days ahead. The possibility of good fortune now felt like an illusion. She glanced at her sleeping children, so young and innocent, oblivious to how their lives were about to change. They missed their father and believed he would be coming home soon after a long trip, as he had done so many times in the past.

She touched the children's cheeks and listened to their breathing for a moment. She pictured being reunited with her own parents, imagining how they would react when they saw their grandchildren. Fanaye felt torn up inside as she struggled to focus on hope rather than on despair. I must be strong for my family, she told herself, no matter how difficult life may become.

Comforted by her own resolve, Fanaye dozed off soundly until she felt her ribs jabbed by Zenite's bony feet. "Oh, you children kick like wild donkeys!" she mumbled, rubbing her aching side as she sleepily pulled herself out of bed. She couldn't believe it was already morning.

She washed herself and prepared breakfast. She reached into the dark wooden pantry for a jar of butter. The jar was close to empty, and there were no eggs and very little dry meat left. She realized there was only enough food for a few days. But hearing the cheerful sounds of her children as they woke and played with their handmade dolls, Fanaye's spirit lightened once again. As long as her children were laughing, she could not complain.

Several days later, when Fanaye glanced out the window, she saw Negash, big and square, thumping his way towards the house. "Have mercy!" she muttered to herself in fear and disgust. "What made that thing come on foot instead of by horse?" She feared that he was coming back to abuse his position and try to force a favorable answer out of her. Before she had a chance to come up with a delaying tactic, Negash was already knocking at the door with an urgency that made her heart sink, knowing she was about to face a very personal enemy.

On his previous visit, even while Fanaye was rejecting his advances, Negash had been all smiles and charm. Now, when she opened the door, his face was hard and serious, as though he were about to divulge his war strategy. Despite his tough exterior, Negash's inner vulnerability was akin to that of a spoiled child, easily upset when things didn't go his way. And in this matter with Fanaye, he was determined to have his way. This was the last chance he would give her. He knew she was stubborn but was her pride really so strong that she'd jeopardize both her own safety and that of her children? If she didn't cooperate with him, her only alternative was to find some other place to live. He wasn't here to dish out charity. He'd made his intentions clear from the first day he arrived, and he was determined that Fanaye should yield to his demands.

Secretly, Negash couldn't help but compare himself to Kebada. His imagined rivalry with Kebada existed, even if his opponent no longer did. Fanaye's open defiance exasperated him because he sensed it was partially rooted in her devotion to Kebada. Clearly, she was still mourning the man's death, which just added to Negash's anger. From now on, he would act forcefully and leave her no choice. I will no longer appease her, he thought. I'm going to get what I came for. When she realizes that I'm going to take the house away, then we'll see a different reaction. Let's see how long she can refuse me now.

Negash's brutal new resolve also meant he would stop acting as a loving, benevolent uncle to the children. No more pampering, no more presents. Now he saw the children as part of the problem. When they came running to the door to greet him with their childish cries of "Agota Negash, Agota Negash," he simply ignored them.

After watching Negash pace back and forth across the room, Sosina tugged on Fanaye's sleeve. "Why is he walking funny?" she whispered. "He's not listening to us. Did he become deaf?" Luckily, Nagash did not seem to hear this.

Fanaye would have laughed, but she was so nervous that all she could do was pray that Negash hadn't heard Sosina. To satisfy Sosina's curiosity, Fanaye whispered back in her ear, "Once a person is deaf, they also act strangely, so try not to look at or say anything to him, okay?"

Sosina looked over at Negash, who was still pacing in anticipation of the confrontation with Fanaye. "I wish Agota Negash didn't have to become deaf," she whispered. "Emaye, do you think he would get better if we prayed for him?"

Touched by her daughter's innocence, Fanaye took her hand. "Yes, I do. Now you two go to the back of the house and stay there until I tell you to come back. I have an important matter to take care of with Uncle Negash."

Negash was still pacing in the living room, waiting impatiently to gain Fanaye's attention. When she finally approached, his eyes were on her, staring ravenously as a hungry dog. "I hope you told the children not to come back in," he said.

It took tremendous patience for Fanaye to refrain from simply shoving him out of the house. Instead, she said, "May I serve you a cup of coffee?"

"No, you know what I want," he said haughtily and moved uncomfortably close to her. When Fanaye backed away, he grabbed her arm and began to pull her toward the bedroom. Fanaye was ready to fight him when, miraculously, the children rushed back inside. Sosina was crying loudly with a bloody mouth. Fanaye yanked her arm away from Negash and hurried over to take care of Sosina. Negash didn't bother to find out what had happened to the child. Instead, he stomped out of the house, fuming and banging the door behind him while shouting, "This can't go on. You'll see."

Chapter 19: Buzunash's Journey

Buzunash was overwhelmed by fear, wondering who would take care of her son if something happened to her. The thought of Daniel being raised by her mother-in-law so terrified her that blood rushed to her head, and she grew dizzy. No! I won't allow my son to be raised by a wicked woman and a drunken old man, she thought. There has to be a better solution.

She wondered what other widows did to survive, especially in times of war, since there were now so many women in similar circumstances to hers. One of these women was Fanaye, whom she'd met once at the christening. She clearly remembered Fanaye's striking and commanding face, which had caused her to stand out among the other women. When they'd met and chatted briefly, Fanaye had seemed confident and friendly.

Buzunash had overheard a woman at the christening gossiping to her friend about Fanaye. "Who does she think she is?" the woman was saying. "She has no shame. She acts as if she were someone important."

"Well, she's nothing but a kept woman," the friend had answered. Some people in Addis Ababa knew about Kebada's wife, Negat, who lived in Gonder with their children.

Buzunash had thought the women were cruel and hypocritical, especially since they were engaging in petty gossip while at a religious ceremony. She suspected that Fanaye had heard them too, and she admired the way she had held her head high and ignored the remarks.

Was Fanaye struggling too, now that Kebada was deceased? Fanaye came from a distant village and had no family here. Just like me, Buzunash thought. If we become friends, that would be good.

Live together, perhaps. The idea was thrilling in its simplicity. Buzunash realized that she didn't have close friends or relatives with whom she felt comfortable enough to ask for help. Maybe she'd spent too much time sweeping her floors instead of joining her neighbors' coffee gatherings. She especially regretted not attending the weekly ceremonies. Each week, about ten women would take turns going to each other's houses. For hours they would eat and chat, laugh and cry, express their joy, but mostly air their complaints about their husbands, children, in-laws, illnesses, and anything else that caused them grief. These groups were as close as families, sometimes even closer. At the end of each meeting, money was collected and given to the lady of the house. And the ritual would go on.

One night, after cleaning the house and washing her in-laws' clothes, Buzunash lay down on a flimsy, uncomfortable cot too small for her to sleep on. She longed for her bedroom. The large bed of firm wood with a cotton mattress—the bed that once belonged to her and her husband, Amara, but was now occupied by her in-laws, Weizero Turunash and Ato Melaku, who arrived at Buzunash's place nine months ago to help bury their son, who had died on the battlefield. Buzunash offered them her bedroom, out of respect, never imagining they would stay for long. But after a seemingly endless month, she waited to hear the magic words, "Sorry, but we must now return to our village." Those words never came.

Buzunash slept little during that night, her mind swirling as she plotted ways to confront her in-laws and reclaim her life. By the morning, these thoughts had consumed her. She knew it would take drastic action to regain her position as the matriarch of her own home, but with her husband dead and the war going strong in Addis Ababa, she had no idea how to escape her mother-in-law's iron-fisted rule of the house.

Meanwhile, Turunash spent the morning languishing on Buzunash's comfortable bed, her fingers twirling her prayer beads, her lips moving silently. Buzunash wondered if her mother-in-law was praying or making a confession. Often Ato Melaku was at the local bar, a habit he'd adopted since they'd moved to the city. "A man cannot spend his days in the house, like a woman!" he was fond of saying.

After finishing her prayers, Turanash expected to be served. That morning, when Buzunash heard Turunash clearing her throat, she dashed off to add water to the kettle for coffee and returned with Kita and some berbere sauce. After a few bites, Turunash called out to Buzunash, "Is the coffee ready? I have a headache. Would you be so kind as to hurry up?"

"I'm sorry," Buzunash said. "Let me put more wood on the fire. It should be ready in a minute."

Turanash sighed. "As I told you before, adding more wood doesn't speed it up," she said in her usual caustic tone. "It's just a waste of wood. You need to judge the amount of water correctly and not fill up the pot as though you were brewing for the masses."

Buzunash's lips quivered, but she didn't say anything aloud. Under her breath, she muttered, "Why don't you make it yourself, you distrustful old witch? I hope you burn your evil tongue!" Turunash had created so much misery for her that Buzunash had begun to think she might be better off dead were it not for her son. She hated her mother-in-law almost as much as she hated her country's invaders. Soon she'd summon her courage and tell Turunash how selfish she was for torturing her and ordering her around while acting totally oblivious to the suffering of her countrymen who

185

were starving and dying like flies. Turunash had never shown Buzunash any sympathy for the recent loss of her husband, and she'd certainly never shown her any respect. Instead, she acted as if she alone had suffered loss from her son's death, and Buzunash should be made to pay for that pain.

When Buzunash brought her coffee, her mother-in-law was out of bed, searching for the source of a slight draft. She traced it to a tiny hole in the wall and placed her arthritic shoulder against the hole to be sure. She turned to Buzunash in an authoritative manner. "Go to Bar Addis immediately and fetch my husband," she ordered. "I need to speak to him about this hole."

"But I don't go to such places," Buzunash answered.

Turunash dismissed her daughter-in-law with a wave of her hand. "I believe my good son has spoiled you," she said. "Now stop acting shy and do what I say. Tell Ato Melaku he must come home immediately."

Buzunash nodded obediently and set off for Bar Addis. She entered through an unlocked gate and was appalled at the condition of the yard, overgrown with wild grass. The neglected garden was a perfect place for poisonous snakes to hide and await their victims. The building had chipped walls and peeling paint, with a sagging, rusted roof. The windows were covered with brown cardboard. Possibly, Buzunash thought, the enemy had come through and killed all the residents. She couldn't imagine that anyone would actually live here under such deplorable conditions. Turunash didn't know that the owner of Bar Addis had moved. Disappointed, Buzunash turned to leave when she heard voices from inside. She looked back at Bar Addis just as a tall young man stepped out of the doorway and asked, "Miss, may I help you?"

"I'm sorry. I've made a mistake. I was looking for Bar Addis."

"You're in luck; this is the place. Are you looking for someone?"

"Ato Melaku. Do you know him?"

The young man laughed. "Of course, I know Ato Melaku, the gabra," he said. "We all know him around here. Such a brave little man."

The man led Buzunash inside. She saw her father-in-law sitting at a table, telling one of his stories that Buzunash had already heard dozens of times. Normally, Ato Melaku was a man of few words, but under the influence of a few glasses of tej, he turned as loquacious as a parrot. Buzunash was uncomfortable since it was the first time she'd ever set foot in a bar, but she waited patiently on the sidelines so she wouldn't interrupt his speech. She looked around at the shabby bar. The owner seemed very old, and she wondered how he managed the place by himself.

An old man, who must have noticed Buzunash standing in the shadows, handed her a glass of water. "It's hot out there, young lady," he said, his eyes soft and kind.

She took the water from him, met his eyes, and bowed. "Egzer yst'lee." She sipped the water and moved closer to her father-in-law, hoping he would notice her, but Ato Melaku was too absorbed in his litany.

"Do you want to know more?" he asked the men in the bar. "Until recently, I was not one to be hanging around idly like this. I used to be a respectable farmer in Gojam until Mussolini's army came. It turned my peaceful life into a nightmare. My farm now belongs to the Italians. They said through a translator that if I stayed and continued farming, my wife and I would be 'compensated.'"

The story never failed to agitate Ato Melaku. He hit the table with his fist, making the glasses rattle. Newcomers to the bar turned their heads in curiosity, but the regular customers didn't blink an eye—they'd heard it all. Melaku described how livid he'd become when the translator treated him like a child. One of the fascists standing beside the translator was so arrogant and sinister that Melaku clearly could tell the man's intentions were evil. The man threatened that if Ato Melaku disrespected the Italian Empire, he would be killed in a way that taught others a lesson. Again, Melaku

188

banged the table and jumped up from his seat, gesturing like a wild man. "I forgot myself and grabbed a wooden mallet," he said. "I swung it with all the force I had at the well-fed white devil who threatened me. I hit him too, hard enough to dislocate his gun arm." He laughed at the memory. "Seeing the devil crawl on the floor and scream with pain would have been worth dying for," he concluded.

He stopped abruptly, noticing his daughter-in-law standing before him. "What happened now?" he asked nervously.

Buzunash understood what happened to Ato Melaku. The Italians destroyed many people in their house-to-house searches looking for stolen guns. Often young Ethiopian men were captured and forced to join the military against their will. Anyone who resisted was killed or jailed. "Nothing happened," Buzunash said. "Mother wants you to repair a damaged wall."

Ato Melaku exhaled. "And that's it?" he asked. "Nothing else happened?"

Buzunash smiled. "I'm sorry if I made you worry."

He shook his head. "I'm angry, but not at you," he said. "I should have killed at least one of those monsters when I had my chance instead of running away. They took my son, my farm, and my dignity. What's left? Just numb my brain with liquor or kill myself in a fit of rage?"

Buzunash took pity on Ato Melaku. He looked so small and wasted. Now she understood a little better why they remained in her home. Unfortunately, she also knew that they'd stay permanently, or at least until the war ended. She couldn't endure the overbearing rule of her bullish mother-in-law and not being the head of her own home much longer. Buzunash longed for the freedom she'd once enjoyed. Since the age of fifteen, she'd been married and managed all the finances and budgets for the family. She'd cooked and cleaned as best she knew how, at least until Amara had gotten a raise and she hired a helper.

As she and her father-in-law finally made their way back home, Buzunash wondered where else she could live. There's got to be a better way than this, she thought.

She still missed her husband very much. He'd always been fair. He'd never raised his hand to her nor taken marital advice from his parents. He'd listened respectfully to his mother but rarely acted on anything she told him. Like his father, Amara had been a quiet man who spoke only when necessary. Buzunash, too, wasn't much of a talker herself, rarely engaging in idle chit-chat. Even when in the company of women, they'd do most of the talking while she did most of the listening.

Her parents had died when they were in their mid-twenties, leaving Buzunash an orphan at the age of twelve.

Rumor had it that someone had poisoned her parents out of jealousy, but Buzunash had always questioned this story. Her aunt Sinquenish had raised her, mostly out of a feeling of obligation. To her, Buzunash had just been one more mouth to feed in a family that hardly had enough, to begin with. Buzunash had been slim and lanky back then, and her eyes shiny and jet-black. She possessed beautiful white teeth that made for a lovely smile. As she developed into womanhood, she grew much taller and seemed uncomfortable in her own body, which threatened to keep growing. To disguise her discomfort with her height, she often slouched.

When the first marriage proposal came, without hesitation, her aunt agreed to give Buzunash away. Luck had been on Buzunash's side because the groom's family did not seem to mind that she was not from their tribe. Her aunt was greatly relieved when Amara's parents accepted a smaller dowry than was customary. One look at Buzunash and the future mother-in-law was satisfied that Buzunash's docile nature would make a good match for her son. Sinquenish and her family were satisfied as well, believing that God was looking after the poor orphaned girl, and until the loss of Amara, Buzunash might have agreed with them.

The next morning, after Buzunash had served her mother-in-law breakfast, Turunash retired again to the bedroom, complaining about her arthritis. "I told you to bring me boiled eucalyptus leaves, and you only bring me hot water!" she yelled at Buzunash. "Are you deaf or just stupid? What's wrong with you? You can't even follow simple instructions!"

Buzunash found her son Daniel and sat down next to him, his tiny arms wrapping around her. After a moment, she pulled him into her lap and, gently rubbing his shaved head, whispered, "I love you the most."

Daniel pushed his mother's hand away. "Why did God take Ababa away? I want to be with him."

Buzunash was startled by this unexpected question. "Not yet, it's not your time," she said. "Only God decides who dies and who lives."

The truth was, she wasn't feeling up to a philosophical discussion with her son. She was focused on how she could leave to visit Fanaye before her mother-in-law came up with reasons to deter her. Daniel's question had so disturbed Buzunash that for once, she was glad to be interrupted by her mother-in-law.

"Buzunash, Buzunash!" Turunash yelled.

Buzunash jumped up and guided Daniel to the front door. "Your coffee is on the table," she shouted back at Turunash.

They stepped outside and started walking. "Where are we going?" Daniel asked.

"To visit a lady and her children."

"Are they boys?"

Buzunash took his hand and struggled for the right response, knowing that if she said they were girls, he'd be disappointed and wouldn't want to go.

"What do you think?" she asked, just to gain enough time to get further away from their home. He shook her arm, asking again if they were boys until Buzunash lost her patience and said, "So, what if they are girls?"

Daniel stomped his feet. "Girls are crybabies," he said. "They don't even know how to play. I hate them."

"That's enough! You don't even know them. I swear, if you act rudely there, I'll whack you with a stick when we get back home. Is that clear?"

The boy remained silent as they walked. When they reached Fanaye's fenced house, Buzunash began to lose her nerve. She heard the sounds of children playing. As soon as she knocked on the door, the chatter and noise ceased. "Who's there?" a woman's voice asked.

Buzunash introduced herself through the closed door. Fanaye opened it and, seeing Daniel, she quickly ushered them inside. "You shouldn't expose your son to such danger," she said as she closed the door. "What if those ruthless Italians saw him?"

"I didn't think of that," Buzunash admitted. Maybe her mother-in-law was right to think of her as a brainless

193

chicken, unable to fetch grain from right under its feet.

"These days, we have to be very careful," Fanaye added matter-of-factly. "But sometimes it's hard to think clearly when we're under such pressure. I hope I didn't offend you." She turned to Daniel. "Why don't you go find something to play with," she said.

Once Daniel unwillingly left the room, Fanaye gestured to a chair for Buzunash to sit. "How long would people be afraid of letting their children play in their own yard? The truth is, no matter how careful we are, we can't protect them from the enemy all the time," Fanaye said. But she swore that Ethiopia would defeat the enemy one day. She also believed that all Ethiopians, including women, should get military training for their own good. "We can't depend on our young men to do all the fighting," she continued. "This is our country, and we all must serve! I'm not saying every woman should get a weapon and fight, but women's duties shouldn't be limited to carrying meals to the soldiers. I swear by the name of Saint Gabriel, if we women fought as well, we would defeat this enemy in no time!"

When Fanaye finished, Buzunash was impressed. "You're a very brave woman!" she exclaimed. Then, following a brief silence, she got to the purpose of her visit. "I heard you're by yourself now, as I am. I don't know about you, but I'm having a terrible time without my husband."

194

Fanaye too admitted, "Things are difficult for me as well, and I hope they will change soon."

Buzunash said, "The other day, my mother-in-law sent me to Bar Addis to fetch my father-in-law. The place was a mess, and most of the customers were either very old or young or were wounded soldiers. And the owner looked very old."

Fanaye listened attentively. "It seems the old man needs help," Fanaye said thoughtfully. "I don't know about you, but something tells me this might be the answer to our problem. We help the old man and, in exchange, we have a place."

Buzunash shook her head. "Live there? I don't even know why I told you about it. So, please forget about it."

"Well, you said the customers seem harmless, and the owner needs help."

"That's not a place for us," Buzunash insisted.

"I am in a dire situation, and we need a place immediately," Fanaye said emphatically.

Buzunash didn't comprehend Fanaye's reasoning but liked her hopefulness. "Okay, I'll take you there."

Daniel walked into the room, hurried over to his mother, and rested his head against her lap. "There's nothing for me to play with," he whispered.

Fanaye looked down at him. "How old are you, young

195

man?"

"Seven," he said, his finger in his mouth.

"Why does such a big boy have his finger in his mouth?"

Embarrassed, Daniel wiped his finger on his pants.

"That's better. Soon those fingers will defend us."

"What's 'defend'?" Daniel asked his mother.

"That means to help others and to protect them," Buzunash answered.

Fanaye called for Zenite and Sosina to come and play with Daniel. Daniel stared at them impassively.

"I just finished making a baby doll!" Sosina said to Buzunash. "Do you want to see her?"

"Sure."

Sosina returned with a tiny doll made of old fabric and sticks and proudly handed it to Buzunash. "You made her all by yourself?" Buzunash asked, holding the doll gently in her palm. "She is pretty like you. Does she have a name?"

Sosina shook her head, "No."

"Take your time in finding the right name for her. You're a smart girl."

After a couple of hours, Buzunash stood up to leave, her voice mellow, "I wish I had met you sooner."

Chapter 20: Visions Of Bar Addis

Fanaye awoke thinking of Bar Addis. With Negash constantly pressuring her, Bar Addis seemed more and more like her best alternative. Almost any option was better than having to sleep with Negash.

A few days later, Buzunash returned to visit Fanaye. When she opened the door, she noticed Daniel wearing a headscarf. Fanaye was happy Buzunash took her advice. Zenite pointed at Daniel. "Look!" she said. "He's wearing a scarf, like a woman." The girls started to giggle.

"Hush!" Fanaye said. "Don't listen to them, Daniel. Do you know even kings wear headscarves?"

"Do they?"

"Hasn't your mother told you that?" She winked at Buzunash over the little boy's head and shooed the children off to play.

As the two women sat down to sip tea, Fanaye steered the conversation back to Bar Addis. "Let's go and see it today," she said, unable to contain her enthusiasm. "Of course, we can't get too excited until the owner approves."

"I warn you, though, Bar Addis is very shabby," Buzunash warned her. "And don't forget, whatever you may think of it, a bar is a bar and may not be fit for mothers with young children."

"Don't worry," Fanaye assured her.

As soon as Tsega arrived, the two women left the children and headed out to Bar Addis on a narrow dirt road. The path was lined with trees, with trunks so thick and branches so low that Fanaye and Buzunash had to forcefully push them aside to pass through. "How do people find this place with all these oak and eucalyptus branches everywhere?" Fanaye asked.

"I hope we don't get lost," Buzunash mumbled.

They saw the old bar through the trees. Bar Addis looked as Fanaye had imagined it from Buzunash's description—dilapidated and unfit for people to live in.

Buzunash whispered, "Fanaye, I'm sorry. It looks worse than I remember. Maybe this is a bad idea."

Fanaye surveyed the bar from a distance, getting a sense of its potential. "Let's go to the backyard and investigate," she said. "We're here now. We might as well check to see if the building can be salvaged."

An old man squinted at them through a shattered window as they approached the building. He stepped unsteadily outside to greet them. "May I help you?" he asked with a warm smile.

Fanaye and Buzunash bowed their heads in respect, but they were nervous. "We have something to discuss with you," Fanaye said. Now that she was in front of this man, she hesitated. He seemed glad to see them despite having just caught them snooping around his place.

He glanced up at the sky and said, "Look how beautiful! Clear blue with white cotton clouds. Ladies, this is a gift to us."

Fanaye and Buzunash were relieved to find Ato Ayle friendly. Fanaye gathered her courage and said, "Ato, our husbands died in the war not long ago. My friend and I are blessed with children. Unfortunately, we have no means to raise them, and we have no other family to turn to. We want to support our children, and we're hoping you will allow us to live here in exchange for work."

Ato Ayle agreed much more quickly than Fanaye thought he would. "Look what they have done to my place!" he said, pointing at the ravaged structure. "At times like this, we need to help each other."

Relieved, the women smiled broadly and nodded. "I can't promise you absolute safety here," he added, "but what place is safe nowadays anyway?"

Fanaye and Buzunash looked around, surveying it more carefully. There were broken windows, large holes in the walls, and a big gap in one corner of the sagging roof.

"I'll leave you ladies to discuss what you'd like to do," Ato Ayle said. "If you decide you want to see more, please come in."

As soon as the old man stepped into the bar, laughter could be heard. Buzunash whispered to Fanaye, "This place is much too dangerous to raise children in! It could collapse at any moment. I wish I'd never mentioned this crazy place to you."

I'm glad you did." Fanaye, full of hope and excitement, was surprised by her friend's lack of imagination. "Ato Ayle will let us live here," she said. "Once we fix things up, it will be much safer. Can't you see the potential in this place?"

Fanaye convinced Buzunash to go inside. The old man smiled, and his eyes creased as they entered. "So you've decided to take the grand tour?" he said jovially. He escorted the women through the house, room by ruined room.

Fanaye stopped at the doorway of one of the larger rooms. "I'd like this one if it's alright with you?" she asked, already imagining a home and how to transform it.

The old man paused for a moment. He had avoided this room until now, for it brought back sad memories and anger. Their son's death at war brought unthinkable sorrow to his wife so that she suddenly became very ill and died.

"This used to be our bedroom, but now that my wife is gone, I can't sleep here anymore."

Buzunash whispered to Fanaye, "Please, let's go before we run into any ghosts."

Fanaye noticed Ato Ayle's moist eyes and glared at

Buzunash to keep her quiet. She placed her arm around the old man's fragile body and said, "You must miss her terribly!"

Ato Ayle squeezed Fanaye's hand and said, "Yes, I'm afraid I do."

As they walked home through the monstrous branches, Buzunash repeated her doubts about moving into Bar Addis. "It needs so much intensive work," she insisted.

But Fanaye was already planning what she'd fix first. "At least we'll have a place to live," she responded. "It will work out; you'll see."

At Fanaye's house, Tsega greeted them and waited anxiously for their decision. "We're moving into Bar Addis," Fanaye said and smiled.

Tsega shook her head in disappointment. "I know you don't want to be with Ato Negash, Fanaye," she said, wringing her hands, "but, please, if not for yourself, go along with his proposal for the sake of your children. He said he wouldn't come here very often. Look at what you'll lose, a nice home and a man who could provide for you and your children and will protect you. All those men and a bar? It will ruin your good name."

"No, my mind is made up," Fanaye said. "Just the thought of being touched by that traitor repulses me."

Tsega shook her head again. "I wish I could convince

you. I never met a woman as headstrong as you." Fanaye put her arms around her to comfort her, but Tsega remained adamant. "I just don't understand. If you're willing to serve all those men at a bar, isn't it better to serve one man instead and live in a nice house?"

"I'm not serving any man! Is that what you think? I told you, Buzunash and I will work in exchange for living there."

"I'm not saying Ato Negash is the best choice, but I think it's a better choice than being a barmaid. A bar is not a place to raise a hero's children."

Fanaye laughed sarcastically. "So you think it's better to be Negash's prostitute?" she asked. "Is that it?" She grabbed Tsega by the shoulders and tried to reassure her. "If Negash ever comes here while I'm out, please tell him that I'm not for sale."

But Tsega persisted, unable to let the matter go. "Let me tell you what happened only a week ago," she began. "I didn't want to frighten you before, but you must know now."

As Fanaye listened, Tsega told the story of Tutu, a beautiful young woman who not long ago caught the eye of an Italian general. He instructed his Ethiopian maid to lure Tutu to his house. The maid lied to Tutu by inviting her over for Italian pastry. Once inside the house, the maid served her cookies and tea and discreetly walked out of the house, leaving Tutu alone. To Tutu's surprise, the Italian general appeared. The poor girl dropped the cookies as she leaped to her feet. The general smiled and offered her candy. Tutu saw the lust in his eyes and ran to the door, but the general grabbed her arm. She shouted for the absent maid as he dragged her to his bedroom, threw her onto his bed, and raped her.

"Can you imagine the anger, shame, and desire for revenge that ravaged the child's mother," Tsega said. "My point is that it's dangerous out there. A woman cannot protect herself." Tsega's eyes filled with tears as she hugged Fanaye tightly. "I'm so worried for you."

But even this dire story of betrayal didn't deter Fanaye. "Please, Tsega, don't worry," Fanaye reiterated. "That doesn't happen to everyone. Where's your faith? Don't you always say that God protects us?"

Chapter 21: Starting Over

While her mother-in-law snored in the next room, Buzunash hurriedly put aside her most valued possessions, including her embroidered cotton wedding dress, her gold cross, and some of her clothing to take to their new home. She opened a small trunk and packed Daniel's clothes and a small pouch containing his silver christening cross. She tucked them all under her mattress. In the living room, she surveyed the rest of her belongings—a painting of Jesus Christ on the cross, a big colorful mesob basket, and a variety of colorful pots. She wished she could take all of these with her.

As soon as Ato Melaku left for the day, she bent under her mattress and threw everything into a sack. She guided Daniel by the hand and, without looking back, walked out of the house toward Bar Addis. Shortly afterward, gunshots rang out in the distance, disrupting the utter stillness of the woods.

"Emaye, Emaye! Is the enemy trying to kill us?" Daniel cried out.

"No, dear. Let's walk faster."

When mother and son arrived at Bar Addis, they found Fanaye's children playing. Fanaye was already busy clearing away the debris and putting them into piles. To Buzunash's amazement, Fanaye didn't even stop to chat. She pointed at the woodpile and said, "Start by putting the rubbish on the pile over there. We'll burn it later."

Buzunash mumbled to herself as she put her belongings down and began clearing the area around the entrance to the house. She'd hoped she could rest a little first. Meanwhile, Ato Ayle sipped his tea, leaning against the door and happily watching the women as they worked.

After a few hours, the children ran up. "I'm hungry." "Me too." Fanaye stopped working, wiped her forehead, and looked at them—happy children, but way too skinny. Still, she felt certain that moving to Bar Addis was the fresh start they all needed.

Fanaye went into the kitchen and made shiro. First, she chopped onions, sautéed them with a little butter, and poured three cups of water. Then she mixed in the chickpeas and boiled the mixture for a little while, adding salt and berbere. Finally, she added the dry injera, and lunch was ready. This was Fanaye's way of cooking: quick and simple, the complete opposite of Tsega.

She fed the children first, then called Ato Ayle for lunch. Just then, she saw a woman approaching the house, carrying a little basket covered with cotton fabric.

Weizero Faniash, a woman in her early forties with piercing black hair, politely nodded to Fanaye, pointed to the covered basket, and said, "It's Ato Ayle's lunch. Are you his relative?"

"We just moved in this morning," Fanaye said, smiling.

A bit taken aback, Faniash gave Fanaye a quizzical look. "Oh, is that so? Ato Ayle didn't tell me he'd hired any helpers."

"We'll be cooking for him from now on," Fanaye said.

Weizero Faniash's smile faded, disappointed that she wouldn't be needed anymore. Then she smiled a fake grin that revealed an entire set of straight white teeth. "I thought Ato Ayle didn't want women in his bar," she said. "He told me women might cause problems."

Ato Ayle was sitting on a low stool under a flowering tree, watching the two women talk. He beckoned them over and, directing Faniash's attention to the children, "Is there a more beautiful sight than children playing?"

Weizero Faniash had ten children and never enough time to be amused by their playing. Her time was consumed by chores: washing, cooking, baking, and nursing a sick child. Her main concern was whether there was enough food to go around, but she didn't want to spoil Ato Ayle's joy, so she nodded and briefly watched the children play, which reminded her of the chores awaiting her. Then, forgetting what she had meant to ask Ato Ayle, she bowed and left.

Ato Ayle, Fanaye, and Buzunash ate their lunch together,

chatting and enjoying each other's company. During their conversation, he learned that Kebada was the father of Fanaye's children. Apparently, he'd been a great admirer of Kebada. "I'm so glad I'm able to give you shelter!" he exclaimed. "His death was a terrible loss to our country. Those brutal fascists knew what a threat he was to them."

After Fanaye and Buzunash cleaned up the lunch dishes, they joined Ato Ayle inside at the bar. A few men were involved in a spirited discussion. When the women entered, the room turned dead quiet, and the men just stared at them. Fanaye ignored the stares and walked into the next room, where Ato Ayle was preparing tej.

"Do you need any help?" she asked.

Ato Ayle looked up from what he was doing. "Have you ever seen how tej is prepared?"

Fanaye admitted that she hadn't. "Would you teach me?"

"Roll up your sleeves. You can begin now!"

Fanaye found that she enjoyed making tej. The smell of honey and a variety of sweet herbs, not to mention the tactile feeling of the mixture on her hands, delighted her. Ato Ayle turned out to be a patient teacher, and Fanaye, a quick learner. The old man had enjoyed making tej throughout his life, even though his hands had become arthritic.

Becoming skilled at making tej would be a good way to make money. The old man had told Fanaye that as long as he was able to provide tej, men would be willing to spend their meager incomes on it. For most men, drinking at the bar was not a luxury but a dire need to relieve tension. The bar had become a second home for many, particularly during this time of war.

When Fanaye thanked Ato Ayle for teaching her to make tej, he winked mischievously and said, "Oh, don't thank me, young lady. I intend to reap the benefits. You'll be the one making tej from now on."

As the weeks passed, Fanaye and Buzunash settled comfortably into life at Bar Addis. Ato Ayle was satisfied with the improvements the women had made, as well as with the presence of the children, which lit up the place. Although Buzunash was working harder than she ever had, she much preferred this life to slave for her mother-in-law. At least Ato Ayle appreciated her hard work. As for Fanaye, she seemed to be in her element at Bar Addis and was particularly happy that she'd learned to make tej.

Finally, the day came for Fanaye to serve drinks to the customers for the first time. She mustered her courage and approached several men sitting at the tables. "Good afternoon, gentlemen," she said in a businesslike manner. "What can I serve you?"

Although there were whispers and covert glances among the men, they remained respectful. Most of the Bar Addis customers were regulars who knew each other fairly well, adding to the sense of community. The men knew not to mistreat the two women. Ato Ayle had forewarned them that Fanaye and Buzunash were widows and not here for the company of men. Any man who could not treat the women with respect, Ato Ayle said, would no longer be welcome at Bar Addis.

But one day, a tough-looking young stranger, seemingly in his twenties, entered the bar and surveyed the room with cold, unblinking eyes. Then he swaggered over to an empty table and sat down without exchanging any greetings first. He loudly shouted his drink order in the direction of the bar. His speech was so slurred that it was clear he was already drunk. Fanaye approached his table, bringing with her a glass of tej, and with a firm voice said, "Here you go."

The man shook his head and looked up. A leering grin appeared on his face. "My, my, who do we have here? Are you sure tej is the only thing you serve?"

Fanaye frowned. "Just drink up your tej, then you can go."

"No, I won't be leaving just yet," the man said, still grinning broadly. "I asked you if you serve yourself with the drinks."

Fanaye picked up his mug and threw the tej in his face. Stunned, the man stared back at Fanaye with a blank expression. "Damn it, woman!" he howled, narrowing his eyes. "You're a clumsy one, aren't you? You need a good spanking to show you how to treat customers!"

Then he rose out of his chair and raised his right hand as if to strike her but stopped when he saw several mean-looking customers staring fiercely at him. One false move, the man realized, and all the bar patrons would pounce on him and give him the beating of his life. Fanaye, too, pointed to the door, ordering, "Get out. Now. And don't ever come back!"

The man had no choice but to leave. Once he was gone, the bar erupted with applause and cheers. That man never came back, which only increased everyone's respect and admiration for Fanaye.

On another occasion, a small elderly gentleman entered the bar one late afternoon with his head down and a forlorn expression on his face. Fanaye wondered if he'd possibly lost a son or a loved one in the war. "Sir, can I bring you a small or large tej?" she asked.

The man only stared up at her vacantly. She repeated her question a little louder. Just then, another man in the bar asked, "Ato Melaku, what's wrong? You don't look so good."

When Fanaye heard his name, she realized this was Buzunash's father-in-law. She served him as quickly as possible and hurried out of the room to find Buzunash, singing outside to the children while preparing lunch. "He's here!" Fanaye said.

"Who's here?

"Your father-in-law."

"Oh no, I was afraid of that." Buzunash's eyes darted toward the bar. Frantic, with shaky hands, she began to pray in desperation. "Please, Virgin Mary, don't let him be a problem. I think I'd better hide," she said. "Please go get Daniel; I'll hide him too."

"You left him your home. What else does he want from you?" Fanaye said. "You'll have to face him eventually. Tell him what's going on. He may not like what he hears, but at least he'll know that you and Daniel are alive."

Buzunash looked unsure. "Maybe after his drink, he'll be easier to approach," she said.

"No sense in talking to him when he's drunk. Take care of it now."

Finally, Buzunash agreed to face him. She slowly walked into the bar, right up to where Ato Melaku was sitting. He looked up at her, startled. "Is that you, Buzunash?" he asked, blinking his eyes furiously.

"How are you, Ato Melaku?"

"Thank God, you're alive! Where have you been? We've been so worried about you and Daniel. We had no idea where

211

to look. We began to think the worst."

Buzunash, though quite nervous, somehow managed to sound calm. She asked to speak to him outside. Once out in the fresh air, Ato Melaku said, "I'm glad you knew where to find me. So where's Daniel?"

"He's playing with friends,"

"Friends!" Her father-in-law seemed surprised. "What, friends? You have no idea how worried we've been and how much we've searched for you. Let's go get Daniel and head home."

"I'll bring him out for you to see, but we won't go back with you," Buzunash said firmly. "Now we live here. Please understand."

"What do you mean by 'here'?"

"I mean here, at Bar Addis."

Ato Melaku looked shocked. "You can't be serious!" he shouted. "This is no place to raise a child! Think of your son. If you can't think of him, then I'm taking him with me."

He turned towards the sound of children's voices. Buzunash darted ahead of him and called for Daniel to come. When Daniel saw his grandfather, he broke away from Sosina and Zenite and ran toward him. Smiling widely, Ato Melaku held out his arms and exclaimed, "Look how big you are, and so strong." He hugged Daniel in a tight embrace.

"Teluko Ababa, look. I made a bow and arrow!" Daniel

held it up for the old man to see. Ato Melaku was the one who had taught Daniel to shoot with a bow and arrow, and for that, Buzunash was grateful.

"Wonderful. What a good job you've done," said Ato Melaku. "Once we get home, I'll teach you how to make a slingshot."

Deeply disturbed by where the conversation was going, Buzunash intervened, "Daniel! Go back to play now!" she commanded.

Daniel hesitated a moment and then reluctantly did as he was told. "Don't go yet!" Ato Melaku called out to the boy. "I miss you." He then turned to Buzunash with a fierce look on his face. "I've lost my son, but I'm not going to lose my grandson," he exclaimed. "So don't try to stop me."

Ato Melaku's face turned a motley red color. "This is not where my grandson should live!" he yelled.

Fanaye saw how shook up Buzunash was. Fanaye's temper flared. She hastened to where Ato Melaku was and stood in front of him, legs slightly apart and her hands on her hips.

"Ato, now you listen to me! Do you think Buzunash wanted to live here? Weren't you aware of how badly your wife treated her? So, you two have not only succeeded in driving her out of her own home, but now you have the audacity to come here to take her son away from the poor

213

woman. Well, I won't stand for it! So, put this in your head and tell your wife also. As long as I'm alive, I'll never let you take Daniel away." With that, Fanaye turned and walked away. After taking a few steps, she turned back to Ato Melaku and said, "But you can come here and visit Daniel."

Chapter 22: Bar Addis

A soldier named Wenda had been coming to Bar Addis regularly. Recently he'd been wounded, and now he walked on crutches. He'd listen to the radio before coming to the bar and pass the news to the other men. One day, he told everyone at Bar Addis that the Italians had sunk their roots deeper into the city of Asmara in Eritrea. They'd destroyed towns and then rebuilt them to resemble towns in their own country. As a result, the Italian population was growing rapidly. "Their fascist government keeps sending more and more unskilled and unemployed Italians to live there," he told the men in the room.

Fanaye raged inwardly upon hearing Wenda's report. But Ato Ayle, who sat nearby, had learned to control his anger because of his weak heart and remained tranquil. Otherwise, he would have gotten furious, like when he'd remember his son's death on the battlefield, followed by his wife's death shortly afterward; he was convinced that his wife had died of a broken heart. Having lost yet another loved one, Ato Ayle had become violently ill, collapsed to the floor, and suffered a heart attack. Everyone said it was a miracle he'd survived.

"Kebada used to tell me about the cruelty of the fascists," Fanaye said when Wenda was finished. "They are lawless, Godless, and brutal." Her voice was strong with patriotic fervor. "Basha Kebada laughed when he found out that the Italians had signed a 'Treaty of Friendship' with our country," she continued. "He knew their tricks. He had a strong belief that the fascist leaders would be incapable of complying with such a benevolent agreement."

When the men asked her to tell them more about what Ato Kebada had told her, she was more than happy to comply. She told them Kebada said that when the enemy pretended to give their support to Ethiopia's governors—the Rases—they had one goal in mind: to divide the people and conquer the country. Some elite Ethiopians fell for it, believing they had become friends with the Italians.

Fanaye paused for a moment, struggling to contain her emotions. "Nothing disturbed Basha Kebada more than knowing how some Ethiopians could be so ignorant and naïve as to believe that the enemy wanted to help them," she continued. Since so many Ethiopians were killed when they refused to cooperate with the fascists, Kebada never trusted the Italians' goodwill, even when Emperor Haile Selassie considered signing an agreement with them.

"Some of Kebada's closest friends grew weary of the fighting and couldn't bear such hardship," she said, "so they sacrificed their pride and honor and are now receiving salaries from the enemy."

"Shameful!" someone shouted, followed by similar

outbursts from others.

"Let the young lady continue," Ato Ayle said. "She's lived with one of the bravest warriors in our country. Listen with your ears, with your heart, and then pass on the words to your friends, wives, and children."

The room went quiet again as Fanaye described how the fascists asked Basha Kebada to work for them in exchange for privileges! He was disgusted by their outrageous requests; he'd rather have died than accept compensation from the enemy. Basha Kebada warned the Ethiopian traitors that by aiding the fascists, they were only perpetuating their own colonization. He was glad that most of the rases and the landlords refused to give up their land, even if that meant losing their lives.

"I pray to God to protect us from these foreign devils," Ato Ayle sighed.

"We can't leave our problems to God while the fascists keep destroying us," Fanaye said and shook a fist in the air. "We must take every opportunity to destroy the enemy!"

Fanaye's patriotism fired up everyone but Buzunash, who wished Fanaye would keep her war stories to herself. All the war talk made her uneasy. She wished people would talk less and pray more. Only prayer could ward off the dangers of war and keep battles far away.

Fanaye went on to explain. "Basha Kebada said the poor

Eritreans were being used as human shields. The fascists trained them and then sent them to the front lines to fight against their own people. They were the first to die, without a clue that they'd been used by the enemy. The fascists go after the poor and the young, giving them food and clothing, and then training them to use their weapons against us," Fanaye said.

"Devious!" someone shouted. "But what kind of people would trust these fascists anyway?"

Fanaye had built slots in the wood of the table and installed trays to carry dirty or clean glasses to the kitchen.

As the conversation continued, Ato Ayle felt a sharp pain in his chest. Slowly, he stood up and signaled the customers to stop talking. "We need to stop upsetting ourselves," he said. "Please, my friends, go home now. Be with your families."

After a brief silence and some lingering and muted conversation, the customers stood up, said their goodbyes, and walked out. Fanaye hurried over to Ato Ayle, slumped over in his chair. She touched his forehead, which was drenched with beads of sweat. "Ato Ayle," she said, "I'm so sorry if I caused you to get sick. Let me get you something. Some coffee, perhaps?"

"I've been ill for some time," he said. "Don't blame yourself."

She worried about Ato Ayle and the war.

"He isn't up yet. He's normally up by now," Fanaye said to Buzunash in the morning as she lined up the coins and bills on the bar counter.

Buzunash agreed. "You're right." She then said, "Fanaye, you spoke so passionately last night. You had everyone spellbound but... did you know what you were saying?"

"I don't know what you're talking about."

"You're very smart and brave, but I don't like the way you spoke about God. It's disrespectful. More than that, it's sinful!"

Fanaye listened quietly to Buzunash's complaints, but they didn't deter her. "These are my opinions, and I'll stick by them," she replied.

Buzunash knew she'd never convince Fanaye to change her mind, so she dropped the subject.

With the onset of the rainy season, Ato Ayle's condition worsened. He still made tej with Fanaye's help and puttered around the house, but he slowed greatly. For a good six months, he kept up this routine, but with each passing day, he did less and less. The love and support of his new family appeared to be his only joy and motivation.

After a while, he seldom left his room. At night, Buzunash, Fanaye, and the children would gather in his bedroom to eat dinner together and take turns feeding him any morsels he could eat. After the meal, one of the women would stay to massage his feet and help in whatever way she could. Although Ato Ayle was weak, he always expressed his gratitude to them.

One dreary morning, Fanaye and Buzunash came into Ato Ayle's bedroom to find him immobile and cold in his bed, a faint trace of a smile lingering on his face. "Finally, he's gone to join his beloved wife and son," Buzunash said tearfully as she crossed herself.

The loss of Ato Ayle caused tremendous sorrow and confusion for Fanaye and Buzunash and the children who— all under the age of ten—had already experienced death several times.

One morning, shortly after Ato Ayle's passing, a young boy showed up at Bar Addis to inform Fanaye that the local priest needed to talk to her, that she ought to go to the church to see him. Puzzled, Fanaye asked the boy, "What for?" The boy shrugged and said, "I don't know. He just told me to inform you."

After she finished her chores, Fanaye headed to the church to learn what the priest had in mind. When she arrived, the priest greeted her and led her into a small room. Seated around a table, the priest smiled at Fanaye and said, "You are a good woman, and God is rewarding you for it."

Fanaye replied, "Thank you. I know that God has rewarded me with two healthy children."

"Well, I'm here to tell you that God has rewarded you in more ways than that. Let me get straight to the point. Before his passing, Ato Ayle had willed to give you all of his worldly possessions. That means you now own everything he left behind." After a pause, he added, "That includes Bar Addis."

Fanaye was speechless for a while. At first, she couldn't fully comprehend what that signified. But, as the import of what she had heard fully sank in, she responded, "You mean he left everything to us?"

The priest added quickly, "No. Just to you!"

"But isn't Buzunash also included?"

The priest shook his head. "No, only your name is mentioned."

"Ato Ayle was very ill," Fanaye explained. "Perhaps he forgot to mention Buzunash."

"Ato Ayle indicated his last wish quite a while ago, and I've no doubt that his mind was lucid then," the priest said. "He was very clear about who should inherit his property. He may have relatives, but he chose you."

"That was very generous of him, but I want Buzunash included as well."

Somewhat impatiently, the priest said it wasn't up to him or anyone else, nor could he alter a deceased person's last

221

wish. "Whether you want it or not, the property is now yours," he said. "As the new owner, you can do anything you want with it. If you want your friend named a co-owner, you can do so. But if I were you, I'd go home and think about it before making any drastic decisions."

"Father, my mind is already made up," Fanaye said.

The priest looked impressed. "You must value your friend a great deal."

In response, Fanaye only nodded in assent. She then rose from her seat and bowed to the priest, who in turn blessed her by doing the sign of the cross by her face with a small cross he produced. Fanaye started home in the wrong direction, shocked by the news.

Back at Bar Addis, Fanaye told Buzunash that Ato Ayle had left Bar Addis and the rest of his property to them. "To you, me, and the children," she lied. "Can you imagine? We're now the owners of Bar Addis."

"Oh my God!" Buzunash cried, stunned. "I can't believe it." Then she looked worried. "What if his relatives come along and tell us to leave?"

"Buzunash, Buzunash, you worry too much. We're the official inheritors, and the will protects us."

As owners of Bar Addis, the two women learned to keep their distance from the customers. When a patron asked for a drink with a promise to pay later, Fanaye offered him work instead. In one year, Fanaye and Buzunash, with help from their customers, managed to fix up the bar and the living quarters. The two women did their best to run the establishment without Ato Ayle. Fanaye emphasized they had to be tough and exert their authority when necessary. Once, when a couple of men who had too much to drink became too forward, putting their arms around the women, Fanaye ordered the men out. When they ignored her, she shoved them out the door. One of the customers, a little tipsy himself, had stood up and said, "Lady, you didn't need to do that. I would've taken care of him for you." Fanaye looked at him doubtfully but thanked him nevertheless.

"I sure feel safe in her presence," another customer whispered to the man next to him, who shook his head and said, "I'm glad I'm not married to her."

After the big scene, Fanaye reminded the others, "Buzunash and I are trying to make a living and raise our children," she said. "We're not women of leisure. We can't and won't tolerate unruly drunks."

The men had listened sheepishly. An older man added, "Ladies, don't worry. We'll try to watch out for the bad ones."

From that day on, the place ran fairly smoothly. But Bar Addis was still in need of a lot of work. Fortunately, some customers pitched in to make the repairs and clear the

223

grounds. They brought cement to patch the holes, and carpenters built new shelves. Tsega, too, participated in gardening: tomatoes, cabbages, pumpkins. Whenever Tsega came to visit, the children would scream, "Ayata Tsega, Ayata Tsega!" She would stretch her arms and embrace them, kissing their cheeks right and left until they were squared away. As poor as she was, she always baked dabo to take with her, which they loved. After chatting with Fanaye and Buzunash over coffee, she would look for the children. She would always tell them Tarik and Mesalee folk tales.

The girls would sit on her lap and Daniel at her feet. So, she would begin, "Once there was a town fool, who carried his donkey on his back, sweat dripping from his forehead..." The children would laugh and watch every expression on Tsega's face.

When Fanaye visited Tsega, she noticed rain dripping into the hut. "How long has it been?" she asked.

Tsega responded, "Well, it has been a couple of months or so, but I kept an empty tela jar under it." Tsega seemed to have surrendered to it, but not Fanaye, who sent a carpenter to replace the whole roof. Within one month, there was a new tin roof. And when the man told Fanaye about the poor condition of the siding that, too, was taken care of. By the time Fanaye was done, the whole place seemed like new. Fanaye enjoyed anything that had to do with renovations and

224

began to save her money to buy a place that she could fix up and rent.

Chapter 23: Sosina

The Mussolini regime used clever tactics and propaganda to gain the cooperation of the Eritreans. They recruited many young, healthy shepherds and farmers and trained them to fight the Ethiopians. After their training, they were given uniforms and generous salaries. Many young Eritreans seized this opportunity to better their lives. They wore shiny medals and appreciated the Italians. So, men eagerly came to the cities to escape the hardship of rural life and farm work. The Italians recruited these young laborers to build new roads, railways, and bridges. By day, these men would learn to shoot, and by night, they would gather in large military compounds to drink wine and toast their good luck.

But other Eritreans steadfastly refused to cooperate with the Italians, though they lived in great poverty, and the farms began to suffer. Underground movements sprang up throughout the country to fight against the Italian invasion.

Early one morning, two Italians and one Eritrean soldier were drawn to Bar Addis when they heard familiar noises from home. Daniel and Zenite were playing outside in full view. Sosina had gone inside to fetch a doll from her bedroom. The men stopped for a moment, taking in the scene and looking at the children. One of the soldiers, a lieutenant, frowned and adjusted his weapon, while the other, named Luca, took something from his pocket and waved it at the children. In his mid-twenties, Luca was not only good-natured for an Italian soldier and quite handsome, with jet black hair and alluring green eyes.

"Have you ever eaten candy?" the Eritrean soldier translated.

Surprised, the children stopped playing and looked at the soldiers. Luca stepped a little closer. "What is that?" Daniel asked.

The Eritrean soldier laughed and translated this to Luca. "Tell them that candy is something sweet," Luca said. "It is delicious! All children love it."

Zenite looked at Daniel as if to say, "Take it! Take it from his hand!"

Luca reached into his pocket again, took out another piece of candy, and handed a piece to each child. "Aren't there any men here?" the lieutenant wanted to know.

Daniel's reply was, "No."

Meanwhile, Fanaye and Buzunash were working side by side in the garden; their sleeves rolled up above their elbows. They were laughing and chatting, unaware that soldiers were approaching, ready to ogle them.

"Where are your husbands?" the translator called out in Amharic.

The women were startled by their sudden presence. Instinctively, Fanaye knew she could show no weakness.

227

"Thanks to Mussolini, we have no husbands; you have killed them all," she called back defiantly. "Go away and leave us in peace!" Then they returned to their gardening.

"How dare you speak of great Mussolini's soldiers in such a rude manner?" said the Eritrean, stepping forward.

"I know only one great man: Haile Selassie, our king," Fanaye shouted, forgetting the danger she was in. "You treacherous cretin! Get out of our place, and take these evil men with you!"

"What's that woman raving about?" the lieutenant asked the translator, adjusting his gun in a way that made Luca nervous.

"She's crazy," the translator said. He looked at Fanaye. "Do you want to get killed?"

"Forget her," Luca said to the lieutenant. "Let's do what we came here to do."

The lieutenant eyed the women and, for a tense moment, Luca feared he would push the matter further. But to Luca's relief, the lieutenant turned away, and they headed for the house to search for men and weapons.

Sosina had just retrieved her doll and was about to come back outside when she heard a strange sound. Peeking from her room, she saw two men with guns coming inside. Terrified, she crawled under the bed and began to whimper in fear.

Once inside, the soldiers heard a sound coming from under the bed. They stopped and gripped their weapons. Luca knew the lieutenant showed no mercy.

"Come out before we kill you!" the lieutenant hollered in Italian.

The noise sounded like a child whimpering quietly. Luca, cautiously approaching the bed, made a motion to hold the lieutenant off. He lifted the edge of the blanket with the tip of his gun. "For God's sake, it's a little girl!" he shouted. "Forget it, we're wasting our time."

In an instant, Fanaye appeared in the doorway with her famous big stick in her hand. "Get out now, or I'll beat you to a pulp!" she shouted.

"Drop that stick, you fool!" the translator shouted back.

"Teach this woman a lesson!" the lieutenant shouted.

"I say we get out of here," Luca said with a persuasive voice. "Look, she's crazy. Let's not waste any more time here."

The lieutenant considered for a moment, then gestured with a broad sweep of his arm for everyone to get out.

Meanwhile, Luca was impressed by Fanaye's courage in protecting her child. She reminded him of his own mother, who had been a widow for many years and had struggled to survive in a man's world. Suddenly, he wished he were in a position to comfort Fanaye. From the moment he'd laid eyes

229

on her, he'd been smitten by her beauty. At least he stopped the other men from killing her and searching the place further.

Fanaye picked up Sosina in her arms and rocked her back and forth. "My little girl, the bad men are gone," she said. "Don't worry. I wouldn't let them hurt you. They'll never come back. If they do, I'll kill them."

After that day, Sosina turned mute, clinging to Fanaye at all times. Two months passed, and the child still showed no signs of recovery.

Abbate, one of the Bar Addis customers, came to visit. It worried him that Sosina's condition was not getting better. "Perhaps a change of location might help the child," he suggested and proceeded to tell Fanaye about his sister, Fantanash, who had recently lost a daughter and was feeling quite bereft. "She does have a way with children," he said. "I'm sure she would be glad to have you and Sosina visit for a time."

Fanaye thanked him for his generous offer. "But would you take us to Wollo instead, to my village that I told you about? It would be so good for Sosina to be with her loving grandparents."

"Oh, no, Weizero Fanaye! That would be quite out of the question. Do you know how far that place is from here? At least ten or fifteen days on horse or mule! And the passage

230

would be so fraught with dangers that, more than likely, we would all be killed before we got here. It's best if you forget about it for now!" Then, seeing how Fanaye looked crestfallen, he added more calmly, "I think you should consider taking Sosina to my sister, as I suggested. For one thing, her place is only a day's trip from here, and the passage there is much less dangerous."

The following morning over coffee, Fanaye told Buzunash about Abbate's suggestion. To Fanaye's surprise, Buzunash was relieved to hear about this possibility. "That might be the best way to heal Sosina," Buzunash said. "Why don't we all go?"

They couldn't abandon Bar Addis just like that. "I was hoping you'd stay here with Daniel and Zenite," Fanaye responded. "I'll ask Samuel to look after you."

Although she wasn't happy about being left behind, Buzunash was glad to have someone like Samuel to rely on. Even though he was the youngest of the customers at the bar, both women trusted him.

Fanaye gathered her bags, taking some dried food and other provisions. When Fanaye was about to kiss her goodbye, Zenite grabbed her hand and insisted. "Why are you taking only Sosina?" she whimpered.

Fanaye knelt down to look Zenite in the eyes. "The mule can't carry all of us," she said. "I need to take Sosina with me just for a while. You stay with Buzunash and Daniel. Before you know it, we'll be back. Now give your sister and me a big hug. Okay, yena leja?"

But Zenite would not stop crying, even after Daniel offered her his kite. Finally, Fanaye had to remove Zenite's tiny hand from her dress so that they were able to leave. Buzunash took Zenite's hand and held it firmly. At last, Fanaye and Sosina departed, but Zenite's crying echoed far beyond the gate of Bar Addis.

While Fanaye and Sosina rode the bigger mule, Abbate rode the smaller one. As a child, Fanaye had ridden mules often, so this trip brought on a wave of memories, and she felt intensely homesick. But soon, she came to her senses and scolded herself for indulging in self-pity. "You didn't think your mother could ride, did you?" she asked Sosina. "If you want me to go even faster, I'll show you just how fast I can ride this mule."

Sosina looked ahead and said nothing.

Several hours later, they arrived at a small but spotlessly clean hut. Fanaye had been told that Fantanash was a gregarious woman, and it was true; she greeted them with a warm smile, a hearty hug, and plenty of small talks. Ever the good hostess, Fantanash rushed to her tiny kitchen to boil water so her guests could wash their feet. She then served cooked millet with sauce. Fantanash, wanting to show off the three orphans she'd recently taken in, called them into the room. The children entered and bowed.

"Tell our guests your names," Fantanash said with pride.

"I'm Etutu," said the scrawniest of the three.

The girl with the big eyes announced that her name was Lemlem.

Wiping his nose, the youngest said, "I am Nega Kebede."

Fanaye introduced Sosina to the other children. "Come play with us," Etutu said, but Sosina just stared at them.

Still, Fanaye was impressed by how polite and clean these children were. It's a sign that Fantanash is a caring woman, she thought.

Because Fantanash was such a generous hostess, Fanaye and Abbate ended up staying for an entire week. By the middle of the week, Sosina still hadn't talked, but her face was more relaxed, and she was content to watch the other children play. Also, she was less anxious whenever Fanaye left the room. Soon Sosina began to leave her mother's side more frequently. Each day she moved closer and closer to where the other children played. Once Lemlem grabbed Sosina's hand and asked, "Are you sure you can't talk? Open your mouth!"

Sosina shook her head and pushed the girl away.

Meanwhile, Fanaye helped Fantanash with whatever chores needed to be done. When the day's work ended,

Fanaye would sit and relax in the shade of a eucalyptus tree, watching the animals graze lazily. This small town reminded her very much of her own village. The river near the house seemed almost identical to the one in Dow-Dow. Now, however, Dow-Dow seemed very far away.

Early one morning, Fanaye filled the water jug at the river. She then dipped her feet into the water. Unable to resist the temptation, she jumped in and swam downstream. Weightless and unencumbered, she felt truly herself—free-spirited, adventurous. After all those years apart from her parents and her village, living under new customs and so many challenges, she let the river enfold her in its cleansing embrace.

She stepped out of the water feeling refreshed and energized. She walked several miles back to the hut, her wet clothes drying along the way. How often she had joined her mother and the other women to fetch water from the well. On the way, the ladies would gossip and whisper about things they knew were inappropriate for the ears of young girls. But Fanaye's sharp ears would always perk up and soak in as many of the juicy morsels as she could overhear.

At breakfast, Fanaye admitted that she was worried about leaving Buzunash and the children by themselves in Addis Ababa for so long.

"If you want me to take care of Sosina until she gets

better, I'd be more than happy to look after her," Fantanash offered.

Fanaye was touched, but she wasn't going to leave her daughter in the care of someone else, especially when Sosina still couldn't speak.

"I can help Sosina speak in no time if you allow me."

Fanaye shook her head. "I cannot leave my daughter," she repeated.

But Fantanash persisted. "If you leave her with me for one month and then come back, you'll find her speaking when you return," she said. "Don't you want that for Sosina?"

Sosina came as if on cue and stood between Fanaye and Fantanash. Fanaye took her daughter's hand, drew her close, and kissed her. She said wistfully, "I wish you would start talking."

Sosina buried her head on Fanaye's chest, but no words came out of her mouth. "It's alright, ligea," Fanaye said as she hugged and kissed Sosina. "Take your time."

Fantanash watched the mother and daughter and then said, "I want a kiss, too."

To Fanaye's surprise, Sosina turned and gave Fantanash a kiss. "How wonderful!" Fanaye said. "She responded to you."

That night and through the following day, Fanaye

235

watched as Sosina interacted comfortably with her new surroundings. Maybe the child would recover faster with this change of scenery and without the constant reminder of her fears.

She approached Fantanash and said, "Alright, I'd be delighted if you would take care of Sosina for a month."

And with that, the matter was settled. Yet, Fanaye still questioned if she made the right decision. What if Sosina's condition worsened without her there? Fantanash tried to ease Fanaye's worries. "Yene ehute, dear sister," she said, touching Fanaye's shoulder. "As a mother, I know how you feel leaving her with someone else, but think of what's best for Sosina."

Later, as Fanaye prepared to leave, she asked, "Sosina dear, I see you like it here. What do you think about staying here for a while? Fantanash said she would look after you and help you get your voice back."

Sosina pulled away and threw herself to the ground. She cried and kicked the floor with her feet until Fantanash came over and held her. In a few seconds, Sosina calmed down, the final reassurance Fanaye needed.

Reluctantly, Fanaye left for Addis Ababa. In no time, she felt empty and was already missing her daughter. Abbate kept reassuring her that she'd done the best thing for Sosina. "It's just one month," he said.

Fanaye apologized, but inwardly, she continued to mourn.

After a while, the wind against her face distracted Fanaye briefly from her worries. She loved riding horses and mules. She rode her mule so fast that Abbate had difficulty keeping up with her. He kept blaming his mule for being slow. When Fanaye reached a fork in the road, she slowed down and waited for Abbate. By the time he caught up, he was sweating heavily. A few hours later, Fanaye and Abbate reached Addis Ababa. Reaching the outskirts of the city, they heard the sounds of gunfire and missiles shrieking through the sky.

They arrived at Bar Addis just before sunrise. The sky was bright, and the air was warm for early morning. Fanaye knocked gently on the door, not wanting to wake the children, but they were the first to hear her. Zenite ran to Buzunash and shouted, "Emaye's here!"

Zenite and Fanaye hugged and kissed as if they had been separated for years.

"Emaye, where's Sosina?" Zenite asked.

Fanaye held Zenite's face and kissed her again and again. "My dear, Sosina needs to stay in a quiet place for a little while. A kind lady is helping her heal. I'll bring her back in a month. By then, she'll be talking. Isn't that great?"

"I miss her!" Zenite cried. "I want her back!"

237

Fanaye tried to comfort Zenite but felt herself becoming emotional, thinking of how much she'd miss Sosina, too, over the next month.

Chapter 24: Fire

The situation with the Italians worsened. They hadn't anticipated such resistance from the Ethiopians. As a result, Mussolini sent more men and more guns. Many young Ethiopian men died bravely while fighting against the enemy, leaving behind wives, children, and elders. Soon the fascists forcefully entered local homes to demand meals or to loot. They would take anything they desired. In time, this included the women. Every time Fanaye heard about such evil acts, she grew extremely agitated and imagined what she'd do in such a situation. She was thankful that her daughters were still so young.

One night Fanaye sat up abruptly in bed and flared her nostrils. There was a clear and lingering scent of smoke. "Buzunash!" she shouted. "Fire! Fire!"

She jumped out of bed and traced the smell to the back of the storage room. Intuitively, she decided not to open the door. Instead, she hurried back to a sleeping Zenite, grabbed the child's arm, and pulled her out of bed while screaming, "Buzunash! Get up! Our place is on fire!"

Confused and still not totally awake, Buzunash mumbled from her bed, "Fire? Now? Why do we need fire now? It's too early, no?"

"Get up and get Daniel outside!" Fanaye yelled. But Buzunash was still mumbling.

Finally, Fanaye forcibly shook Buzunash awake. "Oh, dear God, spare us! Spare the children," Buzunash cried as she climbed out of bed. She dashed into Daniel's room, woke him up, and together they ducked past the smoke that now billowed from the edges of the storage room door.

Once safely outside, Buzunash threw her arms around the sleepy children and looked up to the sky, thanking God for sparing their lives. Zenite became so nervous that she had to pee, so she ran behind a tree to go. When Fanaye didn't see Zenite, she became frantic and dashed into the house. She assumed that Zenite must have gone inside to get her doll. A young man pulled her arm back, but Fanaye shook him loose and ran like a wild animal. Buzunash and others screamed, "Zenite! Zenite!" Clueless, Zenite came round and joined the rest. Buzunash loudly called out for Fanaye to come out of the house… but she didn't.

Getachew and several others who lived nearby saw the flames and came running. They fought the fire, using shrubbery and whatever else they could find until the fire was nearly extinguished. "Don't go back inside!" Getachew warned. "The fire is still smoldering. We don't know if it was set on purpose."

At that moment, Fanaye staggered out and, seeing Zenite, reached out to hug her child before passing out. After ten minutes or so, she refused help and cleaned up herself.

"So where do we go?" Buzunash asked, frightened. "What are we to do?"

Getachew thought for a moment. "My friend's mother, Weizero Amrote, lives close by," he said. "She lives alone. She would welcome having company."

Relieved, Fanaye and Buzunash left Bar Addis with their children, accompanied by Getachew.

A month passed while the women settled into a routine. Initially, Fanaye and Buzunash had planned to clean away the debris left from the fire in preparation for the rebuilding of Bar Addis. But shortly after they'd moved into Amrote's, they found their time was filled by caring for Amrote, whose condition worsened by the day. Seeing the woman at the end of her life, isolated from her son, relatives, and friends, Fanaye felt her own loneliness more keenly. One day she hoped to comfort her own parents in a similar way when their time came. When will the war be over, so I can find a way to go back to Dow-Dow, a home I've longed for so long."

Since Amrote had become bedridden, the regular visits from the priest comforted her. His mere presence was enough to improve her mood. He would sprinkle holy water over her bed and intone, "Oh Holy Father, please have mercy on our sister and let the gates of heaven open for her. " After the communion, Amrote would extend her bony arm and slip some coins into his hand.

One night, several months after Fanaye and Buzunash had moved in with her, Amrote wailed so loudly that Fanaye and Buzunash were jarred out of their sleep. By the time they entered the old woman's room, she was completely silent, lying lifeless on her bed.

Fanaye and Buzunash arranged for a modest burial, attended by a few nearby friends and neighbors. As her plain casket was lowered into the ground, the priest gave his final blessing: "May your spirit fly like a bird to the heavenly gate, where the angels await you." Fanaye pictured Amrote rising like a bird over her modest home.

A week after, Fanaye said, "It's time for us to move back to Bar Addis."

"But it's so damaged!" Buzunash said. "It's impossible to live there!"

Fanaye wanted to resume business, even though rumors were spreading that the enemy was becoming more vengeful than ever toward the Ethiopians. Due to the severity of the Italian aggression, Emperor Haile Selassie had recently made repeated appeals to the League of Nations, asking for their intervention and mediation. These appeals had fallen on deaf ears. Italy was seized by a nationalistic frenzy and wanted retaliation against Ethiopia. Despite this disastrous state of affairs, Fanaye remained unafraid and undeterred, determined to forge ahead with plans to reestablish her residence and business.

Chapter 25: Luca's Dilemma

Luca sat with his long legs stretched out over his metal-framed chair. He was easily noticeable in any crowd for his looks, but it was his gentle manner that separated him from the majority of the men. The Eritrean soldiers who worked under him were well-liked; he treated them as equals. He was criticized for that by his fellow troops.

He was glad the day had ended and looked forward to a restful night. He thought about the woman at Bar Addis and how close she and her child had come to getting killed. Luca hated that his lieutenant was a violent man who had frightened the family. And the woman herself... well, he'd tried to protect her, but he had no doubt she could have protected herself just as well.

Although he was amicable with several of his fellow soldiers, Luca wasn't close enough to any of them to reveal his true feelings. Unlike his fellow patriots, Luca was ashamed of being an Italian. Thanks to Mussolini's regime, Italians now acted superior to everyone else. After spending a year and a half in Addis Ababa, Luca concluded that the Ethiopians were the truly civilized people. In his eyes, they were the masters of dignity and humanitarianism, not to mention exhibiting a unique beauty. And whenever he remembered the face of the woman in the garden of Bar Addis, he lingered on that striking image.

Luca glanced at the two envelopes on his desk. He reached for the one with the large, looping handwriting and tore it open, his face softening. He read the letter with a gentle smile as if he were savoring a fine wine.

My dear Luca,

How much I miss you. Every time I eat a delicious meal, I think of you and wish that you, too, could have a nourishing meal. Please try to take care of yourself. Eat whatever you can. You can't skip meals when you are at war.

My dear son, I pray night and day for your safety. Forgive your old mother for her foolish wishes, but please try to stay out of danger. Let those heartless men be the heroes. This is a crazy war, and I want to see you alive. One more thing, my son: if you can please send me a recent picture of yourself. For now, your photos are the closest thing to having you around.

Your la Madre

Luca became lost in memories of his mother and his life back home. Finally, he decided to open the second letter, which was from Maria, his fiancee.

One afternoon, Luca put together a package containing cheese, flour, sugar, and soap and asked his Ethiopian driver to take him to Bar Addis. When they reached the bar, Luca

245

waited in the car and asked the driver to leave the package by the front door. Luca wanted to see Fanaye, but he knew this would only upset her after what his compatriots had put her through. Did she realize that if he hadn't intervened, his companion would have killed her? If only he spoke her language, he could explain to her that not all Italians were brutes. He could express his admiration for the way she had confronted the fascists. But for now, leaving the package at the door would be a nice token of his affection.

As they drove off, Luca felt empty inside. Halfway back home, on a sudden impulse, he told his driver to turn around and return to Bar Addis. He knew he was being foolish for having illusions about a woman he didn't know and who'd never be able to see him as anything but the enemy. Yet the urge to see her had become irresistible. He had to see her even if she spat on him as she'd done before. He smiled at the memory.

After Luca knocked on the door of Bar Addis and there was no response, a vague dread spread through him. Everything was too quiet. He walked to the backyard and saw the section on the house that had burned down. Frantically, he kicked his way through the mountain of rubble to get inside. He went from room to room with his heart pounding but thankfully found no bodies. He was so filled with an uncontrollable rage that he wouldn't have hesitated to kill the men responsible for this vicious act.

Luca reluctantly returned to his base. An Ethiopian guard at the gate took one look at his face and knew instantly something was very wrong. Luca was one of the few Italians that the Ethiopians liked. Now the guard was concerned for his boss. Once Luca was out of earshot, he quietly asked the driver what had happened.

The driver shrugged. "I don't know for sure, but I think he's in love with one of our women," he said. "He's worried about her safety. Someone burned down the house she lived in—Bar Addis."

The guard nodded when he heard the name. "I think I know the lady," he said. "She's quite beautiful but also a lunatic."

The driver asked the guard who he thought had burned down the house.

"I don't know. It could be anyone she humiliated. She's brutal, you know."

The driver paused for a moment. "I didn't know our women could be so bold," he said.

"Well, she's not your average woman," the guard said. "You have to see her in action to believe it. She's absolutely fearless!"

Chapter 26: Reborn From The Rubble

Fanaye left for Bar Addis to assess the fire damage early the next morning while Buzunash stayed behind with the children. She took shortcuts through familiar streets and alleys, praying that she wouldn't run into any Italian soldiers or anyone else intent on harming her. Along the way, she saw some houses destroyed by fire. Her stomach knotted up as she thought about the people who used to live in those houses. How many had died, and how many had survived? Fanaye could barely control her mounting rage. Everything around her looked bleak and desolate. She began to doubt her lifelong belief in God. Where was His divine intervention when all this was happening? Fanaye wondered.

At the gate of Bar Addis stood a large and menacing dog that barked at Fanaye as she approached. Fanaye picked up a sturdy stick, held it behind her, and began to back off slowly, fearing the dog might be rabid. Fortunately, another dog came running from the side of the building and distracted the first one.

As Fanaye stood at the back of Bar Addis and surveyed the damage, she thought she heard children's voices. Sure enough, four scrawny children, none older than six or seven, came out of the outdoor kitchen from the side of the house. They approached her cautiously. She was about to talk to them when a woman's raspy voice called out, "Children, come and eat." But the children didn't respond; they just continued to stare at the strange woman in front of them.

"Aren't you going to answer your mother?" Fanaye asked.

The children scurried back into the house. "Emaye, there's a lady outside."

"Who is it?" the mother said as she came through the kitchen door. She was quite thin, about Fanaye's age, with close-cropped hair. She wrung her hands together nervously as she spoke. "May I help you?"

Fanaye wondered if this woman was one of Ato Ayle's relatives who had come to claim the place. "What are you doing here?" Fanaye asked, politely but firmly.

"Why do you ask?"

"My family and I own this place," Fanaye answered confidently.

The woman stared at Fanaye for a moment, her mouth agape, then turned and ran back to the kitchen. Fanaye heard her pacing back and forth and wailing, "Ai-yai-yai, ai-yai!" Fanaye was baffled by the woman's exaggerated reaction but waited outside for her to return. After a few minutes, Fanaye began to lose her patience. She went to the kitchen and knocked. "She's at the door!" she heard the children shouting inside, obviously frightened by their mother's behavior.

"Quiet! Don't open that door!" the mother scolded them.

Fanaye shook her head in frustration and knocked again. When again no one opened the door, she tried to peer inside the window, but the woman had already closed the shutters. Fanaye shouted, "Why won't you open the door and speak with me?"

Just then, Fanaye heard someone clearing his throat behind her. She turned and saw a young man in his late twenties. When their eyes met, he took a few steps forward. "Good morning, Miss, I am Berehane!" he said.

Fanaye returned his greeting and then asked, "Are you the husband of the woman I just met? I'm the owner of this place."

The man nodded his head. "I'm so sorry we took the liberty of moving in without your permission," he said, fidgeting with the bottom edge of his tunic, rolling the fabric between his thumb and forefinger. "We meant to ask permission to stay and work, but no one had ever come around until now. We were desperate and had no place to go. We already have three children and my wife, Aberash, has another baby on the way," he said. "You see, Weizero, I'm not a lazy man, but I'd rather die than work for the enemy. So I've busied myself cultivating this vegetable garden. Please come see. Cultivating this garden is my way of showing our gratitude."

250

Berehane pointed behind them. To her amazement, Fanaye saw a delightful vegetable garden surrounded by a wooden fence. There were rows of healthy-looking lettuce, red cabbage, green hot peppers, and herbs. The tomatoes were exceptionally red and plump. Some of the vegetables were ripe and ready to be picked. This is what every garden should look like, she thought.

"I hope the work pleases you, and you'll keep us on," Berehane said, smiling proudly. "My wife will help with cooking and cleaning if you permit." He bowed slightly.

Fanaye was impressed with his manners and his apparent work ethic. "I'm pleased with the garden," she said. "But we planned that my family would live in the kitchen while we renovated the main house and the bar. Now I don't know what to do. How can I be so unkind and ask your family to move out with all your young children?"

After a pause, during which both of them remained silent, Fanaye then said, "If the house were fixed, we'd like to have you stay. But for now, until the repairs are made, I don't see how we can accommodate you."

"Weizero, please forgive my boldness, but perhaps you should see the inside of the house and then make a decision. I'm also a carpenter. As a matter of fact, I've been repairing the walls, and I've already patched the roof. Now at least the rain is not getting in. All you need is a new wood floor, some patches to the walls, and a new paint job."

"Are you saying you've already begun repairs on Bar Addis?"

"Come in and see what I've done. I think you'll be pleased."

As he led her through the house, Fanaye saw an astonishing transformation, including the long solid-oak table as part of the bar. Berehane had repaired Bar Addis almost to completion.

Surprised and very much pleased with the improvement, Fanaye said, "This I never expected! You have no idea how much this means to my family and me. Thanks to all the work you've done, we'll now have a place to live. And so will your family."

"Thank you!" Berehane said gratefully, visibly relieved and bowing with humility. "We will continue to be at your service."

On her way back, Fanaye heard someone call out her name. "I can't believe it!" Fanaye answered. "Bekala! This has to be my lucky day!"

Bekala was a favorite customer at Bar Addis who had always looked after Fanaye and Buzunash. "I didn't know if you were alive or not!" Fanaye shouted. "I'm so glad to see you."

Bekala gave her a strong embrace. "I still keep in touch with some of the Bar Addis customers, but I've lost many dear friends in the war," he said sentimentally. "We all miss Bar Addis. How are you managing with all these problems?"

"I'm glad you miss it," Fanaye said playfully, "because soon we expect to open it again!"

"But I thought it was destroyed."

"Well, now it's almost fixed."

Fanaye was eager to get home, so they said goodbye and parted. Bekala turned around and shouted, "If you like, I'll come and help you out. I'm sure you can use extra hands."

Even though Fanaye was aware that Bekala had romantic feelings for her, he'd never said anything to reveal them. She was relieved that he hadn't, so she wouldn't have to reject him outright. She loved him only like a brother.

When she reached home, Fanaye told Buzunash the good news about the new family who'd live with them at Bar Addis and how Berehane had rebuilt most of what had been damaged. "There's nothing to stop us from moving in any day."

But Buzunash was full of doubt. "Can you be sure these people are trustworthy?" she asked. "Are you certain they won't claim they are related to Ato Ayle?"

Fanaye told her not to worry; if that had been Berehane's and his wife's intention, they would have announced their kinship already. "These people are humble and are grateful to have a place to stay," Fanaye tried to assure her. "They will help us open Bar Addis again. And believe me, Bar Addis is looking better than even before."

Buzunash remained skeptical. "I have a hard time believing these people would put such effort into someone else's property unless they have ulterior motives," she pointed out.

"Buzunash, let go of your suspicions," Fanaye said, growing impatient. "Some people are good."

"Yeah, and Bekala just helps you because he enjoys the work," Buzunash teased and winked at her.

Fanaye reminded her, "You know what a good-natured man Bekala is, how people loved him at Bar Addis, how he used to cheer everyone up. People always left for home with smiles on their faces because of him."

When Fanaye and Buzunash went inside Bar Addis, Daniel and Zenite stayed behind and, noticing the flourishing vegetable garden; they were delighted.

"Let's go pick!" Daniel shouted.

"Yes!" Zenite said. "Let's go!"

Once inside the garden and away from the adults, Zenite snatched up some tomatoes and threw one at Daniel. He ducked and then threw another one back at her. Hearing the racket Daniel and Zenite were making, Berehane's children dashed out to the garden. Seeing the commotion, they were tempted to join in, but their father had forbidden them to set foot in the vegetable garden unless accompanied by a grown-up.

Soon Zenite noticed the other children. "What's your name?" she asked.

"I am Yakob," the oldest one said. The other two introduced themselves as Rebeka and Mulugeta.

When Zenite invited them to come to play in the garden, Yakob explained they were not allowed to set foot in the garden by themselves. But Rebeka, the youngest, ignored her brother's warning and dashed up to Daniel and Zenite.

"Let's play a game," Zenite said to Rebeka. "You go first. Try to hit us with the biggest tomato you can."

Rebeka snatched a very large tomato off the vine and hurled it at Daniel with all her might, striking him right on the forehead. He felt the sharp sting but couldn't admit that a girl had caused him such pain.

Zenite clapped her hands. "Can you hit him again in the same place?"

Giddy with victory, Rebeka began frantically looking for another large tomato when Zenite ran over and handed her a small potato. "Go ahead. Take this. Aim for his head."

Rebeka bit her lip, shifted the potato from one hand to the other while the children counted, "Ande, hulate, sawast!" Then she let the potato loose.

Once Daniel got hit by the potato, he became angry and charged at them like a mad dog, throwing things and stomping over the plants. The children scattered and ran in all directions, screaming at the top of their lungs.

When Berehane heard the racket, he stepped out of the house and saw the damage. He shouted furiously at his children for disobeying him and threatened punishment. Yakob, Rebeka, and Mulugeta froze in their tracks. They knew their father's warning wasn't a bluff. Yakob gathered up his strength and said, "We didn't damage the garden. It was them."

"Yes, they made us do it," Rebeka shouted. "You should punish them."

"Keep quiet! You'll get your punishment later on." Then he turned to Daniel and Zenite. "This is not a place to play, and it's bad to destroy and waste food," he said. "Your mothers won't be happy either."

Daniel, no longer defiant, mumbled, "I'm sorry. We didn't mean to hurt the plants."

That same day, Bekala came to visit with a bunch of newspapers under his good arm. The other arm he'd lost during the war after a particularly bloody battle in which he'd fought selflessly. He'd been collecting old newspapers that Fanaye and Buzunash could use to cover over the clay and straw mixture that was now their bedroom walls. He brought his younger brother along to help him carry a bag of white flour to be used for paste. Bekala and his brother took their time cutting the papers into usable sections and inserting pictures in between so that the walls looked aesthetically pleasing. After they finished decorating the walls, there was a rich collage of text and images. Finally, after much hard work, all of the rooms were nearly renovated, and Bar Addis was ready to reopen.

Fanaye felt such warm feelings for Bekala. Poor man, she thought, it must have been so hard for him to work with only one hand. She remembered how her grandfather used to say, "A man's strength comes not from his physical ability, but from his willingness to do good for others."

Buzunash, seeing all the help and goodwill they had received, felt her heart soften. She looked up to the Heavenly Father and whispered, "Thank you, Jesus. With your help, anything is possible."

One morning, after they had settled back at Bar Addis and Fanaye was preparing Kita for breakfast, Zenite pulled on her mother's dress. "What is it, my child?" Fanaye asked.

"I miss Sosina. I want her to come home."

Fanaye's heart skipped a beat, and she felt as if an arrow had pierced her heart when she heard Sosina's name. It had been three long months since she had seen Sosina, and not a day had passed without her thinking about her daughter. She'd never intended to leave Sosina with Fantanash for so long, but because of the war and one disaster after another, she'd been left with no choice. Fortunately, their life was much more stable again. Just a week ago, Fanaye had gone looking for Abbate to see if he could accompany her back to the village where she'd left Sosina, only to discover that Abbate was away, fighting. Now, Zenite's request increased Fanaye's determination to get Sosina and bring her home.

A few days later, Fanaye went into the city to hire a guide. She prepared herself for the long and perilous journey back to Fantanash's village.

As the sun rose over the hills in the early morning, the guide arrived with two mules. The air smelled fresh, and there was cool dew on the leaves. Fanaye and the guide traveled for seven long hours, stopping only once for a short rest.

As the sun descended in a rosy-hued sky by late afternoon, Fanaye arrived at Fantanash's hut, exhausted but very excited. The first person she saw was Fantanash, sitting on a large stone next to the door with a small flat basket on her lap. Her head was bent as she sorted through some grains.

When Fanaye saw Fantanash, she joyously called out: "I made it! I'm here, finally! I'm so sorry for not coming sooner."

Fantanash looked up at Fanaye for a few seconds without responding. Then, slowly, she stood and approached her with hesitant steps. While Fanaye hugged her, Fantanash barely returned her affection. This surprised Fanaye since she remembered Fantanash as a cordial and gregarious person. "I'm so sorry I couldn't come any sooner, as I had promised," Fanaye apologized. "The threat from the Italians was heavy in our village these past months. Our home was set on fire too." Fanaye couldn't contain her excitement as she looked around for Sosina. "Where is she?" Fanaye asked. "I can't wait to see her! How is she doing? Did she start talking?"

"She's fine," Fantanash answered coolly. "Yes. She has been talking for a while now."

Overjoyed, Fanaye reached out and hugged Fantanash again, but Fantanash stiffened.

"I'm so indebted to you for taking such good care of my daughter and bringing her back to health," Fanaye said, and then she turned and began searching for Sosina. Finally, she spotted her playing with the other children in the backyard. Fanaye let out a whoop of joy and dashed over to hug her daughter, but Sosina just stood there unresponsive, sneaking glances at Fantanash.

"Sosina, dear, come to me; it's me, your mother! Don't you recognize me?" Her arms were outstretched to embrace Sosina, but still, her daughter didn't budge. She just stood there, still as a statue, staring at Fanaye. Confused, Fanaye lowered her arms and leaned forward to kiss her, but Sosina pulled back and turned away.

Tears sprang to Fanaye's eyes. "Sosina, my dear, I've missed you so much. Please, come to your emaye. I want to hug you. Didn't you miss me? Fantanash tells me you are talking. Please talk to me." But Sosina continued staring as if Fanaye were a stranger.

Crestfallen, Fanaye realized that her daughter was probably angry with her. "Sosina, even though it broke my heart to leave you here with Emama Fantanash to look after you, I knew she would take good care of you as if you were her own. You understand, don't you?"

Sosina's face softened a little, but she still refused her mother's embrace. In desperation, Fanaye turned to Fantanash, "Tell me why Sosina is rejecting me!"

"I have no idea," Fantanash said with a shrug.

Fanaye wondered what had caused this woman to turn against her as well. As much as she wanted to know the truth, Fantanash kept her guard up and revealed nothing. Finally,

Fanaye realized she had to take matters into her own hands. "Fantanash, may I speak to you alone?" she asked with a grim expression on her face.

"I have nothing to hide from the children, but if you wish, we can talk in private," Fantanash responded haughtily.

Once they were away from the children, Fanaye asked Fantanash what was going on. "Is it because I didn't come sooner or send you money?" she asked. "If that's the reason, I'm sorry. Circumstances prevented me from traveling sooner. Here," she said, opening her pouch and offering Fantanash some money. "I hope this will cover the entire three months. And thank you for everything."

Fantanash retained that same stony expression. "I don't want your money," she said, pushing her hand away. "I enjoyed taking care of my daughter."

Ignoring the unusual comment, Fanaye thanked Fantanash for loving her like a daughter.

"Sosina took to me right away," Fantanash grinned. "Don't you remember?"

"Yes, she felt close to you. I'm so grateful. I don't know what I would have done without your help."

"Please don't thank me. I did it from my heart."

"You're a kind woman. I know she loves you, too. I hope you'll come to visit us; Sosina would love that."

Fantanash was silent for a moment. "Sosina is very happy here with the children and me, and she prefers to stay here," Fantanash said with sudden assertiveness. "I want her here with me where she belongs."

At first, Fanaye couldn't believe what she'd heard. After a pause, she responded, "Thank you, but I came to get my daughter, and I'm leaving with her." She laughed nervously. "Thank you for all you have done. So, please take the money; you've earned it."

Fanaye extended her hand again, but Fantanash grabbed the money and threw it on the ground. "I told you, I don't want your money, but you can't take Sosina. Now, she is my daughter, so she belongs here with her other siblings, and me. She doesn't want to go with you. It's best if you just go back to the city and your other daughter. Don't confuse this poor girl anymore."

Fanaye's heart was beating so fast she could hardly catch her breath. She thought it was a stupid mistake to leave my daughter here with a total stranger. What was I thinking?

"Please, Fantanash, say goodbye to Sosina," Fanaye said with determination. "We need to leave now."

But Fantanash refused to give up. "Sosina is like a gift from heaven to me," she said, her own voice shaking. "She is my miracle. After you left, I tried to help her get better. I prayed daily. I took her to the herbalist. She also received the

262

holy water, but nothing worked. As a last resort, I took her to the great almighty, Alamayoh." Fantanash went on to explain how Alamayoh saw that Sosina was possessed and her spirit was in transition. He had told Fantanash that Sosina would be fine once the spirit left her for good. Then the witch had said something Fantanash had not expected: "Woman, don't mourn for your dead daughter any longer, for her spirit has entered Sosina's body. Sosina is your daughter now, your own flesh and blood." He assured Fantanash that the girl would soon recover and begin to speak again.

"And he was right," Fantanash exclaimed. One morning a couple of months later, when she was baking injera, she heard the voice of her deceased daughter Negatua saying, "Emaye, I'm hungry." Stunned, Fantanash had turned around, expecting to see her daughter, but it was Sosina who was speaking! "You can only imagine my shock," Fantanash told Fanaye. "I was shaking all over. Sosina came over and hugged me. It was just as the mighty Alamayoh had foreseen."

Fantanash looked deeply into Fanaye's eyes and continued, "Do you hear what I am telling you? It was a miracle! Miracles do happen, but most people are not attuned to them, so they go unnoticed."

Fanaye wasn't sure what to say. "Fantanash, my friend, I think you are confused…" she began in a measured tone.

But Fantanash smiled and rolled up her sleeve. Pinching her arm, she said, "See the skin? It's only a fabric of sorts. It's the soul that matters! What else is there to a person but the spirit?"

Fanaye understood that Fantanash was quite sincere in her own crazy way. Still, all Fanaye could think of was how to escape with Sosina as quickly as possible. Once more, she tried to reason with Fantanash. "I do believe in miracles, too," she said, "but to me, you were Sosina's miracle. You helped her get better with your kindness and your efforts. I don't believe in witches or spells. And that is the end of that."

Fantanash's eyes popped wide open. "Are you condemning the mighty Alamayoh?" she asked.

"No. I am not. I'm not here to judge anybody. I'm only here to pick up my daughter, and I need to leave before it gets dark."

Fantanash looked crushed but said in a steely tone, "I thought I explained to you why Sosina belongs to me now."

Fanaye walked past Fantanash and back to Sosina. She placed her hand on the child's head and said, "Sosina, dear, let's go."

Sosina looked perplexed.

"Come on. Kiss Emama Fantanash goodbye and all your friends so that we can go."

Sosina walked slowly towards Fantanash to kiss her, but Fantanash grabbed Sosina's hand and whispered fiercely into her ear, "Tell this woman to leave us alone."

Sosina looked terribly confused. Fanaye's heart ached for her. "As I said, I'll never forget what you have done for Sosina, but you must let her go."

"You can't take away my daughter!" Fantanash cried, flying into a rage. "She's mine! I won't allow it. Just leave!"

Fanaye wasted no more time. She grabbed Sosina's hand, called the guide over, and firmly said, "Let's go!"

As Fanaye and Sosina walked quickly toward the mules, Sosina kept dragging her feet. Fanaye mounted the mule first, then the guide lifted and seated Sosina in front of her so she could keep a firm hold on her daughter. Fanaye spurred the mule to get it moving.

Fantanash frantically dashed after them, screaming, "Sosina! You're my daughter; you can't go!" Then she paused. An ominous expression came on her face, and she said maliciously, "If you leave with this woman, I will put a curse on you!"

Fantanash's fading voice left echoes in the forest. Fanaye continued to hold on tightly to Sosina, who had begun to slouch in her seat. "Don't believe her, Sosina," Fanaye said. "She can't put a curse on you. She's angry at me for taking you away."

265

The mules trotted down the path into the woods. For a while, Fanaye, Sosina, and the guide said nothing, listening to Fantanash's screams as they receded in the distance: "Sosina! Sosina! Come back! Come back to your mother."

"I'm sorry you had to go through all this, yenilege," Fanaye said to Sosina. "But it's over now. We are now together, and I will never leave you with anyone, never again!"

Zenite and Daniel were playing outside when Fanaye and Sosina arrived. They were sorting out sticks and twigs from a large pile of branches. Daniel was breaking them into small pieces for rebuilding the roof of the toy house. He had assigned Zenite to be his assistant, and as usual, she had accepted the position without hesitation. As part of her job, she was tasked with finding more branches.

Zenite first saw them approaching. Though she couldn't clearly see the people riding them, she assumed they were her mother, Sosina, and the guide. Excitedly, she dropped the sticks and ran towards them. When Daniel saw Zenite running, he too stopped what he was doing and followed her.

"Emaye! Sosina!" Zenite screamed.

Before Fanaye and Sosina had a chance to dismount, Zenite was already tugging at her sister's leg. "You look so big!" Daniel told Sosina. "Are you taller than me? I don't want you to be taller than I am. Boys are supposed to be taller and stronger."

Sosina didn't say a word. Fanaye helped her dismount. "Are you still sick?" Daniel asked her.

Fanaye squeezed Sosina's hand. "Didn't I tell you the children have missed you? Let them give you a hug and a kiss."

Sosina shook her head as though she hardly knew them. Daniel and Zenite were confused by her rejection. "Do you want to see the house I'm building?" Daniel asked.

Still, Sosina seemed uninterested. Eventually, Daniel gave up and went back to his pile of branches. "Let's go and be his helpers," Zenite said and held Sosina's hand.

Again, the older girl refused.

"Why doesn't Sosina want to play with us?" Zenite asked Fanaye. Fanaye shook her head and said, "Just give her a little time. Believe me; she missed you too."

Just then, a stray cat came along and sat next to Sosina. Zenite waved her hand to chase it away, but the cat didn't budge and, instead, began to purr. Sosina smiled and began to pet the cat, which showed appreciation by arching its back and purring louder.

Chapter 27: Fate

Fanaye and Buzunash were almost finished with their morning ritual, which was getting up by sunrise while the maid would come with a pot of freshly roasted coffee beans for them to sniff. The place would be filled with a strong aroma. Over coffee, which would be served in demitasses, they would discuss their daily business, such as what supplies would be needed for the week and how much tej should be made. They would then count the money from the previous day and take care of miscellaneous details in preparation for the arrival of customers. After that, one of them might go shopping while the other would begin making tej.

During one of those mornings, Berehane came in with a dour expression. "What's wrong?" Fanaye asked.

He told them his younger brother Yared had been badly hurt while fighting in the war. Aside from Yared's bullet wounds, the bones in his right leg were shattered and, although the fractures had been set, he was immobilized and needed help with everything. Yared lived in the town of Nazareth and had no one to look after him, so Berehane needed to leave Bar Addis for a while and look after his brother.

"Of course, you have to help him," Fanaye said. "He's your brother. I'm so sorry he was hurt."

"Thank you for understanding. My wife will stay with the children and will continue to work for you."

Fanaye watched Berehane walk away, his arms swinging as if they had a will of their own.

She then turned to Buzunash and whispered, "Do you think we can let Berehane bring his brother here?"

Buzunash wasn't sure if that was a good idea. Wrinkling her forehead and frowning, she asked, "I feel bad for him too, but don't you think we have enough to worry about? Why burden ourselves further?"

"But, Buzunash, his brother fought our enemies and sacrificed himself for all of us. In this case, don't you think we should take responsibility and look after our wounded brothers?"

While Buzunash was debating this, Fanaye dashed out and shouted, "Berehane! Berehane! Come back; we have something to tell you."

Berehane cringed as he retraced his steps back to Fanaye; he was worried that Fanaye had changed her mind about allowing him to leave. "Bring your brother here if you want to," Fanaye said excitedly and smiled. "This way, you can look after him, and everyone can help."

"That's too much to ask, Weizero Fanaye," he responded. "I can never find enough ways to thank you."

"He's not only your brother, but he is also our hero. That's the least we can do for him. He would not be a burden at all."

While Berehane obviously appreciated Fanaye's generous offer, he still struggled with the impracticality of the situation. "Our quarters are already crowded and noisy, with my wife and three children," he mumbled shyly. But no sooner than he said this, he cringed with guilt and embarrassment for thinking selfishly.

"I haven't figured out every detail, Berehane, but don't worry. We'll think of a way to make him more comfortable."

"I am humbled before you." Berehane bowed. "God bless you."

When Fanaye and Buzunash took a break from their work to have a cup of coffee, they continued to discuss where Berehane's brother would stay. Buzunash remained worried that they didn't have enough room for Yared, but Fanaye had an idea about where they could put Yared. "I'm hoping you'd allow Daniel to move into your room," Fanaye told Buzunash. "That way, Berehane's brother can have his own room, at least until we figure out something else."

Buzunash agreed since this was the Christian thing to do.

A week passed before Berehane returned with his brother. By then, Daniel's room had been prepared for Yared's stay. After Berehane helped settle Yared in bed, he dressed his brother's wounds with a poultice of herbs. His hands trembled when he applied the poultices, and Yared winced.

"I wish you hadn't brought me here," his brother complained. "I'm a burden to you. You're not capable of caring for me. Taking care of me is not like growing vegetables or building a chair. You are good at making things, but this is not one of your strong points."

"My brother, it hurts to see you suffer," Berehane replied. "I'm always fearful that I'll cause you more pain."

Throughout the entire week, Buzunash and Fanaye heard Yared moan while his brother tended to him. One morning, Fanaye heard Yared wailing and, without considering if he was decent or not, she barged into his room to find him dressed in a gown, struggling helplessly on the floor.

"I reached for the basin, but I lost my balance and fell," Yared explained. "Would you please call Berehane to help me?"

Fanaye offered her hand to help him up instead, which he accepted, although he was ashamed and avoided looking at her. "Thank you," he mumbled as Fanaye lifted him back into bed. He hadn't expected she would have the strength. "I can tell you've done this before," he said.

"I've had some experience, and I'm glad to nurse a soldier."

271

After this incident, Yared was relieved when Fanaye and Buzunash took over his care. To repay Fanaye and Buzunash for their kindness, Berehane happily threw himself back into his work, his mind at ease, now that his brother was in the hands of two competent and caring women.

Fanaye and Buzunash made caring for Yared look effortless. They helped him wash, prepared him and fed him, etc. The excellent care he was receiving soon helped improve Yared's mood and encouraged him to regain his sense of humor. He always seemed to know how to entertain everybody. Even the children took a liking to him. Of course, he would save his off-color jokes for the company of the rowdier men.

Yared recovered amazingly quickly and, after five months, was well enough to leave Bar Addis.

During those five months, Bar Addis was recovering as well. Berehane busied himself building lots of furniture. As soon as he'd finish putting together chairs and tables, Fanaye would snatch them up and paint them her favorite green color. Often she couldn't get her hands on ready-made paint, so she started mixing her own, using whatever resources were available.

Fanaye invented her own painting technique because she didn't have traditional painting materials or proper brushes. Instead, she took a rolled-up piece of fabric, dipped it into the paint, and then brushed it onto the wall in a circular motion, as if dusting. She painted the tables and the chairs the same way. Surprisingly, the furniture and the walls came out looking pretty decent. No one noticed the unevenness of the paint or the blotchiness of the color here and there. Fanaye herself didn't care much for perfection. She just wanted to create a pleasant and festive atmosphere in the bar.

Once Bekala spread the news that Bar Addis had opened again, customers began to return. As usual, they came to cheer themselves up and temporarily forget their troubles. As had always been the case, Fanaye had no tolerance for unruly patrons and would tell such customers to leave immediately. Should anyone dare to challenge her authority, out would come the trusty stick that she kept nearby just for that purpose. Everyone soon relearned that this was Fanaye's and Buzunash's policy at Bar Addis. No nonsense was permitted.

Once again, the business began to prosper. The two women were exhilarated by their success. Still, Fanaye was in the habit of staring at strangers to determine where they were from, with the undying hope of running into someone from her village. As soon as Bar Addis was profitable again, she vowed to return home. The faces of her family remained permanently vivid in Fanaye's imagination. The images of her mother, father, and her little brother never changed.

Often, she spoke of her brother as though he were still a little boy. But days turned into weeks, which turned into months.

Fanaye was playing with her children before the customers started to come. Sosina was in a mood for rough playing, so she started tickling Zenite and Fanaye. Fanaye saw a resemblance between Zenite and her mother, especially when Zenite smiled. This made her heart ache to reunite with her family. She had to go, she decided. But when she asked the guide to take her and her children to her village, he was adamant against it on account of the children being too young to undertake such an arduous journey. Fanaye didn't want to accept his opinion, so she went on to look for another guide. But all of them said the same thing; the children were too young for the long and brutal trip.

Fanaye found herself in a dilemma. She could not take the children with her on the trip, and she could not leave them with anyone, even with Buzunash, not with Sosina being in such a delicate condition. To her chagrin, Fanaye had no choice but to keep postponing her plans.

Chapter 28: Luca

At the end of the Mussolini era, in Ethiopia, the majority of Italian soldiers left the country. Luca was one of them. He wouldn't have gone back at all, but his mother was getting old, and he wanted to see her.

During his first month at home, Luca's relatives and friends came to visit him. His mother managed to prepare a pasta dish sprinkled with salty cheese and chopped pastrami for the visiting family and friends. The small, dimly lit dining room was filled with laughter and loud chat. Halfway through the meal, one of Luca's cousins said, "You know we Italians are good people. If we weren't, we would have wiped out those savages."

Luca wanted to let him have it, but he decided it wasn't the appropriate time. Some of the time he spent with Maria, his fiancée. But after a few months, his mind would often drift back to Ethiopia and one exotic stranger in particular.

Luca's mother noticed his moodiness. He didn't spend time in the company of his old friends, and her intuition told her that he might not be in love with his fiancée anymore. She loved her son more than anything else, so she decided to have a heart-to-heart talk with Luca. That evening, she mustered her energy, sat up in her bed, and called out for him, "Luca, I need you to sit close to me."

For a moment, she struggled to maintain her composure. "I've wanted to talk to you for some time," she managed to say. "I'm overjoyed that you came back, but you haven't seemed very happy. Can you tell me what's bothering you?"

Luca paused. His answer was diplomatic and evasive since he didn't want to upset her. "I've lived such a different life in Ethiopia. I guess I need a bit more time to adjust to life here."

His mother studied his face. "I sense that perhaps you don't love Maria anymore. You know you can confide in me. Did you meet someone else in Ethiopia?"

No point in denying the truth to his mother. He sighed. "Yes," he said, "there is a woman whom I admire and fancy. As a matter of fact, she reminds me of you. But it's not just about love." He paused, gathered his thoughts, and continued, "I'm afraid I'm not the same Luca that Maria knew before I left for Ethiopia. I feel attached to those people. We invaded their country, violated their people, and destroyed their land. I can't accept that! I feel responsible as a man. Honestly, Mother, my heart is yearning to go back and help them rebuild their country and their lives."

After his fiery outburst, she could no longer hold back her tears. She reached out and touched Luca's cheek. "You always were such a thoughtful boy. I'm just glad I got to see you. Go answer your calling... and don't worry about me, I'll be fine."

Luca hugged his frail mother. "Thank you, Mother," he whispered, tears streaming down his cheeks. "You don't know what this means to me."

Luca had rehearsed what he was going to say to Maria and how he would break the news without sounding too blunt or cruel. However, when he met her, the words just spilled out of his mouth.

Maria was taken aback. "Wait a minute. Why do you think, during all the years you were gone, I waited for you to come back and prayed for your safety and our future together?"

Suddenly everything made sense to her. She had been making up excuses for Luca's aloofness, indifference, and lack of amorousness towards her, blaming it all on the traumatic experiences of the war. Gripping the reality, she lost control, shouting barely intelligible words: "How dare you betray me like this! Get out of my house!" With that, she stood up and scrambled around, looking for things to throw at him. He ducked out the door just in time to miss the shoe that came flying at his head... and that severed the last link that had chained Luca to Italy.

Within a week after he arrived in Ethiopia, Luca found work as a freelance consultant for newly formed companies.

Now that he'd decided to live in Ethiopia permanently, he wanted to assimilate himself into the Ethiopian culture, so he took up a study of Amharic, the official language of Ethiopia.

Luca had already visited Bar Addis once and tried to woo Fanaye through an interpreter, but she hadn't paid much attention to him. One could not expect a translator to express love on behalf of another person. So he promptly hired a tutor and worked with him several hours every day before work started.

Once Luca felt that he'd learned the basics of the language sufficiently to engage in small talk, he decided to visit Bar Addis to test his newly acquired skills. He summoned up his courage and dropped in one afternoon, where he soon found himself face to face with Fanaye.

"I'm so glad to see you. I've been waiting a long time to talk with you," he said to Fanaye in Amharic. Then, after composing his words carefully in his mind, he continued in almost perfect Amharic, "The beauty of your smile is like the sun."

This amazed Fanaye. "I see that you've learned well. You should be proud of yourself." Then she added, "Welcome to our establishment. Would you like some tej?"

"My apologies for bad Mussolini," Luca said in not-so-perfect Amharic, holding his hand over his heart. "I wish to erase… all bad memories. I like to live in this country… and die here."

For the first time, Fanaye felt her heart warming towards Luca. "I think you really mean that," she said. "I would never have expected any Italian to express such sentiments about our country."

Now that Fanaye was relaxed and friendly for the first time, Luca wondered if she was opening her heart to him or merely celebrating the end of Mussolini's rule. Either way, he was glad to see her in such a good mood.

Zenash, the servant, came into the bar from the kitchen area, carrying a good-sized basket tray of food. Fanaye had invited Luca to dine with her and he accepted. As they ate, he remarked, "So delicious! I think your customers would feel the same way." Fanaye shook her head, "I don't serve lamb stew to customers."

"Maybe you should."

Luca continued to visit Bar Addis. To his great sadness, he understood that his feelings for Fanaye were one-sided. She respected him for his humanitarianism and generosity. Since she recognized the part he'd played in her past encounter with the Italian soldiers, she remained grateful to him for saving her life. Now working together, he designed Fanaye's three houses. Although most had never heard of a man and woman spending time together platonically, they truly became the dearest of friends.

The next time he visited, Fanaye was in a good mood. "I'm fixing up that dilapidated shack where we used to store dry goods," she told him. Seizing the opportunity, Luca instantly blurted, "I can help with that too." But Fanaye just smiled and said, "Thank you, but no. There's no need for that."

Chapter 29: A Reluctant Student

With the return of a sense of safety, Fanaye and Buzunash considered sending their children to school for the first time. Most children began their studies in the more intimate setting of a priest's home, and Menuye, an elderly priest who lived nearby, offered lessons.

When the mothers saw Zenite's and Daniel's excitement about the idea, they decided to let the children's schooling begin as soon as possible. Only Sosina was reserved when the topic of school was broached. Still, Fanaye hoped that interaction with her peers might be exactly what Sosina needed.

Early morning on a beautiful sunny day, Fanaye, Buzunash, and the children arrived at Kesu Menuye's place to find him with a long stick in one hand and a book in the other, sitting on a high stool. At the same time, his students were seated on the floor around his feet, reciting the Bible verses that he'd given them. When Menuye saw Fanaye and Buzunash approach, he got up from his stool with difficulty. "Keep reciting," he said to the students. "Don't get distracted."

"Greetings," he said. "Ladies, I believe you've brought your children here today to enroll them in my school." He peered at the children and asked Sosina, "What's your name?"

Sosina shyly looked up at her mother. Fanaye patted Sosina's shoulder and said, "This is Sosina, my eldest."

The priest asked for the names of the other two children and then, without much explanation, said, "Leave the children here today; they'll be fine. Come back at one o'clock. When you come to pick them up, we'll talk about my fee. Don't worry. I don't ask for much."

Fanaye and Buzunash looked at each other and nodded their assent. Then, without any hesitation, they left their children in the hands of the priest and left. And so the children's first day of school began.

When Fanaye came to pick up the children, Sosina complained, "The girl sitting next to me hates me."

"You just started today. Why should anyone hate you? Are you sure about that?" But then Fanaye reconsidered, "If someone bothers you, you should perhaps tell the priest."

"What if he doesn't believe me?"

"Why wouldn't he? If she's done something bad, he wouldn't want a troublemaker."

"No. I don't want to. If the girl finds out I told on her; she'll get mad at me."

Each morning, Zenite and Daniel eagerly prepared to go to school, while Sosina's complaints worsened, even after the priest attempted to resolve the problem with her classmate. Despite Kesu Menuye's daily prayers for Sosina, her erratic behavior interfered with his teaching. After serious consideration, he decided the only solution was to dismiss Sosina from his school.

When Fanaye came to pick up the children, the priest pulled her aside. "Sosina is a bright and sensitive child, but she is having difficulty fitting in with the rest of the children," he began.

Fanaye knew where this was leading. "It's been very hard for Sosina," she said. "I thought perhaps you could help her."

"Believe me," the priest said, "if I could, I would let her continue, but it's not fair to the other children. My teaching has been interrupted too often."

Fanaye was desperate for her troubled child. "Since you're a man of God, you might make a difference in her young life," she pleaded. "Perhaps with your prayers and wise advice, she could be helped. So, couldn't you be more patient with her and give her a bit more time to adjust?"

The priest shook his head. "I've done all that already. There is nothing else I can do. I am really sorry."

After the experience with Kesu Menuye, Fanaye and Buzunash chose to look into more conventional schools. One of the customers told them about a French Catholic school, Alliance Français, where his children attended. He praised the nuns' dedication to teaching. Buzunash was worried that the nuns might try to convert the children, but the customer reassured them. "Catholics are Christians, too."

Fanaye wasn't concerned about the nuns' religion. For her, it was only important for her children to get a good education and for Sosina to find a place to fit in.

The school was a twenty-minute walk from Bar Addis, so Fanaye and Buzunash decided to visit the place before making a decision. As they walked to the school, they heard the school children singing from a distance. "What do you think these farenge are making them sing?" Buzunash wondered.

The school was fenced in and had a big iron gate. Fanaye and Buzunash saw the children in the schoolyard, standing in a circle. Two nuns stood in the middle as they led the children in singing. The nuns wore long black habits with their heads covered, white shirts underneath, and long wooden crosses dangling on their chests. Both had thick wooden rulers in their hands.

"Do you think we're doing the right thing?" Buzunash wondered, looking at the nuns. "To me, they look just like the enemy."

"Yes, we are doing the right thing! We shouldn't deny our children the opportunity. This is a French school, not Italian."

Buzunash frowned. "French or Italian are all the same. If they would just leave us alone and go back to their own countries, we wouldn't have to learn their languages or their customs."

Fanaye ignored Buzunash's concerns. They were led directly into the Prioress's office, where a female translator stood waiting for them. As if reciting a memorized text, she explained that all the children liked the school, that the nuns were totally dedicated to education, that lunch was provided every day, and that the children were taught to read and write in French. Fanaye and Buzunash cast questioning glances at each other. The translator stepped close to Fanaye and Buzunash and whispered, "If you want to see your children educated, I urge you to register them now. The school is getting full. You should hurry and bring your children in tomorrow."

Fanaye turned to Buzunash and said, "Let's do it."

"I don't know, but if you think so... then..." Buzunash said half-heartedly.

Judging from the proper way the two women were dressed, the translator didn't feel the need to explain rules regarding hygiene. So she just brought a few sheets of paper, along with an ink pad, put them on a table, and said, "These are forms you should sign. So, please roll your thumbs on the ink, then press and roll them on the form. These will be your signatures. The children will never have to do this since they will be educated."

It was messy. "It's a good thing the children are learning to write," Buzunash retorted.

At least Fanaye's father had taught her how to count money. Her mind drifted back to her village when she was about six or so... her father spread his ganzeb—money—on a table and smoothed them with his hand. She was curious. "What are those?" His answer was, "These are ganzeb. I received them when I sold the corn and the barley."

Fanaye grabbed some of the ganzeb and coins, crunched them in her little hands, and headed towards the door.

"Where are you going, and what are you going to do with them?"

"I want to play with them with Amsalu."

Her father laughed and laughed. "Your father worked hard for them. They are not to be played with." He extended his upturned palm, so she put the money in his hand. After he got through smoothing them again, he began to explain: "This one is one birr, that one a twenty…" Another time he showed her the difference between coins: amist santim, asera santim...

Fanaye watched intently as if she were looking at fascinating paintings, her quick eyes taking in everything she saw. In no time, she memorized all the denominations of currency.

The next morning, on a typical Addis Ababa September morning—cold and windy—Fanaye and Buzunash bathed and dressed the children for their first day of school. Despite the children's loud protests, both women insisted that they wear shoes. The children complained that shoes hurt their feet. "I hate wearing shoes!" Daniel shouted.

"You'll get used to them; just wait," Buzunash assured him.

The children were required to wear uniforms—light beige dresses for girls and light beige pants for boys.

For a while, everything went smoothly. The mothers took turns taking the children to school. Except for some occasional complaints from Sosina, the children seemed to be adjusting well. Fanaye started to relax and think that perhaps Sosina was improving at last. But after a few months, Sosina insisted that she didn't want to go to school anymore since she thought all the children hated her.

Then one day, when Fanaye went to pick her up, the school translator took her aside and told her of the administration's decision to dismiss Sosina from the Alliance Français. With a sad expression, she explained, "Please understand, the school doesn't dismiss students easily," she said. "We all agreed that Sosina would do better in a smaller school."

"Can't you give her another chance?"

"She's a quick learner and a charming girl, but unfortunately, she's getting into a lot of fights."

Fanaye was shaken by the news. Now she realized that Sosina's problems weren't going away easily. But she wasn't going to give up on her daughter's education.

Chapter 30: The Search

Once, Fanaye took Sosina to an open market and looked around to find a particular woman who sold spices. The woman often had the freshest spices, and Fanaye was always searching for quality.

Sosina suddenly clenched her mother's hand and pulled her back.

"What is it, my child? You look frightened."

Sosina, with great fear and agitation in her voice, said, "They're going to kill us! Please, let us go home! Now!"

Fanaye looked around to see what had upset her daughter. Everything appeared normal: peaceful vendors and customers buying and selling wares. She gently stroked Sosina's head, "Look, do you see anyone trying to make trouble? We have nothing to be afraid of."

Sosina got angry. "You don't believe me. You never do," she protested.

Fanaye, baffled by her daughter's accusatory tone, did not know how to respond.

Sosina shouted, "I want to go home before that woman kills me!" Then she suddenly pushed her mother away and disappeared into the crowded market.

In the blink of an eye, Sosina had vanished. Frantically looking in all directions, Fanaye could not see her daughter anywhere. The marketplace was crowded, and Fanaye's worries mounted. Now Fanaye became like a madwoman, running to and fro and shouting, "Sosina! Sosina!" at the top of her lungs. She pleaded with passersby, "Have you seen a young girl of about thirteen?"

Someone tried to comfort her. "Don't worry, she probably went to buy some candy. Did you check the sweets stand? If I were you, I would go there."

Fanaye dashed to the sweets stand. Many young people waited, but Sosina was not among them. Fanaye was frantic, and her voice grew hoarse from shouting. After searching the entire marketplace and checking all the stands, she was exhausted. For the first time in her life, she wondered why God would test her with such a difficult child.

"I lost my daughter, and I can't find her," Fanaye said to a man selling vegetables.

The man said, "Don't worry. She probably wandered off and lost track of time."

"But she doesn't know this place."

The man sighed. "What does she look like?" he asked.

"People say she looks like me."

"That doesn't tell me much. Is she honey-colored like you? Was she wearing a headscarf?"

Fanaye shook her head and said, "I'm afraid not."

A very dark younger man, overhearing the exchange, barged into the conversation. "How long ago did your daughter go missing?"

Fanaye answered quickly, "Half an hour ago."

"I can find her," said the man with confidence. "But I need to be paid for my time."

This request took Fanaye by surprise. "How could you find her? You don't even know what she looks like."

"I've seen her, standing over there with you. I can find her in no time. I only want a bit of money." The young man shrugged. "Of course, it's not about the money," he said. "I'm only trying to help you. Just give me twenty-five cents."

"Come, come, that's almost a full day's earnings," "said the vegetable vendor.

"Go, go; I'll pay you when you bring her." Finally, the young man threw up his hands and agreed to find Sosina. "I'll go in the other direction," Fanaye said.

The vegetable vendor suggested, "You have to be here to meet your daughter when she returns. Otherwise, we'll have to go look for you as well."

This made sense, so Fanaye agreed. "Alright, I'll do as you say."

Soon, the young man reappeared, leading Sosina by the arm. Sosina was calm, acting as if nothing had happened.

When the vegetable man saw them coming, he turned to Fanaye in a self-congratulatory way: "Didn't I tell you he'd find her? All that worry for nothing! Parents always imagine the worst."

Buzunash, too, was concerned, and she wanted to resolve Sosina's problems. She brought holy water and recited special prayers. For a while, she was pleased with the results of her efforts. But then, Sosina woke up one night screaming, "Emaye, I hear someone telling me to go to my mother."

"My daughter, you were having a dream."

"No, you're wrong! I have to go. She's waiting, and she'll be upset."

"We'll talk about it in the morning," Fanaye said, trying to put Sosina back to sleep.

But sleep would not come to Fanaye. Guilt moved in instead. She wondered which drove her daughter crazier, the incident with the fascists at Bar Addis or Fantanash's curse.

At times like this, Fanaye's heart ached to see her mother. She began to remember some of the traditional rituals she used to see her mother do. So Fanaye began practicing some of the rituals, which helped soothe her aching heart. One Sunday a month before sunrise, she would drink coso—a cleansing herb—and remain in her bedroom, shades drawn, door closed. No one was allowed to go in except to bring her water occasionally. At sundown, she would come out of her room to take a bath where the hot water would be ready.

Another practice that helped Fanaye feel closer to her mother was taking Tese. In the backyard, hidden away and enclosed on all sides with bamboo curtains, a circular pit was dug out of the ground midway. In this pit, Tese, branches would be kindled and allowed to burn down to smoldering ambers. Then Fanaye would strip, sit close to the pit, and let the thick smoke pour all over her body for an hour or so. This would cleanse her entire body by sweating. She would then get up and take a bath, with either her maid or Buzunash helping her by pouring hot water and scrubbing her with a piece of soapy cotton fabric.

To her mother's chagrin, Sosina soon disappeared again.

Chapter 31: Lifting A Curse

After Sosina's disappearance, Fanaye put on a brave face in front of the other children. Each morning she went to different marketplaces and asked the merchants if they'd seen a young girl like the one in the portrait she showed them. Too often, people shook their heads. Some attempted to comfort her by saying it was only a matter of time before her daughter returned. Others frowned and suggested that perhaps the girl had been kidnapped. Fanaye thanked them all for their time, each time her stomach coiling in a tight, anxious knot. Where could Sosina have gone? As Fanaye worried and searched for Sosina, she couldn't help thinking of her own mother, who must have searched just as anxiously for her when she had gone missing.

One night Zenite faced Fanaye with a sober expression. "Emaye, did you send Sosina to her other mother?"

"What do you mean? I am the only mother you and Sosina have." But she could see that Zenite wasn't convinced. She took the child's hand and sat her down on a chair. "What has Sosina told you?"

Zenite hesitated for a moment. "She said she was cursed by her other mother and that she would never be a happy person," Zenite said.

Fanaye broke down and cried. "I love both of you more than you can ever imagine," Fanaye said between sobs. "Without you two, there's nothing left for me."

Zenite was shaken to see her usually stalwart mother yielding to tears and raw emotion. Impulsively, she leaned forward and kissed one of her mother's wet cheeks.

Fanaye hugged Zenite so tightly that the child squirmed, and had to let her go to keep from hurting her. She held Zenite's hands and looked deeply into her eyes. "My love for you and Sosina is beyond words," she said. "You're my world, both of you. I'd never knowingly do anything to harm my children. Don't ever forget that. My own mother used to say to me, 'You'll only understand what you mean to me when you have your own children.' You know, Zenite, she was so right."

As more time passed, Fanaye grew increasingly obsessed with searching for Sosina. She devoted every waking moment to tirelessly going back and forth between the market and the gathering area. Buzunash was also sad and concerned about Sosina's disappearance, but she resented that Fanaye now spent all her time in search of the girl. All the responsibility for running the bar had fallen on Buzunash's shoulders. While she didn't complain outwardly, her manner and attitude became more frustrated and self-pitying. Fanaye understood that running Bar Addis was too much work for one person but felt she had no choice in the matter.

Some nights Fanaye dreamt about Sosina, but all her dreams were hazy, and she didn't remember much about them. One morning, she woke and remembered a dream fragment—she'd seen Sosina when she was about six years old. One of her neighbors read Fanaye's fortune by placing her coffee saucer upside down, then waiting for the coffee dregs to run down and take different shapes. The woman showed Fanaye the inside of the cup and said, "Look here. Do you see that big shape? That's a young woman riding a white horse. I say that's Sosina. There's much confusion and trouble around her, but her path is clear. And she's galloping right through everything."

After five long months, Sosina reappeared unexpectedly at Bar Addis with a very short old woman. The girl appeared in the work area as if no time had passed. "Oh, you're making tej today," she said casually as her mom stirred the honey to make the drink.

The sound of Sosina's voice so startled Fanaye that she dropped the jar of honey she was holding, which shattered into pieces on the hard floor, the sticky substance spreading everywhere. Sosina! Could it be? Fanaye spun around and looked at the young woman standing only a few feet away. The girl was a little thinner than she had been, and there were slight bags under her eyes, but otherwise, she looked exactly as she always had. Sosina giggled at the expression on her mother's face.

With a cry, Fanaye dashed to hug Sosina, nearly slipping on the spilled honey. Soon mother and daughter were hugging and kissing, with tears in their eyes. The old woman, whose shoulders were slumped, stood by silently so as not to intrude on the mother-daughter reunion. Once Fanaye and Sosina pulled themselves away from one another, the woman said to Fanaye, "Could I speak to you in private for a minute?"

"Of course." Fanaye could hardly bear to leave Sosina's side for even a moment. She patted her daughter's cheek one more time before Sosina went off to say hello to the others. Then Fanaye led the old woman into the bar and reached into the money drawer to take some ganzeb to compensate the woman.

"No, no, I didn't come for that," the old woman said. Fanaye, a little surprised, gestured for the woman to sit down, but the old woman also refused this. She said, straight to the point, "When your daughter told me you run a bar, I became concerned and wondered what to do about her," the old woman said, her voice stern and accusing. "A business that gets people drunk is sinful. In addition, exposing your daughter to this unhealthy atmosphere is even more sinful."

The old woman paused, allowing her words to sink in. "A young girl still needs her mother. But let there be no mistake, I do not approve of this kind of business."

Fanaye wasn't sure what to say. She felt immense gratitude that the old woman had brought Sosina home and, at the same time, the woman's meddling and open condemnation irritated her. But her gratitude was stronger, so she held her tongue and simply asked the old woman where she'd found Sosina.

The woman frowned and shook her head. "I've delivered your daughter safely and done my Christian duty," she said. "Please don't ask me any questions. I promised your daughter I wouldn't tell you her whereabouts. Take care of your daughter and make sure she doesn't run away again."

The woman hobbled over to Sosina on the other side of the bar and hugged her. "You, young lady, keep your promise to me as well," she said. "No more running away from home, right?" With that, she turned and walked toward the door. "Don't bother to show me out," she said to no one in particular. "I know my way."

To Fanaye, the old woman's words sounded ominous, so she took Sosina into the bedroom to talk to her privately. Fanaye pulled out the old, tall-backed wooden chair next to the bed and motioned Sosina to sit, herself sitting on her bed. For a long while, she could hardly find the words to speak.

She just sat on the bed next to her daughter and stared at Sosina, hardly believing that she'd actually returned. Still, in spite of her joy at having Sosina home, Fanaye had something to say and realized the conversation was long overdue.

"Do you remember when you went to stay with Fantanash a long time ago?" she asked carefully. Sosina nodded, then pulled at the neck of her sweater and put it between her teeth.

"Of course you remember her. How could you forget? Sosina, I want you to know that you're not cursed. Believe me, once a person is dead, they don't enter a living body." She took her daughter's hand, which felt chilled now and held it. "You're my daughter, not Fantanash's. I want you to believe me."

Sosina's brown eyes darted around the bedroom. "Yes, I am cursed."

"No, Sosina, you have to believe me. That woman's curse will not affect you unless you let it."

"I know it's true," Sosina said, her eyes still downcast.

Sosina became more erratic and moody as the days passed. Sometimes she interacted happily with Zenite and Daniel, while at other times, she wanted nothing to do with them or with anyone else. She would seal herself off in a room or wander out to the garden alone.

299

After a year, one Sunday morning after the church service had ended and it was time to go home, Sosina was nowhere to be found.

Desperately, Fanaye began searching for her daughter all over again. Once again, the entire burden of running the bar and looking after the children fell upon Buzunash. The bar was extremely busy these days; that meant more drinks to be made. Even with hired help, Buzunash was still overwhelmed, and her old resentment returned. Unlike Fanaye, Buzunash believed that Sosina's erratic behavior would continue until the curse was dispelled.

Secretly, Buzunash began searching for a powerful witch. She was led to the most respected witch in town, who also demanded the highest fee. Buzunash was convinced it was worth the money if this man had the power to end Sosina's problems.

She gathered all the birr she could scrape together and headed to the witch's house. After a few hours of a bus ride, she arrived at a modest-looking house, not an impressive one that she was expecting. Instantly, her enthusiasm waned. Surely a famous witch should be with a more-stately place than this place. "Does the honorable Getahun live here?" she asked a woman who squatted in the doorway of the hut.

The woman stood up, "Yes, but wait here until you're called."

Indeed, after a short wait, Buzunash was called into a pitch dark hut. Although the sun blazed outside, all the windows had been covered with thick, black fabric. Buzunash stood in the center of the room, not knowing what to do or where to sit. Maybe it was best to wait for the witch's instructions. Her eyes had barely adjusted to the dark when a booming voice filled the tiny room. "I see troubles, yes?"

Buzunash turned around to face the direction of his voice. "Yes."

"There is a lot of heartache over this problem," he continued.

Suddenly, the room was lit up by a blaze of the wood fire. Buzunash was able to make out a hulking man in a long, black tattered robe. The whites of his eyes gleamed against his dark skin. For a long while, all was silent except for the crackling of the fire, which made Buzunash very uneasy.

"Sit! Sit here!" the witch commanded. With the aid of a long and crooked staff, he hobbled over to a pile of clothes and sat on it. Buzunash regretted not asking the woman at the door how she should approach him and how she was expected to behave.

"You have several children," the witch said. "But one is a problem, yes?"

"Yes, but—"

"I shall begin to dispel the curse," he interrupted. "Oh! Curse!" His voice boomed as he extended his long arms upwards to the heavens. After a moment, he lowered them and spoke again to Buzunash. "Dispelling a curse takes a lot of my energy," he said. "This curse is very stubborn and deep-rooted. I need to contact many spirits, and I need many things to remove this curse. Are you willing to follow my instructions? If not, don't waste my time."

Buzunash bowed to the witch. "I will do everything you ask," she said timidly.

At the witch's command, Buzunash visited him several times after that, each time costing her more birr, but the witch kept telling her to be patient and assured her that the curse would vanish very soon.

After Buzunash had exhausted her savings on the superior witch, Sosina still couldn't be found anywhere. Her faith in the witch diminished. Finally, running out of time and money, she ceased going to him.

On a Friday morning two months after Sosina had disappeared for the second time, she suddenly turned up again, wearing the same outfit she'd been wearing when she left. The outfit now looked worn out and faded, with several tears here and there. Fanaye didn't care about that. Her daughter was back again! She hugged Sosina for a long while. "You are so thin I can feel your ribs," Fanaye said.

"You haven't been eating. I don't understand what makes you run away. Why can't you talk to your mother when you're in a mood to do this? You can say anything to me; just don't keep running away."

Buzunash regained her faith in the witch, convinced that he'd broken the curse. "Thank you, mighty master, and forgive me for ever doubting you," Buzunash whispered to herself. She only wished she could share with Fanaye how her daughter had been healed.

Unfortunately, Sosina's behavior hadn't really changed. She continued her pattern of running away without a word and returning months later as if nothing was amiss. In time, to pacify her, Fanaye gave in and allowed Sosina to sit in the bar with her while she worked. But Sosina remained delusional and often imagined things. One afternoon she confronted one of the customers, claiming that he'd looked at her lewdly and then spat at her. The poor man was caught off guard when Sosina dumped a big jar of tej over his head. As it happened, the man had only spat because he'd inadvertently swallowed a dead fly that was floating in the tej he was sipping.

During one of Sosina's running away episodes, she passed a young man on the street who was playing a flute-like instrument that made some of the sweetest sounds she'd ever heard. Sosina stopped and stood, mesmerized, thinking she could listen to him play all day long. A gentleman with a friendly disposition, seemingly in his fifties, was standing near her. He, too, was enjoying the music. When the musician stopped playing, the man turned to Sosina and introduced himself as Cruebl. "You don't want him to stop, do you?" he asked.

"How could you tell?"

"Your expression alone was enough."

"You're right," Sosina confessed. "I wish he'd keep playing. I have nowhere else to go, really."

Cruebl hadn't expected this response from her. He eyed her carefully. She didn't look like a street girl. "Did I hear you correctly?" he asked cautiously. "You have nowhere else to go?"

Sosina nodded.

"But you do have a home, don't you?"

"My mother doesn't want me anymore, so I just ran away."

Again, Cruebl was surprised by her response. "Listen, it's not a good thing for a young girl like you to just run away from home. Parents don't just stop loving their children. I'm sure, at this very moment, they're worried and wondering where you are."

Before he'd quite finished talking, Sosina was already shaking her head. "I know what I'm saying," she told him.

"My father is dead, and my mother definitely doesn't want me anymore."

"Oh, I'm sorry that you lost your father. So your mother got remarried, and your step-father doesn't want you around, is that it?"

Sosina nodded. "What a shame," Cruebl continued, shaking his head. "But things like this happen in life. I can put you up in my place for a day, but after a good night's sleep, you have to go back to your mother. That's the best way."

"Okay," Sosina said instantly.

"Only for tonight, understand?"

"Yes. Thank you." Sosina bowed.

When they reached Cruebl's house in Entoto, his place was one of the several dwellings located close together in a residential compound surrounded by a wooden fence. The entrance was through a metal gate that squeezed and grated when opened. Cruebl's house was in good shape, modestly built but well kept. He showed Sosina the room where she would sleep and invited her to help herself to any food in the kitchen. "Eat what you want," he said, "and then go to your room and sleep. I'll see you early in the morning. Good night." With that, Cruebl turned around and went straight to his bedroom.

In the morning, he awoke before Sosina did. He quickly dressed for work and fumbled around in his pockets for money for Sosina, who was still asleep. Cruebl shook her awake and announced that it was time for her to leave. She yawned and stretched, seeming to be in no hurry. He needed to lock up his place before he went to work. "Oh, don't worry," Sosina said. "I'll lock up!"

"No, I need to do that myself. So, please, let's get going." He handed her money for her transportation home and to buy breakfast.

Sosina took the money and then stared down at it forlornly. "But sir, I told you I can't go home," she said in a pathetic-sounding voice.

"Your mother is probably very worried about you by now. She'll be happy to see you back."

"You don't believe me," she said. "My mother doesn't want me. Nobody wants me."

Cruebl was a sensitive man and didn't know what to do with her. The girl contradicted him at nearly every turn. To his relief, he managed to get her out of the house in the end.

Upon returning to his home late in the night, he was surprised and annoyed to find Sosina huddled up at his doorstep. He was more annoyed with himself for bringing her home in the first place. Sosina straightened up and, with her arms crisscrossed, her hands hugging over her shoulders, said that she was cold and asked Cruebl for a blanket.

"You don't need a blanket; you need somewhere to stay," he said curtly. "Please leave right now."

"I told you I have no place to go. But if you could lend me a blanket, I'll curl up and sleep right here by the door. I won't bother you."

Cruebl didn't say a word, just opened the door, stepped inside, and quickly closed the door behind him. He paced back and forth in his living room as if waiting for a solution to reveal itself. Soon Sosina began wailing outside. I have to end this nonsense now, he told himself. Enough is enough. She needs to go. I can't be responsible for her. But as soon as he opened the door, ready to send her away, Sosina looked up at him and shivered. "Please, let me have a blanket," she whimpered. "I'm so cold."

Cruebl also felt the chill, which dampened his resolve to send her away. "Okay, okay, come inside," he said.

Over the next several days, as one thing led to another, Sosina remained at his house, despite his friends' and family's advice that he should not let her stay. Actually, Cruebel began to appreciate and welcome the presence of his complicated companion.

To the amazement of everyone who knew him, Cruebl soon married Sosina. As a husband, he was loving, understanding, and patient. Despite Sosina's craziness and challenging nature, he gave her all the passion and love that she needed. Sosina loved and adored him. In return, he was like a true father figure for her, so much so that her bizarre behavior improved under Cruebl's care and nurturing.

As a sign of her improvement, Sosina now wanted to go home and introduce Cruebl to her mother. So he and Sosina made plans to go to Bar Addis on Sunday. But, as if God conspired to give certain people greater challenges than they could possibly endure, another tragedy struck Sosina. Only days before their scheduled trip to Bar Addis, Cruebl was hit by a car and died.

Sosina remained inconsolable. She refused to see people and isolated herself inside the house, often wailing desperately for Cruebl. Her neighbors left food by her doorstep—a plate of chicken wate and gomen with injera—but Sosina rarely ate the food. What was the point of eating?

A couple of weeks passed. One early morning, Sosina's neighbors were awakened by a strong smell of smoke coming from Sosina's house. They dashed out to save Sosina before the fire spread to the entire house, but to their dismay, it was too late. Sosina was already dead. All they could do was extinguish the fire and save the house from burning down completely.

Early one afternoon, Fanaye and Buzunash were enjoying their usual coffee break with two other women from the neighborhood, chatting about the daughter of one of the neighbors who had gotten pregnant from a young man who lived nearby. The girl's parents were pressuring his parents to force him to marry her.

A stranger appeared at the bar. The women had never seen this man before. "We have a new customer," Buzunash said as she got up. "Welcome to Bar Addis."

The man appeared unusually grim. "I'm here to see Sosina's mother," the man mumbled.

Deeply startled and worried, Buzunash signaled to Fanaye with a wave of her hand. "This gentleman wants to talk to you," she told her.

Fanaye immediately sensed that something was very wrong. Her stomach tightened, and her heart began to pound. The man could barely look her in the face. "There's been an accident," he whispered.

She knew something had happened to Sosina even before he mentioned her name.

The man whispered, "You might want to hear this privately."

"There's no one here to hide from," Fanaye said. "Please, just say it."

The man glanced down, then explained how Sosina had fallen asleep while sparks flying from the fire burning in the stove ignited the masoba, a low table made of colorful straw.

Fanaye became dizzy and collapsed into a chair as if the weight of the entire universe had fallen upon her. Buzunash stepped forward. "What happened?" The man explained, "Sosina died of smoke inhalation before the fire could be put out. Because no one knew her parents or relatives to notify, Sosina's body was interred at the local cemetery. While rummaging through the charred remains of the house, someone found a small note in a box, unfinished. The letter was addressed to her mother at Bar Addis. I was put in charge of finding this place and notifying her mother."

"Oh, my poor baby!" Fanaye wailed. "My poor misunderstood baby girl. How could this happen to you?" Thoughts raged through her mind: I let my sweet Sosina leave this world so soon; I could have done more to help her; I should have tried harder to reach her.

For a long time, Fanaye was beyond perturbed about Sosina's short and tortured life. Had she done enough? She wondered. The very thought would overwhelm her. On many occasions, she'd visit Sosina's grave at Saint Gabriel's church. She would bring food for the beggars. Then she would pass the eucalyptus trees standing tall and sycamores spreading their branches wide, finally stopping where the palm trees were gently swaying in the breeze, kneeling and kissing Sosina's gravestone. She'd sit gathering her thoughts. After a while, she would begin talking as if Sosina was listening. "The flowers around you are growing nicely. I am not sure, but I thought I saw a brown cat. Maybe she came to visit you too, knowing how much you love cats. I miss you, and this is the closest I can get to be near you." Her mind would go over many memories, the good and not so good. Sometimes she would be sentimental and cry, "I wish at least you had met your grandparents."

Shortly after Sosina's death, Fanaye decided it was time to go to Dow-Dow with Zenite. But Buzunash had woken up in great agony. Later, the doctor told them that she had kidney stones and needed to be operated on. This left Fanaye no choice but to cancel her trip. Once again, her dream of joining her family was crushed. She had also spent a great deal of money, which she had paid for in advance, for the guide and the supplies for the trip, not to mention the presents she had bought.

Chapter 32: An Infatuation

Mengasha, a friend of Fanaye's family, had a friend named Yeskiash who had mastered several languages and was often tongue-tied in expressing his feelings about women. He was so uninformed about the opposite sex that Mengasha often teased him about this, "You'd make a good husband, but a lousy lover!"

One day, about a year and a half after Sosina's death, the two young men headed out to lunch. Yeskiash noticed two sixteen-year-old or so girls in their school uniforms coming down the street, holding hands while they happily chatted and giggled. Yeskiash focused on the taller two, the one with the captivating laugh. Ordinarily, he wouldn't allow himself to get distracted by a woman. From a young age, he'd been intensely dedicated to educating himself, afraid that he'd likely remain an illiterate farmer, like his father and his father's father, if he didn't find a way to leave his tiny village. At the tender age of twelve, he left his village for the city and never looked back.

But his resolve weakened when he saw this girl in all of her pristine, youthful beauty, her large, wide-set brown eyes and dazzling smile that exuded joy and vitality. Suddenly he was aware that his palms were sweating. He wanted to walk up and introduce himself, but he was woefully ill at ease and much too inhibited. Instead, he whispered into Mengasha's ear, "Will you just look at that girl!"

"What girl?" Mengasha wondered, pleasantly surprised by Yeskiash's interest. "You mean Zenite?"

"Don't tell me you know her! Is she related to you?"

"Well, my mother and Zenite's mother are very good friends."

Yeskiash blushed and asked him to introduce him to her. Mengasha called out to her, waving his arm in the air. The two girls sauntered over. Zenite introduced her friend Abarash, and Mengasha introduced Yeskiash, who was so nervous that all he could say was, "Hello. I also work with Mengasha." Then he stood quietly, as erect as one of Emperor Haile Selassie's guards.

Mengasha thought his friend was pretty hopeless, so he made up an excuse for both of them to leave right away. After they'd gone, Abarash squeezed Zenite's arm. "He's so handsome, isn't he?" she whispered in her ear.

"Mengasha?"

"No, the other one—his friend. What was his name?"

Zenite frowned. "I think it was Yeskiash, but let's just call him Mr. Serious."

"He was just being polite," Abarash said, still staring in the direction where the two men had disappeared. "I like him."

"Then you can have him."

"With pleasure," she said and playfully raised her eyebrows at Zenite. "But would he like me, too, do you think?"

The following day at work at a government office, a part of the Department of Finance, Yeskiash whispered, "I really like Zenite. I've been thinking about her. If she's sixteen, do you think her mother would agree to have her marry me?"

Mengasha smiled when he realized how innocent his friend was. "Just like that?" he asked. "After only one meeting?"

"I've already put a lot of thought into this. I know what I want. I only ask you to introduce me to her mother. Would you do me a favor?"

This was too fast. Yeskiash seemed to know what he wanted, so Mengasha agreed to make the introduction, provided he could speak alone with Zenite's mother first to explain Yeskiash's intentions.

A few days later, he took Fanaye aside in Bar Addis and told her that if Zenite was ready for marriage, he believed his friend, Yeskiash, would make a good suitor.

The whole proposition surprised Fanaye. She'd been preoccupied with the loss of Sosina and completely oblivious to Zenite's blossoming womanhood. "So, who is this special man you think is good enough for my daughter?"

"If I had a sister, I would beg him to marry her."

"Oh, he's that great, then!"

"Yes, he is, and hard-working, too."

Fanaye wondered if Zenite was ready for the responsibilities of marriage. She'd only ask that Zenite's husband be a kind and ethical man. Still, this marriage proposal had come so suddenly and unexpectedly that she needed time to think it over.

Mengasha sensed her indecision. "I know Zenite is very special and deserves someone equally special," he said. "But I think my friend is that special person, which is why I'm mentioning this."

Fanaye decided there was no harm in meeting with Yeskiash. Mengasha was to bring his friend over. On a hot and breezy day, Mengasha and Yeskiash stepped into Bar Addis. Fanaye guided them into the backyard beneath a banana tree. While Mengasha was dressed casually, Yeskiash was formally attired in a blue Italian-made suit and a cream-colored silk tie. His black leather shoes were immaculately polished. Fanaye watched, amused, as he removed a pressed handkerchief from his pocket and wiped the seat before sitting down.

Wasting no time with small talk and the usual platitudes, Fanaye asked Yeskiash bluntly, "I heard you have a good job. Is that true?"

"Yes, and I'll be promoted soon."

He certainly seemed sure of himself. "Tell me what you have in mind."

Yeskiash took a deep breath before answering the big question. "As Mengasha has mentioned to you, I'm very fond of your daughter," he began, "and, with your consent, I'd like her to be my wife."

Fanaye watched him closely; he was all nerves. She trusted her unerring intuition, which told her that underneath his highly reserved demeanor lurked a genuine and honest soul. "My daughter is very special," Fanaye said, looking Yeskiash in the eye. "I'd like her to have a husband who would treat her fairly. I can only give my daughter to such a man. Would you be that man?"

Yeskiash looked at Fanaye and said in all sincerity, "I fully intend to treat my wife as an equal partner."

Fanaye nodded. "Where do your parents live?"

"They live in a tiny village in the Sekota province."

"So you came to Addis Ababa with relatives?"

"No, I came by myself. Otherwise, I wouldn't have had the opportunity to get an education."

Fanaye couldn't imagine herself intentionally leaving her parents for the sake of education, even for a month, so she found Yeskiash's comment a little strange. But she respected his resolve. Mengasha had told her how dedicated and focused Yeskiash was. Fanaye found his manner slightly stilted but decided not to make too much of it, attributing this to the boy's nervous condition.

In the end, Fanaye liked Yeskiash and, although she had a few reservations, she decided she'd be satisfied to have him as her son-in-law. Now, it was a question of how Zenite was going to feel about him.

A few days later, Fanaye decided to bring up the subject of marriage. She took Zenite by the hand and led her into the bedroom, where they sat together for a while in privacy. "Zenite, I would like to discuss something delicate with you," Fanaye said as she gently stroked her daughter's hair. "Something every mother and daughter need to talk about sooner or later."

"Emaye, you're making me nervous. What is it?"

Fanaye chose her words carefully, explaining how Zenite would always be her little girl, but in reality, she was becoming a beautiful young woman. When a young woman reached this age, the question arose of a suitable match for her. "A very nice young man is quite taken by you," Fanaye said. "I met him, and I think you'll like him. He's a good friend of Mengasha's. He's coming over on Sunday to meet you."

"Me? Marriage?" Zenite couldn't believe her ears. She knew immediately that her mother must be speaking of

Yeskiash. "But I don't want to get married yet. I'm still in school. I know who you mean, and I don't like him. He's too stiff and serious." Zenite made a face as if she'd just smelled something bad.

Fanaye was a little surprised by Zenite's answer. "And how did you come to that conclusion?" she asked. "What do you know about him?"

"I've met him already. I know I don't want to marry him."

"My child, I don't want you to think that I'm eager to give you to the first man who comes along, but I was quite impressed with this young man. He's polite and educated, but most importantly, he seems gentle and caring." Then, after a brief pause, she added with a mischievous smile, "Besides, he's also quite handsome."

"Maybe he is, but I still don't want to marry him."

"Okay, that's fine." Fanaye ran her hand through Zenite's hair again. "If that's the way you feel, let's drop the whole subject. I don't want to make you unhappy."

Although the matter was dropped temporarily, Zenite softened over the next several weeks, mostly as a result of Yeskiash's persistence and Mengasha's charm. Finally, largely to please her mother, she agreed to see Yeskiash.

Yeskiash arrived at Bar Addis at exactly two o'clock, looking dapper as usual. Despite all of Fanaye's encouragement, Zenite still wasn't thrilled at the idea of meeting up with Yeskiash alone. And sure enough, when she saw him enter the bar with a dead-serious look on his face, she shrank back in fear. He reminded her of an intimidating teacher.

As she had done before, Fanaye had set up a few chairs and a small table in the backyard. On the table, she placed some dabo kolo and honey drink. A bit awkwardly, Yeskiash handed Fanaye a small box of Italian pastries. "These are for you," he said as he straightened his silk tie, unsure of what to do next.

To give them a chance to break the ice, Fanaye went inside to find a finer plate for the pastries. Zenite sat down, and Yeskiash followed suit, but not before he'd pulled out his handkerchief and dusted off the chair. Then their eyes met, and they smiled at each other nervously.

"It's a good thing you are going to a French school," he said. "Your mother did the right thing by sending you there. It is wonderful to learn a foreign language and become familiar with another culture. I, myself, go to night school since I work during the day."

"What do you study at night?" she asked.

"I am learning Italian and French."

Zenite couldn't help wondering when this man had time to socialize or have fun.

After their meeting, Yeskiash sensed that Zenite wasn't impressed with him. He spent the rest of the afternoon agonizing over what misconceptions she had about him. That evening, Yeskiash met Mengasha at a tea room. When Mengasha asked him about his visit with Zenite, Yeskiash frowned and said, "I don't think I understand women."

"Does that mean your rendezvous with her didn't go well?"

"No, I'm afraid not. I told her everything about me. She didn't seem even a bit impressed."

Mengasha smiled. He knew enough about Yeskiash's nature to envision how the meeting probably went: Yeskiash talked in such great detail about his job that he bored Zenite to tears. "You know, I'm not an expert on women, but girls like to hear personal things from a man, and most girls or women in general love compliments about their looks. So did you tell her how much you like her beautiful eyes or how you were smitten by her dazzling smile?" Mengasha asked. "Did you tell her anything of that nature?"

"Well, she knows how I feel about her. I chose to marry her, didn't I?"

"My friend, you're clueless when it comes to women," Mengasha laughed. "You can't assume that she can read your mind. You have to actually say what's on your mind and what you see in her."

Yeskiash paused to consider this. Why hadn't this occurred to him before? He nodded his head briskly in agreement and vowed to take Mengasha's advice.

Armed with his new knowledge, Yeskiash approached Zenite the next time with unusual openness and candor. He let her see another, more relaxed and personal side of himself. At first, Zenite was surprised by this change in Yeskiash, and then, as time passed, she was even more surprised to discover that she was beginning to find him charming.

Chapter 33: New Beginnings

After six months and several meetings, Zenite and Yeskiash prepared to marry. Lamb was expensive, but Fanaye couldn't imagine a wedding without it. She reached into a chest and pulled out a pouch made of cotton cloth in which she kept her savings. She had plenty of money, so she chose to buy three medium-sized lambs. She was about to celebrate the most important day of her daughter's life.

When the customers of Bar Addis heard about Zenite's upcoming wedding, some of them enthusiastically joined forces and offered generous help. "I will get teff at half price from my uncle," one customer boasted. Another mentioned he knew where to obtain a dunquan, a tent that could seat at least two hundred people. Fanaye's friend Aselafesh, a seamstress, offered to sew the wedding dress. The resulting gown was then beautifully embroidered by a skilled neighbor woman. Another frequent customer and friend, Eyob, announced that he would like the honor of providing the entertainment. Fanaye was delighted, as the man was blessed with the sweetest voice she'd ever heard. In this way, Fanaye's community could give back to their generous friend. Luca, who was busy overseeing the renovation on Fanaye's house, insisted that it was time to add a toilet. Something for the big day.

Fanaye and Buzunash determined they'd need at least 150 kilos of teff. From this, they would make a lot of injera, the flatbread. The vegetables they would serve include cabbage, carrots, kale, tomatoes, potatoes, and onions. Berehane worked hard to produce as many of these as possible in their backyard garden. It took Fanaye and Buzunash a few months to make all the preparations for the food, along with the help of Berehane and his wife.

Weeks before the wedding, they began preparing the spices. They chopped onions, and garlic, and ginger. The week before the wedding, they began cooking. Huge pots of food sat atop several fires that bubbled away rhythmically.

The wedding morning, Zenite crawled tearfully into her mother's bed and put her head on Fanaye's chest. "Emaye, can't I change my mind? I don't want to get married."

Fanaye wiped Zenite's tears and said, "Every bride gets nervous before her wedding. You'll be fine."

"I don't want to be separated from you."

Fanaye nodded. She, too, was feeling sentimental but wanted to appear cheerful in front of Zenite. "We'll see each other all the time," she promised. "This will always be your home."

Soon, three of Zenite's friends gathered to doll her up. They all agreed that her hair should be twisted and put up on the center of her head like a bird's nest. Then, they helped

323

her with her wedding dress. The refined white cotton fabric embroidered with sky-blue, eggplant-purple, mint-green, and paprika-red threads sewn around the edges, from her neck down to her legs, adorned her form. The mixture of the colors and the intricate design were stunning.

Soon, even Zenite was caught up in the spirit of the festivities. Now she basked in the attention of her family and friends as she prepared for the ceremony.

Around noon on the wedding day, Yeskiash and five of his friends arrived in good cheer. His companions shouted, "We've brought the groom to his bride!" and pretended they were going to push their way into the house. Zenite's friends held them off. "Not so fast; let's see the presents you've brought. Where's the perfume?"

"You want perfume? We've got it!"

"Okay, where are the scarves?"

"We have them, too!" Then they put the scarves on the young women and spread perfume until the girls relented and allowed the young men to enter the house.

The wedding ceremony began in the early afternoon; the rich sound of ancient religious chanting filled the church. Two young boys circled Yeskiash and Zenite, swinging frankincense.

The priest walked in, took up his place at the altar, and hunched down to recite prayers in Gues, the old language used for religious purposes that very few people understood. Then, Zenite and Yeskiash approached the altar. The priest then began in Amharic, "Marriage is a covenant not only between the two of you but also between you and God. The bond is not just for joy and happiness, but also for times of sickness and distress until the end of life." He then inquired, "Are you ready for such commitment?" The bride and groom bowed their heads and said, "Yes, we are."

The priest touched the bride and the groom on each shoulder with the silver Coptic cross. "You have taken your sacred marriage vows into this house of God," he said. "May you be blessed as husband and wife, and may God give you long lives and healthy and happy children." He concluded by touching them again with the silver cross on their foreheads.

After the ceremony, the guests began to cheer "Ililillil, Iililil, Iililil!" as they strolled out to the grounds surrounding Bar Addis. There, they continued with more "Ililillil, Iililil, Iililil!" The wedding celebration started in earnest at around sunset. Plenty of stools and tables were set up to accommodate the guests as they arrived in couples and larger groups. The area was filled with the aroma of roasted lamb, chicken, vegetables, and a variety of rich sauces. There was plenty of tej and tella to drink.

When Eyob and his friends sang and played the kirar and the mashinko, everyone cheered, "Ilillil, Ililill, Ililil." Their friends took Yeskiash and Zenite to the center of the floor, made a close circle around them, and began dancing Eskista. Each of their friends took turns dancing. Zenit danced loosely and freely as if she had no bones in her body, while Yeskiash moved his body awkwardly, trying to shimmy his shoulders and leaping up and down to keep up with the music.

Fanaye, Buzunash, and Tsega joined the center. As Zenite began dancing with Fanaye, their eyes filled with tears, their tears flowing and mingling with each others. Despite Fanaye's joy for her daughter, it also brought the memory of the loss of Sosina, as well as the memory of her own mother so far away.

As the celebration died down around midnight, the groom's party escorted the newlyweds to the horse carriage, which took them to Yeskiash's small house. As was the custom, the newlyweds stayed home for a couple of days while their friends and relatives came and brought them food and beverages.

After their honeymoon, Yeskiash returned to work, and Zenite went to Fanaye's almost every day. Zenite stayed at her mother's house and then returned before Yeskiash came home. It didn't occur to her that, now that she was married, her lifestyle had to change.

Yeskiash began to notice that Zenite left all household duties and decisions up to the maid. She remained noticeably aloof from the whole process. Yeskiash was as tidy and organized as a military man. He believed his wife should engage in domestic occupations such as knitting, embroidering, and creating decorative touches to their home. For a while, he refrained from bringing up to Zenite what a wife's duties ought to be, but his disappointment in her grew as she remained unchanged.

The first time he found a big pile of crumpled sheets and clothes on the bed, he assumed Zenite was organizing the closet. But to his annoyance, he found a pile of clothes on the bed again the next day, and the next, and every day after that.

Finally, when he couldn't stand seeing the growing mountain of clothing any longer, he decided to have a serious talk with her. He called Zenite into the bedroom. Pointing his finger at the pile, he said sternly, "I don't ever want to see a single item on this bed that isn't a part of the bedding."

Zenite burst into tears at the harsh sound of his voice. "I always put them away before we go to bed," she mumbled and dashed into the other room, leaving Yeskiash completely befuddled. Zenite sulked the whole evening and vowed to herself that she'd move back to her mother's the next day.

As soon as Yeskiash shut the door behind him when he left in the morning, Zenite rushed off to her mother's. One look at her daughter, Fanaye knew that something drastic had happened. "What's wrong?" she asked as she wrapped her arm around Zenite's shoulders.

Zenite cried. "I don't want to live with that man. I'll never go back there again."

"What happened?"

"He's too serious and fussy."

After listening to her for a while, Fanaye thought there might be some truth to Yeskiash's complaints. So, she instructed Zenite as best she could and concluded with, "The first year of marriage is the most challenging one. Just be patient. You'll see that everything will come naturally to you."

During the subsequent months, Zenite did her best to follow her mother's advice. She began cleaning up the place. After the washing woman finished, Zenite folded the clean laundry neatly and put them away in the tall oak armoire that was the size of a small closet. She began dusting all the cabinets and pictures, the living room and dining room chairs, and other items. After spending hours doing house chores, she immediately washed her face. Doing the housework didn't bring her any satisfaction. Yeskiash was happy about the changes. Over lunch or dinner, he would tell

328

her some news from the hospital that he thought would interest her, but often he would listen avidly to the BBC News and read world history until he fell asleep in his chair.

She tried to adjust to her new role as an obedient wife but still visited her friends and her mother often, which frequently meant she wasn't at home at a time when Yeskiash came back for lunch. Once again, he spoke calmly but authoritatively. "I don't need to remind you again of your wifely duties," he scolded her. "Do you understand?"

Finally, Zenite had had enough. After Yeskiash left for work one day, she hastily threw her clothes into a cotton sack and hurried off to her mother's. She dropped her belongings on the wooden floor with a thud and announced, "I'm never going back!" Shaking her head, "I don't want to live with a husband whose head is buried in his books!" she shouted. "All the neighbors get together and chat over coffee, but he tells me I should stay home and read or do more housework."

Fanaye suggested that Zenite tell Yeskiash how she felt. Zenite responded, "He scares me. I'm scared to talk to him."

Fanaye took both of Zenite's hands in hers. "He's not a bad man. You've only known him for a short time."

"Emaye, I am afraid of him!" Zenite insisted. "I wish you understood! He doesn't even have to say much. Just a glance or one sharp word is enough to frighten me. I freeze up and am unable to defend myself."

329

Zenite was embarrassed to admit she had not inherited her mother's fearlessness.

Fanaye still believed that Yeskiash was a good husband, if perhaps a little too rigid, but she hadn't realized how deeply he upset her daughter. After thinking about it for a minute, she said, "Don't worry. I'll speak with him. I promise that after I speak to him, he'll no longer upset you." Zenite nodded her acceptance.

The next day, Fanaye went to Yeskiash's workplace. He shared a small office with two coworkers. As he led her to his desk, Fanaye noticed how perfectly organized his desk was compared to the others'. As she sat face to face with her bewildered son-in-law, in her usual direct way, she asked, "What's going on? My daughter is very unhappy with you."

Yeskiash answered her directly as well. "I'm a reasonable husband, so I give Zenite a lot of freedo… but I also have to tell her when she's neglecting her duties."

Fanaye understood his point, so she softened. She said, "Look, she's young; you need to be a little patient with her." She pulled her chair closer.

Yeskiash responded, "I'm trying my best to make her happy. In fact, I tolerate her weaknesses. I also give her enough money for the household. If she isn't satisfied, I'll give her more."

Fanaye laughed. "Yeskiash, can't you think of anything else that might be making her unhappy?"

Yeskiash shook his head, dumbfounded.

"Just think about what a young bride might need from her new husband," Fanaye added. "It might be just some simple words of understanding and care." After having said that, Fanaye stood up and left.

Although visiting her neighbors remained a large part of her daily routine, for the most part, Zenite was able to adapt to married life. Within a year, Yeskiash earned a promotion with an accompanying increase in salary. He decided they should move to a bigger home in a better neighborhood, in Kazanchis. He was proud of his achievement and assumed that Zenite also be proud and happy to upgrade their lifestyle. But Zenite didn't want to move. "Please, let's stay in the neighborhood where I've already made friends, not to mention that I'm within walking distance of my mother's home."

Yeskiash couldn't hide his confusion and disappointment. "Moving up isn't pleasing to you?" he snapped.

Zenite had no choice but to accept her fate. "If that's what you want, we'll move," she said. "But I would much prefer to live in this neighborhood. I like the people here. Besides, there are some big houses around here, too. If we moved to one of them, we would still be near our neighbors and also have the house we want."

Yeskiash turned a deaf ear to her arguments. They ended up moving to the area called Kazanchis.

A year later, Zenite woke up one morning, feeling nauseous. The next morning, she was again nauseous. With great effort, she made breakfast for Yeskiash.

After Yeskiash left for work, she stopped at her neighbor's house but declined the neighbor's offer of coffee. "Just this morning, even the smell of it made me feel sick. In fact, I threw up."

The neighbor and another woman who was there glanced at each other knowingly, smiling and shaking their heads. One of the women leaned forward with a serious expression. "Just out of curiosity, have you been menstruating lately?"

Zenite was embarrassed by the question. "I think I missed a month or two," she said.

"Well, dear, you're going to have a baby!"

Zenite's face got flushed. "Of course!" she said. "Morning sickness."

After many hugs, Zenite rose to leave. "I'm sorry, but I must go to my mother's and tell her the news; she's going to be a telukwa enate!"

Zenite barged into Bar Addis and found her mother holding court with close friends. "Guess what?" she said with a big grin as she rubbed her stomach.

The women looked at her, and they all cried out in unison. Fanaye was overjoyed beyond what words could describe. She rose from her chair so quickly that she nearly knocked it over. "Really, it's true?" she exclaimed as she kissed and hugged her daughter.

The women also began kissing her. "I knew it!" one woman shouted triumphantly. "I could sense that you were pregnant."

Watching the other women swarm around her daughter, Fanaye was as thrilled as she was when she had given birth to her own children. But beneath her feelings of joy and gratitude lurked a deep sadness. How she wished her mother could have shared this joyful moment! Even now, there was an empty corner of her heart that her parents should have filled.

To ensure that Zenite would have a healthy pregnancy, Fanaye took all necessary measures. She put together a list of what a pregnant woman should eat: millet, fenugreek, barley, butter, and medicinal herbs mixed with sun-dried ginger and garlic. Unfortunately, Zenite had very little appetite for the first few months. Nor was she diligent about taking the medicinal herbs Fanaye had provided. Despite all this, she did reasonably well until the fourth month of her pregnancy. Then one night, she woke up in excruciating pain. She dragged herself out of bed so she wouldn't wake her husband. Once out of the bedroom, she squatted on the floor and clutched at her stomach. She was horrified by the sight of blood, followed by more blood. She moaned loudly, fell back on the floor, and passed out.

Yeskiash awoke to Zenite's moaning. Alarmed, he rushed to her side and, looking at her on the floor soaked in blood, he noticed that she had had a miscarriage. He dashed to the nearest neighbor's house and rapped frantically on the door. Although she wasn't a midwife, Yetaferash grabbed her netala and dashed off with Yeskiash to help. When Yetaferash saw Zenite sprawled on the floor, she immediately got on her knees, put her head on Zenite's chest, and checked her breathing. Once reassured that she was alive, she turned to Yeskiash. "She'll be fine," she said, "but hurry and bring me some cloth. Let me clean her up a little, and then we'll put her to bed."

A midwife came to see Zenite the following morning. After examining her, with sadness in her voice, she said to Yeskiash, "I'm so sorry that she lost the baby." Then, upon finding Yeskiash so distraught, she put her hand on his shoulder and delivered her well-rehearsed comforting

334

words, "With God's grace and her youth, she'll recover soon, and you'll have many children."

Once Zenite's physical pain subsided, her emotional pain began in full force. She berated herself for not eating as her mother had so strongly advised. Yeskiash was sympathetic. He reassured his wife that the miscarriage was not her fault, but Zenite kept blaming herself. "If I'd only drunk fenugreek and eaten the barley bread," she cried, "this wouldn't have happened. I should have forced myself to do what I was told."

Zenite's guilt and grief lasted for several weeks. Fanaye was heartbroken by Zenite's miscarriage but also immensely grateful that her daughter was alive and well. She knew that childbirth was risky and that some babies were not meant to be born into this world. Still, she wished that Zenite had taken better care of herself during the pregnancy. Maybe she had learned from the tragedy and would do whatever was necessary for a future pregnancy.

Fanaye continued to console Zenite during her grieving while encouraging her to eat. Before leaving, she would embrace Zenite and offer words of comfort.

Yeskiash also tried to reason with Zenite. "Please stop punishing yourself," he said. "You need to think ahead, to the future and our future children." Then he hugged her tightly.

Zenite had never felt closer to her husband in their entire married life as she did at that moment. He had shown empathy and concern.

Three years later, Zenite became pregnant again. This time she was full of energy throughout the entire pregnancy and rarely experienced morning sickness. She gave birth to a healthy baby boy whom Yeskiash named Teodrose. This baby would grow into a strong and active boy with a hearty appetite.

For nearly two and a half years, Teodrose enjoyed the privileges of an only child. Then came a beautiful baby girl Zenite named Negest, after her father's mother. And another baby girl soon followed, whom they named Almaz. This child's resemblance to Fanaye was uncanny.

After giving birth to three children and suffering through two more miscarriages, Zenite, at the age of thirty-six, thought she was done with childbearing. Then, five years after the birth of Almaz, she became pregnant again. While she welcomed the news of her unborn baby, Zenite sensed that something was wrong, something she was unable to pinpoint. It wasn't just the usually early pregnancy symptoms of nausea and craving certain foods. She also felt totally drained and depleted, to the point where even her hands became weak. Her legs constantly ached. Admired for her golden complexion, like her mother's, she now was covered with blemishes and dark spots. Of course, at that time in Ethiopia, there was no way of knowing that her condition was typical of an illness later to be known as lupus.

As if the infant girl understood her mother's fragile condition, she exited from the womb quickly, causing almost no pain. Zenite was elated by the birth of her daughter, and in a burst of excitement and energy, found enough strength to hold her child. The baby was healthy and strong but so tiny. She named the girl Hewait. And in a prayer to God, she whispered, "Thank you, O Lord, for making my baby healthy."

Although he was overjoyed at the birth of his new child, Yeskiash worried more and more about his wife's health. His life with her had settled into one of comfortable intimacy, and he could not imagine living without her. Zenite looked thinner and weaker by the day. He took her to many doctors, and each doctor arrived at a different diagnosis. One doctor said the problem was her liver, while another believed it was her heart. She was subjected to x-rays over and over again. And there was no shortage of prescribed medications. When a particular pill didn't work, she was given another. But no medication seemed to help.

In the midst of Zenite's illness, Yeskiash was offered another promotion. He was offered the position of director, overseeing all hospitals in the Tigre Province. Although happy that his career was advancing, he was reluctant to accept the offer because of Zenite's condition. Her latest prognosis was that the illness might improve in a warmer climate. While Zenite was receptive to the recommendation of moving to a place with more hospitable weather, she hated the idea of living so far away from her mother and friends.

Fanaye, in particular, was adamant that such a long trip was treacherous for a woman in Zenite's condition. "The idea is crazy!" she insisted. "You should stay here with me until you're better." But Yeskiash reminded Fanaye of the doctor's recommendation that Zenite's health would improve in the new location. In the end, Zenite was won over by the practicality of the idea. With this newfound consensus between Yeskiash and Zenite, nothing Fanaye said could dissuade them from leaving, so she, too, resigned herself to their moving and began to oversee the packing of all the items they'd be taking with them.

Chapter 34: Moving

The day of Yeskiash's and his family's departure was a sunny September morning in 1958, the year of prolific developments by the emperor. He was modernizing his country in many ways—such as building factories, roads, more hospitals, etc.—and sending young students overseas for higher education in different parts of Europe. These students were mainly from privileged parents or royal families.

Fanaye, Buzunash, and other family friends gathered to say goodbye, shedding tears. They recited prayers and exchanged good luck wishes. "Please, this is not an occasion for sorrow and lament," Yeskiash reminded them. "It's not like we'll never see each other again. We'll be back often, and you can all come to visit us as well."

Zenite was glued to Fanaye. Yeskiash then took Zenite's hand and gently pulled her away from Fanaye. After the final goodbyes, Yeskiash and his family boarded the van and began to drive away while everyone waved after them.

The trip to Mekale was indeed long and arduous. The narrow roads were often barely wide enough for one vehicle to pass. The children screamed with fear as the minibus went through winding hills and valleys, taking breathtakingly sharp turns and coming dangerously near the edges of cliffs that dropped hundreds of feet. At one point, Yeskiash stopped the minibus, came back and closed the curtains on each of its windows, and curtly said to the children, "I don't want anyone to open the curtains, and no peeking out the windows. Just take a nap."

The children were obedient. They calmed down and soon fell asleep.

As they neared the outskirts of the town they would now call home; they passed a large sign that read 'Mekale Hospital'.

"Why are we going to a hospital?" one of the children asked with surprise.

"This is where we'll be living now," his father said as if that was an ordinary thing to do.

Confused, Teodrose asked, "Like sick people?"

"Just be patient. You'll see."

When they came up to the hospital, a uniformed guard opened an outsized gate. He greeted them with a big smile. "Welcome, welcome, we've all been waiting for your arrival, sir," he exclaimed. "If you follow the path to the left, you will come upon a group of houses. Yours is the big white stucco house, the last one on your left. There'll be someone waiting for you by the door."

They followed the instructions and drove up to their new house. As the man had mentioned, someone was waiting for their arrival. As soon as Yeskiash stopped the van, the man rushed forward to greet them and welcomed them to the house.

"It's like a palace!" one of the children exclaimed, and the others joined in, shouting with excitement. "Who lives here?"

"We do," Yeskiash said. "This is our new home."

Before he could finish his sentence, the children dashed past him and pushed the front door open. They ran inside, up the stairs, and went from room to room, their shrill voices echoed as they called out to one other.

The news spread that the new hospital director and his family had arrived. People who had also been transferred from Addis Ababa were happy to welcome them into the fold. Parties were given in their honor, as everyone was hungry for news from back in the city.

Since it was summer and school was closed, each day was a new discovery for the children. What they liked the most was the garden across from the house. In it were endless varieties of fruit for them to sample. They would shake the trees—figs, peaches, pomegranates, and more fruits they had never seen before—and break off the branches to get them. But their joy had become the gardener's nightmare.

Demesa, a stocky elderly man, had been taking care of the garden since he was a young man. He knew by heart how many fig trees, baby lemon trees, and orange trees were there and could also account for all the garden's vegetables and herbs, including the medicinal herbs. He cherished the time he spent in the garden, enjoying its peace and tranquility, at least until the hospital director's children showed up. They began to frequent the garden almost daily, running all over, shouting and screaming, ruining the peace.

And most regrettably, they often trampled the vegetables and flowers during their rambunctious games. I'd whip their butts if they were my children, he thought. This isn't a playground. Children don't belong here unless they're put to work, even if they are the director's children.

Finally, the gardener firmly explained that there would be no more garden if they continued this behavior, but his scolding fell on deaf ears. In the end, he could take it no more, so he decided to give the children their own little plots of land to cultivate. To his surprise, the plan worked. The children enthusiastically participated in every aspect of gardening, digging, planting the seeds, watering, and weeding. They ran to the garden each morning to see if anything had sprouted overnight. But after several days passed with no visible results, they became disappointed. "What's taking them so long?" they complained.

Yeskiash, never one to pass on an opportunity to impart wisdom to his children, said, "Every good thing comes with a little patience; if you've done your job right, you will soon be rewarded." And just as the children were about to give up, tiny shoots began to appear. Not long after that, one by one, succulent tomatoes, green peppers, bright orange carrots, and crunchy snap peas emerged. Life was abundant in that lush little paradise.

The children's delight was so infectious that Zenite wanted to participate as well. She asked the gardener to clear an area in the yard near the house. Eventually, gardening became one of the family's favorite activities and led to another project: raising chickens.

Now the children's interest turned to the henhouse. Mostly, they marveled at how the chickens knew which egg was theirs and waited eagerly as the tiny, helpless chicks mustered all their strength and pecked their way out of the shells. The children rushed out to the henhouse every day to see what their hens had produced overnight.

Before they knew it, summer had ended, and it was time to start school. However, there was one problem; because Almaz was so young, there was no appropriate school for her in the village. The only school she could attend was in Addis Ababa. So, Zenite and Yeskiash decided to send Almaz back to Addis Ababa to live with Fanaye. Hewait was still just a baby, so she stayed at home.

The first day of school was a bit of a shock for Teodrose and Negest. For one thing, their outfits immediately set them apart from the others. Almost all the girls attending school wore simple off-white cotton dresses and braided their hair in rows. Negest, on the other hand, wore a flowery print dress and a sweater, with her hair in two braids tied with beautiful ribbons. Her leather shoes were polished to a high sheen, and she carried a new school bag made of leather. Teodrose, too, dressed differently than the other boys. He wore full-length khaki trousers, a short-sleeved shirt, and leather shoes, while the other boys wore short pants and sandals. Some even went barefoot. Teodrose's hair was cut short, while many of the other boys had shaved heads, some of them had a tuft of hair leftover in the front of the head.

On the first day of class, Teodrose was asked to introduce himself. He stood up and announced that his name was Teodrose. "I used to go to school in Addis Ababa," he declared. The class went very quiet when he spoke. Everyone was looking at each other since Teodrose was speaking in Amharic, and they were just beginning to learn that language. Yet another palpable difference.

In order to get to school, Teodrose and Negest had to travel quite a distance by car. They also had to travel back and forth for lunch. After several weeks in school, the children had become acclimated to their new environment. Yeskiash decided they should have lunch at school instead of returning home each day. The lunch period was two hours long, leaving plenty of time for the two children to explore life in the small town. The local kids introduced Teodrose and Negest to many things they had never seen or tasted before, such as wild figs and cactus fruit.

One day, Teodrose and Negest followed the kids far up the road to the banks of a fast-flowing river. The boys jumped in and challenged Teodrose to join them. "No," said Teodrose, "I don't want to get wet."

"Come on," the boys taunted him. "We can float down the river back to school." Finally, one of the kids pushed Teodrose into the river and jumped in after him. Teodrose was terrified but tried valiantly not to show it. The water carried him along at such a swift pace that he soon found himself out of control. The boy behind him shouted, "Relax, let it take you." Teodrose did as he was told and tried to relax, but it was impossible. As soon as he started to let go, the water pulled him to the left, and his head hit full force against a rock. Teodrose tumbled under the water, thrashing and kicking until the boy behind him grabbed his shirt collar and dragged him to the river's edge. Blood streamed from a cut on Teodrose's forehead, but he didn't feel much pain. He only felt fear when he thought about facing his father—bloody, bruised, and with his clothes disarrayed.

Nothing he put on the cut helped mask the wound. That evening, as Teodrose feared, his father looked sharply at him and asked, "What's that? How did you get that ugly wound?"

"I fell."

Yeskiash glared straight at him, "While swimming in the dirty river?"

Teodrose could no longer lie to his father. "I didn't want to swim," he said. "They pushed me into it."

Yeskiash shook his head impatiently. "Please stop," he said. "Nobody can drag you from school all the way to the river." "I'm warning you, don't go anywhere near those lakes or rivers again. Now go let your mother put iodine on that cut before it gets infected."

But before Teodrose could leave to go to his mother, Yeskiash went on to lecture him about the dangers of acting silly and irresponsible. His father said he was a city boy and not accustomed to village life. Teodrose nodded and kept his head down. He had been considering himself superior to the other boys, but now he saw that they were superior to him in many ways. They knew how to swim and ride horses, donkeys, and mules without saddles and reins. They knew what was safe to eat and what was not, and they were more daring and fearless in general. Despite all of this, they were

346

still humble and kind. Instead of mocking him, they were willing to teach him all that they knew. Teodrose decided to stop acting superior and, instead, to learn from his new friends.

Teodrose was not the only one who learned to settle into his new lifestyle. Despite her illness, Zenite kept busy hosting frequent parties for Yeskiash's professional colleagues. Her gregarious personality earned her many new friends. In fact, when the children came home from school, they would find her surrounded by friends and visiting relatives. Even though she loved her children without reservation, they had to compete for her attention.

Meanwhile, back in Addis Ababa, Fanaye began to take Almaz to the construction site of her third house. Almaz was fascinated.

Soon, Fanaye had Almaz put the bar's bookkeeping in order. She also took her along to the market when she bought supplies. Almaz soaked in all the new knowledge with great enthusiasm.

Chapter 35: Mamo Gebo

In Addis Ababa, where Almaz went to school, she often ate lunch with her grandmother at the Bar Addis, and sometimes she brought friends along with her. One day, Almaz invited her friend Tutu. Since it was still early in the day, she was allowed to come in through the bar's main entrance. Almaz and Tutu stepped out of the blinding midday light into Bar Addis. As their eyes adjusted to the dim atmosphere, they imagined they saw someone sitting at one of the tables who looked amazingly like Mamo Gebo.

Mamo Gebo was a wild-looking giant of a man with a frightening face, a big matted beard, unruly bushy hair, and saliva dripping from his mouth. Everyone feared and avoided him. It was believed that the infamous Mamo Gebo could even tear lions to pieces! Children trembled when they heard his name. Women screamed when they saw him and would run away in panic. These terrified women wouldn't even take the time to bend down and pick up their netalas or the wallets they dropped. Even strong men turned pale when they crossed paths with Mamo Gebo.

According to rumors, even the most giant guards at the Emanuel Hospital for the mentally ill couldn't hold him down. He could crush an unlucky soul with superhuman strength; he was as strong as the biblical Samson.

Upon seeing Mamo Gebo sitting at a table, Almaz's first thought was that her eyes were playing tricks on her. If he was Mamo Gebo, then no one in the room could possibly survive because he would kill everyone.

"Mamo Gebo! Mamo Gebo is here!" Tutu screamed and ran outside as if a wild animal was chasing her.

Almaz froze, too frightened to make a move. She watched, disbelieving, as Fanaye served Mamo Gebo a plate of food. To Almaz's amazement, her grandmother put her hand on Mamo Gebo's shoulder as if she were affectionately touching a family member or any other average person! Fanaye whispered something to him and then beckoned Almaz with the same arm and hand she'd used to touch Mamo Gebo. Almaz hesitantly came close and held Fanaye's hand. When Fanaye saw the girl trembling, she said, "Don't tell me you believe those foolish rumors about him too?"

"Everybody is afraid of him!" Almaz whispered. "Why is he here? He'll leap up and kill us all, including you!"

"Look at him. Does he look capable of leaping?" Then, on a sudden impulse, Fanaye added, "Actually, I'll introduce you to him."

"What?" Almaz shouted and tried to jerk her hand away from her grandmother's, but Fanaye tightened her grip.

"Stop it!" Fanaye said, with discernible impatience in her voice. "Don't be a silly little girl. Control yourself." She then began to pull Almaz closer to where Mamo Gebo was sitting.

Luckily, throughout the commotion, Mamo Gebo had kept eating without glancing up at them. "But I'm wearing red!" Almaz whispered to her grandmother.

"I can see that. So what?"

"You know he doesn't like red. Let me get out of here!"

Fanaye paused with a frown on her face. She released Almaz's hand and pointed to the other room for Almaz to go into. Almaz bolted ahead of Fanaye so she wouldn't have to be close to Mamo Gebo when Fanaye's back was turned. Once they were in the next room, Fanaye said, "Sit down!"

Almaz did as she was told. Her grandmother sat down beside her and looked at the floor for a moment, composing her thoughts. "There's nothing to be afraid of," Fanaye said. "He's a good man who has never harmed anyone. Frankly, I sometimes think he should each a lesson to some of these fools. Everybody acts cruel and stupid around him as if he were some monster. The truth is, he's a very gentle person."

Almaz was surprised to hear such praise from her grandmother. Was she going crazy? Could her grandmother be talking about the same man Almaz was taught to fear?

"I want you to see that for yourself."

She then took Almaz's hand and began to lead her back to where they were. "I know you're afraid of him, but you really don't know him." She said Mamo Gebo's real name was Gethawen Demesa, and he wasn't born with the condition he now suffered. "When he was young, he was strong and handsome. Unfortunately, he inherited a sickness that made him lose control of his body and shake uncontrollably. When people treat him like a monster, he shakes and drools even more," Fanaye continued. "You can't blame him for turning into an angry man. I'd be angry, too." Then she looked down at Almaz. "Now, I want you to be a good girl when I introduce you to him. I want you to act as you ordinarily would when you meet someone."

After hearing Mamo Gebo's story, Almaz began to feel sorry for him and wished she'd known sooner. She was still a little apprehensive but agreed to meet him.

"You do know I would never make you do anything that would hurt you," Fanaye assured her. "Remember, except for his sickness, he's just like you and me."

With Fanaye by her side, Almaz stood at a slight distance from Mamo Gebo. But against her will, her hands began to shake. When Fanaye noticed this, she held her close. "This is my granddaughter, Almaz, Zenite's daughter," Fanaye said, turning to Mamo Gebo.

Luckily for Almaz, Mamo Gebo didn't even bother to look up but made a grunting noise and kept on eating.

"See you in a bit," her grandmother said casually, leading Almaz away. Relieved that she didn't have to shake his hand, Almaz dashed out of the bar.

On her way back to school, Almaz couldn't help but turn around several times to check if Mamo Gebo was coming after her. But he was nowhere to be seen. Why didn't he come after her if he was such a monster? Slowly, her fears subsided. She realized once again that her grandmother was right. All her fear was based on a myth. He was no longer the terrifying Mamo Gebo. Now he had a real name.

When Tutu saw Almaz coming, she and two other friends rushed to her side. All of them were anxious to hear about Mamo Gebo. "Is it really true that Mamo Gebo was at your grandmother's?" one of the friends asked.

The other one said, "I don't believe it! It was probably someone who looks just like him."

"That scary man looked so much like Mamo Gebo. He terrified me," Tutu admitted.

The first friend said, "I can't imagine Mamo Gebo just sitting down and eating lunch and not killing people."

"Oh yes, it was him," Almaz said, "Please don't call him Mamo Gebo anymore. His name is Ato Gethawen Demesa."

The girls looked at Almaz, appalled. "What are you talking about?" one of them asked. "Everybody knows his name is Mamo Gebo!"

Her friends laughed, thinking Almaz must have lost her mind. "I know it sounds weird, but my grandmother told me who Ato Gethawen really is; he's just like everybody else, except that he's sick."

"Does that mean if you see him on the street, you won't run away?" the other friend asked.

"Not anymore."

"We'll see!" Tutu said. I'll bet you didn't even get close to him."

Chapter 36: Zenite

Despite the doctor's prediction that the move to Mekale would improve Zenite's health, her condition grew worse. Even mild exposure to the sun irritated her skin and left her with more blemishes and lesions. She often said she felt as if her heart was melting between social events and kids' activities, and she found it difficult to breathe. Her joints would ache, and her hands would feel heavy as if she were carrying a heavy load of teff.

Nonetheless, she ran the house smoothly and ensured the children's needs were met. Zenite knew something was seriously wrong and became aware of her own mortality. The prospect of leaving her children motherless made her distraught, and she often wept for their misfortune. She realized she needed to prepare her children for that eventuality. She would take the opportunity to tell them something they would remember. So, one day she pulled them aside, told them to sit down, and began by saying, "I am so blessed to have you, and, as a mother, it's my duty to teach you and make you understand the importance of being good, especially to your sisters and brothers. You need to look out for each other. I know you're very young, but remember, if you love each other, you'll never feel lonely because you'll always have each other."

"And we have you and Ababa," Negest chirped. When Zenite heard the child's innocent comment, her throat ached with emotion, and she fought back the tears.

With her deteriorating condition, Zenite feared that her life might end before she would have a chance to see Almaz. So, it was arranged for Almaz to come back to join the rest of the family at Mekale. Also, now that Almaz was twelve years old, she could attend the same school like her older siblings.

When doctors in Mekale could not help Zenite, Yeskiash knew he must take her back to a hospital in Addis Ababa, the big city. Within a short period of time, he made all preparations to take her to Addis Ababa. On the day of her departure, Zenite felt extremely ill. She didn't want the children to see her in that pitiful condition, so she waited until they were asleep to leave. To not wake them up, she tiptoed to each child's room and said her goodbyes.

In Addis Ababa, Zenite was immediately admitted to the Black Lion Hospital. Yeskiash sent word to Fanaye, who dashed off to the hospital as soon as the news reached her. Losing Sosina had been difficult enough, but the thought of losing Zenite as well was unthinkable. "Dear God Almighty, please heal my daughter," she prayed desperately. "Her children need her. I need her."

Zenite was in the hospital for over a month. Back in Mekale, the children continuously pressed their father. One day, they were eating barley bread with jam for breakfast when Teodrose asked, "Ababa, you promised Emama would be home soon. Why isn't she coming?"

"Please be patient. She'll come home soon." He wished he had a better answer than that, but he couldn't think of any. He hoped the doctors would soon deliver good news about Zenite's condition, which he could then pass on to the children.

When he pressed the doctors, the news wasn't good. The first x-ray showed a spot on her liver. A follow-up x-ray showed the kidney was also damaged. Yet another x-ray pointed to the heart. Because of this, the doctors were not sure how to treat her anymore.

Soon the children started to doubt their father. His usual reassurances became empty promises. Yeskiash was torn inside. "What should I do?" he wondered. "Let them miss school? I can't do that. But on the other hand, what good father keeps his children from seeing their sick mother?"

They were now into the third month since Zenite had gone to Addis Ababa. Every day the children repeated their refrain. "Why isn't Emama coming home? It's been so long."

"She misses you, too," Yeskiash would answer, "but she needs more rest." He would quickly shuffle his newspaper to avoid further inquiries.

Almaz, in particular, soon became so disturbed by Zenite's absence that her schoolwork began to suffer. She couldn't think about anything other than her mother. One day, in the middle of the history class, Almaz heard the hauntingly familiar sound of dogs howling. She was never sure if these sounds were real or imagined, but she knew they must mean something was wrong. She had to see her mother. She shoved her books and pens into her school bag and dashed out of the classroom before anyone could stop her. She hurried to her father's office and barged in. Normally, Almaz would be respectful towards her father, but today was not normal. "I want to see my mother right now," she insisted. "No more excuses."

Yeskiash was sitting at his desk, writing longhand on a pad of paper, when Almaz burst in with her demands. When he took off his glasses, for the first time in her life, Almaz witnessed her father's tears. Yeskiash put on his jacket without saying a word, took her by the hand, and led her out of the office. The silence was oppressive as they walked together.

"Where are we going?" she finally asked.

"We need some fresh air."

"I don't need fresh air," she shouted and pushed him away. "I want to see my mother, now! She needs me."

Yeskiash put his arm around his daughter's shoulders. "Listen, my daughter, I know you have been patient," he began, "and I promise, as soon as…"

Before he could finish what he wanted to say, Almaz covered her ears. "My mother is more important than school," she snapped, angry and defiant. "She'll be happy to see me, to see all of us." She tried to pull away from him. Instead, Yeskiash pulled her closer to him.

Yeskiash, too, was feeling helpless. He believed that attending school was of paramount importance, and he hated the thought of any of his children missing lessons. "As soon as school is out," he said, trying to appease Almaz, "I'll take you to see her."

Chapter 37: The Force Of Inevitability

On an early winter morning, when the banana trees looked skeletal against the grey sky, the day Zenite died in Addis Ababa, a family friend called Mekale spoke with the housekeeper about Zenite's passing. The woman said Fanaye and Yeskiash were on their way and would be arriving by morning. The housekeeper, Tanach, took the news very hard. After crying her heart out, she went to the neighbor's house and told them the sad news.

Unfortunately, the next morning the neighbors came to the house before Fanaye and Yeskiash arrived. They stood by the door and began wailing, expressing their sorrow. The children had already been awakened by the ominous sounds of people shouting and crying in the house. Tanach dreaded telling the children the tragic news, but she had to do it. When she entered, the children sat up abruptly in their beds and looked at each other in fear. "Please, children, get up and get dressed," Tanach said, her voice cracking.

At that moment, Almaz knew that her mother—the mother she'd worshiped and loved so dearly—was never coming back. "No!" she cried out, and when Tanach tried to embrace her, Almaz pushed her away and flung herself on her bed, crying hysterically. Teodrose, too, when he heard all the commotion in the house, jumped up from his bed and ran to his sisters' room. Tanach embraced him with open arms.

"God took our angel away," she said in tears. "I'm so sorry." His sisters, crying profusely, rushed over and placed their arms around their older brother. Teodrose just stood there, stunned by the news.

Fanaye had hoped to be the one to tell the children about their mother's death. But from the crying sounds, she knew that they had learned the terrible news already, so she went to the girls' bedroom, putting on a brave face. But her body betrayed her—her puffy and bloodshot eyes, her slumping from sheer exhaustion. When the children saw her, they ran and flung their arms around her. Fanaye did her best to comfort them and reassure them that their mother was in a better place. "I'm still here, and we still have each other," she told them.

After the funeral, Fanaye remained with the children for a couple of months. Almaz noticed the wrinkles, the hollow eyes, and just how much their grandmother had aged in such a short amount of time. Not only did she look older, but her entire demeanor had changed as well. During those depressing days, Fanaye would often sit in one place and brood, rising only when she had to. In the middle of a sentence, she would often break down, then regain her composure. "You know, she has gone straight to heaven, for her heart was as pure as a white shama."

Bekalach and Saba, a couple of Zenite's friends, came to visit. Bekalach suddenly broke down into tears. "You know it's so true, 'Only the good die young.' That applies to your mother. Jesus must want her by His side."

Teodrose's anger flared up when he heard this. "Well, it sounds like Jesus was selfish," he retorted.

Bekalach's face turned ashen as she quickly pulled out her gold cross and kissed it. "O Lord Jesus, forgive this young man," she prayed. "He knows not what he is saying, for he's truly distressed by the loss of his dear mother."

"Nonsense," Fanaye said and took Teodrose's arm. "You're right!" she said. "You have good reason to be angry!" She turned to the rest of the children and asked, "Do any of you have something more to say?"

"I don't want to blame God, for it's a sin," Negest said.

Almaz took this opportunity to jump in. "I'm angry at God for taking my mother away. All my friends' mothers are alive." She then began to cry.

"O Mighty God, please forgive them!" cried Bekalach, jumping to her feet and raising both hands to the heavens. "They're too young and angry to know what they're saying. Please keep the devil from entering their spirits."

Saba looked intently at Almaz. "Even your manners are so much like your mother's," she said. "I wonder if you're as gullible as well." Then she sighed and, with tears in her

361

eyes, added, "I miss her so much already." Quickly, she got hold of herself and tried to refrain from crying. Instead, she decided to tell them a story that their mother had told her.

"You probably don't remember since you were too young—one of you heard a knock and let a stranger into the house," Saba began. "When the stranger saw Zenite, he said before even introducing himself, 'Weizero, you must warn your children not to be careless. They should ask a man at the door who he is and why he's there before letting him in!'"

"Zenite had never seen this man before. 'Who are you?' she asked. He answered that her husband had sent him, and he apologized for barging in. Zenite didn't know that one of you had already mentioned that their father was away to the stranger. He said that Yeskiash had sent him to tell her that he'd be away longer than he'd expected, so could she send a change of clothes and shoes for him. Your gullible mother not only gave him your father's best suit, tie and shoes, but she also gave the man a basket of food and some money for his long journey back."

Saba laughed with tears streaming down her cheeks. "Of course, your father never did get those clothes. I'll bet the thief was pleased. If everyone were as cooperative as Zenite, he would have an easy job of stealing!"

Teodrose and Negest laughed, remembering the man. "He was a thief?"

"Yes. That was my Zenite," said Fanaye, her eyes filling with tears all over again.

Soon everyone in the room shared stories about Zenite. There was one memory that Almaz did not recount and kept to herself—an incident when Almaz had overheard her father express his disapproval over something that Zenite was wearing. "This dress you're wearing hardly becomes you, given your body shape," he had told her. Almaz had been livid with rage. How dare he say something like that to her mother! She wanted to come to her mother's defense, but she controlled herself. Zenite, looking gloomy, headed to the bedroom to change into the new silver-and-brown flowery dress that she liked so much.

Almaz followed her into the bedroom and challenged her. "Are you really going to change your beautiful dress just because he didn't like it?" she had asked indignantly.

Zenite had looked tired of the discussion before it had even begun. She never revealed anything that transpired between her and Yeskiash, especially to her children. "I don't want to talk about this," she had said.

"It's really mean what he said. You look beautiful in that dress. Don't change it."

Her mother had looked at her with disapproval. "You shouldn't be eavesdropping."

"I wasn't eavesdropping! I was just passing by, and I overheard." Almaz paused and then added, "Telukwa Emaye would never change her dress just because somebody else didn't like it."

"That's because my mother doesn't have a husband," Zenite had replied.

"Well then, you don't have to be married either." But the moment Almaz had said that, she regretted it.

"I don't want to have this conversation with you," Zenite repeated. "Don't forget that you are the child, not the mother. Now go and do your homework."

Almaz was wistfully remembering this memory when Fanaye saw the expression on her granddaughter's face and gave her a quizzical look. "What is it?" Fanaye asked, but Almaz just shook her head, preferring to keep that memory private.

If it was true that Zenite had been gullible, while her grandmother Fanaye was nothing but fearless, a thief could get the upper hand with Zenite but could never scare or outsmart Fanaye. Once, Almaz had witnessed an incident that took place while she was living with her grandmother. After everyone had gone to bed, Almaz was jolted awake by an unusual sound. She whispered to her grandmother, whose bed was just across from hers, "I think I hear noises. Maybe there's a burglar in the house." When Fanaye didn't answer, Almaz tiptoed to Fanaye's bed in the dark and tried to shake her grandmother awake. But Fanaye wasn't there.

Now truly frightened, Almaz stepped out of the bedroom. Had burglars harmed her grandmother? Then she heard Fanaye's angry voice from the entrance to the bar. "You miserable cowards!" she was shouting. "Why in God's name do you bother us in the middle of the night? I'm warning you, get lost now, or I'll break every bone in your bodies!"

Almaz didn't understand why Fanaye was willing to confront burglars, especially when they had no guards or big dogs to protect them as many middle-class Ethiopians had. Almaz hurried over to where Fanaye stood, holding in her hands a thick stick. "Telukwa Emaye, please!" Almaz begged with a trembling voice. "Let's go back before they come in and kill us."

Instead of turning around and going back in as Almaz suggested, Fanaye turned on the lights. She went back to the front door and, with a booming voice, shouted into the dark, "Come on! I dare you to come here so that I can see your miserable faces. If you're not men enough to do that, then get the hell out of here before I kill you!" Then she turned to Almaz, who was cowering behind her. "You see, you have to

365

stand up to these cowardly wimps," she explained. "Never back down and let them see fear. Otherwise, they'll win."

Almaz still was not convinced. She ran to the servants' quarters to get Brekea, the maid. The moment Almaz knocked on her door, Brekea opened it and pulled her inside. "Bandits are going to kill us!" Almaz cried in a shrill voice. "Please go and call all the neighbors!"

Brekea hugged her and told her not to worry. "Your grandmother will make them beg for mercy," she had said.

Brekea then got dressed while continuing to reassure Almaz. "She doesn't need our help," Brekea said. "No one can harm your grandmother." After that night, Almaz viewed her grandmother as some kind of a heroine, and when she had told her friends that her grandmother had confronted and chased off the burglars, they scoffed and said she had made up the story or exaggerated.

Although Almaz loved her grandmother, Fanaye used to perform certain rituals that Almaz and her siblings disliked. When they were young children still living in Addis Ababa, Fanaye would come to their house almost every day. As soon as she'd arrive, she'd remove her netala and get to work. The first thing she'd do would be to seat the children in front of her and inspect their mouths for loose teeth. Each tooth was shaken back and forth gently to detect if it was ready for removal. If it were loose, she would rub the tooth with ashes

366

from the charcoal and continue to do this until the day the tooth fell out.

Another ritual was checking the children's hair for lice. As usual, she would gesture for Teodrose to sit on the floor while she sat hovering over him on a stool. He would approach her reluctantly, for he dreaded this inspection. She would comb his hair thoroughly with a fine-toothed wooden comb. Then she would run her fingers through his hair, parting it until she could see his scalp. As usual, she would find nothing in his hair, so she would let him go. Fanaye was more thorough when checking the girls' hair, believing that lice preferred long hair.

Later, when it would be Almaz's turn, Fanaye would narrow her eyes and bring her face close to the girl's head. No lice could take up residence in her grandchildren's hair under Fanaye's watchful eyes. But on that day, suddenly there it was! Lurking near the roots of Almaz's hair was a good-sized louse nesting comfortably on her scalp.

"How could this happen?" Fanaye cried.

Almaz became frightened—as much by her grandmother's raised voice as by the louse—that she jumped out of her chair. Fanaye pulled her back down with her strong hands. "If you didn't keep looking through my hair all the time, this wouldn't have happened," Almaz mumbled.

Zenite ran into the room when she heard the commotion. "What's the matter? Why are you so upset?"

"I found lice on her head!" Fanaye exclaimed.

Zenite tried to calm her mother down. "We'll just put some lice powder on her scalp, and then she'll be fine."

"No! There's only one sure way to get rid of them. She needs to be shaved."

Almaz stared open-mouthed at her grandmother. She was terrified that her mother might give her consent since Zenite rarely disagreed with Fanaye. But this time, Zenite was firm. "There's no need for shaving," she insisted. "Shaving worked in the past when I was growing up, but nowadays, there are many other ways to destroy them. You don't see girls with shaved heads anymore."

Almaz was relieved that her mother had defied her grandmother, but Fanaye's mind was made up. She would not be dissuaded from her goal and, as usual, she was the one to make the decisions—and was determined to shave Almaz's head. Almaz was terrified of facing her arch-enemies—an infamous gang of four girls at school—with a shaved head. She could die only once, but those malicious girls would ridicule and make fun of her a million times over. She would have to bide her time until they would lose interest and go looking for new prey.

As her grandmother sharpened her razor, Almaz had to rely on herself for protection. With all the strength of an eager eight-year-old, she jumped up, knocking over furniture, spilling a bucket of water, and darted towards the door like a clumsy animal. "I'm never coming back to this house!" she yelled on her way out.

As luck would have it, as she came dashing out, her father was exiting his car. In tears, she ran up to him and threw her arms around him. "What is it? What's the matter?" Yeskiash had asked.

"She wants me to look like a boy!" Almaz wailed. "She's going to shave off all my hair. I'd rather die. Please stop her!"

When Yeskiash learned what Fanaye was about to do, he said, "Come inside with me. Let's go and talk to her."

"No!" Almaz said. "I'm afraid to go in because if I do, she will shave my hair. Then I'll end up looking just like a village girl!"

"Don't worry. I'll make sure that won't happen." With that, he took Almaz's hand, and together they went back into the house. There, Yeskiash said with an authoritative voice, "I forbid you to shave my child's hair." Then, he abruptly turned on his heels and walked out of the room. Almaz stole furtive glances at her mother and grandmother as they sat in awkward silence. She felt invisible, for neither her mother nor grandmother said anything to her. Fortunately for Almaz, Fanaye never again brought up the idea of shaving her hair.

It was through these memories and the act of joining together to share them that Fanaye and her grandchildren found some solace from their grief. Still, Zenite was missed every day.

After Zenite's death, Yeskiash requested a transfer from Mekale back to Addis Ababa so the children could live close to Fanaye. He didn't know what else to do to ease their sorrow.

Fortunately, his years of hard work and impeccable ethics had paid off. He was not only transferred to Addis Ababa but within a year was also made the director of one of the largest hospitals. Once in the city, he rented a brown brick house close to Fanaye's, so everyone could easily make frequent visits to each other.

Chapter 38: America

Yeskiash was filled with paternal pride when he learned that his daughter, Negest, was one of only two pupils chosen from the entire Empress Menen School to go to America as an exchange student. Once she heard the news, the previously reluctant Fanaye was reassured, knowing that Yeskiash would never allow Negest to go abroad without the strictest guidelines for her discipline and conduct, and assurances from the school director regarding her safety and well-being. Weizero Zewidnash, the school director, informed Yeskiash that Negest would be chaperoned the entire time by her host family, even when she was not attending school. "No chance for her to get into trouble," Weizero Zewidnash said with a chuckle.

Fanaye was puzzled by the very idea of 'exchange students.' "If Negest is going to America, shouldn't an American student also be coming to Ethiopia?" she wondered. To Fanaye's dismay, she was told there would be no students coming there, only students going. "Then it should be called something else—not exchange student!"

A week after Negest's departure, a letter arrived, postmarked from Florida. Her siblings gathered around eagerly, tearing apart the envelope. The letter read:

I miss you all very much. My host family is very nice. In fact, they are a bit too nice. They love showing me off to their family and friends any chance they get, which makes me a bit uncomfortable.

In her next letter, Negest wrote:

Dear Ababa,

I miss you all very much. Often I visualize each of you and can almost hear your voices and laughter. I guess I never realized how very much I love you all. So please write to me soon, even if I don't write back. As I mentioned, my schedule is very busy. My English was considered good at my old school, but it's more of a struggle here. I'm trying my best.

Last week I was invited to a meeting of the Rose Garden Society. One of the women asked me, "How many colors of roses are there in Ethiopia?"

"I think one: red," I told her. Someone questioned me if I was sure there was just one. I sensed that she didn't believe me. "When is the bloom season?" another asked, and everyone laughed when I said, "I think all the time."

My host mother finally got annoyed with all the questions. "She's not a horticulturist; she's just an eighteen-year-old student and a very bright one."

I was not upset with them for asking those questions. However, a week before, I had been invited to an elementary school where some of the students were asking me even crazier questions: "Are you a princess?" "Do people have cars there?" "Would children over there like us?" "Do you have a dog?" "Are the dogs different in your country?"

Your Loving Negest

Ababa wrote back:

Dear Negest,

Don't allow anyone to make you feel inadequate, especially those unfamiliar with our culture and our history. You can educate them. Actually, you are there for that very purpose. They are eager to learn, so consider it your job to educate them. I hope you remember your history lessons. If you need to refresh your memory, I can send you some books that could prove helpful for you to refer to in your spare time. That will give you some backup if you are challenged.

Your Loving Ababa

During high school, Negest and Almaz corresponded quite often. After a year, Negest sent her sister an application for college admission. The news didn't surprise the family since Negest and Almaz had always been very close. When

Almaz told Fanaye that she wanted to go to America, Fanaye asked, "As an exchange student?"

"No. I'm going on a student visa."

"Isn't this the same as Negest's?"

In order not to confuse her, Almaz said, "Yes, but mine requires payment."

Fanaye nodded but still looked puzzled. "But why not go to college here and pay nothing?" she asked.

"Telukwa Emaye," Almaz said, "I really want to go to America, so please talk to my father."

"My advice is for you to graduate from high school and go to college here, in your own country."

"Telukwa Emaye, I'm talking about going to an American university! You can't compare the two!"

Fanaye smiled at Almaz's enthusiasm. "What's going on over there that's not happening in Ethiopian colleges?"

Almaz couldn't believe Fanaye was talking crazy about something that she had no idea about. "Telukwa Emaye, if anything, I'll be with Negest and will learn to speak perfect English," she said as patiently as possible and then gave Fanaye a big hug to reassure her. "They also have so many more courses in America that are so important!"

Fanaye hugged her granddaughter back, wishing she could make her change her mind but, above all, wanting happiness for Almaz. Of all her children and grandchildren,

Almaz was most like her. "Your mind is made up, I see," she said and reluctantly gave her consent, gazing into the distance as if she, too, was preoccupied with faraway places.

The idea of Almaz also going to America made Fanaye melancholic. She couldn't imagine not seeing her granddaughter for more than a week. She adored Almaz. Actually, if she were asked whether she favored Almaz above all of her grandchildren, Fanaye would have denied it. But there was no need for asking. The answer was evident by Fanaye's demeanor when she was with Almaz—the gentleness of her voice, the softness of her eyes, the smile on her face whenever she talked to her granddaughter.

Finally, Yeskiash agreed to let Almaz travel to America. Once it was official, Fanaye busied herself preparing Almaz for her trip. First, Fanaye bought the biggest brown suitcase she could find. Every day she added a few items she thought Almaz would need: a gabi, a cotton bed cover; several sweaters; more clothing. Almaz impulsively decided that she wouldn't need any of these things since she was going to America. So she delighted her friends by giving away most of her clothes. Almaz didn't think she would need anything from her homeland. After all, she was going to America, where everything was better.

She gave up asking Fanaye to refrain from adding more stuff since there was no way to stop her. By day, Fanaye would add what she thought Almaz would need, and then by night, Almaz covertly removed whatever items she didn't want from her suitcase. The more items Almaz eliminated, the more items Fanaye added. This surreptitious game continued until the very day Almaz left.

Several neighbors and family members came to the house to accompany Almaz to the Bole International Airport, where they would say their final goodbyes. When Almaz saw Fanaye looking so sad, her excitement began to fade. She couldn't bear to see Fanaye in such a despondent mood; it was rare to see her that way. Fanaye noticed Almaz watching her, so she tried to appear cheerful. "Don't worry. We'll all get used to it," Fanaye said. "It's not the end, after all." She wrapped her arms around Almaz in a big embrace, their two bodies seeming to melt into one. Then Yeskiash came over and tapped Almaz on the shoulder. "Time to board," he said, pulling on her hand. She went with her father, although all the excitement and joy she'd been feeling about going to America had now turned into regret and guilt for upsetting her family.

Yeskiash walked Almaz directly to the departure gate. There he asked the captain and the stewardesses if they would look after his daughter. One of the stewardesses said, "Don't worry. I'll take care of her."

Once the plane was ready to fly, Almaz started to cry. The stewardess sitting next to her tried to comfort her. Eventually, Almaz stopped crying and asked the stewardess, "Tell me everything about America!"

The Ethiopian stewardess began, "To tell you the truth, I don't find America so thrilling." She admitted, "If it weren't for my job, I wouldn't consider going there at all."

"Are we talking about the same America?" Almaz asked with surprise.

"Sorry to disappoint you, but America isn't what you might imagine it to be. To begin with, people of our color aren't treated very well there."

"What does our skin color have to do with anything?" Almaz asked, dumbfounded.

"I know it sounds strange, but you'll find out what I'm talking about."

"My sister lives in America," Almaz continued, "and she never told me this. If Americans were bad people, she wouldn't stay there. I know Negest would never hide such things from me!"

The flight attendant became somewhat irritated. "Well, I'm only telling you from my own experience, as well as from others," she said. "Unless your sister has been locked up in her room by herself, she should know better!"

Almaz pondered over this unpleasant exchange for a few minutes. It was the complete opposite of what she wanted to hear. She leaned back in her seat, closed her eyes, and wished she had never asked.

Later, Almaz saw a group of three young Ethiopian women sitting a few rows ahead of her, laughing and talking. She mustered her courage and went over to introduce herself. Without any hesitation, the girls welcomed her. "What's your name?"

In no time at all, Almaz had become part of the group. They chatted and giggled all the way to America. Almaz was scheduled to change planes in New York before completing the last leg of her journey to Florida. By the time they touched down at the airport in New York, her three lively new friends had just about convinced her to stay in the city for a night. Almaz hesitated to change her schedule, but the offer was tantalizing, and the girls—Dahany, Azeb, and Sebla—became more insistent. "Stay, stay," they chanted, their eyes sparkling. "My big brother, Dawit, is going to pick us up, and I'll ask him to show us New York," Azeb said.

Soon, a friendly man in bell-bottom pants and horn-rimmed glasses stepped up to the group. Azeb let out a whoop and threw her arms around him, smothering him with kisses. Then she introduced Dawit to everyone. When Azeb told Dawit Almaz just had to spend a little time in the city, Dawit said, "What a great idea! So, what's the problem?"

"I'll miss my flight," Almaz said.

Dawit looked at her ticket and pointed out that she had a seven-hour layover, and he'd be happy to show her a little bit of New York. "I'll get you back on time so that you can make your flight," he promised.

Almaz couldn't resist the offer. They all filed out to Dawit's car. The girls piled into the back of the tiny Toyota, and Dawit patted the seat next to him for Almaz to sit. "You'll get a good view of the skyline from here," he said. Dawit slipped a tape of energetic Ethiopian music into the cassette player, and off they went. As they drove west, the sun had set, and the sky was drenched in a yellow-orange glow. In the distance, all Almaz could see was a giant impenetrable-looking silhouette of buildings, a cardboard cutout interrupted by shimmering lights.

"Look," Dawit pointed as they approached the city. Almaz followed his finger to a building with a jutting spire. "It's the Empire State Building, lit up just for you!" They all laughed, filled with the joy of the wind in their hair and this wonderful freedom.

Almaz looked all around her in wonder, already loving everything about New York: the energy, the sights, and the colors. There was only up, with the tops of the buildings

379

culminating in a tiny patch of the sky now turning purple. Almaz's thoughts turned to her family and the thousands of miles that separated them. Yet she was happy at this moment, despite being far away from home.

Almaz was thrilled by a magnificent light show—bright colors, gigantic billboards, and signs with flashing neon. "It's Times Square," Dawit shouted so he could be heard above the din. "Isn't it beautiful? They call it 'The Great White Way.'"

As Almaz looked to the left, she saw the most amazing thing: a huge photograph of a man holding a cigarette with real smoke coming out of his mouth!

They stopped at a sidewalk café for a quick cappuccino. "I love New York!" Almaz exclaimed. "It's everything I thought it would be."

"If you like," Dawit said, "I can arrange for you to stay here."

Almaz smiled at the invitation but said nothing. Soon she grew nervous about the time. "I'd better get back to the airport," she said. "I don't want to miss my flight to Florida."

Chapter 39: Made In China

By the time Almaz arrived in Florida, Negest was away in California. She had been invited to a gathering of international exchange students.

When Almaz arrived at the tiny airport, she was surprised and disappointed. This was not the America she had imagined. It was nothing like New York. The airport was all concrete, small and unimpressive, populated with only a few passengers.

Just outside the arrival gates, Almaz saw a friendly-looking American woman holding up a big sign with "Almaz" printed on it. Almaz waved excitedly. "Welcome to America!" the woman said and gave Almaz a warm hug. "I'm Nancy, the one hosting your sister Negest."

In the parking lot, Almaz found something to be impressed by—the size of Nancy's spacious car. As they drove along, Almaz gazed at the passing landscape; she looked at the boring buildings scattered here and there, a gas station, and a few stores. Everything looked uniform and repetitious. She was anxious to get to the city that she'd imagined so many times. This town is not what America is supposed to be like, Almaz kept thinking. Where are the street singers and bands? She'd heard so much about them. Instead, all she saw was flat land and lots of green. She was anxious for the city to reveal itself around every turn, longing for the restaurants, movie theaters, cafes, and tea rooms.

Through the car window, Almaz saw a sign that read "The Best Hot Dogs in Town." First, she was puzzled, then appalled. Americans eat dogs, she thought. Nobody told me that! Why would they eat dogs? Were all the dogs she'd seen on the streets likely to turn into meals, like chickens back home? This thought made her sick to her stomach, and she wondered if she should mention it to Nancy, who was talking in full tour guide mode, pointing out different sites for Almaz's attention as they drove along the road. But Almaz saw and heard nothing; she was so preoccupied with the dogs. "I didn't know that Americans eat dogs!" she finally burst out.

"What makes you think we eat dogs?" Nancy asked.

"I saw the sign back there—hot dogs!"

Nancy had a big laugh. "Oh, no, we don't eat dogs; it's just a name," She laughed harder and harder. "Almaz, you're right. It's a silly name for food. Sorry for your confusion, I promise you—we don't eat dogs. We love our dogs!"

Almaz nodded, feeling both relieved and embarrassed.

The following morning, they drove into the heart of the college area. Nancy took Almaz to a hamburger joint. When the waitress served Almaz's hamburger, it was three times bigger than what she was accustomed to in Addis Ababa. She took a bite, but to her disappointment, it tasted bland. She set the burger down and didn't finish it.

Back at Nancy's house, Almaz opened her suitcase to change her clothes and discovered that she had little to wear. She'd packed a great deal of small baskets and jewelry, but very few clothes because she wanted to buy American clothes. She couldn't wait to go shopping. Since Nancy had a tight schedule, she asked her nephew, Michael, to take Almaz shopping. Michael dropped her off in front of the main entrance to a store called K-Mart, saying he'd be back to pick her up in one hour.

K-Mart was the largest store Almaz had ever seen. She didn't know where to look first. The store was blazing with fluorescent lighting but was also freezing cold due to the air conditioning. The clothes looked as if they'd been made for giants, and there were silly cartoons on the T-shirts. The fabric felt flimsy, not at all like her tailored outfits from Italy or Paris. She took a sweater off the rack and looked at the label: 'Made in China'. Why was an American store selling clothes from China?

Almaz roamed around the store looking for American clothes, but they all seemed to be made in places like India, Indonesia, etc. After nearly an hour of searching, her eyes started burning. Maybe it was time to ask someone to direct her to the American section. Almaz found a pretty sales clerk standing alone. "Miss, where are the American-made clothes?" she asked.

"Oh, you're a little one; you want the small sizes," the woman said, looking her over. "Follow me."

Almaz followed the woman, who clattered along in her high heels. They stopped at a section near the back. "Honey, here, these ought to fit you. They're small sizes," the clerk said.

Almaz eyed the clothes, then the clerk, and tried to explain again. "Small, yes, but I want American clothes."

The clerk smiled. "Oh, I get it! You want something with the American flag on it for the Fourth of July! Sort of patriotic-like, eh?"

Almaz shook her head. "No, not like that."

Now the saleswoman was getting frustrated. Almaz felt more and more baffled by their lack of communication. What did the Fourth of July have to do with American clothing? I must be confusing her with my accent, she thought.

As if she were reading Almaz's mind, the woman said, "Don't worry, I'll find someone who speaks your language," and went to find the manager. She returned with a man whose round stomach hung over his belt. "Senorita pweydo ayudartay con algo?" he asked with a smile almost as big as his friendly American drawl.

Almaz shook her head hopelessly.

The manager smiled. "Maybe my Spanish just isn't good enough," he said. "What can we do for you?" he said slowly, in English this time.

"I just want to buy some American clothes!" she said, a little louder now.

Finally, the manager seemed to understand. "Honey, you won't find any American-made clothes at K-Mart," he said with a laugh. "All our clothes are made overseas."

By this time, Almaz had come to the conclusion that K-Mart was an Asian store.

Why hadn't she listened to her grandmother and brought her own beautiful clothes along? Whenever she wore outfits from her Ethiopian wardrobe, she received many compliments, even if she was wearing old clothes. "You're dressed up. Are you going on a hot date?" people often asked her. Almaz noticed that Americans—young and old alike—wore blue jeans on most occasions.

Chapter 40: Change Of Time

When one of Fanaye's youngest customers, Amara, handed Fanaye a letter from America, she grabbed the letter and held it to her chest, her face brimming with joy. Then she handed the letter back to him with the excitement of a child. "Please, read it for me?"

August 16, 1973

Dear Telukwa Emaye,

It's only been a week now, but I miss you terribly. Most of the things you said about America have turned out to be true. It's not as exciting as I thought it would be—in fact, it's actually kind of boring. Nothing much is happening. I guess things will get better once Negest returns and school starts.

I find this part of America very strange. You would never believe the way Americans treat their pets. They build stores just for them! There are special foods, toys, and beds just for dogs! Even beauty salons! It's called "pet grooming," and I'm told it costs a lot.

Teluka Emaye, you were so right to insist that I take many clothes with me. I should have listened. I'll never find clothes as beautiful as the ones I had in Addis. I went shopping the other day and what I saw was unimpressive. Can you imagine you can't even find clothes here that are made in America! Telukwa Emaye, would you please send me the clothes I took out of my suitcase? That would make me so happy.

Another thing I have noticed is that none of the houses I've seen have fences the way we have back in Addis. Yet it's almost as if the fences are invisible because people don't visit without calling first. Here people don't come in and out of each other's houses the way we do. The women don't even get together daily for coffee. When I asked Nancy why there were no coffee gatherings, she just said, "That sounds nice, but who has time for that kind of thing here?" Please write to me soon. I can't wait to hear from you.

Your Loving Almaz

September 3, 1973
My Dear Almaz,

I hope this letter finds you healthy and happy. I miss you terribly. I know you aren't thrilled with America so far from your letters. I'm sorry to hear that; I'm not surprised. Our imaginations are more adventurous than what is real. But don't worry, you'll get used to it. The main thing is that you get an education and are healthy.

As you know, I've never been to other countries, so I can't say much, but I think it takes a while to adjust to anything new. In your case, going so far away to a foreign land with a foreign language and a different culture sounds overwhelming.

Of course, I'd be thrilled if you were near me. I know that going to America has been your dream, so give it some time. My only concern is for your well-being. Almaz, if you aren't happy and unable to adjust to life in America, you can always come home.

May you be healthy and happy.

Your Telukwa Emaye

December 20, 1973
Dear Telukwa Emaye,

How are you? I'm just fine—don't worry about me. I'm not too thin; it's just the photo. Did I tell you that being skinny is not a sign of poverty in America? It's a sign of sophistication, I think. It's considered good. Someone told me that poor people are more overweight here in America than rich people. Can you imagine that? Maybe that's why many people talk about diets (it means eating very little for a few months or so, to reduce weight). There are some people whose job is telling people what to eat and in what proportions.

Would you tell Akesta Meskeram not to worry about being skinny! If she were in America, everyone would envy her.

As always, I can't wait to get your letters.

Your loving Almaz

February 7, 1974

Telukwa Emaye,

I have good news. I joined the international club, and I can't tell you how my life has completely changed. Already I've made lots of new friends, and we seem to have a lot in common. The club has many activities, and some of the professors are interesting and very friendly. They take us on different outings, like football games and boat trips on local lakes and rivers. Some of the professors have even invited us to their homes for barbecues. I really appreciate their generosity.

Negest and I have already been invited somewhere for Thanksgiving and Christmas. One of the professor's wives attempted to cook an Ethiopian dish just for us to make us feel at home! She found a recipe for cooking chicken wate and injera, which made us very happy.

Her husband, Tom, told us his wife had been in the kitchen all day long. Finally, Mrs. Falstein came out with a steaming platter in her hands. With a big grin on her face, she said, "Here you are, girls. It was a labor of love."

When we sat down at the table, we were all so hungry and ready to eat. Telukwa Emaye, you should have seen what Mrs. Falstein cooked for us. The injera was as thick as kita—most of all, it was unrecognizable as injera.

But she worked so hard we couldn't disappoint her. "Well, it took a long time, but I did it," she said, smiling. "So please eat as much as you want; there's plenty more." Negest and I had great fun laughing about it later on.

Your granddaughter,
Almaz

May 10, 1974
Dear Telukwa Emaye,

I wish you were here with me; we could have gone together to the International party. I can't tell you how much I enjoyed it. The room was alive with the music, talking, and vibrant colors of flags from nations. I'd left behind my traditional dress. The other students wore their native clothes, and the table was even covered with ethnic fabric brought by the students. Unfortunately, I was the only one who wasn't wearing a traditional costume. When we were asked to bring a native dish, I was first worried that I wouldn't be able to cook something Ethiopian. I didn't have the knowledge or memory to come up with anything. Too bad that Negest was away and wouldn't be able to help me with this in any way. As you know, we never did learn how to cook.

But after thinking about it a bit, I remembered an Ethiopian woman in town named Tezeta, so I immediately called her. She agreed to cook for me. You wouldn't believe it! She took it on as though it was her duty as if she were a representative of Ethiopia. Instead of one dish, she prepared two kinds of chicken, lamb stew, kale with potatoes and carrots, one red lentil dish, shuro, and tons of injera. As you can imagine, she must have been up all night. So many students liked Tezeta's cooking and, for almost all of them, it was the first time they'd ever eaten Ethiopian food. I was happy to be able to display such wonderful plates.

That day I ate a lot and tasted just about every food on the table. I liked the tabouleh the best, the mixture of color and the tangy flavor. I found it yummy beyond description... I couldn't stop eating it. Right then, for the first time, I decided I wanted to learn how to make it. Yahoudit, the student who made the tabouleh, came from Israel. When I told her how much I enjoyed it, she was pleased and asked if I'd like the recipe. Jokingly she told me, "Almaz, you'd

391

better sharpen your knife because you'll be chopping vegetables forever if you want to make tabouleh!"

But a girl from Morocco told me that tabouleh comes from her country and that they make the best. I didn't care. I was happy with Yahoudit's tabouleh. It has become my favorite food (except, of course, for Ethiopian food).

I was glad everybody enjoyed the Ethiopian food, except for a few people who said it was too spicy. But it will never be too spicy for me.

Forever Yours,

Almaz

Almaz sat down to write another letter to her grandmother. She picked up her pen and tapped the pad. She wanted to share so much, yet she couldn't convey her thoughts. Could she tell her Telukwa Emaye about Brian? Almaz was dying to share her happiness about the young man who had taught her how to swim and was now teaching her to drive. She loved him too much to keep the secret to herself. Her thoughts drifted and came back to the letter. Better not tell Telukwa Emaye this news. Instead, she began writing:

July 16, 1974

Dear Telukwa Emaye,

Do you remember that headscarf, the dark green one? You were wearing it when you were walking quickly to Saint Gabriela's Church. Do you still walk fast? If you were living here, you probably wouldn't walk. Almost everyone has a car, even students. Can you imagine? I've started learning to drive and already have a learner's permit. It's so much fun to drive. My friend lets me drive her car when it's not crowded. She thinks I'm ready to take the driving test. When I come back to Ethiopia, I can be your personal chauffeur.

Guess what? Last week I went to Miami Beach. I saw a crew filming a movie. Anyway, a very nice girl invited me to go with her to the beach. She taught me how to float in the ocean. At first, I was scared, but everybody jumped over and under the waves, so finally I got brave and jumped in. Very scary but fun. I wish I could be as good a swimmer as you.

Until I hear from you, I will reread your letters. Telukwa Emaye, write me soon.

Your loving granddaughter,

Almaz

August 10, 1974

Dear Almaz,

You have no idea how much I miss you and how much pleasure your letters bring me. I don't know if I mentioned to you, but Buzunash's son Daniel has been working for Ato Demesa, an elderly gentleman who owns several factories in Addis and Debre Markos. Ato Demesa has appointed Daniel to be in charge of his business. Daniel has a good head for business. Buzunash couldn't be happier, as she was worried about Daniel's future.

So, Almaz, how are you doing in school? Most importantly, are you eating well and taking care of yourself? Write to me soon. As always, I'll wait for it like a hungry child.

Your loving Telukwa Emaye

Every week Almaz received a letter from home. Her father's letters were predictable and always contained the same message:

Study a lot and try not to get involved with the wrong crowd. We all miss you, so please remember to write back.

Almaz's letters were predictable as well. She reported back what she knew he wanted to hear. These reassuring letters appeared in his mailbox about two times a month.

I'm doing very well and studying hard. I received my grades yesterday, mostly A's. I thought you would be pleased to know.

Her father had said that he had left his family and his hometown at the age of twelve and gone to Addis Ababa in

394

search of education. As hard to believe as it was, he'd traveled for months by himself, barefoot and with little to eat, his journey long, arduous, and fraught with danger. He didn't travel by car or train. People in the villages traveled on mules, horses, or trekked on foot in those times.

When Yeskiash arrived home from work, unfailingly, the first thing he'd do would be to check the children's schoolwork. Anything marked as wrong by the teacher was totally unacceptable to him; even two errors out of fifty were too many. "What are those ugly marks?" he would ask in a disappointed tone. Throughout their school life, the children worked hard not to get poor grades so they wouldn't upset their father.

Chapter 41: Upheaval

By 1974, substantial changes had taken place in Ethiopia. Following a turbulent transition period after the ousting of Emperor Haile Selassie, the communist regime of Mengistu came to power. The military junta's taking over the country, followed by the emperor's death, was all too swift and confusing. Initially, people were so overwhelmed and in such a state of shock that they didn't know what to make of the transition. Public opinion was divided over the issue of welcoming or opposing the new government.

When Haile Selassie was overthrown, the country's youth was, at first, enthusiastic about the changes proposed by the new communist government. But they quickly turned disillusioned when the Mengistu government became oppressive and started to severely restrict people's freedom. The resultant opposition led to complete chaos, including the torture and murder of countless innocents.

Fanaye was devastated by the cruel treatment of the country's former leaders, who had bravely fought off the Italians and rebuilt the country, restoring every fiber of Ethiopia's strong and independent identity. But she soon cast the disturbing thoughts out of her mind and focused on accomplishing her usual daily chores around Bar Addis; continuing to fix up homes for her family's future security.

After the communist government came to power, they extorted money from the public in a variety of ways, all for *the good of the people.*" Office workers were asked to donate money to the state for the benefit of their country but, in truth, they had no choice in the matter. Soon, deductions were taken automatically from the employees' paychecks. This was accompanied by more restrictive rules and regulations that deprived people of their freedom. Even slightly critical comments against the government brought trouble. People were taken away, interrogated, tortured, jailed, or killed. One carpenter working for her and Luca disappeared. Disgruntlement spread quickly among the previously enthusiastic public. Their hope that the extreme measures would make everyone equal and share the wealth was wrong.

When one of Fanaye's customers defended the new government, Fanaye couldn't resist challenging his foolishness. "This could happen only in your dreams, not here or anywhere else," she said.

"We never had such an opportunity before. Why are you against it?"

"Do you really believe what you are saying?" Fanaye asked. "That lazy men and hardworking people should be compensated equally? No, my friend, I don't think that's what you want. But it's not going to happen anyway."

Fanaye had begun to express her disapproval of the government's practice openly. Many of the regular customers began to fear Fanaye's dangerous ideas, so they began to visit the bar less frequently. Even Fanaye's closest friends grew concerned about her persistent defiance of the new government; their usual carefree gossip and exchanges became noticeably subdued and restrained over coffee. Idle chit-chat had turned into a kind of forced conversation, punctuated by political outbursts from Fanaye that set everyone on edge.

A couple of months after Mengistu came to power, Fanaye and Buzunash were having breakfast when they heard a forceful knock at the front door. At first, they ignored it, thinking it was someone anxious to have an early drink, but the knocking grew persistent. Fanaye headed towards the door and shouted, "We're not open yet! Come back later."

"Open the door!" a woman's voice shouted. "I'm an officer of the Women's Community Association."

"Whoever you are, just go away!" Fanaye shouted back.

"It's an order from an officer of the government," the woman said, her voice strong and authoritative.

"Officer or no officer, just go away!"

The word "officer" terrified Buzunash. She pleaded with Fanaye to open the door. Fanaye ignored her and returned to enjoy her coffee. But Buzunash was so distraught that Fanaye finally allowed her to go and open the door.

A stern-faced young woman stepped inside, briskly walked over to Fanaye, and held out a piece of paper. "What do you want us to do with this?" Fanaye asked, grabbing the paper but not even looking at it.

"That's an official order. All of you are expected to show up tomorrow at the Community Center at 7:00 in the morning." She saluted, "Ethiopia Tikdem! Ethiopia First."

Fanaye sarcastically asked the woman, "And if we don't show up, what will happen?"

"Those who don't follow the regulations will be fined accordingly."

"And why do we need to go there?"

"To start with, you'll be exercising. We're concerned about the public's health and fitness."

Fanaye was enraged to hear this. "Here at Bar Addis, we're the officers who make the rules," she said. "So get out of here!"

The woman complied, but not before she curtly told them that they had better cooperate and show up the next morning at the Community Center. Fanaye made a dismissive gesture with the back of her hand, not even bothering to look in the officer's direction.

Buzunash remained deeply worried for the rest of the day, hoping that Fanaye would reconsider and go along with her the next morning. But Fanaye wouldn't budge. "Don't we get all the exercise we need here, all day long?" she asked. "What kind of a crazy idea is this, lining up in rows, moving the body this way and that way? I'm not going. You go if you want to."

Buzunash furrowed her brow. "We can't keep breaking the rules," she insisted. "You know they don't fool around with people who challenge them." Buzunash didn't sleep well that night. She awoke early and dressed for her appearance at the Community Center. Maybe Fanaye had calmed down overnight and changed her mind about going. But to her disappointment, Fanaye was more resolute than ever. "I'm not a monkey to jump at their command," Fanaye told her. "Let them come and try to drag me there. They'll have to take my dead body out of here."

So Buzunash went to the Community Center alone. When she arrived, the female officer, Meron, who had come to Bar Addis, recognized her immediately and said, "Good, you're here. Where's your boss?"

Buzunash pointed out that Fanaye wasn't her boss but her partner. "She couldn't come since one of us has to be there." The official looked down for a moment as if

400

considering. "Alright," she said. "But make sure she comes the next time."

One afternoon, three young men barged into Bar Addis, drenched with sweat and panting. Two armed, uniformed men appeared at the door behind them. One of the uniformed men pointed at the boys and ordered, "You there! Get out, let's go!"

When the young men didn't move, the other uniformed officer raised a heavy wooden cane over one of the boys' heads. Fanaye immediately approached and stood between them. "No, you get out!" she shouted. "Don't bother my customers."

The uniformed men looked at her with disbelief and then grabbed the boys by their arms to drag them away. Fanaye's loud voice rang out once more, "Didn't you hear what I said? Leave!" She paused for breath. "Look at you!" she continued. "You're no better than Mussolini's army. I wasn't afraid of their evil tactics then, and, by God, I'm not afraid of yours now. I said, get out of here, and don't touch these young men again!"

Buzunash, terrified by what was happening, summoned her courage and timidly approached the soldiers. "Officers, please, these are just kids," she said, cringing and rubbing her hands together. "What do they know? Let them go. Why don't you sit down and have a drink instead? It's on the house."

The officers ignored her offer. "We're only doing our job," one of them said. "It's for the good of our country."

"No, it's not," Fanaye butted in. "So don't waste our time." With that, she grabbed the cane from one of them and gave him a good whack on the shoulder.

Shocked, hurt, and humiliated, the soldier almost raised his hand to strike Fanaye, but he managed to restrain himself at the last instant. Such was the power of the taboo against disrespecting an elderly person.

Meanwhile, the boys watched with anxious eyes, uncertain about what they should do. At that point, the second soldier said, "Let's just go."

The angry one considered this for a moment and then abruptly turned and stomped out of the bar, followed by his buddy. Fanaye did not soften. "Now you young men, you go, too," she said, "and don't go around making trouble."

As time passed, the political situation increasingly affected the business at Bar Addis. Even the more vocal customers became quiet and subdued, seemingly coming to the bar just to drink rather than to socialize and discuss issues. Only Fanaye kept expressing herself about the political situation.

Buzunash continued to plead with Fanaye not to talk about the regime. When she told her son Daniel about Fanaye's reckless attitude, her son listened with sympathy. "There's only one solution to this problem," he said, "and that's to close Bar Addis."

She looked at him in surprise. "That's impossible," she said. "That's where we've lived and worked since we were young. I can speak for Fanaye, too, on this. Bar Addis is all we know."

"How about moving in with me?" Daniel suggested. "We have plenty of space. You could stop worrying about your situation, and I could stop worrying about you two."

Still, Buzunash was uncertain. "Even if I were to agree, you know Fanaye," she said. "She would never go along with this."

Daniel said it was Buzunash's decision and not Fanaye's. "I love my Aunt Fanaye, but she has no right to control your life," he said. "Besides, if I know her, she'd never try to prevent you from doing what you want."

After enduring the tension following a few more of Fanaye's outbursts, Buzunash finally understood that it was only a matter of time before the regime would bust them. The prospect of going to jail, being interrogated or even tortured terrified Buzunash so much that she approached Fanaye. "Look, I do not feel safe here anymore," she said

403

bluntly. "I constantly live under the fear that, any day now, they will come and take us off to jail. Daniel is also very worried. He really wants both of us to move in with him." She paused, weighing her words. "I'd like to take him up on his offer, and I think you should consider it as well. I'm not abandoning you, but I also hope you will understand if I move."

For a moment, Fanaye looked deep in thought. "Buzunash, I understand how you feel," she said. "Of course, you're free to do as you choose. But I'm staying here."

After she went to bed that night, Fanaye pondered Buzunash's decision. They had lived together for over fifty years. They'd worked side by side and eaten together. Buzunash is the sister I never had, she thought, like Yenanish back in Dow-Dow. Fanaye couldn't imagine them not living together anymore. She realized that any day now, they would have to say goodbye. She wondered how one said goodbye to a person with whom one had lived for such a long time.

Bar Addis was her home. It was where she had raised her children and known many loyal customers who had become a second family to her. Fanaye wouldn't exchange that for anything.

On a Monday afternoon, Daniel parked his blue Mercedes in front of Bar Addis. One of the customers who had been a regular for at least thirty-five years, an old man who knew Daniel when he was just a little boy, spotted him through the window. "Is that your son, Daniel?" he asked, squinting for a better look.

"Yes, it is!" Buzunash said proudly.

"Is Daniel old enough to drive?" the old man asked. "And whose car is that?

"It's his car."

Another customer overheard this and moved to the window for a look. "You know, this is not any old car," the customer said. "It's a Mercedes!"

"He's been blessed for being a good son."

The younger customers still couldn't get over it, but Daniel remained humble. The status and money he'd gained from his association with Ato Demesa had not gone to his head. Nonetheless, he did enjoy all the comfort and material goods that money could buy. He had no problem adjusting to a life of luxury. Buzunash, on the other hand, worried for his safety, especially under the new regime. She was convinced that it was only a matter of time before they'd take everything away from him.

The finality of leaving Fanaye and Bar Addis suddenly filled her with sadness. She had never imagined she would walk away from Bar Addis, and it was unthinkable for her to live without Fanaye. It had not been an easy decision. She wished she could change Fanaye's mind.

The day Daniel came to Bar Addis to take Buzunash away, she tried one last time to convince Fanaye to go with them. Daniel again tried to persuade Fanaye to move into his big stone house. "I think it would be good for both of you to be together, and we have plenty of room," he pointed out. "Why not come with us, Aunt Fanaye?"

Fanaye reached over with open arms and gave him a big hug. As much as she appreciated his kindness, she wasn't about to change her mind. Buzunash threw herself to the floor and rested her face on Fanaye's foot, crying profusely.

Fanaye pulled her friend back up and wiped away her tears as if she were a weeping child and said, "Buzunash, we can always visit each other. It's not the end of us, right?"

Buzunash nodded. Living apart from Fanaye would not be the same as living with her. But Buzunash knew she had to face the reality of the situation. She mustered her strength, stood up, clutched Fanaye's hand, and said, "No, of course not. It's not the end."

After moving to Debre Markos, her son gave Buzunash a huge bedroom with fine oak furniture. Even the bedcover had an intricate wool design, manufactured in Europe, which Buzunash had never seen before. The walls were adorned with paintings, such as the Last Supper, the Virgin Mary with the Baby, and the church of Lalibela. When she saw a painting of the crucifixion in her room, she fell into a trance in front of it. With tears in her eyes, she thanked God for the blessing of her son.

Buzunash thought this was indeed God's doing; otherwise; she could not comprehend how his boss would leave a young man his entire wealth and trust him to look after his wife and children. From Buzunash's point of view, the now-deceased Ato Demesa had wanted to ensure that his young wife and children would be well taken care of. He knew his wife, Lakash, was not capable of running a big factory. Obviously, as young and beautiful as she was, she would not remain a widow either. She would not lack suitors, but could he trust the man she would choose to look after the business and his young children as well? Ato Demesa had been an entirely practical man.

The man had not only chosen Daniel to run the business but also to marry his wife and become a stepfather to his children. Buzunash became convinced that Ato Demesa had chosen well when she noticed that Lakash appeared more like a happy bride than a grieving widow. Whenever she saw Daniel, Lakash's eyes sparkled in a way she couldn't conceal.

After a few months, Buzunash discovered that she'd grown accustomed to getting up early and working until the time came for sleep. She was not able to rest, nor did she enjoy doing nothing. But Daniel insisted that she shouldn't work while living at his house.

Dearest Fanaye,

I hope to God this letter finds you healthy and content. I cannot seem to get you out of my mind. Every day I think of you and our life at Bar Addis. Oh, how much I miss our customers, even the noisy ones! Yes, I do miss everything... I just don't seem to be settled here. Daniel and Lakash have been so good to me. Anything I desire has been provided— and more. Daniel thinks it's time for me to do nothing but relax. And Lakash, God bless her, insists that I don't lift a finger. She thinks she's doing me an honor by insisting I don't go in the kitchen and help out. I really need to get it into Lakash's head that not every woman enjoys doing nothing.

I sure feel that if you would change your mind and move here with us, things would be much better. I don't think it's good for both of us to be apart after such a long time together.

I still can't get over Daniel's unusually good luck in how he became the head of a household. I pray for his safety, for I hear a rumor that Ato Demesa's relatives are pretty upset with the will that allowed Daniel to retain this position. Yes, I know you told me not to worry about it, but you know me. Please do write to tell me you are coming soon.

Your loving sister,
Buzunash

Chapter 42: Old Days

After several more incidents and close calls that could have landed Fanaye in serious trouble with the authorities; her son-in-law and grandchildren insisted that she should leave Bar Addis and move in with them. Fanaye didn't want to move and was vehemently against this idea, "This is my home and my business," she said. "I'll stay open if I have only one customer left," she'd insisted.

Her son-in-law pointed out that even Buzunash had known when it was time to leave and move on. "You should follow her example."

"Buzunash did what she had to do, and I'll do what I have to do," she answered him back.

After Fanaye received a letter from Almaz, she decided to pay a visit to Girma, her favorite translator, and composer of letters. He was the only writer that seemed capable of transcribing her feelings into words. Fanaye paid no attention to the crowds as she hurried to her destination. When she entered his cramped office, Girma's eyes widened with surprise. Fanaye pulled up a chair and dictated her letter without delay. Before long, Girma paused and said, "Weizero Fanaye, I don't mean to be impolite, but I don't think it's safe to write a letter like this."

"Young man, nothing is safe in this world. Please just write what I say and don't contradict me."

Obedient, Girma lowered his pen to the paper and continued to write.

September 6, 1975

My dear Almaz,

As you know, I'm writing to you less often these days. Mail delivery is much slower than usual. I hear they are censoring every letter that leaves the country now, but I won't allow this to affect me. I'll write to you as I always have. I never thought I'd say this to you, but I'm relieved that you're not in Ethiopia right now. At this moment, I'm not proud to be an Ethiopian.

Almaz, our country is descending into chaos. Even my customers at Bar Addis are divided in their political views. Some say that the military is good for the country, while others tell me that Haile Selassie's grandson will soon be in power. Others are talking about overthrowing the communists. Bar Addis is no longer the relaxing place it used to be, and the atmosphere has become very tense.

When we Ethiopians fought the Italians, we were united, but now we're fighting each other. This will only lead us down the road to a bleaker future. There's no way I could find the words to express my feelings of disappointment

411

about our country. How I wish I could have you near me again.

Your Telukwa Emaye

As a letter writer, Girma was supposed to withhold judgment about what people wrote and not fabricate any details. But after Fanaye left, he reread the letter before he put it in an envelope to mail to Almaz. He knew beyond a doubt that sending this letter would seal the fate of both Fanaye and himself with the authorities: Fanaye, for expressing those views and him for being an accomplice to the crime by transcribing and mailing the letter. After careful consideration, he acted in a way he never had with any previous customer's letters—he would write and send an edited version of the letter, which would solve the problem. Fanaye would never know, and everything would be fine.

After a week or so, Almaz received the letter. As usual, her face lit up upon seeing the familiar white envelope with red and blue edges.

September 6, 1975
Dear Almaz,

How are you, my child? We're all doing fine. The winter seems colder than last year, and it is raining more. It's God's

412

Will. One can do nothing but accept such circumstances. How about where you live? Does it rain there a lot as well?

I'm glad you enjoyed your trip to Washington, D.C., to spend time with your Ethiopian friends. You mentioned that you ate injera every day. I'm glad about that. We're doing very well, and I hope to hear from you soon.

Your Telukwa Emaye

The letter puzzled Almaz. This just doesn't sound like Telukwa Emaye's letter, she thought. Perhaps the previous letter writer had been replaced by a new and impatient person? She wished Fanaye were able to write on her own.

That night, Almaz was filled with memories and couldn't sleep. She laughed when she remembered what she and Negest used to do when they were youngsters in Addis Ababa. Almost every Saturday morning, they'd visit Fanaye's place. In her bedroom, they'd pull out the big brown trunk from under her bed and sit on the floor, facing each other, with the trunk in between. They would grab handfuls of birr—paper money—from the trunk and toss it into the air, as if they were tossing dead leaves in the air, all the while screaming with laughter. Then they'd settle down to business. Fanaye taught them how to divide the birr into stacks of proper denominations. Soon they would count out loud and have neat stacks of fives, tens, and twenties.

413

After all the money had been counted, it'd be placed back into the trunk with the amounts indicated on small slips of paper. They really liked the job of cutting up pieces of colored paper and writing down the totals.

At some point, Fanaye would remind them to wrap the stacks of fives, tens, and twenties with a string. After they completed the job, Fanaye would praise them and hand them some birr for their work.

Almaz always knew that Fanaye was good with money. Once Fanaye accumulated enough, she put the money back into projects that she could see and touch. She liked building houses. Eventually, she ended up owning four houses, all of which were rented out and provided her with a stable income. As far as Almaz knew, she was never tempted to move into one of those spacious houses herself. Apparently, Fanaye had little need for luxury, so she continued living in the modest and small Bar Addis.

For some reason, this memory dovetailed into another memory. Almaz remembered her second day at summer school. Her Telukwa Emaye had never missed going to church on Saint Gabriel's day to pay homage to the saint's icon. Before she left for church, Fanaye had instructed her maid to ensure that Almaz and Negest didn't cross the street by themselves. Later, when the maid was ready to take the children across the street, she remembered she'd forgotten something and needed to go back to the house. She warned the children to remain where they were and not cross the street. But as soon as the maid was gone, Negest ran out into the street.

Suddenly, a big Cadillac came speeding around the corner. The driver honked his horn as he slammed on the brakes. The car screeched to a stop as Negest disappeared under the hood. The crowd gasped and screamed. Several men rushed to lift the car, but suddenly Negest appeared from the back of the car without a scratch and stood up. The crowd was in awe—it was a miracle!

Almaz couldn't help but smile at all these memories. On nights like this, when her memories got the best of her, she longed to return to Ethiopia and to that life that she'd left behind at the age of nineteen.

Shortly after Buzunash left Bar Addis, her old customers, Amara and Bekala, got engaged in excitedly discussing a variety of matters as usual. Soon two young men, casually dressed like college students, came in. Fanaye had never seen them before. While enjoying their tej, the new customers complimented Fanaye.

"This tej tastes great!"

Fanaye didn't think so since she had to use less honey and not enough ingredients due to shortages of supplies. Amara had heard the young men's satisfaction over their tej.

415

"You never had tej here before?" he asked. "Well, before this madness started, no tej bar could compare with Bar Addis."

"We are visitors, but so far, this is simply the best we've had."

"Where are you from?" Amara asked curiously.

"From Harar," the men answered simultaneously.

"Are you visiting relatives, or have you just moved here? Oh, I am not probing; I'm just curious."

Bekala laughed. "He loves questioning people. One might consider him nosy, but he means no harm."

The taller one of the new customers turned towards Amara with a smile, "No, it's okay if you want to get to know us. We arrived a couple of days ago from Harar to visit our sick grandmother, but our timing was not right. All these demonstrations are making us scared, but the students are right to fight back."

Amara responded strongly by vigorously shaking his head up and down in agreement. "Yes, I totally agree with you!"

Amara had seen a dead body thrown on the street a couple of days ago and, ever since, he had been deeply disturbed. So he felt like sharing his disgust with these young men. They should know the cruelty of the regime, regardless of the consequences, he thought. So he continued excitedly,

"I'd say, join the young people and fight to overthrow this evil regime."

Fanaye was glad for his bravery and reaffirmed his feelings. "I agree. They need to be stopped before they cause more harm to our young people and our country. What do you say?" Fanaye gestured towards the new customers.

At this point, the new customers both got up abruptly, looking severe, no longer friendly. One of them announced loudly, "We are commissars of the people! You are charged with subversion against the state!" Then he barked orders to Amara and Bekala. "Get up, let's go!"

The old customers were dumbfounded. They had not expected such a sudden twist to ugliness from these innocent-looking young men. The men roughed up and cuffed Bekala and Amara and shouted, "Move, move! Don't waste our time!"

At that point, Fanaye shouted fiercely as she shook her fist at them, "You two, get out! Both of you. And never come to my bar again!" Then, turning to Amara and Bekala, she said, "Don't let these cowards intimidate you!"

The tall and skinny one gazed at Fanaye menacingly, then said, "Well then, you too, join your customers."

Fanaye didn't even flinch.

The men took Fanaye and her customers to jail. She was among a handful of the elderly but was the only older

417

woman. The place was very crowded, and most people had been there, waiting for hours. Several armed guards in dark brown uniforms paced around the prison.

Fanaye had enough. "Do what you're planning, you cowards!" she shouted.

One of the soldiers commanded her to keep quiet, but Fanaye wasn't to be silenced.

"That's what the crooked regime wants us to do, be like lambs and be butchered in silence!"

Another soldier approached Fanaye, looking quite angry. "Are you crazy? We asked you to keep quiet. You are causing a lot of disturbance."

"I am supposed to stay silent while there are acts of injustice?"

The soldier stared at Fanaye. He looked like he was about to say something, but instead, he turned towards the other two guards and whispered something. After exchanging a few words, the guard came back to Fanaye and stood uncomfortably close to her. "You have to obey the rules. That's an order!"

She shouted even louder. "What rules? What do any of you know about rules?"

The guards didn't know what to do with a stubborn old lady like Fanaye. So they decided to take her to the prison office. When Fanaye came into the office, the clerk sitting behind a desk got up and went into one of the officers' rooms. A few minutes later, an officer came and escorted Fanaye to another room. Once inside the room, the relatively young-looking officer closed the door behind him, told Fanaye to sit down, then sat down himself. He was wearing a khaki uniform and a matching military-style cap. When he looked up at Fanaye, he suddenly exclaimed loudly, "Emama Fanaye! What are you doing here?" It was clear he had not expected to see her there. Then he promptly got up out of respect.

With his cap and uniform, Fanaye had not recognized him at first either. "Why, it's you, Mebrat! How could you become part of these murderers? Does your mother know what you are doing for a living?"

Mebrat smiled, then spoke softly. "I wish you would understand what this movement is about. It is for the good of Ethiopia. I am part of the progress. Our country should be for everyone, not just for corrupted greedy people who feel entitled to everything. It has to stop. No more!"

Fanaye listened but didn't believe this was the same sweet boy she knew. "They've brainwashed you! Don't you see they are no different than our enemies?"

"Emama Fanaye, you are a good person, but there are plenty of selfish people with no consciousness. They need to be awakened. The motto of the new regime is distribution and equality. Don't you want to see that happen?"

"I don't want to hear you talking about these evil people as if they were saints! Maybe in your dreams!"

"Emama Fanaye, you have been so kind in helping my mother and me for as long as I remember. You see? I call that communism."

"Are you trying to convince yourself that your job is your salvation? No, it's not." Fanaye laughed sarcastically. "It's an inhumane act to our people."

Mebrat stayed silent for a while. Then, with sudden resolve, he declared in an even voice, "Emama Fanaye, I am letting you go this time. But please don't get in trouble again. Just remember, if it were another officer, you would have been in great danger. There is no tolerance for dissidents here, even for ones at your age."

"I suppose I should thank you, but I pity you for getting involved with these devils."

She turned to him and made another demand. "Make sure my customers are released as well."

Mebrat froze for a second, then started to breathe heavily, as if he was about to suffocate. "Emama Fanaye, why are you putting me in such a difficult position? I could lose my job or even my life. I can't do it. It's impossible!"

"Well, then these innocent men could be tortured or killed, too. Look, if your mission is indeed to bring equality and fairness like you said it was, then do what's right. You know, thousands and thousands have died for their country, so you wouldn't be the first one to take a risk for your fellow countrymen. If you don't let them go, then lock me up with them, for I am not leaving without them."

Mebrat got up, looking flabbergasted, then sat down again with his head down. Finally, he said, "Okay, I'll do it. But please, you go first. Then I'll do what I have to do to release them. Your staying here will only make my job difficult. Please trust me; go home."

But Fanaye was not to be satisfied with mere promises, so she uttered her final words: "Alright, I'll go now. But I'll be waiting around the corner to see them released. If they are not out in exactly one hour, I am coming right back in here to raise hell!"

Mebrat agreed. Fanaye turned around and left, unescorted.

After repeatedly bailing out Fanaye, Mebrat had it, so he told his mother that he wasn't going to help Fanaye anymore. He was frustrated. Zewida warned her son, "If Wizero Fanaye gets arrested, I don't even want you to come to my funeral! And don't forget who fed you after your father passed away and I became too sick to work for her. Weizero

421

Fanaye continued paying me my full salary until I got better, which took me a year. Ha! Who would do that? Tell me!"

Now he had no patience. "Why is she so defiant? Why can't she stay at home?"

"Because she cares," his mother raised her voice. "Do you blame her for caring?"

He puffed, "All I know is that she is making my life difficult. I may get arrested instead. How would you like that!"

To that, Zewida stared at her son and left the room.

Six months later, in addition to more unfortunate encounters with the authorities, shortages of supplies made Fanaye's life difficult. In particular, she could no longer get the honey and other ingredients from suppliers required to make tej. In a way, this was just as well, since there were fewer and fewer customers every day; more often, there would be no more than three or four people. Finally, she realized that she could not run Bar Addis any longer, even if she wanted to. So, towards the summer of 1982, Fanaye reluctantly yielded to the family's demands and agreed to move in with Yeskiash and her grandchildren.

On the first morning of her arrival at Yeskiash's house, Fanaye awoke early and went outside. She thought it was unusually quiet. If she'd been at Bar Addis at this time of the day, she would have heard cars, horse carts, and the voices of many passersby. Although it was still early September, the month of Yekatit's sun was blindingly bright. The red and pink roses caught her eye as she browsed the flower garden. She bent down and sniffed them; the sweet smell of the flowers lifted her spirit. She then went back into the house and opened the wooden window shades to let in the sunlight.

Amsalach, the maid, entered with a colorful tray made of china. On it were two coffee cups and a brown clay coffee pot, barley bread, jam, and boiled eggs. Fanaye drank her coffee without waiting for Yeskiash. Soon Yeskiash appeared, holding a newspaper. He greeted Fanaye with a cheer, "Good morning! How was your sleep?"

"Not bad at all, considering I was surrounded by pictures of strange people staring at me." It took Yeskiash a few seconds to realize that Fanaye was referring to the posters on the walls depicting famous movie stars and sportsmen. He laughed and said, "Yes, I know what you mean. Teodrose never got rid of those pictures from when he was younger."

Although Teodrose had a good job and was a little over marriageable age, he was still single and living with his father. He had courted several beautiful young women, but when the time came to proffer a marriage proposal, Teodrose had ended each relationship, not out of selfishness so much as consideration for the women. He didn't want to waste their time while they waited for him to be ready. When people asked him why he didn't marry, he'd simply say that he just wasn't ready to settle down yet.

Yeskiash said to Fanaye, "Perhaps we should have Teodrose take the pictures down."

"No, they don't really bother me. Let's leave them where they are."

Yeskiash nodded, then raised his newspaper wide open in front of his face which was his usual habit... lost to the world.

Hewait burst into the room and embraced Fanaye. Fanaye then asked, "Aren't you going to be late?"

"There's no school for a whole week because of the demonstrations."

"Good for them!" Fanaye said. "Somebody has to do something about this regime."

"I wish father thought like you," Hewait responded.

Although Hewait, with her sparkly brown eyes, would have loved to join her college friends at the demonstrations against the regime, Yeskiash had instructed her not to do so. She glanced over at her father, whose head remained buried in his newspaper, oblivious to the conversation.

Noticing this made Fanaye wonder about her son-in-law. How could he remain so calm and indifferent to the world at a time like this? she wondered. "Yeskiash, you can't pretend

424

not to be affected by everything that's going on in this country."

Yeskiash set down his newspaper and said his primary responsibility was to raise his children in a safe environment rather than fill their heads with ideas that would put them in danger. Actually, Yeskiash was very knowledgeable about the politics of his country, as well as those of other countries. He possessed a deep-rooted conviction that all the ills of society came from a lack of education.

Yeskiash's impeccable honesty, integrity, and work ethic had paid off by saving his life. Throughout the earlier years, when some of the people in power were cheating, stealing, and building fortunes for themselves from the meager wealth of the nation, Yeskiash had never taken any money other than his legitimate salary. As a result, he had established a reputation for being honest and incorruptible. If he had only been corrupt, as director of a major hospital, he would have been in a perfect position to become very wealthy. Although he was in charge of choosing among the bidding merchants, he'd never accepted bribes or gifts from them. In fact, it was well known by all merchants that he'd even refuse to see them if bribes were in question.

When the communist party took over, one of the first things they did was eliminate corrupt functionaries, who were tossed into jails, and some were even killed. Yeskiash

425

was spared from these purges. Everything about him and his work was found to be in order. While this helped save his life and spared him from imprisonment, he was still removed from his job and replaced by one of the new regime's own men.

The regime also committed unspeakable cruelties by imprisoning or killing many intellectuals, dissidents, and people who spoke against them in general. Yeskiash not only lost his job, but the new government also took away a piece of land he owned, which Emperor Haile Selassie had given him. Yeskiash accepted his fate calmly since he had never thought of that land as his anyway. He had let the farmers live there and use the land to cultivate their crops, the profit from which they kept. Many of his colleagues had found him quite unique in this respect.

After staying for a week in Yeskiash's house, Fanaye began to feel restless. To make her situation even more complicated, Yeskiash's house was located on the outskirts of Addis Ababa, surrounded by good-sized houses, all isolated from each other and fenced in by stone, metal, or wooden walls. The cement-and-brick house may have been beautiful, but because of its isolation from people and other activities, Fanaye felt cooped up as if she were under house arrest.

How would she live the remainder of her life this way? She missed Buzunash and her old neighbors, not to mention the company of her customers. In this house, surrounded by a stone fence, she couldn't even see people strolling by. No use moping, she told herself. The past is behind me. I'll make the best use of my remaining years.

But despite her resolve, she spent a good deal of time feeling restlessly nostalgic for her old lifestyle where, for years, she'd been at the hub of activities. At Bar Addis, each day was full of novel and unexpected events, and all the news and gossip came readily to her. The memory of how many marriages she had saved and how often she had settled disputes and conflicts brought a wistful smile to her face. She lived on these memories every day when she couldn't see beyond the walls.

Idleness didn't agree with Fanaye. She tried to busy herself with the house and the family that lived in it, so she went into the kitchen to help out. There she saw the cook preparing elaborate dishes, which carried Fanaye's memory back through many years, to the time when Tsega had found her cooking too simplistic and tried to teach her a more urban approach. Some things never changed! Fanaye decided to leave the cooking to the cook and instead went out to explore the world beyond the surrounding stone wall.

She walked a great deal to get to one of the markets. There she saw four uniformed guards bearing arms. She approached them and asked indignantly, "Why are you standing here with these guns? Is the enemy coming?"

Startled, the guards just stared at her. "We're guardians, so we're guarding,"

She persisted. "I can see that, but what is it that you're guarding?"

Politely, but with a menacing undertone, one of the other guards said, "You don't need to concern yourself with that. Why don't you just move along and have a nice day."

Fanaye was not to be intimidated. "You're stupid enough not to know what you're guarding?"

As she walked away, one of the guards, enraged, shouted after her, "Do you know who we are?"

"No, you're nobody to me," Fanaye said as she crossed the street.

Another time, Fanaye went to Haile Selassie's palace and stood in front of it, feeling sentimental. To her, the idea of ousting their emperor was inconceivable. She approached the guards and dared them, "Who do you think you're guarding with our beloved king gone? Where were you when they took him?" The guards simply ignored her.

While most people were afraid of criticizing the new regime, Fanaye kept confronting all kinds of authorities. A friend of the family was so concerned about her reckless behavior that he asked Yeskiash, "Is Fanaye trying to get herself killed? It sure looks that way to me."

Yeskiash knew that changing the mind of his mother-in-law was as difficult as moving a mountain. He tried very hard to figure out what he might say to her, but he couldn't determine anything effective. Finally, he decided that perhaps she should hear it from her grandchildren. So, one night after Fanaye went to bed, Yeskiash gathered the children around in the living room. They sat patiently. "I've been worried about your grandmother, and so have her friends," he began.

"Is something wrong with her?" Teodrose asked.

"No, not physically. Thank God for that."

"What happened, then?"

Yeskiash lowered his voice and explained how Fanaye's defiant behavior against the new regime worried him. All of her criticisms of the new government could get her into trouble.

"I think she's brave," Hewait said. "All parents should be like her and join efforts to overthrow this savage regime."

Yeskiash raised his hand to exert his authority. "We're not here to discuss politics," he said sharply. "On these subjects, you know where I stand anyway. So just stop and listen." He paused for a moment before continuing. "All I'm

429

saying is that if your grandmother keeps going around and condemning the regime, she'll place herself in grave danger." This produced the desired effect. Visibly shaken and having nothing to retort, Hewait lowered her head and remained silent. "If you want your grandmother alive, talk some sense into her. Do you understand?"

They nodded in unison.

The following evening, Fanaye's small family gathered around her. Hewait wrapped her arms around Fanaye's shoulder while Teodrose got straight to the point. "I think you're very brave, and we're proud of you," he said. "But we're worried that you might get arrested, Telukwa Emaye. The police are cruel. They've killed and tortured so many people."

"Yes, and that's what they want. To terrify people into submission."

"Yes, but we love you so much; we don't want anything to happen to you."

At this point, Hewait started to cry and abruptly got up to leave. Taken aback, Fanaye grabbed her hand. She'd never considered the situation from their viewpoint. After quietly mulling over her feelings for a moment, Fanaye softly said, "Okay. From now on, you don't need to worry about me. I will not say or do anything to put myself in danger."

For the most part, she kept her word. She continued getting up early and had the maid bring her the roasted coffee to sniff. Yeskiash would join her and, as usual, he would resume reading his newspaper after exchanging a few pleasantries. This routine would remind Fanaye of Zenite's early marital complaints about his excessive reading. Fanaye found it hard to blame him. Wasn't every man obsessed with something?

Since there was not much else to do, Fanaye's passion increasingly focused on the past, and the wonderful memories that looking at the pictures of her children and Kebada evoked. As she settled into more of a sedentary life, doing so little, her body rebelled. Unfortunately, she developed a stubborn cold that wouldn't go away, even though she was taking all of her revered herbal remedies.

After some time, Yeskiash became concerned that Fanaye's cold had lingered for too long. "Emama, I think it's time I take you to see a doctor," he said.

At first, Fanaye was reluctant to go to a doctor, but she finally agreed when the cough persisted for several more weeks.

Chapter 43: The News

Dr. Toshoma was a slender man with a balding head and a straightforward manner. He studied Fanaye's x-rays with a stern look before setting them down on the table. He looked at them again, wondering if he had read them incorrectly. He took his time, pondering, looking for a different result, but to his disappointment, the x-ray pictures remained the same.

He wanted to talk to Yeskiash before Fanaye. Just then, his nurse stepped into his office and announced, "Ato Yeskiash is here."

After Yeskiash entered and sat down, Dr. Toshoma, looking sad, said, "I wish I had good news," he said, "but things don't look promising."

Yeskiash frowned. "I know she's been coughing for a while, but I didn't think it was that bad. She's a strong woman."

"Unfortunately, her x-rays don't agree," Dr. Toshoma said.

In disbelief, Yeskiash picked up the x-rays and stared at them. Yeskiash was familiar with medical information and reading x-ray films. What he was looking at was an advanced tumor.

Back at home, when Yeskiash was sure that Fanaye had gone to her room, he called his children into the living room.

After they gathered around the table, Yeskiash began, "As you know, your grandmother hasn't been feeling well lately. I don't want to alarm you, but the doctor thinks she has cancer."

The word cancer left them speechless. "How bad is it?" Teodrose asked, with fear in his voice.

While Yeskiash tried to think of how to answer honestly without making things worse, Hewait said abruptly, "I think she just has a bad cold. Not cancer."

Yeskiash admitted that he also had a hard time believing the diagnosis. Still, he believed she could be cured. "I'll make sure she gets the best treatment," he assured them.

"I think they made a mistake," Hewait added.

He took a breath and said, "I wish that were the case, but the x-rays look otherwise."

Hewait's eyes widened. "That means Telukwa Emaye could die!" she cried.

Her father reached for her hand. "Your grandmother is a strong woman; don't worry. But it's time you all do your part, which is to spend more time with her."

Yeskiash could see the gloomy expressions on their faces. He hated having to give them such bad news. Later that evening, he sat down next to Fanaye and, after mustering his courage, he told her the truth. "Emama, the x-rays showed that something is wrong with your throat."

433

"What's wrong with it?"

Yeskiash lowered his voice and said, "It seems you have a kind of cancer." He hoped that the news wouldn't depress her too much.

Fanaye took the news calmly. "Well, I'll just have to take some more herbal remedies then."

Yeskiash nodded. "Yes, that's a good idea. Also, the doctor is going to prescribe a medicine to shrink the tumor."

"At least we know why I've been coughing."

Her response was so calm, that Yeskiash wondered why he'd been so worried about how Fanaye would take the news. I should have known how well she would take it, he thought. "Herbal remedies are fine, but I think you need to take the doctor's prescriptions as well," he added. But this was where Fanaye drew the line. "Thank you, son, but I think I prefer to stick to my own remedies. Look what happened to my Zenite from taking all those drugs!"

"Nowadays, doctors are far more advanced," he argued. "You should take advantage of what they have to offer."

"Well, I'll give it some thought," Fanaye said casually, although she said it only to pacify him.

After a couple of months of taking her remedies and seeing little improvement in her condition, Fanaye considered giving modern medicine a chance. "Well,

Yeskiash, maybe you're right," she admitted. "I should try the doctor's prescription. Who knows, maybe it will work."

Yeskiash smiled and said joyfully, "I'm glad you've changed your mind." He got up and retrieved the bottles he had kept waiting in a cabinet.

The almost empty medicine bottle stood on Fanaye's bureau next to her bed. It was the second refill. She'd been taking a pill twice a day as the doctor had instructed. However over the past few days, her throat had grown much worse, and swallowing had become extremely difficult.

She picked up the pill bottle and began to talk to it. "It's hard to imagine what good can come from taking you little things." Still holding the bottle, she told it her decision, as if it would understand. "It's time I stop taking you."

Just then, Amsalach came into the room with freshly roasted coffee and passed the pot under Fanaye's nose. The familiar aroma lightened Fanaye's mood. Nothing else mattered much; coffee remained one of life's little pleasures.

Yeskiash approached Fanaye cautiously. "Did you get a good night's sleep?"

To spare him the details of her new aches, she just said, "Yes, I'm okay."

"Good," he said. "This coming Monday, I'll take you to see your doctor. I'm sure he will see the improvement."

"I'll see how I feel by then." She decided not to tell him that she was no longer taking the pills.

As planned, Yeskiash took Fanaye to the hospital on Monday. After a little chat with the doctor, he left Fanaye and Dr. Toshoma alone. Dr. Toshoma was cordial as usual. In the few times that he'd seen Fanaye, he'd concluded that she was a fighter. He pulled up a chair for her. "How are you feeling?" he asked.

"Not well."

"Can you tell me more?"

"You should know since you took so many x-rays. Can't you tell my condition?"

Her confrontation took him by surprise. He was not accustomed to patients like Fanaye. On the contrary, his patients usually humbled themselves before him, as if their humility would help them gain favors and heal them more quickly. Now, sitting face to face with a challenging woman, it was he who was seeking respect from his patient. The doctor smiled and lowered his voice as if he were a little boy trying to please his mother. "Weizero Fanaye, the machine reveals a great deal, but I would also like to hear from you. So, please tell me how you feel. Is your condition better or worse?"

Fanaye was not smiling. "You tell me what you see in that x-ray. Otherwise, my coming to see you is of no use."

436

Dr. Toshoma lowered his voice, even more, attempting to calm his patient. "From the result of the x-ray, I suggest we increase the dose for two weeks, and then we'll take another approach," he explained. "I understand your frustration, but in the end, you'll see good results. And I'll continue to do my best."

Fanaye's friends and family had been noticing that she was losing weight and that her spirit was ebbing. They came to visit her more often.

One morning, Hewait came in to check on Fanaye. At a quick glance, she thought the bed was empty. She left the room, assuming that Fanaye was in the bathroom, but she noticed that the bathroom was empty as well. She then went to the dining room to see if Fanaye was there, but she found only her father, having his breakfast. "Where is Telukwa Emaye?

"She's not in her room?"

"No, she isn't there."

When they went back to Fanaye's room, Yeskiash looked at the bed and whispered, "Yes, she's here."

"But, Ababa, the bed is empty."

He put his finger to his lips and whispered again, "Shhhh, she's asleep." He then added, "Hadn't you noticed how much weight she has lost?"

437

Hewait was appalled. "How could this happen in such a short time?"

Fanaye was having more and more difficulty sleeping. When her throat started to hurt, she would wake up and, after tossing about, would get up and open one of the windows. Luckily, the windows faced north and south, so plenty of sunshine flooded into the room during the day, which Fanaye welcomed. She would stand by the windows at night and look up at the moon and the stars. This reminded her of her childhood when she would ask her father, "Why only one moon, but many stars? Why is that one very bright?"

Now, as she looked up at the sky, in her mind's eye, she saw her parents and her little brother, as young as they were when she'd last seen them. She remembered herself as a young girl, running up the rocky hill overlooking Dow-Dow village faster than most of the other children, including the boys. She was agile, and she loved the challenge of climbing trees, which worried her mother.

It was hard to believe that over sixty years had passed since she'd seen her family. Now, as she stood by the window, taking in the chill of the night and the fragrance of the flowers, she deeply regretted that she hadn't tried harder to overcome the difficulties and superstitions that had prevented her from returning to the village of her birth. No doubt her parents had died, never knowing what had become of her. That pained her greatly. She closed the window and shuffled back to her bed. With great effort, she managed to pull herself into the bed and closed her eyes, heaving a great sigh and thinking, What good will regrets do me?

Later that night, she woke up from confusing dreams when, suddenly, a long-lost memory sprang into her mind, a memory that had faded away like the flowers on an overwashed dress. Now, in her mind's eye, she could vividly see Kebada's young gardener, Alula, the one she had liked so much. He was staring back at her, too. He was still handsome, and when he smiled, she could see his strong teeth, the color of white cotton. He still squinted when he smiled, and his eyes sparkled like two black pearls under a beam of light. He was naked from the waist up, sweat glistening on his muscular chest.

Fanaye smiled, remembering the incident that had led to his dismissal. She was amazed that the memory was so fresh after the passage of so many years. So many things had happened since then, a lifetime of happiness and joyful things, the friendships, the house building, and the bar—the births of Sosina and Zenite. And painful things, too, like losing them both at young ages. With the passage of time, even the memory of Kebada had begun to dim.

Just then, Amsalach came in with the roasted coffee beans for Fanaye to smell. This time, Fanaye waved her away. The maid was appalled at this gesture. "But I roasted it just the way you like it!"

"I'm sure you did. I just can't take the smell of it today. Please don't bring it anymore."

"I'm sorry," Amsalach apologized and hastily left the room.

Fanaye could no longer bear the thought of becoming a burden to her family or anyone else. This was hurting her dignity. Slowly, she began to accept that it was time for her to leave this life. Knowing she was still in charge of her own life brought her as much freedom as she'd ever known.

To hasten her journey to the other side, Fanaye stopped eating. No amount of pleading and cajoling made a difference. After another day, Yeskiash finally consulted with the doctors. They suggested that Yeskiash bring her to the hospital to feed her intravenously.

That evening, Yeskiash approached Fanaye and said diplomatically, "Emama, I spoke with the doctors at the hospital. They'd like to do some tests. How about if I take you to the hospital for a few days?"

"Absolutely not!" she said. "I'd rather die than go to the hospital. I know I'm very sick. Just let me spend whatever days I have left in this world with my grandchildren."

She sounded so firm and resolute that Yeskiash bowed his head in painful acquiescence. "As you wish, Emama," he whispered and left.

When her old customers heard Fanaye was sick, they didn't hesitate to visit her, even though for most of them, the trip wasn't easy since Yeskiash's house was on the outskirts of the city. They had to take a bus which took a good hour or so, and then walk for about twenty minutes. It was customary to bring something when visiting someone. On those days, thanks to the regime, everybody was short of money, but still, they couldn't go empty-handed. So, they brought dabo kolo. Their visit was like medicine to Fanaye. They would surround her and begin talking about the good old days, joking and teasing each other, laughing and laughing. Later on, when Fanaye got weaker and stayed in bed, chairs and a small table were brought into her bedroom. They came once or twice a week. On days they would stay longer, and on rainy days, Fanaye would ask Yeskiash to give them a ride back when he came home. And Yeskiash complied.

Fanaye awoke in the middle of the night to pee. After she finished, she looked at the mirror above the sink. She stared at her reflection as though she were a spectator. Her famously admired complexion was no longer there to be seen. Instead, she saw a skinny, ashy complexioned, and wrinkled woman. No wonder, she thought, her visitors looked at her pityingly. I might as well be dead, she thought. She headed to her bedroom and sat on a cushioned chair that used to be in the dining room with the light off. "What now? Waiting for my death?"

She closed her eyes; her mind was buzzing loudly like the Mercato on a Saturday morning. Every memory was visually coming back to her as if she was watching old movies but loaded with emotions. Memories of her life from the day she had left her parents' village: the unfortunate incident of being accosted by bandits, meeting Kebada, her destiny which brought her to Addis Ababa, then her beloved children and their untimely deaths.

No, she thought, I am still alive; there is still a chance for me to go back to my village. All day I am in pain anyway, whether I am sitting or lying in bed. So what's the difference if I am sitting on a car traveling while I'm in pain. The thought energized her.

That morning, when the maid came in to check on her, Fanaye greeted her warmly. Amsalach noticed Fanaye's cheerful mood, which delighted her. Right away, she offered, "May I bring you something to eat?"

Fanaye surprised Amsalach when she asked if there was any fenugreek. "Fenugreek! Is that what you said?" The maid couldn't believe what she heard.

Fanaye smiled, amused by her confused expression. "Yes, that's what I said. So, is there any?"

"There is no problem. I will go get some."

"Don't rush yet; first, finish what you have to do."

Amsalach nodded but immediately headed to Hewait's bedroom and frantically knocked on the door, which made Hewait jump out of bed. "What's wrong? What happened to Grand Emaye?"

"Nothing to worry about. Can you believe she asked for fenugreek?"

"That's a good sign, don't you think?"

"Yes, I think so. She wants it for a medicinal purpose. It's known for building strength. Let me go and buy it." And with that, Amsalach grabbed her netala and left for the nearest grocery store while Hewait rushed to Fanaye's bedroom.

That afternoon, Fanaye drank a glass of fenugreek tea with a little honey, then another one before going to bed. The following morning, Amsalach entered Fanaye's bedroom again with a glass of fenugreek tea. Amsalach hoped the fenugreek would bring back her appetite. She asked if she should bring her a piece of barley bread with butter. "Good idea, but bring just a little piece," was the reply.

The next day, Fanaye asked Alemuwa, the cook, if there were any suff, sunflower seeds. If not, let Senit, the washing

443

woman, get some. "I don't think Senit can tell fresh from stale ones; suff is a bit tricky to tell. I'll go get it myself, and I would still have enough time to cook lunch after I come back," the cook said. "Wait, don't you need money?" Fanaye asked as she took out a twenty-birr bill from her pouch and handed it to her. "Buy what else you think is needed, and that's for your transportation as well."

It was the third time Almaz called, and again Hewait told her Fanaye was out. She asked impatiently, "Don't tell me Teluka Emaye is out partying. Tell me what's happening? Is she arrested?"

"No, she is not."

"So, where is she? Whatever it is, don't hide it from me. My mind is going crazy. So please, please tell me!"

Reluctantly Zenite said, "She is sick."

"How sick is she? Let me talk to her then."

"She is asleep."

"Please wake her up. I won't keep her for long."

"Please, Almaz, let her rest."

"If I don't speak to her now, I'll keep calling all night. Do you want me to do that?"

"She is very sick."

"I am coming in a couple of days."

"I don't think that's a good idea. Why don't you talk to Negest?"

"Okay, I will; she would want to come as well."

Almaz hung up the phone and immediately called Negest in California. Negest knew about Fanaye's condition and was planning to tell Almaz.

"You mean you knew, and didn't tell me? I am flying on the earliest flight. Do you want to take the same plane?"

"Almaz, I love Telukwa Emaye too, but this is not what she wants us to do. Are you aware of the dangers of going back home at this time? These days, nobody goes back home, even to their parents' funeral. People are fleeing the country like the plague. It would be like throwing ourselves into a war zone if we go. We could be put to jail right from the airport, and God knows what they'd do to us."

"Yes, I am aware of all that, but that's not going to stop me. I am willing to accept my fate. Now I have to hang up and get busy."

"Please, Almaz, don't do it. I beg you."

"I need to go and take care of her. God forbid, if she dies and I never see her again, that would be my saddest day. Not seeing Mother when she died was bad enough; I still feel the pain every time I remember it. No, never, nothing can stop me. So, I have to say goodbye to you."

She then put the phone down while Negest was still trying to talk her out of it.

445

Meanwhile, Almaz remained by the phone, thinking where to begin. She called her boyfriend, but when she told him what she intended to do, he started questioning her. So she cut him short, saying, "I love you. Talk to you later. I've got to go now!"

She then called her office, hoping they would understand, but was ready for the outcome regardless. Her boss was surprised to hear about her plan to go to Ethiopia, but luckily, he agreed to her request. Earlier, she had told him she wouldn't go to her country because of the communist regime. But he knew how foreigners were devoted to their parents.

She dialed her favorite travel agent, hoping she was in her office. She liked her efficiency, and she always managed to find her the best flight at a reasonable price. Luckily, her agent cheerfully answered her call. She told her she would save at least forty percent if she waited one more week. But nothing could change Almaz's mind. The following night she flew by Air Lufthansa.

After one night and day and another day, Almaz arrived at Bola Airport around 3:00 pm. Where she stood to check out, there were five lines. All the officials were young, not more than thirty years old; they all wore dark uniforms. Almaz looked for a friendly-looking clerk and stood in that line to wait for her turn. She was holding her American passport.

A man next to her kept looking at Almaz; she pretended not to see him. A little later, the man whispered, "Don't you have an Ethiopian passport?"

"Why?"

"If you have it with you, you'd be better off showing that instead."

When her turn came, she handed over her passport. The clerk looked displeased. "Are you an American? Are you?"

She disguised her fear and managed to look relaxed. "No," she replied. She wished she had her grandmother's fearlessness.

"So, why are you traveling with a foreign passport?"

"I am a dual citizen."

"You need to go over there!" he commanded, pointing with his right hand.

Almaz obeyed and headed to the area where it said "Foreigners." She entered a small room and handed her passport to a beautiful woman. The woman looked at it carefully. "Oh, you have been in America for a long time! Why did you come back now?"

"To be with my sick grandmother."

"For real?"

"Isn't that a good reason?"

447

The woman was seized with emotion. "You look sincere... I believe you. Did she raise you?" she asked as she stamped Almaz's passport. "I wish her well. She is a lucky grandmother."

Relieved, Almaz thanked the woman and walked to claim her luggage. She wanted to take a taxi instead of calling home. But, just as she was about to go outside, she saw her father standing there, still looking distinguished, with more grey hair. He had aged well, despite the stressful political climate. As usual, he looked calm. Almaz shouted with joy. "Ababa! Ababa!" They hugged tightly. Yeskiash looked at his headstrong daughter lovingly and kissed her on both cheeks several times. "How did you know I was coming today?" she asked.

Yeskiash paused, then asked her, "How was your trip?" It was his way of not being willing to answer her for whatever reason, and Almaz, who knew him so well, didn't push him for an answer.

The reunion with her family was very emotional; her siblings were grown up and looked somewhat different. But when Almaz saw Fanaye, she threw herself on her grandmother's frail body. She tried to hold back her tears, but to no avail. Almaz cried uncontrollably, still hugging Fanaye. After a while, Fanaye looked tired and overwhelmed with joy since she had not expected to see Almaz.

448

"Children, why don't you go wash up, so we can have dinner," Yeskiash said as he left Fanaye's bedroom. Reluctantly, Almaz stood up, and her siblings followed her, leaving Fanaye by herself.

"I'll be back soon, Grand Emaye," Almaz shouted.

Fanaye wanted to join this happy gathering in the dining room, not lie in bed, so she got up from her bed, opened her clothes chest, and picked out her festive dress. "What's more festive than seeing my Almaz?" she reasoned.

Seeing Fanaye all dressed up and looking much better somehow surprised all of them. "Oh, Grand Emaye!" Hewait exclaimed with a delighted smile. She then turned to Almaz and said, "Just know that she is dressed only for you."

Almaz teased her sister, "Don't you know coming from America has its advantage!"

They all laughed and chatted and asked Almaz lots of questions about life in America. Despite her exhaustion, Almaz tried her best to answer them. Yeskiash noticed Almaz struggling to keep her eyes open. "I think you should go and take a nap," he suggested. Almaz was glad to hear him say that. She was exhausted, and all she wanted was to spend more time with Fanaye. Insisting on staying with Fanaye, she went to sleep in Fanaye's bedroom on a cot.

A couple of days later, Almaz and Fanaye were sitting outside on the veranda, where the sun was cheerful and golden yellow like meskel flowers. Almaz couldn't stop expressing her delight with the warmth of the sun, the clearness of it. When she left New York, it was shivering cold. According to the weather report, it was the coldest day of the year. Her grandmother was surprised by Almaz's continuous delight over sunshine. "Almaz dear, is the sun that different in America?"

Almaz laughed. "No, the sun is the same; it's just that we don't get enough of it, not like here, for sure."

Fanaye laughed. "Well, that's the only free thing these days. Who knows, they may start charging us for that too."

Almaz got closer to her grandmother. Fanaye put her delicate hand over Almaz's shoulder and tapped it. Then they were quiet, each left to her own thoughts.

"I am overwhelmed with your determination and devotion!"

"I told you there is nothing that would make me happier than being here with you. And I want you to know that I am planning to go to your village before I go back to America."

Fanaye straightened up and stared at Almaz with a look of disbelief.

Ten days later, against Yeskiash's futile opposition, Fanaye and Almaz left for Dow-Dow. The driver, Mekonen, an energetic middle-aged man with the quick movements of a teenager, was the son of one of Fanaye's old customers.

She knew his father before Mekonen was born. She felt right about him. He cleaned his van as he had never done before. It was always clean anyway, but his father had instructed him to look out for Fanaye and Almaz and make sure that Fanaye was comfortable.

On beat-up roads, Mekonen drove very carefully. He would apologize for every pothole as if it were his fault. Upon Almaz's insistence, Fanaye lay down on the back seat. Almaz kept reminding her, "Telukwa Emaye, don't forget you need your strength." But Fanaye was too happy to feel tired or even to feel pain. Her mind was back to when she was a child. She was remembering when she and her friends would dash out of their homes and embrace the rain with delight, screaming, jumping up and down, and cupping their little hands to collect the rainwater, then chasing each other to throw the water at each other's faces. When they would get tired of chasing each other, they would move on to another game: digging the wet mud to build a mini bridge. Some would dig; others would go around to find twigs. Finally, they would build their bridges. And when satisfied with their games, they would go back to their homes, drenched from top to bottom.

Fanaye smiled, remembering she was good at that. Where would they be now? She wondered. Would they remember her? Would she recognize them? She had to find out.

After nine hours of driving, Mekonen stopped in front of a medium-size hotel called the Blue Nile. "This is where all the Ferange stay," he said with exaggeration. And then he added, "It's expensive!"

"What makes them the best?" Almaz asked.

"Well, it's just very nice. Even their furniture is from Europe! The Ferange appreciate a good place like this. I guess they have more money. That's why they are willing to pay a high price."

Almaz thought about that and wanted to discuss it more, but this wasn't the time and certainly not the place, not in front of Fanaye.

The Blue Nile was clean, but the furniture needed upgrading. They had checked in for the night anyway. Mekonen refused to stay at the same hotel because of the fee, even though Almaz was willing to pay for him.

Almaz woke up, stretched her tired body, and turned around expecting to see Fanaye sleeping, but her bed was empty. She quickly got dressed and went to the main room, where she saw Fanaye talking to a young couple who were having breakfast. Fanaye introduced them to Almaz, and then they headed to the table that the waiter had set for them.

Almaz wished they had sat with the couple and had breakfast with them. Reluctantly, she followed Fanaye to their table. Already, the waiter had brought them a plain omelet, a roll of dabo, and orange juice.

"I am glad he brought dabo instead of Italian bread. It's so delicious!" Almaz exclaimed.

"The waiter was surprised when I told him you prefer to eat a country bread."

"Doesn't he know the traditional bread is the best! I want to learn how to make it."

Fanaye ate a tiny bit, while Almaz, pleased to find the eggs and the bread so fresh and tasty, was eating voraciously. "Simple yet delicious! And the macchiato? Nobody makes it like Ethiopians!"

Fanaye nodded, but her mind was busy with thoughts of her family. She wondered if she would find her parents alive and be able to see her brother and her distant family. Would anybody recognize her at all? The more she thought about her family, the more anxious she became. At the same time, she was also gaining strength. Her memory was becoming more clear now than ever. Suddenly, she became too impatient and got up.

"Almaz, hurry up and finish your breakfast. I'll be waiting outside."

"Grand Emaye, you need to eat; you need your strength."

453

"I know; you keep reminding me," Fanaye replied jokingly.

Almaz shook her head helplessly, reached for her backpack, pulled out some birr from her pink leather wallet, and paid the bill, leaving a generous tip for the overly polite waiter.

Mekonen was outside, waiting for them. Almaz didn't know he was already there.

"Why didn't you come inside? You could have had breakfast with us."

"Thank you; I ate already." He appreciated Almaz's consideration, which he had not expected. Throughout their trip, she showed him respect and care.

"Let's go then," Fanaye exclaimed.

Five hours later, they arrived at the much-anticipated village, Dow-Dow. Both Fanaye and Almaz were nervous but joyful. Mekonen drove on a dirt road of red earth on which children were playing. Fanaye noticed the increase in the size of the village and its population, which seemed more than double to her. There were more clustered huts and, as a result, smaller lots. Children were ubiquitous. Fanaye was amazed to see so many crowds. Donkeys carrying heavy loads and moving side by side with pedestrians more visible than ever. There were also mules carrying piles of goods or people riding them. Fanaye noticed changes in the style of

454

houses she had never seen when she was growing up. There were even some houses with flat roofs and broader doors and windows, and here and there were two-floor houses. But what had not changed was the building materials; almost all the huts were still made of a mixture of mud and dung. Fanaye lovingly watched the passersby; she wanted to hug and kiss them and tell them she was one of them. She wanted to start looking for her family immediately; she didn't want to waste a second, but she had promised Almaz they would first get some rest.

Later, the driver took them to a two-floor inn. Mekonen had been asking around if anyone knew a nice hotel in Dow-Dow. Since it was not a tourist attraction, there were no accommodations better than this one. A widow named Wasena and her son ran the place. Wasena had a similar complexion and body shape as Fanaye, though she was much younger by at least twenty-five years. Almaz wondered if she could be related to Fanaye. She couldn't wait to find out.

"Are you by any chance related to the Adaferaw family?"

Wasena shook her head, revealing sharp white teeth, "No, I am not, and I don't know any family by that name. I came here from Gonder with my husband when his company transferred him about eighteen years ago. God bless his soul;

he passed away three years ago." She sniffled. Then, raising her eyebrows, she asked, "Why do you want to know?"

"My grandmother is from here, but she should talk to you all about it soon."

Fanaye was unable to take a nap, but she stayed in the room to not worry her granddaughter. But when she couldn't take it any longer, she got up and left the room. Outside, she saw Mekonen talking with a man leaning on a big oak tree. Nearby, there was a three-wheel scooter with a beige top cover, seating for two passengers in the back. Fanaye couldn't be more delighted. Did this man appear here by pure chance, she wondered? She had been thinking about what would be the best way to look for her family. Walking all day would be out of the question for her. She would soon be tired and would hardly be able to cover more than a small area. Driving in the neighborhoods in the van wasn't a sensible idea either. That wouldn't give her much opportunity to talk to people and ask questions since most of the houses were very close to each other, and cars wouldn't be able to pass through them anyway, especially a big van like theirs. So, this scooter was the perfect solution.

The owner of the scooter was more than happy to rent his vehicle. Every morning he brought his scooter for them to go wherever they wanted to go. He was so glad to be getting paid a generous sum of money. He had already figured out from the very beginning that a substantial amount of income would be coming to him. He wished he had these kinds of clients more often.

Mekonen sat at the front, driving the vehicle, while Fanaye and Almaz sat back. Their search continued for hours each day, which worried Almaz about Fanaye's health condition. She wished Fanaye would listen to her and rest at the inn while Mekonen and her comb through the neighborhoods. But Fanaye wouldn't hear of it.

After a week of searching but gaining no clue about where her family was, Fanaye and Almaz began to wonder what they should do next. Suddenly, Fanaye uttered, "I have an idea!"

Almaz was curious, "What is it? What?"

"Why didn't I think of this from the beginning!"

"Think about what?"

"Hire several people to look for them! That would speed our search."

Almaz was amazed at Fanaye's smart thinking. That same day, they recruited ten young men. Fanaye chose them by their pleasant personalities and their eagerness for the challenge of finding her family. But, after yet another couple of days of fruitless search, Almaz's spirit started to dwindle. But not Fanaye's! Instead, she decided to extend the search beyond Dow-Dow. Upon acting on this, the first thing she

457

found out was that her cousin Yenanish's nearby village didn't exist anymore. Their community had merged with some other bigger town. Which one? Nobody knew. The news was upsetting to Fanaye and Almaz.

The following day, Fanaye decided they should go to the town called Fenfeye. The drive there was pleasant. That village was about two hours away, and seemed even greener than Dow-Dow. It was a Saturday morning when they arrived. Shoppers were coming and going from the marketplace. With anticipation and excitement, Fanaye stretched out her arm and pointed. "Let's go in there!" she shouted. "To the marketplace!"

Mekonen stayed by the van while Fanaye and Almaz strolled around. Smelling familiar spices, looking at the people, the handicrafts, and the variety of vegetables that she hadn't seen in Addis Ababa, Fanaye felt very much at home. They kept asking about her family, but it was all in vain.

Towards the late afternoon, Fanaye was exhausted. Almaz became worried and wanted to take her back to the inn, but Fanaye dismissed the idea. "I'll just take a little rest in the car. That's all I need." But, instead of getting into the car, she decided to sit outside, next to the van. Mekonen brought her a little stool. On it, Fanaye sat, watching people as if she were watching an outdoor movie. The passersby, too, were watching them curiously as they were trying to figure out who they could be. Then, overcome with fatigue, Fanaye's head slowly fell forward, and she began to snooze right there where she sat.

A short while later, two women were coming towards Fanaye and Almaz. One was about forty, the other much older. They were perhaps mother and daughter, Almaz guessed. The younger one was carrying a basket of goods, and the older one was carrying a small tote bag. As they got closer to where Fanaye was sitting, one of them began to stare at her, casting glances at Almaz. From the way the woman was staring at Fanaye, Almaz became overwhelmed with the hope of having run into a member of her Grand Emaye's family and her own as well.

Pointing at Fanaye, Almaz excitedly asked the woman the same question she had routinely been asking everyone. "Do you know who she is? She was born here but left a long time ago." The woman paused, looking intently at Fanaye's sleeping figure for a while. Then, tilting her head up to the sky, she exclaimed loudly, "Could that be Fanaye?" She looked at Fanaye one more time, then spat into the air and began hollering, "Elel, elel, elel! Jesus, Geta! Jesus, Geta! You brought Fanaye home!" And then she fell on her knees.

The commotion woke Fanaye up. Almaz quickly wrapped her arm around Fanaye's shoulder, afraid she might be too overwhelmed and may fall. "Grand Emaye, there is someone here who knows you," she said excitedly.

Anxiously, Fanaye looked down at the woman, who was still kneeling on the ground. Not being able to see her face, she asked, "Can you please look up, so I can see you?" The woman tilted her head up and squinted to look at Fanaye. She began muttering, "Is this true? Is this Fanaye? Please let it not be a dream."

With one look at her, Fanaye instantly recognized her cousin Yenanish, despite all the deep wrinkles on her weather-beaten face. Fanaye felt as if her heart would jump out of her chest.

"Yenanish!" she shouted with disbelief. Almaz and the younger woman pulled the woman up. Once on her feet, Yenanish threw herself into Fanaye's open arms. The two cousins held each other tight for a very long time, as if they were afraid of losing each other again.

Every now and then, they would pull apart just to look at each other, then resume hugging, kissing, and more crying. Almaz, too, became very emotional. She was thrilled to witness her grandmother's life-long wish come true.

CPSIA information can be obtained
at www.ICGtesting.com
Printed in the USA
LVHW081959280922
729507LV00002B/312